RECONCILIATION OF HATE

RECONCILIATION OF HATE

EXCEPTIONAL S. BEAUFONT™ BOOK 11

SARAH NOFFKE
MICHAEL ANDERLE

DISRUPTIVE IMAGINATION

LMBPN Publishing
PMB 196, 2540 South Maryland Pkwy
Las Vegas, NV 89109

First US Edition, January 2021
Version 1.01, January 2021
eBook ISBN: 978-1-64971-394-0
Print ISBN: 978-1-64971-395-7

THE RECONCILIATION OF HATE TEAM

Thanks to the JIT Readers

Debi Sateren
Veronica Stephan-Miller
Diane L. Smith
Deb Mader
Allen Collins
Angel LaVey
Peter Manis
Jackey Hankard-Brodie
Larry Omans

If we've missed anyone, please let us know!

Editor
The Skyhunter Editing Team

For Bep, for all your thoughtfulness and support.

— Sarah

To Family, Friends and
Those Who Love
to Read.
May We All Enjoy Grace
to Live the Life We Are
Called.

— Michael

CHAPTER ONE

Roughly three hundred and some-odd years in the past...

Slain dragons lined the battlefield, most of them not moving. Some tried to make a last-ditch effort to survive, but this war was over, and everyone present knew it. Smoke and the smell of burning flesh wafted through the thick air—a would-be sign to those in the distance that a battle had been fought on these grounds. However, no one was near enough to know the events that had come to pass on that day.

No one would know until it didn't matter anymore.

The moans of the riders sprawled beside their dying dragons was an insufferable sound to Talon Sinclair, a Councilor for the House of Seven. He yanked a handkerchief from his robe pocket and covered his nose and mouth, unable to stomach the smell much longer. He'd stepped through a portal moments after a deadly blow assaulted the final demon dragonrider.

The five Warriors for the House of Seven that he'd enlisted stood on the battlefield nearby, wounded from the fight, but none of them close to death. That had been because the demon dragonriders hadn't seen this battle coming and walked right into the ambush. To make the fight even more decisive, Talon Sinclair had all of their magic locked at the House of Seven without them knowing it—a magical governing device that he'd invented and would use to control all in the magical world one day. It made it so that an unsuspecting magician's magic suddenly was gone, rendering them defenseless in most situations.

Everything was going to plan.

One of the oldest magicians to ever live, Talon Sinclair had worked hard to take over the magical worlds slowly. That had involved making it so pesky mortals couldn't see magic and erasing them from the House of Seven, which had once comprised them and made it the House of Fourteen. No one would remember that though, because he'd erased that history and written a new one.

Taking control over the other magical races hadn't been hard. The elves, giants, and gnomes didn't care, keeping to themselves and minding their affairs. The fae were too much in a drunken stupor most of the time to realize that the world had pretty much changed overnight after the conclusion of the Great War. Magicians would do what the House of Seven wanted, which Talon Sinclair now controlled.

But dragonriders... They'd always been a thorn in Talon Sinclair's side, upholding justice and putting mortal affairs at the top of the priority list. At first, it had been easy to dwindle the dragonriders' numbers, pitting the Dragon Elite and Rogue Riders against each other, encouraging both sides to fight one another. Brother against brother. Few fights had more vengeance and personal gain behind them than between Hiker Wallace and Thad Reinhart.

Then it appeared that Hiker Wallace had won, sending Thad Reinhart to the depths of defeat. However, the leader of the Dragon Elite hadn't seen what was coming next.

Overnight, mortals weren't able to see magic anymore, and suddenly the precious moral adjudicators for the mortals were utterly useless. Talon Sinclair had felt no better victory than when the Dragon Elite sulked away to their headquarters, not to be seen again.

However, the Dragon Elite was composed of angel riders—those who wanted to do right by the world. The biggest nuisances for Talon Sinclair because they poked their noses where they didn't belong.

Once they were gone, there was only one group to take care of—the demon dragonriders. They kept to themselves without Thad Reinhart's leadership. However, they were still individually powerful, and if left unchecked, they might reform a group, one that could take over the magical world. Talon Sinclair couldn't allow that to happen.

Expertly, he'd called all the demon dragonriders to that spot, inviting them on false grounds, using personal reasons that appealed to the rider's particular interests. It wasn't hard since they were selfish-minded. Once there, the demon dragonriders' magic was disabled at the House of Seven, and the ambush commenced.

Talon Sinclair looked out over the battlefield littered with dead bodies and smirked. Dragon and rider must have been so perplexed without magic that they didn't see the first or second blows coming. By then, their swords and fire were useless against the five Warriors for the House of Seven that Talon had enlisted for the tasks, led by his very own relative—Cassius Sinclair.

The Councilor strode over to where the Warriors all stood at attention, their focus on him. Many gave Talon looks of fear. He'd told them that the demon dragonriders were threats and convinced them that they needed to exterminate them. These Warriors wouldn't question Talon, which was why he picked them: Cassius Sinclair, Solope Chienne, Lucille Mantovani, Jazebella Acker, and Enzo Bernardi.

Talon left the Beaufonts and Takahashis out of the lineup, knowing that they'd ask too many questions. They'd argue that there were other methods besides murder. They'd ruin everything. But they hadn't, and now he'd done it.

There might be a few demon dragonriders left in the world, but like the Dragon Elite, they were powerless in this world that Talon Sinclair was quickly taking over.

Talon halted beside Cassius, the Warrior he trusted the most. Like Talon, his hair and beard were all white, having shared the same albino genetics. Their light-colored eyes briefly met as Talon leaned close and whispered in Cassius' ear.

"Wipe their memories," he ordered while cutting his gaze to the other Warriors.

It was better if there was no way the others could talk about this incident. Having a memory of it would pose too many risks.

Cassius nodded, a determined expression on his pale white face.

"If you have a problem with anyone, you know what to do," Talon finally finished before marching forward and opening a portal back to the House of Seven.

He didn't wait for Cassius' reply. The Warrior would know that he should murder those who potentially could be trouble, the same as the demon dragonriders. That might be for the best anyway since it was high time there were new families in the House of Seven. Ones that Talon Sinclair could more easily control as he poised to take over the magical world further.

CHAPTER TWO

Present day...

"What's a breakfast burrito?" Evan stared at his plate of food like it might jump back and bite him instead of the other way around.

Trin, the housekeeper for the Gullington, gave Sophia a confused expression. "They don't know what breakfast burritos are?" She swept her metal cyborg hand at the others at the table: Wilder, Mahkah, Hiker, Ainsley, and Quiet, excluding Mama Jamba for obvious reasons.

"They didn't know what tacos were when I first got here." Sophia laughed at Evan continuing to regard the tortilla stuffed with eggs and bacon and veggies.

"How is that possible?" Trin rested her hands on her hips while shaking her head at the group.

"Because we're not Americans," Evan stated, then pointed at Mahkah. "Well, he is but that doesn't count because I don't think his tribe spent much time at taco joints before he came to the Gullington."

Everyone looked at Mahkah as though expecting the stoic Native

American to answer. He swallowed his bite of hash browns, unhurried. "Not much. No."

"Anyway," Trin indicated the burritos she'd made for breakfast. "I thought I'd switch it up. That's what you'd expect from a burrito, but it has eggs and bacon in it."

"Weird." Wilder grimaced at the platter of burritos.

"Says the vegan." Evan laughed.

"I made you a tofu scramble one," Trin offered. "I'll go and fetch it."

Ainsley shook her head while picking out the center of the burrito, obviously against the idea of lifting it to take a giant bite out of the thing the size of her head. She took a dainty portion. "Remember when you used to tell me to fetch things for you? Almost like I was NO10JO." She batted her eyelashes at Hiker, a smile hiding below her expression.

"I never treated you like a dog," Hiker grumbled while indicating the cyborg dog stationed on the other side of the threshold to the Castle's dining hall.

"Oh, no," Ainsley teased. "Dogs get treats and told how good they are."

Hiker set his coffee mug down on the table with a little more force than he probably intended. "Are we truly doing this? I thought we were past all that."

Ainsley coyly held her cup of steaming tea up to her chin, hiding her grin. "Oh, where would the fun be in letting go of centuries of being your housekeeper because I'd lost my memory saving your life?"

Hiker shook his head. "Obviously nowhere."

Trin returned, carrying a plate with a single burrito on it, and laid it in front of Wilder.

"Thanks." He looked at the rolled-up tortilla with uncertainty.

Sophia laughed and picked up her mammoth burrito. "You simply lift it and stick it in your pie hole."

He watched her and copied the movement, cramming a bite into his mouth.

"Why is it that Mama Jamba and Wilder get custom orders every morning?" Evan pointed at Mother Nature, who was polishing off what would probably be her first of many plates of banana nut pancakes.

"Well," Trin began, "I think it's obvious why Mama Jamba gets whatever she wants."

"Because of my southern charm," Mama Jamba remarked, then handed the empty plate to Trin and pulled the next short stack toward her.

"Because she made everything on this planet," Wilder corrected. "Including the planet."

Evan, who still hadn't touched his burrito, folded his arms over his chest. "I once made a table out of old wood."

Mama Jamba patted Evan on the arm. "It was very nice. Not sturdy or well-made, but nice nevertheless."

"Thanks." Evan cheered up slightly.

Trin continued, "Wilder has special dietary needs."

"Wilder," Evan held up a single finger and corrected, "has special dietary preferences because he's a special pain in the ass due to the way he was born."

"It's true," Wilder affirmed and ate a bite of his burrito. "What's your excuse?"

Trin ignored their banter, pursing her lips. "I made the breakfast burritos because I thought you'd like them. If you don't, then fine. I won't try anything new."

"Sounds good to me." Hiker eyed his burrito, which was also untouched.

Trin stormed back to the kitchen, her black boots making noise as she stomped.

When the kitchen door swung shut, Wilder shook his head at Evan. "Smooth move, mate. Please teach me your ways, Casanova."

Evan kept looking over his shoulder, back at the kitchen—worry on his face. "Man, I didn't mean to offend her."

"Still, it's who you are, and there's no way of avoiding it," Wilder stated.

"It would seem," Evan grumbled, turned back, and glared down at the burrito.

"Don't worry." Ainsley sounded sympathetic. "You guys will find your way. It's hard when you serve someone and also are in a more complex relationship."

Evan nodded and picked up the burrito, not at all looking sure about the food.

"Does anyone want to know what I think about Evan fancying the housekeeper?" Hiker speared a roasted potato with his fork.

"Not really, son." Mama Jamba snapped her fingers, and a skiing magazine appeared beside her half-eaten short stack of pancakes.

"You also could be a little nicer to Trin," Ainsley said to Hiker and nodded at the burrito. "She's trying and putting her spin on the job."

"You seem to have loved the change to the menu," Hiker teased and eyed the burrito she dissected with a fork and knife but didn't eat much of.

"I thought it was an interesting adventure," Ainsley said smugly.

"I like eggs for breakfast, not adventures," Hiker argued.

"This is delicious!" Evan exclaimed, having taken a bite finally. "What's wrong with you old sticks in the muds? Breakfast burritos are the best thing ever!"

Wilder leaned forward in the other dragonrider's direction. "I think she heard you in the kitchen," he whispered. "I think the chickens who laid those eggs far outside the Gullington heard you."

Evan took another bite and chewed with a delighted smile. "You miss eggs, don't you?"

Wilder shook his head. "The only thing I miss is stealing your bacon."

Both guys' eyes darted to the tray in front of them where there was one hash brown left. They seemed to both have the same idea, rushing to pick up their fork to snag the potato. Sophia had less decorum. She reached out and grabbed it with her fingers, stuck it in her mouth, and winked at Wilder and Evan, who both regarded her with offended expressions.

"While you two battle, the real culprit will steal your treasure," she said through a mouthful of hash brown. "So be careful what you spend your time doing."

Hiker cleared his throat and pushed away his plate. "Speaking of which. I want you all in my office straight after breakfast. We have to discuss this Rogue Rider situation. Something tells me that it's going to get worse before it gets better."

"Sir, your optimism is always so inspiring," Evan commented and continued to eat his burrito.

Hiker stood, his presence commanding. "I'll see you all momentarily. We have much to discuss."

CHAPTER THREE

"What company makes the best snow gear?" Mama Jamba asked no one in particular from her place on the Chesterfield in Hiker's office. She was thumbing through a magazine and eyeing a pair of skis.

Hiker scowled at her from behind his desk. "How am I supposed to know?"

"How do you not know that?" Evan asked Mother Nature from where he perched against the far wall next to the bank of windows overlooking the Pond. "Don't you pretty much know everything?"

She shrugged. "Who has time to keep up with all that stuff?"

"Papa Creola," Sophia answered from her seat beside the old woman.

"Where do you plan to go?" Wilder asked Mama Jamba, hanging over the back of the sofa, draped between the two women.

She shrugged again. "Maybe the Alps or the Rockies, or I'll make a new mountain range."

"Or you can help us with our latest enemies, the newest set of Rogue Riders," Hiker urged, irritation in his voice.

"I could." Mama Jamba hummed while turning the magazine's page. "I've never skied. I wonder if it's hard."

Anger flared on his face. He was about to voice his complaints, but Evan cut him off.

"Aren't you good at everything by default?" he asked Mama Jamba.

She shook her head. "Oh, no. We all have our limitations. No one is all-powerful. I create. That's what I do. I don't fight or have superpowers. That's why I have you all."

"We'd love to do our job if you lot would focus already," Hiker muttered before glancing at Ainsley, who perched on the corner of his desk. She wore a silver gown with red rose patterns throughout. It was elegant and sophisticated at the same time and made her look like she was professional and also ready for a posh affair. "How are things with the elves after the Rogue Riders invaded their homeland?"

"They're very grateful for the Dragon Elite," Ainsley began, her tone neutral. Clinical. "However, even with the protective barrier we put up, they're still very shaken. It will take a while before those on the island don't fear that the Rogue Riders will return."

Hiker nodded. "Understandable. I wish I could reassure them that it won't happen, but I can't since I don't know where the Rogue Riders are. They've been quiet since fleeing the island."

"More like tucking tail and running for their lives." Evan puffed his chest out.

"What about the tracking device that Mama Jamba made to locate the demon dragons?" Sophia looked around Hiker's desk where the orb had been the last time she saw it.

The leader of the Dragon Elite shook his head. "It stopped working once we located them. Maybe you can help with that Mama?"

The old woman shook her head of curly bluish-gray hair. "Oh, no. I already did that. I got you acquainted with the demon dragons and their riders so you all could track them down once. I'm not giving you something to keep constant tabs on them. That's your job, son."

Hiker's eyes fluttered with annoyance. "Yes, and I've devoted that job to looking for disturbances worldwide. Something tells me that the Rogue Riders won't remain quiet long. Under Versalee's leadership, I suspect they'll create trouble somewhere else very soon."

"Yeah, there's evil, and there's really evil." Evan whistled. "There's no reasoning with a demon dragonrider like her."

"I'm afraid you're right," Hiker stated with an edge to his voice. "I've met many a demon dragonrider in my day. Some are selfish. Some will abuse their powers to get what they want. Then there are ones like Versalee who are crazed with evil and diabolical."

"She remind you of anyone?" Ainsley asked him.

Hiker nodded bitterly. "All too well of my brother, Thad Reinhart."

"By definition, shouldn't all leaders of the evil demon dragonriders be corrupt?" Evan asked.

"Maybe," Hiker allowed. "In the past, demon dragonriders either laid low or created tyranny depending on who their leader was. Everything always depends on leadership."

"Which is why we're in such good hands," Evan gushed.

Wilder coughed, and it sounded very much like, "Suck up."

"Yeah, I want to believe that under the right leadership," Sophia began while ignoring the guys' banter, "the Rogue Riders could contribute to the world order by governing mortal criminals, rather than by exploiting and benefiting from them."

"Do you also want to believe that the Earth is flat, Pink Princess?" Evan asked in a teasing tone. "Because there's reality, and there's fiction."

"You're fiction," Wilder quipped before returning his focus to Sophia. "I think you're right. The demon dragonriders were created for a reason. They have to have a purpose."

"Regardless, they're ruining our good name." Hiker strode around his desk looking individually at each of the riders. "The world simply sees dragonriders creating problems and doesn't know that it's not us, the Dragon Elite."

"Was this a problem in the past?" Sophia asked. "When there were Rogue Riders under Thad Reinhart?"

Hiker shook his head. "No, because the world knew there were two groups. We'd been around for a long time, and things were established. In these times, we've simply popped up and have battled with reputation from the beginning thanks to stigma and the mortal world easing back into seeing magic after so long."

"So it seems there's an opportunity for education," Sophia offered.

"I agree," Hiker stated. "Evan and Wilder, I want you to continue on one of the goodwill campaigns you worked on in the past. We need to make ourselves known as the Dragon Elite. I'll send out a press release stating that we have nothing to do with the Rogue Riders and don't condone their behavior and crimes."

"I can help you to craft it and get it out to the other magical races," Ainsley offered.

Hiker nodded without looking at her at his back. "Thank you. That would be helpful." He turned his attention to Mahkah, who was beside the door, standing straight, his chin high. "I want you back on adjudication missions." Hiker pointed at a stack of files on his desk. "I have a few cases that have come in recently, and that way our actions will follow my words. We will try to bring justice and peace to the world, whereas I suspect the Rogue Riders are doing the exact opposite."

Sophia drummed her fingers on her knee while thinking. "So the Rogue Riders aren't a new society of dragonriders?"

Hiker shook his head. "I'd guess the shared consciousness of the dragons informed them of the organization that was started centuries before, and they took the name."

"What did they do in the past?" Sophia asked.

"It depended but it was usually self-serving," Hiker answered.

"Was it always composed of demon dragonriders?" Sophia continued to question.

Hiker thought for a moment. "Yes, as far as I'm aware."

"What happened to all of them?" Sophia drummed her fingers on her knee, feeling like she was on the brink of understanding something if she drilled down a little more.

"Well, under Thad's leadership, unfortunately we had to kill many of them," Hiker stated, regret in his voice. He shook his head, his blond hair knocking him in the eye. "He didn't leave me any choice in the matter. Thad couldn't be reasoned with and had to be stopped. Killing our own has never been my first option."

Evan drew in a loud breath. "I agree with that sentiment as despicable as those guys on the island were. I tried not to kill any, but they left me no choice."

The other dragonriders agreed with nods.

"At one point," Hiker stated, "most of the demon dragonriders fled from Thad's Rogue Riders, knowing they were fighting his war and weren't going to win it. Demon dragonriders have always scattered, preferring to be drifters and loners on their own if not led by someone like Thad."

"I know that Thad went after some for their dragons," Sophia began slowly, as though trying to work out her question, "but there had to be a lot. More than he could have wiped out. What happened to all of them?"

Hiker blinked at the question as if he hadn't expected it and was broadsided. "I honestly thought they did their own thing, keeping to themselves. I was shocked when I learned there were no more out there once we returned to the waking world when mortals could see magic once more."

Sophia let out a long breath. "That doesn't make any sense though. Like, Thad went after some, but according to the *Complete History of Dragonriders*, there were quite a few demon dragonriders after the Great War."

"It doesn't say what happened to them?" Mahkah questioned.

"No. It cuts off after then."

"Doesn't sound very complete," Evan observed.

Sophia laughed. "I think because the House of Fourteen—or rather the House of Seven then—rewrote history, that the *Complete History of Dragonriders* paused, not knowing how it should tell the events. I suspect that it's sorting out the details now and will write those chapters soon, once things settle down on the timeline."

Wilder shook his head. "A book that writes itself. That's impressive."

"It records events," Hiker imparted. "I suspect you're right, Sophia, and the book was confused. To your point, it is curious that demon dragonriders disappeared seemingly overnight, but we were locked here, and it seemed that they probably got themselves killed off."

"I think it would be worth looking into what happened to them," Sophia stated. "We know that Thad was the last one from the old generation. Maybe if we find out what killed off the rest…"

"We can find that and use it again?" Evan jokingly supplied.

Sophia smirked but shook her head. "No, we can figure out what went wrong the first time."

"Why?" Hiker arched an eyebrow at her, a deep curiosity in his gaze.

"Because we were almost extinct," Sophia began, trying to piece everything together in her head as she spoke. "It started with us warring with each other, the angel and demon dragonriders. It feels like that's where we're heading once more. Magicians loathe us right now. Tensions are high. Mortals don't trust us. We're fighting to stay alive against our own. What if history repeats itself? There are only so many of us left and no more dragon eggs to replace us."

"Are you offering to dig into this matter?" Hiker asked. "Can you figure out the missing part of history?"

Sophia nodded with determination. This felt right—the most logical next thread to pull. "Yes, and I know exactly where to look. It's through understanding what went wrong in the past that we correct the future. We have to figure out what went wrong and fix it this time."

CHAPTER FOUR

In Los Angeles, Sophia was used to steady warm temperatures. If constant was what she wanted, Scotland offered that, reminding Sophia of her childhood hometown. However, it wasn't nonstop sunny weather in Scotland, but rather the persistent rains. At least Sophia knew what to expect day in and day out—rain.

Sophia didn't have a predictable job, so having predictable weather was nice, even constant showers. She didn't mind it so much. It was humbling, and Lunis had explained the weather in Scotland was chosen by the first generation of dragons as their home because they believed it made them hardy, but more importantly, it strengthened their riders. Only the tough could ride on the cutting winds with their heads held high, and their shoulders braced against the cold.

The rain had let up for the time being when Sophia stepped out onto the Expanse of the Gullington after the meeting in Hiker's office. However, she didn't delude herself into thinking that meant the sun would break free from the blanket of thick clouds and bask the grounds in rays of golden light. It merely meant that she wouldn't get drenched during her meeting with Lunis.

The blue dragon flew down from his new place, a cave opening beside the Nest known as the Pad. It wasn't cold and damp like the

Cave with the elder dragons. Nor was it filled with dragonettes like the Nest. It was all Lunis' and pimped out to his taste with surround-sound speakers, tons of electronics, snacks, and a cozy bed for him to sprawl out on.

Lunis landed on the soft ground beside Sophia with a new serenity on his face. They were quiet for a long moment, not even greeting each other but rather soaking in each other's presence without words.

Finally, Sophia said, "So, the new place—"

"It's incredible!" Lunis exclaimed, cutting her off, his tone vibrating with excitement. "I couldn't sleep. There were so many fun things to check out. I have a Nintendo Switch now and don't need your stupid phone or to rely on my cracked iPad that you got me secondhand from Liv—"

"You're welcome," Sophia said dryly.

"Then I got a stomachache from eating too many spicy Cheetos," Lunis continued.

"Which is why you have cheese dust under your claws," Sophia observed after glancing down at the dragon's feet.

"I took a long soak and finally fell asleep listening to rock music at full volume, without a care in the world for waking the baby dragons who haven't let me have a good night's rest since they defiled my world with their repugnant existence." Lunis finished with a dreamy quality in his green eyes.

"You get that the new generation is supremely important and the world's future rests on their existence and growth," Sophia blandly stated.

Lunis gave her a dismissive look. "Whatever. It doesn't mean I have to like them."

"Well, I'm glad you like the Pad and that you're able to have your space and quiet," Sophia offered.

"By quiet, you mean I blared Metallica until my ears bled."

"Metallica, eh?" Sophia questioned, surprised. "That's a bit different than your usual pop music choices."

"I'm in a particularly angsty mood, displaying my independence from the colony."

SARAH NOFFKE & MICHAEL ANDERLE

Sophia nodded, enjoying the cool mist laced in the wind that swept across the Expanse. A few dragonettes flying low in the sky followed it, gaining height as they headed for the Barrier.

"They're leaving." Sophia indicated the almost full-grown dragons.

Lunis nodded. "That's the second group today. They're ready, it seems. Or they're bored without me around the Nest for them to annoy."

"See? You forced them to spread their wings by moving out of the Nest." Sophia laughed.

Lunis gave her an irritated look. "Your puns know no bounds."

"You're welcome."

"No, they really should. Leave the puns to me. I'm better at them. You're the pretty one. I'm the funny one. Let's not step on each other's roles."

Sophia shook her head. "I won't be confined. You do you, boo. I'll do me."

He rolled his eyes at this. "Leave the hip talk to me too. Otherwise, you'll get all this shade thrown at you, and it will be big yikes."

"You're straight up trippin'. I totes know the current hip slang," Sophia argued.

Lunis shook his head. "You're so cringy, you potato."

"What are you even saying right now?"

"You not understanding the current lingo of the zoomer generation is a 'you' problem," Lunis said smugly but playfully winked at Sophia.

She laughed and pointed at the Barrier where the dragons were about to fly through. "Do you think they'll return?"

"Yes. I think they'll return with riders."

Sophia smiled wide. "So it begins." She glanced around at the Expanse and the Pond in the distance. "Our once quiet little home is about to get a lot busier."

Lunis nodded, suddenly turning mildly serious. "Soak it in while you can because I have a feeling that when the new generation of dragonriders come to the Gullington, things will become more complex. More than that, I think our roles will be more demanding."

CHAPTER FIVE

The founders' ancient language danced under Sophia's fingertips as she ran them over the walls in the entryway of the House of Fourteen. The gold lettering swirled and sparkled like it was coming alive from Sophia's touch. She couldn't read it since she wasn't a Warrior or Councilor for the House of Fourteen, but many of those who were didn't know the language either. It was something that they inherently could understand, but had to work at—like many abilities in life.

What do you say? Sophia wondered to herself, half-expecting Lunis to pop into her head with a sarcastic answer.

She didn't mind that she'd never become a Warrior for the House of Fourteen, taking the position that Liv at first fulfilled until she was old enough. Liv was the perfect Warrior, and Sophia was destined to be a dragonrider. However, now and again, she longed to know the secrets that only Warriors and Councilors knew, like how to read the founders' ancient language.

Deciding to push the thoughts out of her head, Sophia shrugged. *Oh, well. I guess I'll never decipher the ancient language, and that's okay.*

"As I once said," a voice sang at Sophia's back and startled her. She thought she'd been alone.

She didn't see anyone when she first spun, but then her eyes found the small unassuming black and white cat sitting at the far end of the long corridor. Plato smirked at her.

"Ignorance, the root and stem of all evil," the lynx continued.

Sophia narrowed her eyes and tilted her head. "Where did that come from? That bit about ignorance? Were you in my head, hearing me give up about ever understanding the ancient language?"

The cat strode in her direction with his tail high in the air, its white tip flicking from side to side. "I have no idea what you mean."

Sophia sighed. "Why would I ever need to read the ancient language? Liv can if I ever need information. It's not like I need it to control the House of Fourteen. What they do is separate from the issues the Dragon Elite faces."

"If you do not take an interest in the affairs of your government, you are doomed to live under the rule of fools," Plato imparted, a sneaky grin under his whiskers.

"Why are you quoting the philosopher, Plato?"

His light expression disappeared. "I'm not. That man quoted me."

Sophia nodded, realizing she should have expected this. "I know that Lorenzo Rosario and Bianca Montavani on the council for the House of Fourteen are corrupt. Probably that newbie Marty Martinez too. I think they're mostly harmless, trying to benefit personally from their public positions."

"Don't you think they'll be intimidated by anyone or anything that stands to steal that power?"

"Well, of course. It's been a constant struggle with the council to accept the Dragon Elite. They don't like what we represent or that it outranks their authority in the world. I'm certain that things are tense with the Rogue Riders out there giving us a bad name."

"I can assure you that they are."

Sophia sighed. "Yeah, well, I'll have to deal with that soon, but I'm not sure how."

"Good actions give strength to ourselves and inspire good actions in others," Plato stated sagely.

"So serve through example," she replied, a doubtful edge in her voice as though she were trying to unravel the threads of wisdom Professor Plato dangled in front of her. How was it that she felt like the feline playing with a string in that scenario?

He nodded.

"I guess," Sophia replied. "It's hard to do that and not react in other ways, defending the Dragon Elite. Fighting for our good name."

"Oh, but we're twice-armed if we fight with faith."

Sophia stuck her hands on her hips. "Are you going to keep answering me with lines of Plato, the philosopher, who apparently plagiarized them from you, although the whole timeline of that hurts my head and confounds me?"

"In the words of the great Confucius," Plato began, "the man who asks a question is a fool for a minute. The man who does not ask is a fool for life."

Pretending not to be amused by her sister's familiar, Sophia batted her eyelashes at Plato. "Well, here's a question you probably won't answer. How is it that I'm supposed to find the Rogue Riders so that I can stop them from doing whatever they're doing and therefore protect the Dragon Elite's reputation?"

Sophia firmly believed she'd hear another Plato quote, or maybe one from another famous philosopher. However, Plato replied, "When I'm looking for a mouse, I don't search for the rodents. Instead, I seek their cheese. When I find that, it's not long until I locate my prey."

A laugh popped out of Sophia's mouth. "When have you ever eaten a mouse?"

Plato didn't at all appear impressed. "That's the takeaway from my advice that I obviously shouldn't have given you?"

Sophia wiped the laughing expression off her face, becoming suddenly serious. "No, and thank you. I get what you're saying. I need to go after what the Rogue Riders are interested in—criminals. Still, there are so many in the world. How am I supposed to find them, and how am I supposed to know which ones? Then there's how am I supposed to—"

"There is no harm in repeating a good thing," Plato interrupted, quoting once more. "Unless it's the blasted question of how. I trust you know someone who can help you find criminals and figure out which ones will be best to target."

Sophia nodded while chewing on her lip. "Yeah, I have a few resources." Her eyes lifted to meet Plato's. "Thanks for the tip. It's a good idea to find the Rogue Riders by going after their own. Now I have to figure out how to get the world to trust us again, which will be difficult since our job as the Dragon Elite always makes enemies for us."

"When men speak ill of thee," Plato began, "live so nobody may believe them."

Sophia thought about this notion. "I think that strategy involves a long game. For the time being, the world isn't buying everything we have to say, even if it's the truth."

Plato nodded with understanding. "No one is more hated than he who speaks the truth."

"You know," Sophia mused. "You had some pretty good lines."

"Had?" he questioned, raising an eyebrow.

Sophia nodded. "Had. Have. You get the point. Anyway, I was looking for information on the history of the old demon dragonriders. You wouldn't happen to be willing to fill me in on it?" There was a hopeful edge in Sophia's voice.

"Your first inclination to seek out your brother for the information was right."

Sophia lowered her chin. "You're not allowed in my head."

Plato sauntered past her and wiggled his tail in the air. "Get on the list of those who tell me what I'm not allowed to do."

"Fine," Sophia seethed. "Stay in my head. Don't tell me about lost history. Still, maybe you'll impart something."

Plato turned, seemingly willing to entertain one last question.

"Did the philosopher, Plato, steal all your words?" Sophia asked. "Or was he real at all?"

"He was," Plato answered. "He had one original quote."

Sophia gave the lynx an expression that said, "Go on then."

"He was a wise man who invented beer," Plato stated and vanished without a trace.

CHAPTER SIX

Sophia found herself laughing as the lynx disappeared, leaving her alone once more in the entry hall of the House of Fourteen.

Plato had been strangely helpful, giving Sophia the idea of going after the criminals of the world to find the Rogue Riders. That was still a lofty goal and a little overwhelming, but she had some ideas to make the monumental task a little easier.

She didn't like it one bit that Plato could poke into her head, but Sophia also recognized that trying to keep one of the most powerful entities on Earth out of her mind was a waste of her time. Instead, she focused her attention on finding Clark, who she knew wasn't at the apartment since she'd already stopped by there on her way over. There also wasn't a meeting happening in the Chamber of the Tree for another hour.

Thankfully for Sophia, Clark was a creature of habit. He wasn't at the apartment he shared with Liv and Stefan, so he was somewhere in the House of Fourteen. Her brother wasn't the type to hang out at coffee shops or taverns on his time off.

For starters, there wasn't really time off for Clark. There was merely the in-between when he slept, ate, and got ready. Also, he wasn't the type to hang out. Living with Liv had softened him up a little and now and then he'd chill on the sofa. However, Liv had argued that while they were vegging and watching Netflix, he was quietly plotting out his ten-year plan, finessing it to the smallest detail.

After checking a few of Clark's usual haunts, Sophia realized exactly where to find her brother and wondered how she hadn't guessed that first. Her feet brought her up to the House of Fourteen's top level, where one of the best and strangest parts of the building resided—the library.

The library in the House of Fourteen wasn't as majestic as the Great Library, which held every book ever written and instantly updated with new editions as they occurred. However, it had mostly all magical books, which made it a fascinating place to visit. The books were alive in one regard, due to the magic they held, and therefore the volumes greatly influenced their home.

Finding Clark in such a big area usually would have been difficult, but the library in the House of Fourteen, much like the Castle, responded to people's thoughts. That's how one found the book they were looking for or found themselves completely lost, depending on how they directed their thoughts. All someone had to do was think about what—or in this case who—they were looking for, and the library would rearrange itself accordingly to lead the searcher to the right aisle, row, and book.

However, patrons in the library had to be diligent because their thoughts led them to what they were looking for, but those were fickle things that often changed without warning. One small diversion in thoughts and someone could go from being led to a book on shrinking spells to finding themselves shrunk and stuck in the belly of a beast. Magic was a tricky thing, and even those who understood it well knew better than to think they could fully understand it all.

Moreover, the library didn't hold up signs that led the way to whatever a person was looking for. On its path to continue to be tricky, the library offered clues on where to go and the person following them had to be on the lookout, following the right direction and not getting fooled.

Clark, Sophia thought to herself. *Where is Clark?*

"Beaufont," she hastily added. "The person." She didn't want to go to a shrine for Clark Gable or books on Dick Clark. Both of whom were magicians, but few knew that.

"I need to find my brother, Clark Beaufont," she said to the quiet library that seemed to go on for miles.

She did her best not to focus on the overwhelming size of the place or the many other things vying for her attention. Her job was to stay focused.

Sophia closed her eyes and clearly saw her brother's face in her mind. She focused on that, as if his flesh-and-blood body stood in front of her right then. Her foot moved forward without her consent.

Her eyes sprang open, and she almost wished they hadn't as the library spun all around her, turning into a blur and making her instantly dizzy. Although she was used to spiraling through the air on her dragon, the rotating library made her sick—probably because it was unnatural to her, she reasoned. Nothing was more natural than to fly through the air on her dragon.

Libraries that spun on their own, well, that was by far a more unnerving experience, especially because Sophia didn't know what to expect when it quit moving. All she could do was remain still, hoping that one of the many shelves of books speeding by her didn't knock her over or flatten her with the speed at which they moved. Also, Sophia was well aware that moving even an inch could mean she walked out a window at the back of the whirling library and fell to her death.

The House of Fourteen's library patrons risked their lives every time they ventured to find a book. Such were the dangers one faced when searching for one of the greatest treasures in the world —knowledge.

Sophia was about to close her eyes again when she noticed the spinning slow, as though she was at the center of a disc that rotated itself to a stop. She drew in a breath, expecting to see an aisle in front of her that led to another one, then a set of clues and more spinning. Instead, she found herself face-to-face with her brother, who started and screamed as he fell backward, stumbling onto his backside and hands.

CHAPTER SEVEN

Sophia stopped herself from laughing at her spooked brother, who was all white as his chest heaved. He must have been tracking unsuspectingly through the library, reading the book he'd since dropped on the floor, and suddenly found himself nose-to-nose with Sophia. It would have scared most anyone, but Clark was also a little more excitable than many. It didn't take much to make him reach for an anti-anxiety potion.

Clark was still on his tailbone, looking up at Sophia from the floor as though trying to decide if she were real or an apparition.

She extended a hand to him as she smiled sensitively. "Sorry that I scared you. I blame the library."

He nodded and looked around, trying to get his bearings. "It stuck you right in front of me. You must have really focused on finding me."

She smiled. "I'm glad it worked, and so efficiently. Yes, I need your help with something and thought you could save me the time of looking."

A forced chuckle fell from Clark's mouth as he took Sophia's hand and allowed her to haul him up to his feet. "You don't seem to have any difficulty finding things, or me, in this case."

Sophia nearly threw Clark into the air when she lifted him to his feet, forgetting how light he was. Unlike the other dragonriders she was used to sparring with, who were all muscle, Clark was rather skinny and hunched over most of the time, making him close to her short height. However, where Clark was weak in strength, he was strong in knowledge. Sophia's brother had to be one of the smartest people she knew, and that was saying quite a lot since she knew the brightest in the world.

"Are you all right?" Sophia looked her brother over when he was on his feet.

He pressed his starched suit down as if it had been wrinkled in the ordeal, although it looked as flawless as when he probably ironed it that morning. Clark couldn't be any more different from the T-shirt and jeans-wearing Liv. They were complete opposites, and for that, Sophia was grateful that they had each other.

Liv made Clark cut loose and eat ice cream in bed, and Clark reminded Liv that she couldn't leave the empty container on the floor afterward or they'd attract ants. Sophia was the luckiest of the three because she had the best sister and brother that anyone could ask for. She might have lost her parents and Ian and Reese, but she was still so rich in life, and she never wanted to forget that. At the end of the day, it wasn't about what someone lost, but about how much they loved that which they had.

"I'm fine." The crease between Clark's eyes deepened as he looked Sophia over. "Are you? Is this about the Council?"

Sophia blinked at him. "What about the Council?"

"Their request for your attendance at today's meeting," he said with surprise as if he thought she was already aware of this.

She shook her head. "I wasn't aware that they'd paged me."

"Oh, so that's not what this is about then?"

Sophia folded her arms over her chest. "Let me guess. The Council is pissed about all the trouble the Rogue Riders are making?"

Clark nodded solemnly. "I'm sure you can reassure them that it's all under control."

"I can lie," Sophia joked, which didn't get a laugh from her brother whereas Liv would have thought it was funny.

"Beaufonts don't lie," he warned, his tone punishing.

"Of course I won't." The playfulness disappeared from her tone. "I don't think I have much to offer that will make the Council feel better. The Dragon Elite aren't lying down, that's for sure. That's why I'm here. I need your help with filling in the history, and since you pretty much memorized the Forgotten Archives, I thought you could save me the trouble of doing the research."

Clark perked up. Now Sophia was speaking his language. Talking about books was how Clark kept himself calm. It was his Prozac. "Yes, I've read through the Forgotten Archives a few times. What can I help you with?"

Sophia sighed with relief. "Oh, good. I thought so. You see, I think the best way to keep the dragonriders from repeating history is to figure out what went wrong in the past. It should be recorded in the *Complete History of Dragonriders*, but there's a lag on the information."

"Lag?" Clark didn't follow her casual jargon. Sophia almost laughed while thinking of Lunis trying to use his hip lingo on her brother.

"Yeah, the history of what happened to the rest of the demon dragonriders after Thad Reinhart hasn't been recorded, not in its entirety," Sophia explained. "I'm not sure why I'm looking for the information, but I thought it could be helpful. I have this sick feeling that we, the Dragon Elite and Rogue Riders nearly killed each other to extinction. If that's the case, then we're quickly heading back down that same path, and I have to turn us around before it's too late."

Clark's gaze slid to the side with an uncertain expression on his face. "You don't know that part of history?"

Sophia blinked at him, not expecting the question. "No. Not even Hiker knows because the Dragon Elite were stuck inside the Gullington after the Great War when mortals couldn't see magic anymore. We know that some demon dragonriders left after Thad Reinhart went into hiding too, but when things went back to normal, almost all of them had disappeared. I want to figure out what happened." A thought occurred to her that made her mouth pop open with shock. "Oh, could the demon dragonriders have gone after each other? I know that Thad used some for experiments when trying to fix his dragon, Ember. That doesn't account for all the rest. There would have been a lot—at least a dozen or so."

"Thad Reinhart didn't have much respect for his own," Clark said through a long, heavy breath. "However, he's not what nearly brought the demon dragonriders and dragonriders in general to extinction." He gave her a grave expression, reluctance heavy on his face. "It was the House of Seven."

CHAPTER EIGHT

S peechless. Sophia felt like he'd punched her in the throat. She'd expected to learn the many horrible things her own had done to each other, nearly sending the dragonriders into extinction. What she hadn't expected was for the betrayal to come from the House—also one of her own.

Sophia found a chair nearby, suddenly feeling lightheaded, and sat in the sturdy straight-back. She hadn't remembered seeing the chair there a moment before but was grateful for its sudden appearance and the fact that it supported her when she felt sick to her stomach from the spinning library and news from Clark.

"Tell me what happened," Sophia urged when she'd collected herself.

Clark nodded, taking a seat opposite of Sophia's that also wasn't there moments prior. He was still pale and appeared as uneasy as her. "It's a dark part of history. Well, darker. We as magicians don't have a lot of positives in the last few hundred years. Not until Liv came to the House did things start to turn around, and now we're not writing such a bleak history anymore."

Sophia smiled, swallowed, and enjoyed the first piece of good news so far. "I'm grateful for that. It only takes one to change things."

"Unfortunately, that's true on both sides," Clark stated darkly. "It was the one known as the God Magician who was responsible for slaughtering many of the remaining demon dragonriders."

"Talon Sinclair," Sophia gasped, remembering when Liv and the others had to battle the oldest remaining magician who had done so much to take over the House and tried to extinguish mortals. Apparently, he'd tried to get rid of the dragonriders too.

"That's right," Clark affirmed. "From what I learned from the Forgotten Archives, which aren't complete but rather pockets of our history, the dragonriders were divided. It's good to note that when a race is separated like that, either by choice or force or by views, it's easy to break them up further and get rid of them."

The revulsion rose higher in Sophia's throat. She knew her brother was right. Worse, the dragonriders were headed back in that direction, having been divided by interests. The Dragon Elite wanted peace and justice, and the Rogue Riders wanted to capitalize off crime and gain by taking that which didn't belong to them. It seemed like such a distant possibility that the two organizations could come together, but would they end each other if they didn't?

Maybe sensing that Sophia was struggling with this new information, Clark paused. After a moment he continued, his tone careful, "With the dragonriders divided, the Dragon Elite hiding away, and the Rogue Riders pretty much ineffective without a leader, the remaining demon dragonriders were scattered. Talon Sinclair lured them to an empty field and had the Warriors for the House take them out. I don't think the dragonriders saw it coming, and with their magic disabled, they were at several disadvantages."

Sophia gasped, thinking of how disoriented those dragonriders would have been. "As dragonriders, we think we're the strongest out there. But it's that assumption that can put us in real danger. No one should ever convince themselves they're invincible because that's when someone can strike a lethal blow."

Clark nodded. "That's very true. I'm glad you recognize it. Usually, the strongest are taken down by a sideways blow they never saw coming. Remember that you're only as strong as your perception is clear. If it gets muddied, then you'll be vulnerable to all sorts of attacks."

"So Talon Sinclair murdered the remaining demon dragonriders," Sophia stated, her eyes looking without seeing.

"Most of them," Clark answered. "Not all came when he called, but yes, I think we can credit him with taking out a vast majority of them."

"Why?" Sophia asked. "Besides the obvious that he was after power and control, and the dragonriders outrank everyone else."

"There's that. It will continue to be an uphill battle for you, as you already know from dealing with the Council. However, the problems long ago are still part of the current ones. Chiefly, I think Talon Sinclair firmly believed that erasing mortals from seeing magic and taking out dragonriders created a better world. Like many presently, he didn't think anything good could come from demon dragonriders. That's the hardest perception you'll have to change. The Rogue Riders aren't doing the Dragon Elite any favors."

Sophia nodded. "I agree they're out of control. Under their current leadership, there are many problems. I can't believe that all demon dragonriders are bad. Thad Reinhart did a lot of amazing things. They're talented. I think they have to be controlled."

"Who is going to do that?" Clark asked, an edge to his voice. He was in Councilor mode all of a sudden. Still, he only echoed the tone she'd soon face from the Council for the House of Fourteen and Sophia was grateful for the chance to practice.

"The Dragon Elite," Sophia stated with confidence. "We're going to control the new dragonriders, and we're going to keep history from repeating itself."

"I hope you're right, Soph, because there are a lot of magicians who don't want you all ruling this planet." Clark shook his head, regret on his face. "The dragonriders have more enemies than ever before. I dare say, there are many who don't want the dragonriders on this planet at all."

CHAPTER NINE

S ophia knew that Clark was only trying to help, preparing her for what she'd meet when she faced the Council. However, after learning that it was the House of Fourteen, then the House of Seven, that had taken out many of the old generation of dragonriders, it was difficult not to be overly sensitive about all the matters.

She knew she couldn't blame anyone on the current Council for what happened to the demon dragonriders, but that didn't make the news any easier to digest. It felt like such a personal betrayal, her magicians' race taking out her society—the dragonriders.

Acutely, Sophia felt the raw emotion and vengeance Liv had expressed when she learned that the House of Seven was responsible for mortals not seeing magic and going to great lengths to bury the secrets. One of those was murdering Guinevere and Theodore Beaufont and their children, Ian and Reese.

That had been personal, no doubt, but the Sinclairs who were responsible for that were gone, and with it, mortals could see magic once more. However, Sophia wasn't convinced that the same Council that had murdered dragonriders all those centuries ago was much different than the current one. Something told her that if the majority had their way, they'd dispose of dragonriders again.

There were too many variables with the dragonriders that people didn't understand and therefore feared. She had to change all that. The Dragon Elite was already working on it. Still, it wasn't only about perception, and she instinctively knew that. Something had to change with dragonriders in general, or history would repeat itself. Sophia didn't know what though.

The vibe in the Chamber of the Tree did little to relieve her tension when she stepped through the Door of Reflection. Anger flared in her chest at the sight of the Council, although again she knew these weren't the people responsible for slaughtering the demon dragonriders.

It's the institution you despise, Lunis offered in her head, having learned everything that she had.

Did you know about what happened to the demon dragonriders? Sophia asked, realizing that the events could have been locked away in the dragons' shared consciousness.

If I did, I would have told you, he stated with remorse. *Those were my ancestors, and the information hasn't come easily. Talon Sinclair must have done something to block it.*

Sophia strode through the domed room and took her place in front of the Council, intending to make her presence known rather than waiting to be called from the back. There were only a few Warriors present, Liv being one of them. Beside her were Trudy DeVries and Stefan Ludwig, Liv's husband.

Talon Sinclair was a very powerful magician, Sophia related to Lunis, the chatter between the council and Stefan mostly on mute in her head. *If anyone could have blocked the memory from the dragons, it would have been him.*

You're right that the dragonriders have to change, Lunis observed, having followed her thoughts. *I don't know what has to happen there either, but the current structure isn't working, and we're heading for more doom and extinction at this point.*

You think the institution of the House of Fourteen is a problem too? Sophia asked curiously. *They've adapted the structure. Now mortals sit on the Council and vote on issues, as well as other magical races.*

It's more balanced than it used to be, but I think there's still corruption at its core, Lunis stated.

Can that ever be fixed entirely? Sophia wondered.

I want to believe that it can, Lunis answered. *It's about who's in power. There are those who lead because they want to make the world better. Because they want to protect justice.*

Like Hiker with the Dragon Elite, Sophia offered.

Yes, Lunis affirmed. *Then there are those who lead because they want to gain personally and they're motivated by fear and their selfish desires.*

Sounds like a lot of people I know. Sophia glared up at the Council, her eyes on Lorenzo Rosario, who she knew had betrayed the Dragon Elite already when Nevin Gooseman was in power politically. He was motivated by fear and the idea that power could be lost if not hoarded, and threatening entities like the dragonriders cut it down a notch or two.

Then there were Bianca Montavani and Marty Martinez. Sophia didn't know if they were inherently out for selfish gains or motivated by fear. Bianca had no doubt been a pawn in the Sinclairs' vie for power. Maybe she wasn't totally evil, but those on the Council were supposed to be individual thinkers who voted based on their knowledge and expertise. If anyone voted based on pressure, then Lunis was right, and the institution was corrupt.

It appeared that Sophia had more to figure out than how the dragonriders needed to change to create balance. It sounded like the other very powerful organization of the House of Fourteen had to change.

"I don't see why you can't assign the case to me!" Stefan's voice flared, pulling Sophia from her thoughts on how to fix the broken world and all its broken parts. She shoved it all to the side for the moment, deciding it wouldn't be an easy fix or one that she could discover right then when about to meet with the Council.

Lorenzo Rosario leaned forward, looking down his crooked nose at the Warrior in all black. Stefan wore a long traveling cloak that matched his jet black hair and the mud that splattered his boots could also be found under his fingertips when he wasn't gripping his fists.

"I don't believe your opinion on how the Council assigns cases is relevant," Lorenzo stated, authority in his tone. "You have your cases hunting demons. Ms. Beaufont has hers."

"Mrs. Beaufont," Stefan corrected through clenched teeth.

"I prefer to go by Mrs. Warrior Beaufont-Ludwig because it's a real mouthful," Liv joked, obviously trying to break up the tension building between the Councilor and her husband.

"She returned from a mission this morning," Stefan argued. "Neither Trudy nor I have had a case in days."

"That's the nature of how the cases came in," Haro stated matter-of-factly. "We've had some demon cases come to our attention."

"Fine, I'll take that one," Stefan said at once, determination in his voice. "Give the squabble between the giants and the gnomes to Trudy."

Lorenzo narrowed his eyes at Stefan. "Liv is better at negotiating with the giants, and we all know that. Whereas Ms. DeVries has her strengths, they aren't in the area of dispute resolution."

"The only way to resolve this ongoing quarrel will be with bloodshed, and we all know that!" Stefan exclaimed as his face flushed red.

Sophia had never seen him like this. Based on the annoyed expression on Liv's face, she had and wasn't in the mood to put up with it.

"It's fine, Stef," Liv encouraged, her tone full of irritation. Sophia couldn't decide if she was annoyed at her husband or the case she was being assigned. Something told her it was a little bit of everything. Liv didn't seem like her usually chipper self, but if she had returned from a case that morning, she could be exhausted on many levels.

"It's not fine, Liv," Stefan said urgently, not taking his eyes off Lorenzo. "She only returned this morning from dealing with those goblins that had taken over that mall in Alabama."

"It wasn't as much a mall as it was a series of stores that looked like they'd been thrown up by an Abercrombie and Fitch and Cinnabon," Liv joked.

"She nearly lost a finger from a goblin trying to bite her," Clark stated to Lorenzo, obviously in favor that Liv deserved a break.

Liv held up her middle finger and flexed it at Lorenzo, essentially flipping him off. "But I didn't. Still works. See?"

Lorenzo rolled his eyes.

The Councilors beside him scoffed.

"Oh, really, do you have no dignity?" Bianca asked rhetorically. "A Warrior should never show such disrespect to the Council."

Liv directed her middle finger at Bianca. "I'm simply showing you all that the little goblin didn't get the best of me. Don't you care, B?"

She scowled at Liv, her expression hot with anger.

"As I was saying," Stefan cut in, "you don't have a case for Trudy, but you're already sending Liv out again."

"That is not your concern," Lorenzo stated. "Ms. Beaufont showed up for this meeting. She shouldn't have done that unless she was prepared to be assigned a case."

"In truth," Hester DeVries began. "It was so she could give her report on the goblin incident."

"Clark and I carpool, and today was his turn to buy donuts," Liv added playfully. "I didn't want to miss that. He made us go to this organic donut shop that serves only vegan fare. We spent his hard-earned money on an eight dollar donut. I'm going to tell you, watching him shell out the money for a donut I nibbled on and refused to eat was worth coming in today to see all your chipper faces. Especially when I could have used the morning to sleep in after having to peel a goblin from the ceiling of a Macy's department store."

"Oh, really, the Council doesn't need you derailing this with breakfast stories," Bianca complained and shook her head, her hair tightly pulled back into a bun that slanted her eyes.

Sophia realized she probably should have taken this opportunity to exert authority and interrupt, demanding the Council give her audience, but the things going on were too interesting to her, and it seemed many others in the Chamber of the Tree. Hester and Raina appeared entertained by Liv's breakfast story. Clark was irritated, as usual. The rest of the council seemed ambivalent, everyone but Lorenzo.

"The point remains that we need a Warrior to intervene in the giant and gnome situation," Lorenzo stated. "Liv is the best option. The Council has made its decision."

Based on the sour expressions on Hester's, Raina's, and Clark's faces, Sophia guessed they hadn't voted for Liv to take the case.

"Ms. DeVries will remain on call for the next available case that comes up," Haro added, sorting through his files.

"This is ridiculous," Stefan nearly shouted again. "We all know that the giants and gnomes are on the verge of war."

"Not if a Warrior for the House of Fourteen does something about it," Marty Martinez said in a shrewish voice.

Lorenzo nodded. "That's right. These clans can find peace if offered a solution."

"They will battle first," Stefan argued.

"Stef," Liv said from the corner of her mouth. "I've got this. Don't worry."

"Fat chance of that," he fired back, still not taking his eyes off the Council.

"You two have been assigned cases," Bianca stated smugly from the bench. "You are dismissed."

Neither Warrior moved as Lorenzo directed his attention to Sophia. "Now it's time that we discuss the dragonriders and the global crisis that they've single-handedly created."

CHAPTER TEN

"I'm not sure that expression works there," Liv interjected. "You see, dragonriders would have two hands. Then I think their dragons have, like, four. So, I don't see how the plural of dragonriders can singlehandedly do something. Maybe solely is a better word."

"Ms. Beaufont!" Lorenzo yelled, his eyes bulging slightly. "You've been dismissed. The Council has had enough of your interruptions."

"I think that when it comes to word usage, I can be of help," Liv argued, mischief in her voice. "I mean, you yourself said I was the queen of negotiations."

"I didn't say that," Lorenzo fired back.

"Potato, potato," she replied, saying both words the same way. "Anyway, what I'm great at is getting separate societies to understand each other, like giants and gnomes. It's a family thing, I think, because Soph here is a master arbitrator. If you're referring to a collective organization as having a single hand—"

"That is quite enough," Bianca interrupted, her cheeks flushing red.

Liv looked like she'd had enough, having gotten the Councilor flustered. "Okey-dokey."

"You're dismissed," Lorenzo stated.

"Yeah, but I'm taking my sister to lunch, so I should stick around," Liv argued. "I saved money on breakfast so I can buy her nachos."

"If you're going to stay, then we're going to require that you're quiet." Lorenzo glared down at Liv.

"I can do that," Liv sang, rocking forward on her toes and back again on her heels.

"I'll believe it when I see it," Bianca retorted arrogantly.

"Technically," Liv drew out the word. "You would believe it when you heard it, or rather when you didn't hear anything."

"Ms. Beaufont, will you stop making a mockery of these meetings?" Lorenzo questioned, his expression severe.

Liv pretended to zip her lips closed and threw the imaginary key over her shoulder. She then bowed as though giving the floor back to the Council.

Sophia had trouble hiding her laughter. From the looks of it, so did Hester, Raina, and Clark. However, their brother's reaction was more brooding disapproval. He never appreciated it when Liv acted out at meetings, which Sophia could have told him only encouraged her.

"Ms. Beaufont." Lorenzo turned his attention to Sophia.

"That one is a Miss," Stefan interrupted the Councilor.

"Although I think it would be more appropriate to call her by her title." Hester nodded at Stefan.

"Yes," Raina agreed. "That would be Rider Beaufont."

Lorenzo appeared ready to come unglued, his eyes growing wide. Liv hadn't said a word, as she promised, but she'd done her job and encouraged others to copy her defiant behavior. "Titles aren't our concern here."

"They should be," Haro Takahashi corrected. "Titles are a form of respect and if we, as the Councilors, don't honor the importance of prestigious roles such as those held by dragonriders, then I think we set ourselves up for a whole host of problems."

"Quite right," Clark affirmed. "How are we supposed to demand the respect we deserve if we don't offer that same thing to others?"

Lorenzo sighed. "Can we all focus on the matter at hand? The dragonriders are creating problems on a global scale."

Bianca nodded adamantly while holding up a report. "That's correct. Crime is up worldwide, reaching unprecedented levels. It isn't even the demon dragonriders that are the biggest contributors to this trend, directly, although they are responsible for much of it. The real problem seems to be that criminals are now under the protection of dragonriders, making it impossible for mortal police to quell the rise."

Marty shook his head, staring down at Sophia. "How do you respond to the allegations, Rider Beaufont?"

Sophia had to give it to the newbie to the House of Fourteen. At least he called her by the right title, even if he talked to her like she was a toddler.

"The important distinction here is that these criminal offenses and the spike in misconducts aren't the results of dragonriders in general," Sophia began, her chin high and voice clear and loud. "It's the result of a new or rather existing organization that's reformed known as the Rogue Riders."

"Which is comprised of demon dragonriders, isn't that correct?" Haro asked.

"Yes, but—"

"Which supports the case that Nevin Gooseman made against the demon dragonriders," Bianca interrupted Sophia.

"Nevin Gooseman was a madman," Sophia argued. "He went to dangerous lengths to try and take out the Dragon Elite."

"Although we can all agree that Nevin Gooseman wasn't of sound mind and went to extremes, he might have been right regarding his concerns about the demon dragonriders," Marty stated.

"He wasn't," Sophia countered through clenched teeth.

"Are there any demon dragonriders that serve on the Elite?" Lorenzo asked.

"Well, no, but—"

"Your mission as the Dragon Elite is to protect justice," Lorenzo cut in. "What do these Rogue Riders do?"

"Besides cause mayhem." Bianca harrumphed.

"They've taken on the role of governing criminals," Sophia

answered and immediately regretted it. The stir this admission caused across the Council was abrupt. There were sounds of protest, whispering, and plenty of sighs and groans.

"Well, no wonder the world is out of control," Bianca said shrilly over the commotion.

"The new generation of demon dragonriders do need to learn boundaries," Sophia began. "The Dragon Elite are working on it, but like a rebellious teenager, the Rogue Riders might need to make mistakes before they listen to reason."

"Likening magicians who ride on dragons to teenagers is exactly where the Dragon Elite is failing the world at large," Lorenzo criticized.

"They're young and inexperienced though," Sophia stated, careful to keep her chin up although she felt the pressure from every direction and it made her feel so small. "These new demon dragonriders have a lot of sudden power, and it has gone to their heads, but we're hopeful that we can control them."

"When?" Marty asked at once, on the heels of Sophia's statement. "When they've already destroyed the world? When do you plan on intervening and taking control of these teenagers, as you call them?"

Note to self, Lunis said in Sophia's head. *Marty needs me to torch his pants.*

Sophia refrained from laughing but silently agreed. The real answer to Marty's question was as soon as they could locate the Rogue Riders, but that would only make her and the Dragon Elite sound even more like they didn't have things under control. She needed to fix that perception even if it wasn't entirely accurate. Hopefully, soon it would be, and the Dragon Elite would be on their way to governing the Rogue Riders.

"We pushed the Rogue Riders out of the elfin homeland," Sophia began with confidence. "And—"

"What lands are they taking over now, I wonder?" Bianca interrupted.

Sophia held her breath, reminding herself that murder was wrong even if the person was begging for it. She nearly laughed out loud, thinking that Liv's proximity must be inspiring her naughty behavior and rebellious humor.

"I'm not aware of any lands that the Rogue Riders have commandeered," Sophia replied when she was sure she was in control of her temper, her tone neutral. "When the Dragon Elite kicked them off the elfin territory, we made it clear that they weren't to take over lands that didn't belong to them."

"So instead they're running a crime ring." Lorenzo huffed.

"They've elected themselves as the ones to govern the criminal world," Sophia corrected.

"Which shouldn't be governed at all, as if criminals deserve rights like nations and citizens," Bianca said. "They need to be locked up, and instead they're being encouraged."

"I agree!" Marty exclaimed.

Lorenzo nodded.

This was the problem with the Council, Sophia observed. The others who were more objective and voted based on justice—Clark, Raina, Hester, and sometimes Haro—were the quietest. Yes, they listened and contemplated whereas the others were reactionary, their agenda already formed based on their greedy desires. However, the Council couldn't have any balance as long as the "good" ones didn't have the same level of voice.

"I disagree," Sophia stated, making everyone freeze. They hadn't expected her to argue this point, but rather that the Dragon Elite were doing their job.

"The Rogue Riders might be new, and they need to learn boundaries," Sophia began, looking each of the Councilors in the eyes. "However, I applaud the initiative they've taken."

"You do?" It was Clark who asked this, quickly followed by Liv. She'd surprised her siblings, which meant the others were probably totally perplexed.

Not allowing herself to become flustered by the reaction she'd gotten, Sophia nodded. "I do. Policing horrible crimes such as murder and the like should happen. The mortal police's biggest concern should be going after those who brutally harm others. However, it's unrealistic to think that we'll ever control all crime."

"Spoken like a true underachiever," Marty spat.

Bianca nodded. "*And* she's a part of the Dragon Elite who want us to bow to them as a higher authority. If this isn't proof that we shouldn't, then I don't know what is."

"We have the support of Mother Nature," Sophia argued.

"So you say," Marty retorted.

"I do say, because it's true." Sophia narrowed her gaze at the man who so boldly questioned her honesty. "I stand by what I said. We can't abolish all crime, and the Rogue Riders have had the good sense to realize that. Yes, they're going about it the wrong way by capitalizing on the crimes, but there's something to be learned. If we try and blot out all illegal activity, then the criminals of the world will find a way around our laws. Isn't it better to keep tabs on the drug users of the world and make them pay into the system rather than hide under the radar where we can't do anything about them?"

"She has a point," Hester said, musing on the idea.

"Oh, you can't be serious!" Bianca challenged. "Now we're going to condone working with criminals?"

"I've been doing it for ages," Liv admitted.

"Why am I not surprised," Lorenzo stated dryly.

"It's true," Liv chirped. "There's a slew of gnomes who used to trade illegal magical artifacts on the black market. The stuff was usually harmless, but now and then, something really dangerous got traded. When they thought I was going to shut them down, they ran every time they saw me. It was only when I told them I wouldn't close their business as long as they adhered to some rules that we found an even ground. Now I stop in every so often to ensure the products are up to snuff and only sold to those who know what they're getting."

"So you're admitting to aiding illegal activity as a Warrior who has vowed to stop such things?" Bianca questioned.

"I pick my battles," Liv corrected. "In return, the gnomes don't shut me out, and when I need a favor, they're receptive." She turned and winked at Stefan. "Like when I need negotiations with giants to go smoothly, I'll have the right people on my side."

He nodded and released some of the tension from before.

Clark combed his hand over his chin, thinking. "This idea has merit. I mean, the mortal world saw its fair share of problems with the war on drugs. It did little to curb the problem. The dealers and users found other means."

"Exactly," Sophia said, keen to keep the excitement from her voice after getting the extra support from her siblings. They needed to remain professional and not like they were banding together merely out of nepotism. "It's not like we should allow bad things to happen, but we have to ask ourselves, just because something is against the law, does it make it wrong? Many things are wrong that aren't against the law, like lying and being mean to one another. I believe that in an ideal world, we could have some order in the criminal world so that things ran smoother. Criminals don't pay taxes, but if they were allowed to operate on some level, well, then they would. Think about all the horrible crimes we could prevent if a group of dragonriders had insight into what was happening on the black market level. We might avoid all sorts of things."

"So is this what the Rogue Riders are doing?" Haro asked.

Sophia bit her lip. "It's what they should be doing. However, they're a bit out of control."

Bianca laughed. "A bit out of control? They're encouraging crime, not regulating it."

To Sophia's dismay, she couldn't argue with that. "I realize that. However, we're going to get them under control. That's our responsibility as the world adjudicators and the supreme governing body."

Lorenzo shook his head and leaned forward. "You want to keep throwing around *that* title, but it's high time you showed us that you deserve it. The rest of the magical races are fed up with the dragonriders, having suffered from things done to them by the Rogue Riders. We're your last hope. If we turn our backs on you, you'll find a war on your hands."

"Is that a threat?" Sophia was surprised at how serious this had gotten. And fast.

Lorenzo tilted his head, not backing down. "It is. The Dragon Elite better figure out how to get the Rogue Riders and demon dragonriders under control. Otherwise, we'll have to intervene, and I fear it won't end well for you all."

CHAPTER ELEVEN

Sophia stared angrily at the thali platter that sat between her and Liv on the table in the Indian restaurant called Anarbagh in Woodland Hills. It was off their usual beaten path, but Liv had said she had a craving and nothing else would do. Not caring what they ate or even if she did, Sophia went along, simply wanting to get as far from the House of Fourteen as she possibly could.

"Can you believe him? That stupid lizard-licking toad, Lorenzo." Sophia narrowed her eyes at the naan, which had done nothing to deserve her hate except sit there like little pillows of goodness, ready to soak up the extra spicy makhani sauce.

Liv also didn't look as keen about eating as Sophia, although she was the one who insisted they come out to this particular spot. She nibbled on a piece of papadam and gave Sophia a sympathetic expression. "I think I can believe that behavior from Lorenzo. Your problem is in expecting perfectly unreasonable people with egos the size of a dragon's fart to react to complications in the world in a perfectly reasonable way."

Sophia scooped rice onto her plate to give herself something to do with her restless hands. "Yeah, there was my mistake. And I don't think dragons fart. They're way too civilized for that."

Liv leveled her gaze at her sister. "Your dragon once burped the entire chorus of *Hotel California* for me."

"That's a classy song," Sophia argued. "I mean, it's not like he burped *Baby Got Back*."

"No, that was later," Liv joked. "I've had enough experience with Lorenzo and the dumb Council to know that they overreact when there are problems in the world. It's like they think that we should be all dancing around totem poles and singing kumbaya by now." She stuck her nose up, doing her Bianca impersonation. "Why are there still problems with the trolls? How are they even still alive? Why don't the elves do what we say? Why yes, I look like I'm sitting on a pine cone."

Sophia laughed, wondering if Liv's sudden shrill voice entertained anyone else in the restaurant. No one in the other booths seemed to notice them as the waiter brought over another platter of food. The man had seemed hesitant when the sisters ordered so much, and Sophia had looked forward to showing him that he underestimated the wrong set of sisters but viewing the spread on the table, she had her doubts. Neither of them had touched much of it.

"The problems in the world are never going to fully go away," Sophia said through her continued laughter. "That's the mistake in their thinking. Our job as the Dragon Elite is to arbitrate the mortal affairs, which are constantly at odds in neighboring and competing governments. The House of Fourteen's job is to govern the magical world. It's an endless and thankless job, but that's the way it is. It's not like we'll wake up tomorrow and decide that we don't need to eat anymore. The same is true for conflict. It's part of life. We eat, we breathe, we sleep, we fight. Maybe in an ideal world we do the latter less, but still, without tension, there's no growth."

"Amen, sister," Liv sang and eyed the new food in front of them. "Speaking of eating, you need to dig in already."

"You're one to talk." Sophia looked at Liv's empty plate. "I thought we were going for nachos."

Liv shook her head. "I have to deal with giants, and they take the fun out of everything, so we're going with Indian today."

"Because Indian food isn't as much fun?" Sophia questioned.

"It's more serious than nachos. I mean, you can't be angry when eating nachos. It's simply impossible to pull apart those chips covered in cheesy goodness and have a bad attitude."

"You can be angry when eating Indian food?" Sophia challenged.

"I think," Liv began while taking a vegetable samosa and tearing into it, but still not taking a bite, "that you can be whatever you want when eating Indian food. You can be happy or sad or angry or indifferent, but with nachos, you can only be happy."

Sophia studied her sister. There was something off about her. "Is this about Stefan being worried about you taking on too many cases? Is everything all right? Are you overdoing it?"

"What's my name?" Liv replied.

Scooping vegetable masala onto her rice, Sophia laughed. "Obviously, you're overdoing it. That's clear to me. Why is Stefan all of a sudden protective of you?"

Liv pursed her lips and studied the food as if trying to decide what to attack next. "I don't know. Maybe the demons have him down."

"Isn't that what the demons do?" Sophia joked.

In a rare "Liv" move, she pulled the bowl of mulligatawny soup toward her and went at it, spooning mouthfuls to her lips. "I don't know. He's going through a thing. I really am the best person for the negotiations. He's probably tired of Netflixing with Clark at night, and who can blame him? That guy wants to watch *Downton Abbey*, and we both know that Stefan is more of a *Lucifer* kind of man. He misses me, I guess."

Sophia couldn't blame Stefan. Without Liv at the apartment, it was probably lonelier for both Clark and Stefan. "Is war imminent with the giants and the gnomes?"

Liv decided that she'd had enough soup, which wasn't much, and pushed it away. She shrugged. "The gnomes and giants do this at least every century as far as I can tell. They own similar industries and fight for common resources. Every hundred years, they step on each other toes and the House has to intervene. Usually, there's a skirmish, maybe more, but I'm working on a strategy that will hopefully avoid both. I didn't want to unveil it today because I like it better when Lorenzo and Bianca think I'm in over my head. Then I return with the case solved, no battle wounds and a more peaceful resolution than they thought possible. It always puts them in a sour mood."

Sophia laughed. "Wow, they really want you dead, don't they?"

Liv was good-natured enough that she agreed with a chuckle. "Not as much as Adler Sinclair, but yeah. I mess up all their power plays."

"Why don't the rest of the Council members stand up to them?" Sophia dipped her naan in some sauce. "Hester, Raina, and Clark aren't corrupt."

Liv arched an eyebrow. "I don't know. That Clark guy is pretty suspect. I have my eyes on him."

Sophia laughed. "He's our brother. You live with him."

"Exactly. You know what they say about keeping your friends close." Liv hid a grin.

"So Clark is your enemy now, is he?" Sophia challenged.

"He got mad at me yesterday because I forgot to tell him the plumber was coming over."

"That seems like an overreaction."

Liv shrugged. "Well, the guy *did* come in while Clark was in the shower. I thought he'd like someone to hear his singing so I sent Mr. Plumber in there unbeknownst to either him or Clark."

"You're wicked."

"What can I say?" Liv poked at her uneaten samosas. "I get bored and need entertainment via torturing my friends and family."

"How on Earth are you bored?"

"Coming from you, that's funny," Liv stated. "I see the way you handle your leadership role with the Dragon Elite and knock out cases and juggle all the rest. If I were a betting woman, which I'm not ever since losing a ton to some gnomes when playing Blackjack, I'd wager that you need more on your plate."

"You're crazy," Sophia retorted. "I have enough to manage, and half of it I don't know how to solve."

Liv nodded. "That's a good thing. If you're ever given a case or a problem, and you're like, I know exactly how to handle this, you probably better check out of this business because you're finished. I think we thrive on the not-knowing aspect of all this."

Sophia swirled raita into the makhani sauce, enjoying the way they mixed, white and red creating a subtle pink. "Good, so as long as I feel in over my head, I'm doing okay, then?"

"Exactly!" Liv affirmed. "If you find yourself doing the back-stroke easily, then watch out because you're about to get hit by a tsunami."

Sophia laughed. "Okay, well, I'm struggling to stay afloat right now."

"No one knows," Liv related. "You're making it all look easy."

For a moment, Sophia didn't say anything. She simply watched her sister. Liv was the one who showed signs of not staying afloat. Maybe that's why Stefan had been worried about her and urged the Council not to give her back-to-back cases. Something was going on with Liv, but by the way she studied her food and didn't touch it, Sophia doubted her sister would confess anything.

Maybe something more had happened with the goblins than Liv was letting on. Or perhaps the giant and gnome negotiations would be incredibly dangerous. It wasn't that Sophia wasn't worried for her sister. She was. That had been the case since the beginning when Liv took the role of Warrior. However, Sophia always had a quiet confidence that Liv would persevere. Still, something new in her sister made her worry that she might quit before she could win.

"Is everything okay?" Sophia began and realized that wasn't the question that would get answers. "I mean, how can I help you out? You and Stefan recently helped the Dragon Elite with the Rogue Riders. I hoped that we could repay the favor. Do you need me to accompany you on the negotiations with the giants and gnomes? Lunis could come."

Liv shook her head. "Gnomes are afraid of dragons ever since they started referring to them as appetizers, and giants are still offended that they never qualified for rider status due to their weight, but thanks."

"Oh, well, I guess that makes sense. We wouldn't want to make things harder for you. I could accompany you if you'd like. If you think I could help. I could leave Lunis at home. He's busy anyway."

I'm not, the blue dragon said in her head. *I beat Animal Crossing on the Nintendo Switch.*

That game isn't one you beat, Sophia argued. *It's an ongoing thing.*

Yet, I dominated.

Sophia nearly laughed, but then she'd have to explain that she was talking to her dragon in her head and that never went over well.

"There is something I could use your help with." Liv pushed the plates in front of her away.

"Really?" Sophia asked, her interest piqued. "What is it? One of your cases? Research for the House of Fourteen?"

Liv shook her head. "Have you heard about a genie who once worked for King Rudolf Sweetwater?"

Surprised by the question, Sophia leaned back. "You mean Stan?"

She couldn't believe it, but Rudolf had mentioned the genie and his interactions with him recently. It had been a very typical bizarre Rudolf conversation.

Liv slapped the table. "I knew I came to the right person. How did I know that you'd have heard about that genie?"

"Because I obviously have nothing better to do than hear Rudolf's strange stories."

Liv nodded. "Me too. We should get hobbies. Maybe we'll join a bowling league."

"I'd rather not."

"Agreed. Anyway, I know that you're working with Ru a lot lately for the new business and since I have to buzz off for a while, I thought you might be able to find out the location of the genie's bottle."

"Stan?" Sophia asked. "I think Rudolf said he dropped it in the ocean."

"Yes, but where would be the question. I think we need specifics if we're going to recover it."

"Recover it?" Sophia asked.

"Yeah, it's for a case." Liv's eyes slid to the side.

She's lying to you, Lunis stated in Sophia's head.

Liv wouldn't do that, Sophia argued.

She would if she's lying to herself about something, Lunis countered.

What does that mean?

She has a secret, and she's not ready to talk about it, Lunis answered.

Like what?

Maybe she's been poisoned again, Lunis offered, referring to the many times that Liv had tried to downplay how sick she was when recovering from some beast she should never have encountered if not doing stuff that the House shouldn't have known about.

Maybe, Sophia admitted, looking at the many untouched plates of food on the table.

Or maybe she's spelled not to talk about it, Lunis suggested.

That's a possibility. Sophia studied her sister.

Finally, she said, "So you need me to find the location of the genie's lamp? I was going to see Rudolf soon and could ask."

Liv's face brightened with a smile. "Thanks. That would be great. Then we need a way to recover it from the bottom of the ocean."

"Didn't you use a spell to pull the Forgotten Archives up from the ocean floor?" Sophia asked.

Her sister nodded. "Yeah, but it was taxing, and fishing isn't easy."

Sophia gave Liv a skeptical glare. Something was definitely up with her. This girl hadn't been taxed in all her life. Deciding it was best to help without question, as she would have wanted if it was Sophia doing the asking, she simply let out a breath and thought. Finally, something occurred to her.

"Hey, Evan and Coral can swim underwater and hold their breath for long amounts of time," Sophia offered. "Maybe they'll help recover the genie's bottle."

Liv smiled, her eyes lighting up. "That would be great. Can you ask them?"

Sophia nodded. "Yeah, Evan owes me a favor or four hundred."

Liv laughed. "That seems about right."

Sophia lowered her chin, her face going serious for a moment. "When I recover the genie's bottle for you, are you going to tell me what it's for?"

Her sister reached across the table and patted the back of her hand. "Of course, Soph. I have to work out some things first. Then I can explain the details."

Sophia knew Liv wasn't lying with what she'd said. She also knew she was holding something back.

CHAPTER TWELVE

The desert air was anything but refreshing as it swept past Versalee's face and tangled her hair, high on the rooftop of the Cosmopolitan Hotel and Casino. The demon dragonrider didn't like anything about the desert. What was there to like?

However, she liked the idea of the Las Vegas Strip with all the debauchery and crime and potentials for the Rogue Riders to profit from. Once she'd secured her rightful place inside the building where she stood with Ash, her dragon, she wouldn't know that they were in the desert. She'd only breathe in air-conditioned oxygen and be bathed in fluorescent lights.

The Rogue Riders' leader had started with a bang, only to be momentarily defeated by the Dragon Elite. She had to give it to them. They were skillful. However, they were out of practice and conditioned to the old ways. Not only that, but they were good at their core and unwilling to do what it took to be a real dragonrider. They were born to dominate. To rule. To soar in the skies and roast the lands if they desired.

Versalee had no idea why those given majestic beasts used them to serve the weak mortals. It made no sense, and she wasn't going to be defeated once more by the Dragon Elite. No, this time she'd sneak up on them, quietly building her army and presence until the Rogue Riders were strong enough to squash the Dragon Elite decisively. Never again would she have them ride into her territory and challenge her. She'd be the one storming into the Gullington when the time came. First, she needed an empire to rule.

Versalee pointed at the Las Vegas Strip below, traffic rushing by on the roads, bright lights flashing in the dark, the Bellagio fountains cascading, and smiled. "This is the perfect place to build the Rogue Riders' empire."

Beside her, his boot on the edge of the rooftop and a pursed expression on his face, Nathaniel gave Versalee an uncertain look. "I thought the Las Vegas Strip was the property of the fae. Didn't they create it?"

Versalee shook her head. She had a lot to teach her second in command. Well, if he lasted long enough for such things. "They did us the favor of creating it. I'm not worried about taking something away from a magical race who can't fight and only know how to indulge in drinking, eating, sleeping, and other things."

Nathaniel scrutinized her for a moment before his eyes skipped to his green dragon, stationed close by Ash. Versalee thought that he and his dragon were probably conversing telepathically. She sensed his hesitation, which would also be his death sentence.

"What about the Dragon Elite?" Nathaniel finally asked. "They ordered us not to take over any more lands that don't belong to us. Won't they storm back in here and force us out? Wouldn't it be better to find a place that's not already taken?"

Versalee sighed and considered pushing Nathaniel over the building's side but thought that would only cause more issues for her. Then she'd have to recruit a new number two and explain to the mortals on the streets below why a falling body had crushed someone. Instead, she shook her head and let out a calming breath.

"The Dragon Elite won't know we're here until we own this place," she answered. "By that point, we'll have such a stronghold on the Las Vegas Strip that it will be too late. Unlike with the elfin island, we're not going to storm in and take over this city. We'll do it stealthily. By we, I mean you."

"Me?" Nathaniel questioned, surprise making his freckled face crease with confusion. "What about you?"

"I have other things I need to attend to. I need to secure forces that will help ensure any battles with the Dragon Elite deliver us a decisive win."

"Forces?" Nathaniel asked. "Like what?"

"It's better if I don't say," she answered at once, her tone clipped, ending that part of the conversation at once.

He nodded. "So you want the Rogue Riders to take over the city quietly?"

"That's right. Take over the criminal rings. Infiltrate and spread our rule. The fae are cowards and will naturally shrink away when a new, stronger force comes into their city. By the time the Dragon Elite get wind of it, it will be too late. We'll own this place. It's the perfect place for us."

Nathaniel's green eyes lit up with greed. "Yeah, think of all the riches we can get here taking from the criminals."

Versalee nodded. "When you kill the king of the fae, once we've taken over, be sure to thank him for setting us up with such a nice empire."

She turned at once and strode for the orange dragon, feeling the confused expression at her back from Nathaniel. Swinging her leg over the side of her dragon, Versalee secured herself on top of Ash. Only once she had the reins in her hands did she look back at Nathaniel. As she guessed, he wore a bewildered expression.

"Me?" He pointed at his chest. "You want me to kill the king of the fae? When are you going to be back? How long will you be gone?"

She tightened her hands on the reins. "It's hard to say. As long as it takes. Yes. I want you to do whatever it takes to secure the Las Vegas Strip as our territory. If the Dragon Elite show up, throw them off our scent. When the time comes, kill the king and show the world that we mean business."

Versalee yanked back on the reins, making Ash back up from the edge of the building, giving them enough space for a takeoff. Her dragon tugged her head from side to side and resisted the command, but still ended up acquiescing.

"How will I get in touch with you?" Nathaniel asked. "What if I have questions?"

Versalee shook her head while commanding her dragon forward. Ash ran like a bull for the edge of the building and nearly fell off the side before springing into the air, soaring over the Las Vegas Strip and away. She looked back over her shoulder at Nathaniel left standing on the top of the Cosmopolitan. "I'll be in touch with you. Don't screw this up."

With that, she soared to the west to lands that were better suited for what she was looking for—something that would make her an unstoppable force.

CHAPTER THIRTEEN

At the threshold to Hiker Wallace's study, Sophia paused and took in the strange sight of Mama Jamba watching television on a small handheld device, all curled up like a grandmother although she was much, much more.

Behind his desk and digging furiously through the drawers was Hiker, his brow furrowed with frustration.

Both Hiker and Mama Jamba seemed absorbed in their tasks, and although it was kind of nice to watch them doing their thing, Sophia felt wrong spying on them, even from such a public place as an open doorway. However, for a moment she allowed herself to lament about how these two were as close to a mother and a father as she could ever remember.

Well, it was sort of an overstatement since Mama Jamba was quite literally the mother of all. Hiker, well, he wasn't a father at all. However, he had father-like qualities, and she had to admit that she looked up to him—both literally and figuratively.

Sophia decided to make her presence known and cleared her throat. "I have news," she said from the doorway while knocking on the frame for good measure.

Mama Jamba didn't look up but instead simply nodded. "They're out of the blue ski boots. I know, it was a bummer for me too."

Sophia narrowed her eyes at the woman as she tilted her head, trying to figure out what she was watching.

Apparently following her train of thought, Hiker motioned in Mama Jamba's direction. "It's some home shopping network thing she's been watching all day. Who knows what that is or why she's wasting her time on it."

Sophia's brow scrunched up more. "I know what it is but didn't realize that was still a thing. Can't you buy your snow boots off Amazon? Or I don't know, manifest them?"

"I could," Mama Jamba answered. "Where's the fun in that?"

"Nowhere, apparently," Hiker grumbled and continued to dig in his center desk drawer. He looked close to having his body sucked into the desk he had his arm so far in.

"What are you looking for?" Sophia asked, curious.

"My sanity," he answered at once. "Have you seen it?"

"Not since we met," she replied. "I don't think it would be in there regardless."

He pulled his arm from the drawer and stood while shaking his head. "Probably not." He nodded in Mama Jamba's direction. "That one knows what I'm looking for, but she isn't talking, now is she?"

"I can, if you want me to," Mama Jamba sang, not taking her eyes off the screen as the announcer described a thermal coat that kept out the wind and snow. "Do you want me to tell Sophia what you're looking for?"

"Are you going to tell me where it is?" Hiker countered.

"Most likely not," Mama Jamba answered.

"Then no," Hiker muttered while looking around the desk, which he seemed to have destroyed in his quest for the mystery object.

"Maybe the Castle can help you find whatever you're looking for, sir," Sophia offered.

Hiker laughed dully. "The Castle. Why, I thought of that. The entity that's always quick to hide my stuff and not give it back. It's probably the Castle that has what I'm looking for and won't give it up until I'm six feet under."

Sophia nodded. "So I take it you tried asking, then?"

"You'd be right," he replied, his attention off in thought before he looked up at her. "You said you had news. What is it?"

Sophia wished she had good news, especially because Hiker seemed frustrated by his current situation. However, she needed to tell him what she'd found out and hoped to then soften the blow with something light that might help, although she realized it was probably more for her morale than his.

"I found out what happened to the demon dragonriders after the Great War when the Dragon Elite stayed inside the Gullington," Sophia said in a rush and realized that her tone gave away the grave nature of the news.

Hiker's eyes skirted to Mama Jamba. "You know, don't you?"

"What do you think, son?" she answered, her eyes going wide at the screen, apparently intrigued by whatever the salesperson was showing.

"Tell me," Hiker urged, looking straight at Sophia again.

As succinctly as she could, Sophia explained what she'd learned about the history from Clark. As she'd expected, the news made Hiker's face contort with anger.

"Those damn Royals have always been out for us," Hiker muttered, still looking around his office for the misplaced item.

"Sir, I'm a Royal," Sophia informed him.

He nodded. "You're the biggest pain in my ass. Probably not out to kill me, although I think it depends on the day."

She nodded. "It does cross my mind on occasion."

"So your thoughts..." Hiker knew that Sophia had thought through a couple of different scenarios based on what she'd learned.

Drawing in a breath, she explained how they didn't want to repeat history and played through a few different ideas she had. When Hiker appeared annoyed by her bold plan, Sophia launched her thoughts for finding the Rogue Riders.

"Go after criminals." Hiker combed his hand over his beard. "There are a few of them. You do realize, right?"

Sophia giggled. "Yeah, I'm aware. I think we can narrow it down. It's a start anyway."

"The lynx gave her the idea so it's worth pursuing," Mama Jamba called from behind the screen in her hands as though she'd been part of their conversation the entire time.

"The lynx?" Hiker arched an eyebrow at Mother Nature.

She waved a hand at him dismissively. "One of the most powerful entities in the world. Tricky little creature with more mystery than even I can fathom. Also a friend to the Beaufonts and offered this advice she's using."

Hiker gave Sophia a skeptical glare. "When were you going to tell me you had such powerful friends?"

"I don't really," Sophia admitted. "They pop up on occasion and sometimes help me, and sometimes annoy me."

Hiker nodded. "I know how that goes." He glared at Mama Jamba, who had her attention solely on the screen.

She looked up suddenly. "Do you think that thermal underwear will be too bulky under my snowsuit?"

"Why does it matter? You don't need a damn thing, you batty old woman," Hiker replied. "You're Mother Nature. Stop with this lunacy of planning a trip. We have a crisis on our hands, and you're over there wasting time."

She lowered the screen and regarded Hiker with a pursed expression. "The point isn't whether I need something. I simply want to have a human experience. It's been a while."

"Why?" Hiker asked. "You're not human. You're better."

Mama Jamba shook her head and clicked her tongue dismissively. "That's not how it works, son. There's no better. There's only different. I have my strengths and weaknesses, and so do humans and every other creature and plant and pebble on this Earth. That's the way it goes, whether you like it or not. We weren't created equal, but I'll be damned if we were created better than one another."

Hiker sighed and gave Sophia a commiserating look. "There's little reasoning with this one lately."

"So my idea about finding the criminals." Sophia tried to steer the conversation back on track.

He nodded, not at all seeming that interested. "Yeah, that's fine. It might work. Whatever. What do we have to lose?"

Sophia lowered her chin and regarded Hiker with some annoyance. He was distracted. Not only that, he was starting to seem like he was losing his steam. She needed him to be motivated. It would take all of the Dragon Elite for whatever came next, which unfortunately she had no idea what all that would include.

"Also, there's another thing, sir," Sophia began, more nervous about the next thing she wanted to ask about than telling Hiker about the morbid demise of the demon dragonriders.

Sensing the caution in her voice, he glanced up. "What is it?"

"Well, I know we have a lot going on, but I think that keeping up morale is important for the guys. Especially right now with so many changes and the potential for more to happen."

He glared at her. "What are you trying to plan? Is this like your Halloween thing?"

"That was fun," she argued. "Yes."

"I had a lovely time at the Halloween party, dear," Mama Jamba stated. "Although Hiker kept stepping on my feet when we danced."

"I did not," he retorted. "Now, what's this request you have, Sophia?"

She nodded and drew in a breath. "Well, I get that it's not a big deal here, but I thought that since Trin and I are American and Mahkah too, technically, that we could have a Thanksgiving meal. It's more about the idea of gratitude rather than the historical aspects."

To her surprise, Hiker laughed. "Oh, right. Good old Scottish Thanksgiving. What exactly are we celebrating?"

Sophia blinked, not having expected this reaction. "Well, I guess it's when we showed up on your island, and you offered us whisky, and we asked what you wear under your kilts."

Mama Jamba nodded. "I remember that. It was a sunny day. I saw to that."

Hiker shook his head. "Yeah, I'm fine with a Scottish Thanksgiving, but you have to get Trin and Quiet to sign off on it. They'd be the ones responsible for the details since I want your attention fully on the Rogue Riders and everything connected to them."

Sophia smiled, grateful for the small victories. "Great. I'm sure it won't be a problem."

Hiker cut his eyes at her. "I'm sure. Because when you want the Castle to do something, it erects a big top and throws a lavish party. I lose something small and it won't so much as offer me a clue about where it is."

Sophia offered him a sympathetic smile. "I'm sure that when the time is right, you'll find what you're looking for."

Mama Jamba smiled broadly. "I couldn't have said it better myself."

Hiker nodded, his gaze unfocused in thought as he chewed on the inside of his cheek. "Yeah, maybe you two are right, for once. Maybe the timing isn't right yet."

Sophia shook her head at Mama Jamba. "I think we're supposed to take it as a compliment that we're finally right about something."

"Oh, honey." Mother Nature waved her hand through the air at her. "We're always right. Hiker is the one who's willing to admit it for once."

CHAPTER FOURTEEN

The commotion down the block on the far end of Roya Lane made Sophia tense as soon as she stepped through the portal. There was something wrong, and she would go ahead and assume that it was her.

She couldn't make out much as she hurried in the opposite direction toward Heals Pills, but she saw more than a few angry faces and many of them charged her way. Not thinking that this was the time for a peace-building mission, Sophia decided to disguise herself and run for cover. There would be a time to explain to the world about the Dragon Elite, the Rogue Riders, and the difference.

However, for some reason, Sophia didn't want to tear the Rogue Riders' reputation apart. Right then, she believed that the problem was leadership and if they could get Versalee out of that position, maybe someone with a more balanced and healthy mindset could productively lead the demon dragonriders.

If the Dragon Elite slandered the Rogue Riders, there might not be any recovery for the groups later. Sophia wanted to believe in a future where the angel and demon dragonriders got along. They didn't have to work together, but they also couldn't murder each other to the point of extinction.

Sophia was banking on a long game, which meant she had to run right then rather than defend. There would be time for education, but when she was outnumbered and trying to avoid violence and looked like the bad guy they all thought she was, now wasn't the time for confrontations.

Slipping into the shop, Sophia nearly tripped over one of the Captains. She was fairly sure it was Captain Morgan. The little girl had her mother's dark brown hair, hanging in ringlets around her cherub-reminiscent face and her father's piercing blue eyes. She held up a bottle of Heals Pills. "Buy. You ugly."

Remembering that she'd disguised herself as an old man magician, Sophia pulled the disguise off. The halfling giggled like the magic trick was merely entertaining and not a huge display of spell work. The Sweetwater triplets wouldn't ever know normal, it seemed. The extraordinary would seem common and mundane, but such was the way when King Rudolf Sweetwater was one's father.

Sophia's new appearance seemed to change the child's sales strategy. Captain Morgan thrust the bottle of pills at her again. "Still buy!"

Taking the bottle from the toddler, Sophia smiled sweetly. "Thanks. I'm good. I own the shop."

Sophia caught sight of Captain Silver and Captain Kirk toddling around the other aisles. Like their sister, they'd grown quite a lot and didn't resemble normal mortal children. Nor did they give off the impression they were fae. The halflings were something else. Something new. No one knew exactly what to expect of them since mortal and fae was a rare combination.

"Captain Silver," Rudolf bellowed from the back, coming through with his head down as he carried a box of products. "Are you taking another break? I'm docking your pay again unless you get back to work. There are customers to attend to."

Rudolf was right. The shop was full of several people, but thankfully they didn't seem to need any help. They were lined up at the cash register where Rudolf's wife Serena was checking them out.

Captain Silver had sat down in the middle of the aisle and was chewing on a bottle of Heals Pills. She revolted from her father's order to get back to work by drooling on the bottle and exclaiming, "Ghah!"

"The labor union can't help you," Rudolf argued while setting down the box and stocking the shelves. "I know my laws. Although mortal children can't be forced to work before a certain age, the fae have no such laws. Quite the opposite. We're required to earn our keep, or our parents will toss us back in the wishing well we crawled out of. So your fae side better get to work and drag your mortal self along with it before your butt that belongs to both gets a warning."

Serena smiled sweetly at the customer, who regarded the whole display as if it might be cause for alarm. "Don't worry. They're empty threats."

The old gnome nodded while taking his change and bag of products.

"Now remember to rub that ointment straight onto your face to fix that rash," Serena offered.

His grimace deepened. "I don't have a rash."

Serena's expression brightened. "Good news. Then it will be that much easier for the Heal Pills ointment to fix your ugly."

The gnome spun and stomped for the door, his face flaring red... well, redder.

"Question." Sophia strode over to Rudolf, careful to step over the toddler who was cleaning the floor—with her tongue.

"I'm only the stocker," Rudolf said, his head down. "I don't know anything about the products, and my boss hasn't permitted me to talk to the public. Ask the insubordinate employee behind you for help."

Sophia glanced at where Captain Silver gnawed on a bottle of Heals Pills, looking close to breaking the safety seal. She leaned over and plucked the bottle from the toddler's hand, earning an offended expression from the child.

Sophia held out her hand. A colorful teething ring appeared that had plastic keys and a small stuffed elephant attached to it. She handed it to the child and offered a kind expression. "Here, chew on this instead," Sophia insisted.

Captain Silver took the ring and launched it into her mouth so fast she nearly fell backward. She didn't appear to have ever seen such a thing.

Spinning back to Rudolf, Sophia cleared her throat. "Your boss hasn't permitted you to talk to the employees, eh? You don't know anything about the products, huh?"

The fae froze, his hands in mid-air as he withdrew items from the box in front of him. From the corner of his mouth, he whispered, "Serena, is the person in front of me a dragonrider lacking a sense of humor and a stickler for telling the truth always?"

Thankfully, Serena had rung up the last customer in the shop, and it was empty again. Otherwise, Sophia worried she'd have to start defending herself if people found out she was a dragonrider.

"I don't know," Serena answered, sounding bored behind the register. "She's pretty for a magician and has a sword, but if she has a dragon, it's in her pocket or invisible because I don't see one."

"It's in my pocket," Sophia said dryly. "Yes, Rudolf, I have my sword and some questions for you."

Rudolf glanced up as a smile sprang to his face. "Sophia, I'm so sorry to hear that you've been hallucinating lately and seeing and hearing things that aren't real."

Sophia shook her head. "That hasn't been the case since I got the mark erased from my soul."

"Are you sure you did, though?" Rudolf slid products onto the shelf. "I mean, it seems like you're still suffering."

"Why are you refusing to talk to customers?" Sophia's hand went for the hilt of her sword and paused there, a mock-murderous expression on her face.

"See!" Rudolf exclaimed. "I knew it didn't cure you. You're still seeing and hearing things. I bet you see three children who you're mistaking as shop employees."

"Was Serena, your wife, insulting a customer part of my delusions too?" Sophia asked.

Rudolf shook his head. "Oh, no. Serena is the worst. She constantly offends the gnomes. Well, pretty much everyone." He leaned forward and cupped his mouth. "Finding good help is so difficult these days. I was going to fire her, but she threatened to make me sleep in the doghouse, and the pig's pen she makes me sleep in is already small enough."

"You all need therapy," Sophia stated blankly. "You remember how we had a conversation about how the triplets aren't qualified to work yet?"

"I remember." Rudolf tossed the empty box over his shoulder where it landed in the doorway for the back room.

"Are you ignoring my advice?" Sophia asked. "Because this is my shop too, and I don't think toddlers make good employees."

Rudolf pointed at Captain Silver, who was blowing spit bubbles on her lips. "Especially that one."

"Ru…" Sophia said, a warning in her voice.

He threw up his arms. "Fine. I won't have the Captains work for me. That means you too, Serena. Sorry, Sophia's orders. No family at work."

The mortal glared up from the cash register with a seething look in her eyes. "What?"

Rudolf shot a finger at Sophia. "It was the mean old dragonrider. Not me. I love having you all here."

"Well, what are we supposed to do then?" Serena asked grumpily.

"Look into preschools," Sophia encouraged. "Really good ones. The best your riches can buy. Your children will need that."

"Good idea," Rudolf cheered. "What will we do with the Captains while Serena is at school?"

Sophia clapped her hand to her forehead. "The preschools would be for the children."

"Serena could go too?" Rudolf questioned, an uncertain expression on his face.

"I guess so," Sophia answered, wondering how they were having this conversation.

Rudolf nodded and smiled at his wife. "Okay, go find something that will make the kids into geniuses. You know, someone who knows the punchlines to knock-knock jokes."

"Okay." Serena picked up Captain Morgan and stuck her on her hip. "I don't want one of those uptight places where they grade them based on performance."

"You mean tests?" Sophia questioned.

Serena picked up Captain Silver with her free hand and quite nimbly stuck the child to her other hip. "Yeah, those things are so demeaning. They always make me feel stupid."

"Imagine that," Sophia stated dryly.

"Good idea, dear," Rudolf stated. "Find a school where the curriculum is relevant to our ideals. No math. Science is a maybe. They better not learn how to read until they've mastered seamless costume changes in small spaces. I'm not raising a nerd who can't take on a last-minute main role in a Broadway show with no notice. Priorities."

Serena nodded. "I'm in complete agreement. I'll find this school." She snapped her fingers at her back, and Captain Kirk glanced up from tracing shapes on the floor. "Come on Kirky. We have to find a place to unlock your genius."

Sophia was impressed at how the mortal handled the three children. That was the mystery and conundrum that was the Sweetwater family. Rudolf and Serena were simultaneously unbelievably dumb and also incredibly gifted in strange ways.

When the door to the shop swung shut, Rudolf clapped Sophia on the back and smiled. "Just like we rehearsed. You did great. Good job following the script. Now, mission accomplished. Serena is out of my hair once more, all because of you. If she ever finds out this was all your idea, she'll no doubt murder you."

CHAPTER FIFTEEN

"What are you talking about?" Sophia questioned the fae who had trotted over to the back counter where the cash register was.

He sighed. "Your memory is horrible these days."

"I'm certain that it's not." She picked up an ointment tube of Heals Pills.

"Anyway, remember I told you that Serena and the Captains were driving me crazy here at the store?"

"When and more importantly, how was that?" Sophia asked.

"Through our telepathic link, last night," Rudolf answered while organizing the cash register area.

"There you go," Sophia said, mostly to herself. "You realize that we don't have that mode of communication?"

Rudolf shook his head. "Yet, you showed up here and got Serena to quit and take the Captains. They were driving me crazy. So much workplace drama. One of the employees was always crying about this or that. Then Captain Kirk constantly slept on the job."

"They're babies," Sophia argued.

"There's always an excuse. Anyway, we played that perfectly, you all questioning me about why I wouldn't talk to employees and pretending to be mean about me not doing my job."

"You weren't doing your job, telling a customer to get help from a child," Sophia stated, her eyes fluttering with annoyance.

He nodded. "Great acting. Then when you pretended to be offended about how Serena insulted a customer."

"I was offended by that."

Rudolf waved her off. "They're gone now. You can drop the act."

Sophia decided that she'd let the whole thing go, mostly because she didn't want to spare the brain cells. She held up the tube of ointment. "We're expanding our product line?"

With a triumphant pride in his eyes, Rudolf nodded. "Another good idea you passed to me along the telepathic wire."

"I wish I could take credit for this," Sophia admitted. "I think you get the kudos here."

Rudolf shook his head. "It couldn't have been my idea. I'd finished off a case of strawberry wine and could hardly operate the blimp."

Sophia blinked at him, wondering where to start with that admission. "You have a blimp?"

He nodded. "Yeah, but the dragons keep getting in my way, which makes it hard to navigate it through the skies, especially when I'm bleary-eyed, if you know what I mean."

"Wait; what?" Sophia suddenly tilted her head. "Where are these dragons that you're flying this blimp around?"

He pursed his lips as if the answer should have been obvious. "Las Vegas, of course."

"There are dragons over the Strip?" Sophia asked, not aware of this. It could be angel dragons. It was also likely to be demon dragons and the Rogue Riders.

Rudolf shrugged. "I guess so. I mean, they could be something else."

"Describe them to me," Sophia ordered. "Tell me specifically what they've been doing."

"Well," he began, drawing out the word. "They're large and are like airplanes, except that they have wings."

Sophia worked hard to keep her hand from pulling out her sword and ending the king of the fae. "You do get that airplanes have wings, right?"

Rudolf shook his head, clicking his tongue at her. "Maybe you want to go to the preschool we send the Captains to. I'll pay."

"I'm good," Sophia said dismissively. "What have these dragons over Las Vegas been doing?"

"How am I supposed to know?" Rudolf asked. "I see them flying around and hand the blimp's wheel over to the captain before I pass out."

"Please tell me in that instance; you mean that you hand the steering wheel over to a qualified captain and not a child."

His eyes slid to the side, a coy expression on his face. "Sure…"

Sophia sighed. "Okay, well, keep an eye on these dragons and report to me if anything happens."

Although Sophia wanted to go check out the situation, she had enough going on, and if it was the angel dragons, she wanted to give them space so they could magnetize to a rider. If things progressed, then she'd go to Las Vegas and check things out, but it sounded like there wasn't much going on besides soaring dragons.

Rudolf sat on the stool behind the counter and let out a long breath. "It's our first lull all day."

"That's great." Sophia noticed that many of the shelves were empty. "I'm glad that business is going so well."

He nodded. "Yeah, but keeping up without the Captains will be difficult. They were excellent salespeople."

"Have you considered hiring someone to replace them and Serena?" Sophia asked.

A loud gasp came from Rudolf's mouth as he clapped his hand to it. "My gods, Sophia. You can't hire people to replace your family."

Sophia laughed at this. "I was referring to hiring someone to replace them as employees. You know, maybe someone to do the stocking and clerical stuff and another as a salesperson. You have the business starting up with Lee at the bakery so I can't imagine you should be spending so much time here."

Rudolf considered this. "I keep playing with the idea, but it's hard to turn my baby over to someone else. We built this business from scratch, and it brings so much goodness to the world. I'm proud of it and want it to flourish."

Sophia was momentarily speechless, hearing Rudolf talk in such an altruistic way. "Wow, I didn't realize that it meant so much to you."

He nodded, passion in his eyes. "Yeah, not seeing so many ugly magicians when I stroll down Roya Lane has helped to increase my appetite. Your kind can be sickening to look at."

"Of course." Sophia realized she should have seen that one coming. "Well, regardless of your reasons for the business, I agree that we need good employees. I trust you'll find some who can keep the shop successful."

"Your trust is well-placed." Rudolf bowed slightly.

Sophia held up a finger suddenly. "But! No children as employees. The job description can't require the workers to do anything illegal. You must give them all orders verbally and not through a bogus telepathic link."

The king sighed. "If I hire two employees that I think could be a good match, I can require them to breed, right?"

"No," Sophia said decisively.

"I can require them to marry, right?"

"Absolutely not."

Rudolf shook his head. "Fine, but I don't see what's the point in having employees if you can't control every aspect of their lives. I like playing matchmaker...well, really just God. I like playing God."

Sophia shook her head. "You'll be their boss and assign them work," she stated and quickly added, "to do with the shop, and that's it. No playing God. Only a boss who has limited authority and answers to me."

"Who do you answer to?" Rudolf challenged.

"God, I guess, in a way." She thought of how she worked for Mother Nature and the angels in so many ways.

"So I got tossed down the managerial ladder, I see," he muttered grumpily.

"Yeah, sure," Sophia said dismissively. "I came here for other reasons besides to see how you were making bad employee decisions."

"Oh?" Rudolf appeared curious. "Is this about the location of the genie lamp that I tossed in the ocean?"

Sophia nearly fell over. "How did you know that?"

He tapped the side of his head with a victorious smile on his face. "Telepathic link. Sounds like your end might need some maintenance. Mine is working fine."

Sophia was about to start questioning everything she knew when Rudolf added, "Oh, Liv called and mentioned it. Said you'd be stopping by and I should draw up a map of Stan's location."

"There we go." Sophia realized she never needed to question her judgment and sanity where the king of the fae was concerned.

He rummaged in the drawers of the counter behind the cash register. "I put something together for you that I hope helps. A little sketch that should help you find the genie's lamp."

Rudolf laid what appeared to be a blank piece of paper on the counter between him and Sophia. She glanced at it and his broad, prideful grin.

"I'm not criticizing you, but I feel like you could have offered a little more detail," Sophia commented and added, "Well, any detail would have been good."

He jerked his head up in surprise. "You don't see it? Oh, of course, you don't. You look with your eyes."

"Imagine that," she dryly replied.

Rudolf tapped his finger on the paper, and it instantly transformed to show land masses and churning bodies of water around it. Different labels for the lands and seas appeared as well as a compass in the corner. In the center of the map was an X.

Sophia was about to express her complete astonishment at the map the fae had created, which was no doubt full of helpful details she hadn't seen before. However, before she could, he tapped the paper again, and the area where the X was zoomed in and gave them a view of the ocean. Suddenly, she saw an underwater picture of where the genie's lamp was, showing different obstacles that they'd have to navigate like around coral reefs, rocks, sea life, and a sunken ship. At the bottom, sitting on the ocean floor was Stan's lamp.

Sophia looked up, total amazement written on her face. "You did this?"

"I think so," Rudolf replied. "I mean, I passed out halfway through, but I was the only person present when I awoke, and there the map was. So sure, I'll take credit. Plus, I'm the only one who knows where I put Stan's lamp."

"Wow, Rudolf, this is really helpful. Thank you."

He flashed her a toothy grin. "I'll do whatever it takes to help Liv get away from that self-centered husband of hers that's always off galivanting with ugly ladies."

"Those are demons," Sophia corrected.

"Oh, that does make more sense, now that I think about it." Rudolf shrugged. "Anyway, once Liv uses the wish from the lamp to dump Stefan, then we can hang out once more, just like, well we never really did."

"I don't think she's using the wishes from the lamp to get rid of her husband, who I know she loves endlessly."

Rudolf sighed. "Well, what is she using it for?"

Sophia shook her head. "I'm not sure."

"Well, remember to tell her that when she uses the last wish, she'd better be careful because then Stan will want his freedom, which he only gets if he murders his master, the person who used the three wishes and possesses the genie lamp."

Sophia nodded, suddenly feeling very uncertain about this mysterious mission Liv had enlisted her for. "Copy that. Use wishes, then drop the lamp back into the center of the ocean and run like hell."

"Well, you can't run on water," Rudolf corrected. "I'll get you enrolled in that preschool. Then you'll know that kind of stuff."

Sophia picked up the map and slipped it into her cloak. "You do that. Thanks for the map."

"You're welcome," Rudolf called at her back. "Oh, and one last thing."

Sophia turned at the door, giving him a questioning expression.

"One way to avoid Stan trying to murder his master is not to use all the wishes," Rudolf offered. "I'm not sure what Liv wants it for, but that's a thought."

Sophia drew in a breath, hoping they only needed one or two wishes. However, the idea that her sister was relying on wish magic was the most unsettling part of all. That wasn't like Liv. Something was definitely wrong.

CHAPTER SIXTEEN

The commotion at the end of Roya Lane was ongoing when Sophia exited Heals Pills. She threw on her disguise as the old man magician and studied the street ahead. It didn't make sense that the disturbance was still going on once she'd disappeared into the shop if it involved her. She reasoned that it didn't. Still, she wasn't looking forward to finding out what had gnomes, magicians, and other magical races yelling in the distance, all gathered around someone or something.

These kinds of disturbances on the magical lane fell under the jurisdiction of the House of Fourteen. Sophia wasn't looking to intervene and sorely wished that a Warrior was there to break things up. Otherwise, she might have to act. She'd avoid the disturbance if she could, but the place she needed to go, the Official Brownie headquarters, was in that area.

Sighing, Sophia started down the lane, paying careful attention to the things being shouted.

"Get out of here!" someone yelled, by the sounds of it, an angry gnome.

"How dare you bring that beast to Roya Lane!" another shouted.

"You'll pay for what you've done!"

"Okay, break it up!" a familiar voice yelled, dividing the crowd that Sophia could see as she approached. Over the top of the group, she noticed a head of short blonde hair. Trudy DeVries, Sophia guessed. She was instantly relieved that the House of Fourteen had someone on the scene to take care of things. Now she wouldn't have to worry about it because whatever was happening wasn't her problem.

Sophia slipped around the back of the crowd, trying to go as unnoticed as possible, which wasn't hard in her plain gray cloak and wearing her old man features and balding head. She went a lot more ignored than if she sported her usual look with her silver and blue armor and carried Inexorabilis. Still, Sophia kept her head down, and her face mostly obscured, blocking much of her peripheral vision.

"He's a thief and a scoundrel!" someone yelled from the other side of the crowd.

"A tyrannical bully," another person screamed, fury heavy in their voice.

"As far as I can discern," Trudy DeVries yelled above the crowd, "he hasn't done anything wrong."

"Thief! Thief! Thief!" the magicians around the center of the commotion chanted.

Sophia was almost to the other side of the angry mob, where she could see a break in the crowd and the Official Brownie headquarters up ahead.

"I don't think this is the villain you think he is," Trudy said, her voice clear and loud but also even. "As far as I can tell, he's brand-new and simply confused."

Shaking her head, Sophia was grateful that this hadn't become her problem and that Trudy DeVries had shown up. She didn't know who this guy in the wrathful center of a horde of pitchfork-carrying magical creatures was, but she was glad it wasn't her. Or one of hers. The Warrior for the House of Fourteen would dispel the situation, Sophia told herself while breaking through to the other side where there were fewer people to navigate around.

"He's one of them!" someone yelled from Sophia's back.

"They're all bad!" another said, and that made her pause. What were they referring to? Or more importantly, who?

She looked over her shoulder and saw Trudy's long arms rise into the air. The woman's above-average height made it so everyone could see her even at the center of the crowd. "That's not true. You must learn to be fair and reasonable."

Sophia nodded, silently commending the Warrior for her level-headed approach. She was one of the good ones. The DeVries had always been allies of the Beaufonts, and Sophia was grateful for that.

Turning back around, she hurried for the brick wall where the invisible door to the Official Brownie headquarters was.

Over the grumbling and protests of the crowd, Sophia heard a disgruntled gnome challenge, "Like the House of Fourteen has always been reasonable?"

Sophia suddenly felt sorry for the Warrior, having to deal with the wrath of a mob that she didn't deserve.

"Yeah!" someone yelled from the crowd. "I'm not surprised to see you defending him! Of course you'd work together! The House of Fourteen and dragonriders are both corrupt!"

Freezing, Sophia held her breath. Tensed. Turned to face the angry group of magical creatures.

This just became her problem.

CHAPTER SEVENTEEN

S ophia pushed through the crowd, making quick progress although the group had tightly knitted together. It was probably because she was wearing her disguise and those she passed simply thought the hunched-over old man needed to be closer to see better.

When Sophia was close to the center of the ring of protestors, she saw something she thought she'd never find on Roya Lane—a dragon.

Standing next to a scrawny young magician with dark blond hair, glasses, and a tentative expression was a seafoam green dragon who was quite beautiful and young. Sophia recognized the dragonette from the Gullington. It was an angel dragon, and she'd grown a lot and also magnetized to a rider, it appeared.

The dragon had her head down low, cowering from the many angry fists brandished in her and her rider's direction. That explained why Sophia didn't spy the dragon towering over the crowd before. She suspected that this particular dragon could blast the horde of protestors if she wanted to. Still, the dragonette didn't appear to be considering it as she snaked her neck around her rider in a protective stance, her large head cupping him to her.

The new dragonrider also didn't appear ready to defend himself.

He was weaponless, and his face was pale with fear. He kept blinking wildly and rubbing his eyes under his glasses.

Trudy DeVries held up a hand as Sophia approached, looking much more defensive than the pair next to her. "Stay back! We don't want trouble! You all need to disperse."

Sophia let her disguise fall away and took her normal form, earning gasps from the crowd. "I agree!" she yelled clear and loud and nodded at Trudy DeVries. "You all need to disperse."

The Warrior for the House of Fourteen gave her a relieved look. She was probably happy that she didn't have to fight an old man and that Sophia had come to help, the situation quickly having gotten out of hand.

Sophia heard whispering from around the crowd, but they weren't yelling at her as they had before. A few had shrunk away, their angry faces turning to ones of hesitation. Insulting a cowering dragon and unarmed rider was one thing. However, this group knew who she was and what she was capable of, and they didn't appear as ready to challenge her.

When close to Trudy and the young dragon and rider, she turned, put her back protectively to them, and faced the crowd.

"The House of Fourteen is not your enemy," Sophia stated in a confident tone. She pointed at the stranger next to the green dragon. "Neither is this rider of the Dragon Elite."

"Dragonriders are taking over the world," an elf called.

"You all think you own this planet!" a gnome complained.

"Taking what's not yours," a female magician remarked in a disapproving tone and shook her head.

However, the complaints were more subdued than before.

Sophia cleared her throat. "We do own this planet."

There were mutters of protest around the crowd.

Sophia ignored it and continued, "We own this planet as protectors. Some dragonriders are abusing their powers. The Dragon Elite will work to bring justice to this situation. Right now, I need you all to trust that we aren't your enemy. In time, we will prove that, but for now, you'll simply have to believe me."

Silence fell over the crowd. Sophia watched as many shifted their gaze between her and those at her back, then to others around them, as if looking for an indication from one of their neighbors about what to do next.

If it had been only Sophia there, she didn't know how things would have panned out. The world at large was angry with dragonriders and not showing any distinction between the different groups. They feared all dragonriders at that point. They didn't understand, and that was to be expected.

If it had only been Sophia, she believed the fear and bitterness over the recent abuse would have riled up the crowd, and they would have rebelled, taking what they saw as an opportunity for retribution. However, she wasn't alone.

Trudy DeVries stepped up beside Sophia, her sword in hand and a punishing look on her face. "Those who are still gathered here in the next ten seconds will be held and charged by the House of Fourteen for disorderly conduct and threatening a Dragon Elite member—the highest-ranking official on this planet."

That didn't meet with instant acceptance. There were terse words and much grumbling after Trudy's ultimatum.

However, when she started to count and held her large sword higher, the group lost their resolve to rebel. Many of the gnomes skirted away while throwing glares over their shoulders.

Magicians, fairies, and elves all trudged away, albeit it a little reluctantly. Regardless, when Trudy had counted down to five, almost all of the crowd had dispersed.

Sophia let out a relieved breath and turned to the Warrior for the House of Fourteen and the brand-new rider and dragon.

CHAPTER EIGHTEEN

Trudy DeVries stayed tense as those around moved off, her eyes skirting from side to side as if she expected someone to double back and attempt an attack. She was a seasoned warrior and knew never to let down her guard. Something that Sophia thought she could learn from her.

When there was no one in the general area, the Warrior for the House of Fourteen turned her attention to Sophia. "I'm glad you showed up when you did."

Sophia's gaze flickered to the new dragonrider, and she offered him a calm smile before glancing up at Trudy. "Me too. I didn't realize you were defending a dragonrider at first. Or that the House of Fourteen would come under attack too."

Trudy nodded gravely. "Things have heated up a lot. If the House doesn't do something, then we're going to be seen as complacent. The matter with the Rogue Riders involves you, the Dragon Elite, and I support you handling it the way you see fit. I mean, you're not intervening on House of Fourteen business and never have, and I think minding those boundaries is important."

Something in Trudy's tone put Sophia on guard. "The House or rather, probably the Council, isn't as level-headed as you, are they?"

The Warrior nodded. "Some of them are. You were there and know how reactionary those others are."

Sophia nodded. She did know, and it worried her. "Well, I'm working on some solutions. That's why I'm here."

"Good timing, being here." Trudy nodded at the dragon and rider who hadn't moved since Sophia had approached through the crowd. She was starting to wonder if they had a statue spell placed on them. "I guess I can leave you in charge of these two."

Sophia glanced at the pair and nodded. "Yeah, and thanks for defending them. I don't want to think what the crowd would have done to them if you hadn't shown up."

Trudy offered a tight smile. "Good luck, Rider Beaufont." The Warrior gave the new dragonrider a curt nod before she strode forward and disappeared down Roya Lane.

CHAPTER NINETEEN

Drawing in a breath, Sophia focused her full attention on the new rider and dragon, still aware of those passing. The light green dragon made it so they got way more attention than was necessary. Sophia had no idea what this guy was thinking, bringing his dragon to Roya Lane. He obviously didn't care that the world was disgruntled about dragonriders. Or maybe he didn't know any better. Based on the innocent expression in his eyes, Sophia guessed the latter.

"You're Sophia Beaufont?" the guy asked in awe, his eyes flicking to her sword and her face, then doing another double-take.

Sophia nodded slowly, wondering for a moment if she should be proud of this or be on guard. This guy had paired with an angel dragon, but that didn't mean much to her yet. Everything was so new with this generation that she wasn't making any assumptions.

"You're the one who helped to defeat Nevin Gooseman when he attacked Dallas, Texas," the guy stated, his eyes wide behind his glasses. "You were also part of the forces that took down Thad Reinhart. Also, wasn't there something about Olento Research and cyborgs?"

Sophia couldn't help but grin. The guy was harmless, she realized, and was more likely to harm her with a hug than a punch. "You know your stuff."

He nodded adamantly. "I've followed everything I can about the Dragon Elite. You all make the headlines a lot lately, but the news hasn't been very reliable."

Letting out a breath, Sophia combed her hand through her hair. "That's true. The media tends to sensationalize stuff. The news gets delivered in a way that benefits those pulling certain strings."

"Like when Nevin Gooseman was in power," the guy guessed.

"That's right." Sophia extended a hand. "Why don't we start from the beginning? I'm Sophia Beaufont with the Dragon Elite. This is a dragon who recently left the Gullington." She indicated the green dragon who still had her head low and an uncertain expression in her eyes. "You are?"

The guy straightened. Gulped. Extended a shaking hand. "My name is Cooper. This is Sage."

"Sage?" Sophia mused while shaking his hand. "As in wisdom?"

Cooper nodded. "Also as in the brush. Sage's elements are plants and trees."

"That's lovely." Sophia realized the color of the young dragon's scales was reminiscent of the herb sage. It would be fascinating to meet the dragons again when they returned with riders and discover their true names and the elements they possessed.

She might have seen the dragonettes on the Expanse before they left, but it hadn't been her responsibility to train them so this was like meeting them for the first time. In truth, a dragon, like its rider, matured and changed a lot after magnetizing.

Sophia drew in a breath, pulled her gaze off Sage, and focused on Cooper again. "However, you shouldn't have brought Sage here. The mortal and magical world is very distrusting of us right now because of the Rogue Riders."

"I know." A shameful expression covered Cooper's face. "That's the thing. I followed everything I could about the dragons and saw that the public was growing fearful of dragons and riders. I magnetized to Sage a few days ago. My mom kicked us out of the house, saying that we would bring doom and hate to our family. I'd kept her in the garage before that. Anyway, with nowhere to go and no money, I didn't know what to do. I knew I needed to find the Dragon Elite, but I didn't know where to look."

Pity made Sophia's chest ache. She couldn't imagine being out in this world as a new dragonrider. It must have been terrifying, especially since Cooper's family turned on him. Fear made people do awful things. When Lunis hatched, Sophia had her sister and Clark and lots of friends to help steer her through the new situation. Then Hiker's note came, and Sophia knew that she had the Dragon Elite to help her. That thought made Sophia tense.

"Have you received a note?" Sophia thought that the Elite globe should have alerted Hiker about the new dragonrider. However, there was a massive influx of new dragons, and many had recently left the Gullington. Sophia could see how his tracking methods might have fallen through the cracks, especially with everything else going on with the Rogue Riders.

Cooper shook his head. "No, but something could have come to my parent's house." A saddened expression fell on his face, making him suddenly look so much younger and vulnerable. "I haven't been in contact with them."

"I'm sorry, Cooper." Sophia offered him a sympathetic expression. She glanced over her shoulder at the Official Brownie headquarters. That business would have to wait. The main priority was getting Cooper and Sage to safety, which meant inside the border of the Gullington. It was hard to believe that new dragonriders would be joining them. Things were shifting. The Dragon Elite were growing. Never again would the Gullington be the same, and that was a wonderful and scary thing.

"I need to get you out of here." Sophia noticed they were still attracting attention. It was unlikely that the new rider could fly, or fly well on his dragon. That was fine because Sophia hadn't been able to ride Lunis when they entered the Gullington.

"Yeah, I don't think it's good for me to be here." Cooper pulled off his glasses and rubbed his eyes. "I've been getting headaches since I got here and can't see so well."

Sophia smiled at this, put out her hand, and stopped the new dragonrider from putting on his glasses. "The chi of the dragon must have taken up residence in you."

"What?" Cooper's eyes looked puffy without his glasses on.

"It's bad timing," Sophia related, "but it happens when the dragonrider is ready, and probably venturing here cued your independence."

"What are you talking about?" Cooper asked.

Sophia took his glasses from his hand. He allowed it although he wore a confused expression. "Cooper, blink and look around."

The guy did as told, his vision most likely taking a moment to clear. Then his face transformed into one of amazement, and he rubbed his eyes again before looking up and down Roya Lane with a smile lighting up his mouth. "I can see. I can see without my glasses!"

This exclamation got the attention of a few gnomes making deals on a nearby corner, but they soon ignored them again.

Sophia wore a wide grin. "That's right. The chi of the dragon would have given you better than perfect vision. When you're not here and learn how to hone your senses, you'll be able to see for miles. The Dragon Elite will teach you all about your new abilities."

"New abilities..." Cooper said slowly, as though trying to digest the brand-new concept.

Sophia nodded. "As a dragonrider, you'll be stronger and faster than ever before and have superior senses, thanks to the chi of the dragon. Not only that, but you and Sage, having connected your lives, will live longer than if you two hadn't joined. As a dragonrider, you're now one of the most powerful magical creatures in the world."

Cooper's mouth fell open, and for a moment, Sophia thought he was about to pass out. She was prepared to catch him if that happened. He finally shook his head as though trying to shake away the amazement. His short blond hair whipped back and forth.

"For real?" he asked. "This is all happening?"

Sophia smiled wide. "Yes, and—"

An envelope drifted down from the sky that carried a familiar wax seal on it. Sophia reached into the air and grabbed it.

"What's that?" Cooper glanced at the note. It was addressed to him in Hiker's handwriting.

"This," Sophia handed him the letter, "is your invitation to the Gullington to see if you want to be part of the Dragon Elite. Looks like your change in address delayed it from finding you."

"Dragon Elite?" Cooper asked, his eyes wide. "Join you all? Of course. There's no question. You all are superheroes and make the world a better place, and I can't think of a better purpose." He indicated the meek dragon behind him. "Now that I have Sage, we should put our powers to good use. I know that she wants nothing more than to help. She talks about the Gullington fondly all the time. She says she only left there to find me but couldn't figure out how to return after the fact."

Sophia smiled. "Well, when you're ready, open the letter. It will give you directions for how to find the Gullington. Then you both can use portal magic to get there and meet the others."

Cooper paused as if waiting for her to say, "Just kidding."

When she didn't, he tore into the letter, his eyes scanning it before he glanced up at Sophia.

"This is all real…" His voice vibrated with excitement. "I'm going to the Gullington. I get a chance to be one of the Dragon Elite. I'll do whatever I must to qualify to be a part of that. Especially if I'll eventually get to help the world and also make my mom proud."

Sophia clapped a hand on the guy's shoulder. "You'll make her proud. The chance to join the Dragon Elite is open to all riders who want it. You qualify by wanting to make the world a better place."

CHAPTER TWENTY

Sophia waited until Cooper and Sage had stepped through the portal to the area outside the Barrier to the Gullington before she strode to the Official Brownie headquarters down the lane.

She wasn't surprised that Cooper had mastered portal magic as a magician—a powerful spell that not all could do so easily or so young. He had magnetized to a dragon for a reason. All the dragonriders would have enhanced and above-average skills, hence one reason that a dragon had chosen them.

Still, the new dragonriders would need a lot of training, which was where the Rogue Riders would no doubt fall short. They seemed to think they already knew everything. That simply being a dragonrider made them incredibly powerful. However, one can have strength and still not be able to lift a large boulder if they didn't master the skill of leverage.

Strategy was about doing something the most efficient and skillful way. So far, the Rogue Riders seemed to rely on their brute strength, not realizing that riding a dragon wasn't like driving a car. One didn't simply press on the gas and expect it to go. A real dragonrider became the vehicle, moving it as they would their legs for walking. Controlling a dragon should be as easy as a command to the brain, but as

Sophia had witnessed when around the Rogue Riders, they missed crucial parts of being dragonriders because they were unwilling to learn.

Cooper would be trained by the very best. The Dragon Elite would be his new family if he so desired, not rejecting him because of fear or the world's perceptions—which Sophia would one day change.

It felt good to know that a new dragonrider headed to the Castle. What worried her was that Cooper would meet Evan first and be scared away. She laughed to herself while thinking about poor Cooper striding up to the Castle and not knowing that it was sentient or that Mother Nature called it home or that their housekeeper was a cyborg...and their dog.

A warm sensation suddenly spread over Sophia's chest. The place that she called home wasn't normal even by a magician's standard, but she loved it. The Gullington was perfect with all its eccentric ways and peculiarities. She even thought it was fun that the Pond had a dangerous sea creature in it and that on the far side of the Gullington was Falconer Cave that had dozens of strange uses, only a few that she'd explored. She could spend centuries exploring the Gullington and not unearth all its secrets—and she planned on doing that.

Right then, Sophia needed others to do some exploring for her. After announcing her title to the seemingly solid brick wall, she watched as the small door to the Official Brownie headquarters materialized. She crouched and army-crawled through the opening, having gotten used to the undignified manner in which she had to enter the small office frequented by tiny elves.

Sophia half-expected to find Ticker, the son of the Brownies' head official, sitting in the reception area as before. The little guy had taken over for his parents when they were gone, but to her surprise, the front room was empty.

From the back office, Sophia heard muttering and suspected that Mortimer was back in his office. She called to him as she strode forward, careful to keep her head ducked so she didn't bump it on the low ceiling.

"Mortimer? Is that you? Is this a good time?"

Sophia felt bad, always showing up to the Brownie headquarters without warning. However, they never seemed to mind and always helped her out. She only hoped that she could return the favors when they needed it.

"Sophia Beaufont of the Dragon Elite," Mortimer responded in his squeaky voice from his office. "I'm here, and this is a fine time."

Peeking her head through the cracked door, Sophia expected to find someone besides Mortimer in his office. However, he was alone. The office was a little messier than usual as if he'd been rummaging through the file cabinets for something.

"Hey." Sophia looked around and tried to keep the curiosity off her face. "How are you?"

The small elf sighed and tapped his bony fingers on the surface of his desk. "I've had better centuries, but this too shall pass."

Sophia's gaze fell to the map sitting in front of Mortimer. She'd seen Ticker using it the last time she'd visited the Brownies. From everything she could tell, it was an incredible map, about like the one that Rudolf had given her with a similar level of detail. Mortimer's was even more interactive though and responded to the user's touch as though they were moving pieces on a chessboard. By pieces, that meant actual Brownies through the mortal and magical world.

"What's going on?" Sophia brought her gaze up to meet Mortimer's. His eyes were large and round and full of stress.

He seemed to realize this a moment too late and replaced the tense expression with a fake smile. "It's fine, Sophia Beaufont of the Dragon Elite. Silly Brownie politics."

Sophia dared to sit in the chair on the other side of Mortimer's desk. It felt like she was sitting in one of those small chairs that preschoolers had in their classrooms—or so she imagined. Sophia had never been to preschool or in a classroom or really done any of those normal things usually considered milestones. She'd watched television though, and that pretty much counted as experience.

"The last time I was here, Ticker told me that you and Pricilla had to deal with union affairs," Sophia explained. "You'd left him in charge, and he seemed to be doing an incredible job."

Mortimer smiled broadly, his long ears perking up. "That's wonderful to hear. Ticker is very reliable. Yes, it appears he kept everything in order." He glanced down at the map, and his light expression fell away. "However, there are certain problems that he can't fix and I probably can't either."

"When you say union problems," Sophia began. "What does that mean?"

"Well," he drew out the word, his tone full of hesitation. "It would appear that some of the Brownies who work for me find that some of the business I engage in contradicts our mission and have said I'm potentially in danger of violating the union agreements."

Sophia tilted her head as she picked up on the tension in the elf's voice. "What kind of business?"

"Working with magicians," he answered in a rush, suddenly shuffling around papers on his desk and making noise that Sophia believed sought to cover up his words.

She pursed her lips. Lowered her chin. Batted her eyes at him. "Let's be straight with each other, Mortimer. By magicians, do you mean when you've helped Liv and also me?"

He continued to flip through pages, not looking at them. "They don't get it at the union. It's been that way for ages. They think we have to remain separate from the rest of the magical community. There's us, and them. There are mortals who we serve and everyone else who we don't. When Liv came to me and asked to form a partnership, well, it was the single most helpful thing I've done in centuries."

"So what's the problem?" Sophia asked.

Mortimer stopped messing with the papers and looked at her directly. "The problem is that it's progress. It's evolution. Most aren't comfortable with it. They can't see that it leads to something good for all because all they can see is that it endangers their way of doing things, which if you ask me are outdated and ineffective."

Sophia couldn't help but smile at Mortimer. She knew exactly what he meant. She'd faced similar challenges when she came to the Dragon Elite, having to force Hiker into the twenty-first century. Even now, she felt resistance from the magical world, which didn't want to embrace dragonriders because they were new. The ironic part was that they were old. They'd merely been out of practice for a while.

"I can understand your plight," Sophia stated with a thoughtful expression.

"You can!" he exclaimed, relief on his face.

She nodded. "Yes, but that doesn't mean I want you getting into trouble to help Liv and me."

He shook his head furiously. "I don't mind it. The thing is, they don't get that we've remained separate for too long. It's hard operating alone. Yes, Brownies are supposed to go unseen, but that doesn't mean that we have to be unknown. We have a lot to offer the other magical races, and I dare say they, us."

Sophia tapped the front of the desk. "Now, we're talking. How can we help you, Mortimer? How can we make your job easier? Or help you to fix this problem with the union?"

"That's the thing, Sophia Beaufont of the Dragon Elite," Mortimer began, the enthusiasm receding from his voice. "The union doesn't want to deal with anyone. If you did anything to help us, they'd resent me more. They want you out of our affairs, not in them."

Sophia sank back in defeat and nearly toppled over, forgetting the chair's small size and the odd weight distribution she had to maintain to stay upright. "Oh, well, that's disappointing. I wish there were something I could do to help."

Mortimer's eyes brightened once more. "Oh, but there is!"

"There is?"

He nodded. "Yes, there's only one thing you can do to fix this problem for me."

Sophia leaned forward again. "Okay. Anything. What can I do?"

"You can let me help you with your problems!"

CHAPTER TWENTY-ONE

"Wait." Sophia wondered if she'd heard the Brownie correctly. "To help you with your problems, you want to help me?"

He nodded, his ears flapping back and forth. "Yes, that's right, Sophia Beaufont of the Dragon Elite."

"I'm honored and do need your help, but I'm not sure I follow the logic," Sophia admitted.

"Well, your problems trickle over into the rest of the world's problems," he explained. "I get that. Pricilla gets that. Ticker understands that. There are a few other more progressive Brownies who also appreciate this principle."

When he paused as though waiting for a reaction, Sophia nodded. "I follow you. Please continue."

"It's the same with your sister, Liv Beaufont, Warrior for the House of Fourteen," Mortimer explained. "I saw that from the beginning. I could have turned her away when she first tried to form a partnership with the Brownies, seeking our expertise. However, I knew that as leaders of the magical world, that helping out the magicians would improve mortals' lives and therefore improve Brownies', then it would help out everyone."

Sophia nodded at the brilliance of it all. "Yes, it's truly a cyclical process."

"Exactly!" Mortimer exclaimed. "My predecessor operated in a vacuum. That's how most magical races work. I knew there was something inherently wrong in our system. So when your sister approached me, I realized this was the solution we were looking for. Now I help you two with things that are relatively easy for me, and you all fix big problems so that I hardly see too many small problems."

"Now you have issues with the union," Sophia reminded him.

"I have a problem with Brownies who refuse to see progress happens from doing things in new ways," he corrected.

"So even though you're under fire, you still want to help us?" Sophia questioned.

"Especially so," Mortimer answered. "I'm going to prove to all those old-thinkers that we aren't separate but rather all connected. Then when you fix global issues, I'll be able to explain how that made our smaller, seemingly less important jobs easier."

"There are no less important jobs," Sophia stated thoughtfully.

"Maybe so." He laid his hands on the surface of the desk and threaded his fingers together. "So, what can I help you with?"

"Okay, well, if you think it will help you all out, while also helping us, and incidentally helping the world."

He nodded. "I do. What did you come to me for today?"

"I need you to give me a list and location of all the mortal criminals in the world."

CHAPTER TWENTY-TWO

For a long moment, Mortimer simply blinked at Sophia as though waiting for her to follow up her request with, "Just kidding" or "April Fools...in November!"

When she didn't, he gave her a tamed smile and grabbed a hard candy from the dish on his desk. "It's funny because for a moment, it sounded like you asked me for a list of mortal criminals."

Sophia nodded. "That's right. You heard correctly."

He popped the butterscotch into his mouth and sucked for a moment before popping it into the side of his cheek, making him look like a squirrel preparing for the winter. "The thing is that Brownies are excellent at finding good mortals who behave in extraordinary ways. We do this so that we can serve them, thereby rewarding their good behavior."

"I understand." Sophia pointed at the candy dish. "May I?"

"By all means, Sophia Beaufont." He waved her toward the dish.

She took a chocolate kiss and unwrapped it. "I realize what I'm asking for is a little unorthodox."

"I'm not sure that word does it justice," Mortimer argued. "This is like going to a gnome and asking them to classify fish." He laughed and slapped his desk. "Can you even imagine?"

Sophia didn't know what to say, so she simply shook her head for a moment before replying out loud. "I can't."

"Well, we both know how gnomes can't stand water or anything to do with it," Mortimer related. "In the same way, Brownies only have dealings with good mortals. I wouldn't even know how to find the criminals of the world."

"I thought about that." Sophia chewed on her chocolate. "You know how to find the well-behaved mortals based on what, some sort of magical spell?"

"An equation," Mortimer answered.

"Even better!" Sophia exclaimed and took another piece of candy, this one with peanuts and caramel. "So you reverse the equation. Instead of looking for well-behaved mortals, you look for the opposite. Or look for the good ones and eliminate them. What's left is who I'm looking for."

Mortimer drew in a breath and continued to suck on his butterscotch. "Technically, I guess it could work. I mean, it's simply a reverse operation. Are you certain that it's necessary? As Brownies, we've always considered that positive reinforcement is the best practice. We reward those who do good and ignore those who don't."

"I think that's a great operation. It's perfect for the Brownies. Sometimes, we have to focus on the criminals to stop bigger evils before they get out of control. I think that if you help me find the mortal crime offenders of the world, I might be able to find the really big bad guys of the magical world and hopefully make both our lives easier."

Mortimer stood from his desk, his height not changing much. He extended his tiny hand to Sophia. "Then you have yourself a deal. I'll find you the mortal criminals of the world, and you help me to prove to my race that we should all work together."

Sophia took his small hand and shook it in earnest. "Hopefully, together we prove that we can make this planet a better place for all."

CHAPTER TWENTY-THREE

Returning to the Gullington felt different. Maybe it was because Sophia knew that it was with a new dragonrider inside it. Or perhaps it was because she felt different after all the developments. However, she reminded herself that change was progress in many ways and she had to embrace evolution rather than be like the Brownies who were giving Mortimer trouble because they didn't want to do things differently.

When Sophia stepped through the portal, she found not one newish dragon flying high in the skies, but rather a few. She remembered them from when they were dragonettes, but outside the Gullington, having magnetized to riders, the dragons had matured fast and grown to almost their full size. Now they sped through the air, circling. Their riders were on the ground, looking up at them.

Sophia didn't approach Cooper or the other two or three riders that she saw standing in the distance. Instead, she stopped next to Hiker and Mahkah, who watched from the other side of the Expanse, simply observing.

"We have new riders." Hiker sounded proud, almost boastful.

Sophia nodded. "I met Cooper and Sage on Roya Lane, where they almost got their butts handed to them by a bunch of angry magicians, gnomes, and elves."

The light expression dropped from Hiker's face, and Sophia almost regretted having said anything to spoil his good mood.

"You were right to call me back here then, sir." Mahkah took up the conversation in a rare turn of events. "It's better that we train the new generation rather than go on a goodwill tour and educate the world about who we are. There will be time for that later after the new dragonriders are trained and ready."

That seemed to bolster Hiker, and he nodded. "I think so too. We'll always have time to fight a brewing war, but it's not every day that we have new riders. It's not every year or decade." He chuckled and shook his head.

Sophia didn't think she'd ever seen Hiker Wallace like this. There was a spark in his blue eyes that she'd never witnessed before. He seemed…almost hopeful. Excited. Maybe even giddy.

She could get behind that emotion as she watched the dragons, who were half a size bigger than they were when they left the Gullington, circle each other in the sky. On the ground were Cooper and another two guys, both looking up with mesmerized expressions.

"So you'll train them how to fly," Hiker stated as Evan and Wilder walked up from the Castle, both fully geared up as though about to go into battle.

"Yes, sir," Mahkah agreed.

Hiker turned to Evan and Wilder without having to be alerted to their presence. "You two." He pointed at the pair.

"Are your greatest assets." Evan tried to complete Hiker's statement.

"Hardly," the Dragon Elite's leader countered. "I pulled you off your current missions because of the new dragonriders. They need training in combat and strategy. I'm counting on you two to do that."

Evan knocked into Sophia as he sidled up. "Sorry, Pink Princess. Guess you're going to be left with the task of retrieving my weapons while I teach the newbies how to hold a sword."

"Actually," Hiker cut in after clearing his throat. "I want Sophia's attention fully on investigating the Rogue Riders. We can't let them get too far ahead as we train our army. The new dragonriders deserve our attention. They deserve your help as they bond with their dragons." Hiker glanced at Evan, Mahkah, and Wilder. "Sophia needs to be the one to keep an eye on the Rogue Riders. They're our greatest enemy, and when our army is ready, she'll be the one ready to lead them into battle."

Sophia elbowed Evan in the side. "Then you can retrieve my sword for me buddy, and watch me ride into battle."

He gave her a cutting look but still smiled. "Whatever it takes. I'm a team player."

"It's about time," Wilder teased.

"Okay, we all know what we need to do," Hiker cut in, drawing everyone's attention back to him. "Are we ready?"

"Yes, sir!" Mahkah answered.

"Are we prepared to make this new generation the best yet?" Hiker called to the foursome.

"Yes, sir," Wilder answered.

"We won't be defeated by those who challenge us, will we?" Hiker asked again.

"No, sir," Sophia stated with confidence.

"Because we are the Dragon Elite and we're meant to rule this world, right?" Hiker asked rhetorically.

"Yes, sir," Evan answered and headed back to the Castle. "Right after I get a snack."

CHAPTER TWENTY-FOUR

"Why is there nothing to eat in this Castle?" Evan complained while inspecting an artfully arranged platter of assorted cheeses on the table in the dining hall. Beside the tray were artisan crackers and breads filled with nuts and dried fruit. Alongside that were jams and spreads as well as fresh vegetables and ripe fruit. There were also assorted finger sandwiches and little cakes and cookies, all so pretty they looked like art rather than food.

"Ha-ha," Trin said from the other side of the room, her Inspector Gadget arm stretching across several yards to slap Evan's hand as he went to grab a slice of smoked gouda. "Those are for the new dragonriders."

He straightened and gave her a look of offense. "Are you kidding me? I'm an old dragonrider who they need to pass along my wisdom so that they don't get their dragons' butts handed to them on the battlefield. I need snacks, woman."

Not at all deterred, Trin shot him a defiant glare as she marched in the direction of the kitchen, retracing her arm as she did. "I have some trail mix for you. I'll get it."

Evan spun and shook his head as he plopped down on a chair across from Sophia and Wilder. "I don't want stupid trail mix. I'm a dragonrider. How am I supposed to maintain my strength with squirrel food?"

"I find trail mix to be very hearty and great for keeping up my endurance," Wilder commented.

"And there my point has been made," Evan replied. "Some of us, like the real men in the Castle, need real food."

"Or is it that the real men can sustain themselves on a plant-based diet and the rest of you need to slaughter harmless creatures to perform at the same level?" Wilder countered.

Evan shook his head and reached for a piece of cheddar. "I don't think—"

"Don't you dare," Trin hollered from the kitchen, making Evan pull his hand back.

He glanced over his shoulder toward the closed kitchen door. "How does she do that?"

"She has eyes in the back of her head," Wilder answered and added, "Literally."

Sophia laughed, picked a grape from a bunch on the table, and popped it into her mouth. "Evan, I need your help with something."

His eyes widened. "Are you serious? How come you don't get in trouble for nicking the newbie, day-old baby dragonriders' food?"

Trin strode out from the kitchen and laid a platter of cured meats in the center of the table, followed by a bowl of trail mix in front of Evan. "If you're going after the fruit and vegetables, then I'm not stopping you. As far as I can tell, you're going to eat all the cheeses and sandwiches and leave none for the new guys."

"So?" Evan retorted and pointed at the meats. "Is that fair? You know that dried prosciutto is my favorite." He batted his eyes at her, and the cyborg softened slightly as her gaze darted between the platter of meats and Evan.

"Yeah, fine, have some meat," she acquiesced. "Also have some fruit. It won't kill you, you know."

Evan darted forward, grabbed a slice of prosciutto, and stuffed it into his mouth. Talking with his mouth full, he said, "I don't know. I think it might. I hear there are bugs on fruit." He shook his head and glanced at Wilder. "Oh, think of all the innocent bugs you've killed when you've eaten fruit. You're a murderer."

Wilder picked up a broccoli floret and took a bite. "It doesn't count if I don't know about it."

Evan went to reach for another piece of meat, but spied the challenging look on Trin's face, redirected his hand to a pile of strawberries, and grabbed one. "Oh, look a strawberry. It's red like meat. Fleshy like meat." He took a bite and stifled a grimace as he chewed. "But tastes nothing like steak."

"I was thinking of making watermelon steaks on the Expanse at some point," Wilder offered. "You know, we could build a bonfire out there and grill up watermelon or cauliflower steaks."

Evan put the half-eaten strawberry on the plate in front of him and shook his head. "You are the worst person ever to live. If I didn't know that you'd struggle to make a friend, even with new blood coming into the Castle, I'd ditch you from my friends list."

"So you're my friend out of pity?" Wilder sounded amused.

"Yeah, sorry the truth had to come out this way. I mean, and it was a lack of options thing. Proximity also worked in your favor."

Wilder laughed, not at all offended. "Now you've got new mates you can try and impress with your..." His voice trailed off, and he scratched his head. "I mean, I'm sure they'll like that you're..." Wilder glanced at Sophia. "I'm sorry, I'm drawing a blank on any redeeming quality of Evan's. Can you please remind me of one?"

Sophia pretended to think while plucking another grape from the bunch. "Well, as far as people go, he's very much...alive. When he speaks...it's out loud. Oh, and when he enters a room...he's present."

Trin laughed and shook her head as she made for the kitchen. "Good one."

"Hey." Evan snapped his head in the retreating cyborg's direction. "I thought you liked me."

"I do," Trin sang. "That's why I can laugh at you."

Wilder and Sophia joined in, chuckling at Evan's expense.

"Hey, you Trin, are cute and fun, so you can't laugh at me," Evan warned.

"Thank you," Trin called from the kitchen.

"You're welcome," Evan replied over his shoulder.

"I'm cute," Wilder argued.

"I'm fun," Sophia added.

"Those are your opinions," Evan stated. "You're safe as my friend for a little longer, Wilder. I'm not going to buddy up with the infant dragonriders yet. I think it's better not to get too friendly with them since they need to regard me as a leader who they respect and admire."

"How drugged up are you going to have to get them to accomplish that?" Wilder asked.

Evan shook his head. "You've started to take me for granted after all these years. People love me. Look at Pink Princess. She was obsessed with me when she first got here and kept trying to get my attention."

"I believe I threw a knife at you my first week to get you to stop bullying Quiet when you stole all the pastries," Sophia offered.

"I know, you had to pretend to care about the little guy so you had a reason to stalk me," Evan gushed. "It was really cute. Then I turned you down, and you settled for Wilder." He winked at his friend. "You're welcome, mate."

"Thanks!" Wilder chirped.

Evan leaned forward. "Are you worried that your gal is going to dump you now that there are more choices at the Gullington?"

Wilder grabbed a carrot and smiled at Sophia. "I would worry more that she'd dump me every single day because she's the best gal in the world."

Sophia smiled back at him fondly. "That won't happen because you're the best guy, and no one is as lucky as us."

"That's so true." Wilder took a bite of the carrot. "We should start that charity we discussed."

"Which one?" Evan asked.

"One where we raise funds for all the sad people in the world who aren't us," Wilder responded. "The rest of the planet doesn't know what it's like to be so happy. It's impossible that they could."

Evan pretended to gag. "Okay, I take it back. You and Sophia are the worst humans ever. As a pair you two outdo everyone."

"Thanks!" Wilder stated.

"You're not at all welcome." Evan tapped the table in front of Sophia. "You said you needed my help with something. If it's making it so other people can tolerate you or your boyfriend, I don't have those kinds of magical powers. No one does, I'm afraid. Not even Mama Jamba."

"I'm good," Sophia stated. "Yeah, my sister needs help retrieving a genie's bottle from the bottom of the ocean. I hoped that you and Coral would help out."

"This sister of yours," Evan began. "Is she cute?"

"I heard that," Trin called from the kitchen.

"I'm asking for a friend," Evan replied.

"She's Liv Beaufont," Sophia stated. "You know, the Warrior for the House of Fourteen that brought down the barrier when we battled the Rogue Riders at the elfin homeland."

Evan shook his head. "Don't recall that."

"She helped fight the cyborgs when they invaded the Gullington," Sophia added.

"I was too busy looking at Trin to notice anything else," Evan stated.

"Thank you," the cyborg sang from the kitchen.

"You know it's all about you," Evan replied.

"Anyway, it has to be important, or Liv wouldn't ask," Sophia stated. "Can you please help out?"

"Well, since you're begging."

"Asking," Sophia corrected.

"I'm supposed to devote my time to training the newbies," Evan stated. "I can probably pull away for a little if you know where the genie's bottle is."

"I have a map that should make it easy to find."

"Fine." Evan stood from the table, still eyeing the cheese platter longingly. "Then let me know when you need me to save your butt, and I'll come to the rescue. In repayment, you and your horrible boyfriend have to sit at the far end of the dining hall table so I don't have to look at your faces while I eat."

Wilder grinned and patted Sophia on the arm. "I didn't think this day could get any better."

Sophia leaned into him. "When you're us, it always can since we're the luckiest people in the world."

Evan shook his head, mock revulsion on his face as he made for the entrance hall. "The worst. The ultimate worst two people on the planet and I have to share *my* castle with them."

CHAPTER TWENTY-FIVE

Wilder and Evan strode off to the Expanse, leaving Sophia alone in the Castle. She was waiting on Mortimer to give her leads on the Rogue Riders. She knew that tracking down criminals was a long shot, but Plato had reinforced the plan, so she figured it had merit. Other than that, she didn't have other ideas for how to deal with the Rogue Riders.

With all the guys out on the Expanse training, it left Sophia alone in the dining hall, looking at all the artfully arranged food Trin had laid out. She pulled out her phone and messaged her sister.

"Evan is on board to retrieve the genie's bottle," Sophia typed. "I have the map from Ru. Let me know what you want to do next."

"Jump into a ravine," Liv responded a few moments later.

Before Sophia could reply, another message from her sister came through. "Oh, you meant about the genie's bottle. Yeah, let me get back to you on that. That's too stressful for me to think about right now."

"Is everything okay?" For the second time, Sophia sensed that things weren't okay with Liv.

"Well, there's an avalanche of rocks speeding in my direction, so not really," Liv responded.

"So when you said you want to jump into a ravine..."

"It was literal," Liv replied.

"Be careful," Sophia warned.

"I will, but I have to dive right now."

"Isn't jumping into a ravine going to get you buried?" Sophia had to ask.

"No, it's how the fairy godmother I saved earlier told me to get out of danger. There's a tunnel down there. I have to get to it..."

"Okay, message me later when you've survived."

"Copy that, Love Bug. XOXO."

Sophia lowered her phone, feeling like everyone had a job right then but her. She often found herself in the middle of these lulls between missions where she waited for a lead to come in. Sophia knew it would be smart to use the time to conserve energy, but it was difficult for her to sit around when she sensed that she could help the world to be a safer place.

Suddenly, something that Liv had mentioned occurred to Sophia. She didn't know why she hadn't thought of it before. Yes, Mortimer was a godsend. Yes, she had eyes and ears looking for signs of the Rogue Riders. Still, she didn't know why she hadn't thought of this option until then. It should have been a no-brainer.

Sophia eyed the little cakes and confections on the dining room table before her, tempted to grab one for the road. However, she remembered that where she was going, she wouldn't need to fill up on dessert. That she could do once she got there.

CHAPTER TWENTY-SIX

Happily Ever After College didn't look anything like how Sophia remembered it. The grounds were still lush and green, and the temperature was perfect, reminding Sophia of a warm spring day with a mild breeze carrying hints of floral aromas. However, whereas the college's grounds used to be manicured like a school campus with a lawn and sidewalks, now it resembled more of a forest.

Large oak trees with long hanging branches dripped luscious leaves and blossoms of every color. The grounds weren't even and filled with flat green grass. Instead, they bumped and rolled with many tree roots and other plants obscuring the path.

Everywhere Sophia looked, there was something to delight the senses, whether it was strange flowers in a rainbow of colors, or mushrooms growing from the ground that were the size of a bread box, or the large owl that blinked at her from inside the hole of an immense tree.

Mist rolled across the ground, making her think it was either early morning or right before sunset. It was hard to tell under the forest canopy.

In the distance, she could just spy the outline of a building through the trees. It didn't resemble the red brick building that used to be there and was the center hub of Happily Ever After College. There was a sliver of the old building still intact, Sophia observed as she moved through low-hanging branches and approached the college, the view becoming clearer through the trees.

The new Happily Ever After main building, or at least what Sophia guessed it was, looked like ten different whimsical buildings were stuck together and made to look like one. The center part was pink with columns and tons of windows. Along one side were multiple different pastel buildings that reminded Sophia of the townhomes one found in San Francisco, except these were all glued to each other to make one. Around the other side was a clear turret that rose to the top of the building with a large spiral staircase that Sophia could see going all the way up to the rooftop, which was seven stories up.

It was like something out of...

"A fairy tale," Sophia whispered, nearly laughing at the realization.

"That was the idea," a familiar voice said at Sophia's back.

She turned around to find her fairy godmother Mae Ling gliding through the air on a tree swing.

Sophia hadn't noticed the two ropes or the small board attached to the tree when she walked by. She definitely hadn't seen Mae Ling swinging from the large oak tree, her feet gliding through the air as she leaned back while holding onto the ropes for support.

"The college..." Sophia looked around, every moment noticing something else that was new.

Mae Ling smiled. "We were overdue for a renovation."

Sophia noticed a toad hopping through the grass at Mae Ling's back, making its way for a notch in the tree's base. "Is this a result of the toxic slime? Did the college not recover?"

"It did," Mae Ling answered. "In so many ways. It's like when a storm comes and pulls the front porch off your house, and you realize that you didn't like it in the first place. The storm did you a favor, and now you can build things the way you want them."

"Oh, so the green sludge pulled the front porch off the college, and this is how you really wanted it?"

Mae Ling nodded and fondly looked around at the enchanted

forests. "It makes a lot more sense. The old college was the result of an older generation of fairy godmother professors. They were a little more regimented than the current faculty. I would venture to say that we'd lost some of the whimsy over time." She shrugged and continued to swing. "I get it though. My predecessor wanted to combine the virtues of fantasy with the logical factors that often surround love. However, it's often those same factors that pose challenges to true love's destiny, so Willow and I saw no reason to continue to embrace the old ways. Instead, we're going back to our roots."

Sophia drew in a breath, smelling both chocolate chip cookies and gardenia blossoms at the same time. It was an intoxicating aroma. "This is whimsical. The new building…"

Mae Ling giggled. "You like it? We couldn't decide on the architecture. All the professors submitted building ideas. At the end of the day, Willow put them all together into one so that we'd all be happy. Who says you can't please everyone?" Mae Ling pointed to the pink part of the building with columns and plenty of windows. "That one in the center was mine. I don't think you can ever have too much pink."

Sophia nodded. "I would have to agree with you there."

"One of the many reasons we get along," Mae Ling gushed with a smile.

"So the college is good then?" Sophia asked. "After the evacuation and the damage caused by the toxic sludge?"

"I think we're better than ever." Mae Ling leaned back as she continued to glide through the air. "We have a new college that nurtures our purpose. Before, the old one was nice and open, but it was overly manicured, and that doesn't promote the right message. We're about creating love here and that never blossoms if pruned too much. No, the best place for love is in a fertile forest where trees grow on top of trees and seeds are allowed to be scattered on the wind, rather than planted by a gardener."

Sophia smiled, enjoying the sentiment.

"Furthermore, we learned some valuable lessons," Mae Ling continued. "We tried to engineer a love potion, and now we remember why that doesn't work. You can create spells that encourage love, that provide the right environment for it to flourish, that support its growth. Under no circumstances can you make love happen."

"That makes sense."

"Well, it does to you, and it does to me now, but over time, we need these lessons as reminders," Mae Ling informed her. "I think returning to an environment that's organic and whimsical will be good for the fairy godmothers. We've already benefited."

"How is that?" Sophia asked, and in the distance, she heard giggling and saw shadows moving through the trees.

Mae Ling indicated that direction with a nod. "We're playing again. It's been ages. We got so bogged down in curriculum and regulations handed down from the head office that we forgot who we were. As fairy godmothers, we help our charges, but it's not through discipline but rather through creative expression. If we aren't enjoying life, then how do we expect to lead others to a life they love?"

Sophia suddenly felt infected by the spirit of the grounds and wanted to frolic and play in the woods, maybe swim in the babbling brook she heard not too far off and catch the fireflies that buzzed around through the trees. Although she wouldn't keep the fireflies. Maybe she'd dance around them.

Suddenly, she felt like she'd passed out and awoken in some sort of nirvana. She shook her head, feeling intoxicated. "This place truly is a new kind of magical."

Mae Ling nodded and slid off the swing. "All thanks to you."

"I'm glad I could help."

"Now, it's my turn to help you," Mae Ling offered, striding in front of Sophia and indicating that she follow. She led her through the trees dividing the forests and the college. In the thick branches hung little paper lanterns of every possible color, shaped like various flowers.

Sophia expected that they were headed for the college, but Mae Ling stopped before that and waved her arm. At first, Sophia didn't know what the sparks of magic that fell from Mae Ling's arm did, or the sound of a bell that followed. However, a moment later she noticed that a tree stump had risen from the fog and ferns, and sitting on top of it was a tea tray, a series of desserts, and little fairies who went straight to work pouring and stirring and slicing.

The tray was breathtakingly beautiful and also looked scrumptious. Sophia was suddenly glad that she hadn't filled up on the food at the Castle. Although Trin's desserts had looked delicious, these were heavenly.

Mae Ling swept her arm through the air again, and two neighboring tree stumps rose, offering the perfect stools so they could sit at the table for tea. "Shall we?"

Sophia grinned, grateful that she'd thought to visit her fairy godmother. Now she had to hope that Mae Ling could offer her some help.

She nodded and sat, and almost immediately as if sensing her thoughts, her fairy godmother said, "I'm glad you came to see me, but I must let you down straight away and inform you that I can't give you any information to help with the Rogue Riders."

Sophia deflated instantly as a tiny fairy with lavender wings dragged a full teacup on a saucer in her direction. "Oh…" Although Sophia had worked to keep the disappointment out of her voice, it was still there.

"Sorry, my dear." Mae Ling picked up her cup of tea, which a fairy the size of a monarch butterfly and with wings to match had delivered to her. "However, sometimes my job is to help you with the things you don't expect or think you'll need, and that's what I'm doing today."

The fairy with lavender wings had gone back to work, dragging a plate of assorted desserts over to Sophia. The tiny sprite had piled it high with a slice of vanilla cake, fudge brownies, cookies with fat sprinkles, and truffles.

"Are you going to help me fix the Dragon Elite's reputation with the magical world?" Sophia didn't touch her tea or desserts.

Mae Ling shook her head.

"Oh." Sophia thought for a moment. "Are you going to help us with the mortal world and how they view us?"

Again, another headshake.

"Oh, well, maybe you can—"

"I'm going to give you the name and address of the perfect employee for Heals Pills," Mae Ling interrupted.

She deflated instantly. "Oh, that's not something I was working on. Rudolf was supposed to hire for that position, and it's not really a priority for me."

"It should be." Mae Ling sipped her tea. "Heals Pills is an important endeavor that will help the magical world. Having the right staff is important for it to flourish."

"I don't disagree. It's just that—"

"King Sweetwater has other ventures that he should devote his attention to," Mae Ling stated. "So my best efforts can be in helping you to find not a good person for the role of running the shop, but the best person."

"That's very thoughtful of you." Sophia again masked her disappointment. Heals Pills was great, but in the big scheme of things, it wasn't her biggest concern.

"Now, based on what I know, this person needs to be resilient," Mae Ling stated.

"Because Rudolf will be their boss?" Sophia offered.

Mae Ling shook her head. "Because it's a dangerous job and they will encounter many fatal situations."

Sophia lowered her chin. "At Heals Pills? We are talking about the same place, right?"

"We are," Mae Ling answered. "I'm privy to things that I can't disclose, but I will say that's one reason that the king shouldn't be in the shop any longer. It's a powerful place that sells miracle things. That won't go unnoticed."

"So what do you have in mind as far as an employee goes?" Sophia asked.

"Well, you need someone who has multiple lives," Mae Ling explained.

"Like a cat?"

"Sort of. There's a particular individual who had an accident when he was younger. He fell into a fountain, and when they fetched him out, they determined that he'd be different in a few ways."

"And these ways?"

"Well, he has many lives and can't easily be killed," Mae Ling answered.

"Was this fountain the one for youth and longer life?" Sophia guessed.

Mae Ling waved her off. "Doesn't matter. It's since been destroyed. Anyway, there's something else about this individual."

"Yes?" Sophia braced herself.

"He sort of attracts trouble. It's part of the counterspell that adhered to him when he came out of the fountain. Everything comes with a price. You can have multiple lives, but there will be something one pays in return."

"Then why would I want to employ him?"

"Because he's the best person for the job according to my findings," Mae Ling stated. "The shop will have trouble regardless. It's inevitable. So it's better to have him with his defenses than to have someone vulnerable. Otherwise, you'll go through employees left and right."

"Okay, then where do I find this guy?" Sophia questioned.

Mae Ling snapped her fingers, and a card materialized in the air. "This is his current address."

Sophia took it with a grateful smile. "I look forward to meeting this strange fellow."

"Oh, but you've already met him." Mae Ling returned to her tea after handing off the card.

"I have?" Sophia read the name on the top of the card. Her eyes widened as she groaned. It read:

Ramy Vance

Previous bodyguard to Zac Efron

Current bodyguard to Henry Cavill

"That guy?" Sophia asked. "That's the guy who can't be killed?"

"Can't be killed easily," Mae Ling corrected. "Yes. He's the right person to run your shop. Give him socks for Christmas—and lots of cheese."

Sophia nodded, wondering how she'd gone from trying to save the world to recruiting a shop clerk. She had the strangest job of anyone she knew.

Mae Ling pointed at the plate of desserts. "Now eat up. And drink your tea. It's getting cold, and I had it laced with an herb that will help with negotiations."

"Negotiations?" Sophia tentatively regarded the teacup.

"Well, you don't think you can just offer Ramy the job, and he'll take it?" Mae Ling asked.

"No, I wouldn't dream of it." Sophia picked up the tea and drank it in one gulp before wiping her mouth.

CHAPTER TWENTY-SEVEN

I t was ironic to Sophia that her job so often brought her back to her hometown of Los Angeles. She didn't know the many roads well or all the back routes for navigating around the city to avoid traffic. However, she knew the way the city felt. It always filled her with a gentle hum in her chest. That was the city's energy, and Sophia felt it the moment she stepped through the portal onto the movie studio lot in Hollywood.

"Oh, it's good to be home," Sophia said to herself, careful to stay out of view as camera technicians and makeup artists hurried to their stations.

It wasn't clear what movie was underway, but by the looks of the set, it had to be something action-packed. There were pads for falling on the set area's floor, and wires rigged overhead with various objects. Smoke from a machine billowed around the staged site, obscuring a lot of it.

"Okay, let's take five," a guy in all-black clothing said, not noticing Sophia as she stepped out of the shadows.

She had a spell on her that would make her blend into the surroundings in a way. She wasn't invisible, but she didn't stand out. An unsuspecting person would simply see her and dismiss her presence right away as unimportant. It was only if she talked to someone that she'd stand out and only for them. It was a complicated spell and draining, but Sophia thought she could risk the magic.

How hard could it be to recruit this Ramy guy? Sophia thought to herself. It wasn't like she would have to fight him. Negotiate, yes, but that wasn't so difficult, she reasoned. Why wouldn't a magician want to work on Roya Lane, rather than as a bodyguard in Hollywood, protecting a mortal?

Sophia hadn't realized when she first met Ramy that he was a magician, but something must have blocked his powers from registering for her. Maybe he had them turned off by the House of Fourteen. That was a possibility. Or there was a host of other potentials like strange planetary alignments, or it was Leap Day or Ramy had too much curry for lunch.

A very striking man strode from the set and grabbed a towel from a nearby rack to wipe his face. That's when Sophia noticed Ramy approach, carrying a bottle of water. He handed it to the man with a smile.

"That was amazing, Mr. Cavill," Ramy said, his eyes full of stars as he stared up at the actor.

Cavill took the bottle, unscrewed the lid, and took a long drink. "How many times do I have to tell you to call me Henry?"

"At least once more, Mr. Cavill, as always." Ramy winked.

"I wish you'd stop quoting lines from *Pirates of the Caribbean*," Henry shook his head.

"Is there another movie you prefer, sir?" Ramy asked. "The *Terminator*, maybe? *Jurassic Park*? Maybe one of your films? *Man of Steel* is my favorite. What was it like playing Superman?"

"You can't be killed, and you want me to tell you how it was to play a man who can't be killed?" Henry drained the water bottle.

"Easily," Ramy corrected. "We can't be killed easily."

"I used to think that was a good thing," Henry said dryly.

"We need you on the set," the director called to the actor. "We need to block out the action sequence. Will you come stand over here?"

Henry hurried over, giving Sophia her chance. She approached

Ramy, who didn't notice her as he only had eyes for the handsome actor walking onto the stage.

"Hey, so we meet again." Sophia stood beside Ramy and watched the actor the same as him. They were like two people at a rendezvous point, pretending to focus on something else and not talk to each other, or so Sophia imagined, her imagination inspired by being on a movie set.

"Like it's the first time," Ramy said in a strange voice.

Sophia blinked at him. "No, it feels like the second time. You remember me?"

"How can I forget," Ramy stated.

"Oh, because of the dragon thing," Sophia guessed.

He shook his head. "No, because of the stealing Zac thing."

"He agreed to help me," Sophia argued.

Ramy's eyes didn't move from watching Henry Cavill as he blocked out an action scene. "Are you here to take Mr. Cavill from me now?"

Sophia nearly laughed. This guy was a piece of work. "No, I'm here to offer you a job."

That surprised Ramy, and he looked at her now. "Do you need me to be The Rock's bodyguard? That's the only job I'll give this one up for."

"I'm pretty sure The Rock doesn't need you to be his bodyguard," Sophia countered. "No, it's come to my attention that you can't really die."

"Not easily," he added. "Yes, I have suffered many fatal deaths, only to rise again from the ashes like a phoenix."

"But not nearly as majestic, I'm guessing," Sophia teased.

He shook his head. "Usually I look like death, but thankfully I don't feel any pain."

"Wow, that was some fountain you fell into."

He arched an eyebrow at her. "How do you know about that?"

"I have sources," Sophia answered. "She told me that you were the right person for a job I need to fill. Apparently, it could become dangerous, and I need someone who can't die."

"Easily," he added.

Sophia nodded. "I'm not sure how this magical multiple life thing of yours works. You're a magician, right? Why is it that I don't sense your magic?"

"Much like the great Warrior for the House of Fourteen, I gave up my magic," Ramy answered.

"You mean Liv Beaufont?" Sophia asked, surprised by the reference.

He nodded.

"She took back her magic so that she could take the role as Warrior," Sophia explained.

He waved his hand. "That's irregardless."

"Regardless," Sophia corrected. "Liv has her magic now. She's my sister, you know?"

Ramy's eyes widened. "Does she need a bodyguard?"

"She's a Warrior for the House of Fourteen," Sophia dryly stated. "Others use guards against her."

"But still... I would die for her multiple times."

"I don't think that's necessary. Anyway, I need your help to run a shop on Roya Lane."

Ramy grimaced at her. "That doesn't sound very glamorous at all."

"We sell a magical elixir that heals and makes people prettier," Sophia offered in an enticing tone.

"Let me get this right. You want me to give up my stardom and prestige to run a cash register in a store?" Ramy asked, skepticism heavy on his face.

"Ramy, I need my sweat rag," Henry Cavill called from the stage, gaining Ramy's attention.

He suddenly glanced up and looked around. Finding the towel that Henry had left on a nearby table, he picked it up and brought it over to the actor.

"Thanks." Henry mopped his sweaty brow.

Ramy nodded like an obedient puppy and returned to his post beside Sophia.

"Wow, and to think I would take you away from all this prestige and stardom," Sophia said dryly.

"It isn't always like this," Ramy argued. "Sometimes I get Mr. Cavill other things."

"When do you do any guarding?"

Ramy shrugged. "He's a pretty tough guy, and no one really would dream of messing with him. Mostly I keep back screaming women who want to tear his clothes off, but they can be pretty feisty. I got scratched the other day."

"You poor thing," Sophia joked. "Well, I can't say that you won't be attacked at my shop Heals Pills, since apparently, it's going to be the epicenter for danger in the future. We can make the perks worth your while."

"Why is it going to be so dangerous?" Ramy asked.

Sophia held up a hand, listing off reasons. "It's co-run by the king of the fae, and he's offended more people than a diva wearing white to a wedding." She ticked off another finger. "Second, I'm involved, and trouble follows me around per an agreement I apparently made before I was born."

Ramy nodded as if this made perfect sense.

"Third, what we sell is valuable, life-changing, and vital. When you have that sort of combination, I'm guessing people will go to great lengths to steal what we have, take the formula we use, or abolish something that could have such far-reaching effects. There are people, after all, who don't want others to live long lives."

"My tremendous intuitive sense of the female creature informs me that you are troubled," Ramy observed, again quoting a line from *Pirates of the Caribbean.*

Sophia rolled her eyes. "I have a lot of problems and didn't think playing a human resources rep was going to be on the list today, but according to people I don't argue with, this is important. Will you take the job?"

"You mentioned perks. What are they?"

"I don't know. What do you want? Six-figure salary? Lots of vacation? A retirement plan? We have pretty deep pockets, and this business is about making the world better, not about money, although it's hugely profitable."

Ramy combed his fingers over his chin, thinking. "I want you to buy my lunch on Fridays and give me the days off that there are major award shows like the Emmys and Oscars."

Sophia pursed her lips, wondering if she should play hardball with this guy. She decided she didn't have the time, energy, or inclination for it. "Yeah, that's fine. We would have bought your lunch every day and gotten you into the Emmys and Oscars."

"No to buying my lunch every day," Ramy stated as if offended, then his mouth opened and closed as his eyes widened. "D-D-Did you say you could get me into the award shows?"

Sophia nodded. "Yeah, I don't see why not. There's not really anything off-limits for us. I mean, I'm a Dragon Elite. Rudolf is the king of the fae. We have magic, which you do too, but refuse to use for whatever reason."

"It's a virtues thing," Ramy stated. "I'll probably get over it soon when I'm back in the magical world again. Mortals always judge me for using magic, as if it makes me better than them. Like I could ever be better than Henry Cavill."

"Wait, does that mean you'll do it? You'll take the job?"

"If you're going to get me into award shows, then yes!"

Sophia tilted her head, confused. "Don't you get into those events as a bodyguard?"

"Nooooo." He drew out the word. "Mr. Cavill thinks I'll embarrass him. The other celebrities, well, they seem to think that trouble follows me and I'd ruin their big event."

"Oh, yeah, about that..." Sophia gave him a careful expression. She didn't sense anything strange about the guy, and yet, Mae Ling had said that he attracted problems and now he admitted to it. "What sort of trouble do you have following you around?"

He held up his hands. "I don't think I do. Not more than anyone else."

"Well, how many times have you died and come back?" Sophia asked.

"Only two hundred and six times."

Sophia laughed, then regretted it when the people on the set gave her rude stares. "Is that all?"

"I know, I don't know what the big deal is and why everyone says I'm accident-prone."

"I couldn't imagine…" Sophia started to have doubts about inviting this guy to manage Heals Pills. However, Mae Ling had recommended him, and she trusted her wisdom.

"Okay, well, I'm glad we could agree, and we didn't have to pretend to fight like last time," Sophia related.

He scoffed at her. "Why fight when you can negotiate?" Ramy elbowed her in the side. "That's a line from *Pirates of the Caribbean*."

Ignoring this, Sophia said, "When can you start?"

"Do I get a relocation package?"

Sophia shrugged, not really caring.

"And business cards?"

"Sure," she answered noncommittally.

"How about a fancy title?"

"You can have a company car for all I care," Sophia offered.

"Not all treasure is silver and gold, mate," Ramy replied, his eyes on Henry Cavill, who was getting into place to run through the action scene again. "That was another line from *Pirates of the Caribbean*."

"You don't have to inform me of that each time," Sophia related. "I'll assume that as an honest man, the lines are mostly yours."

"I'm dishonest. And a dishonest man you can always trust to be dishonest."

Sophia lowered her chin. "Another quote from *Pirates of the Caribbean*," she guessed.

"Right you are," he nearly exclaimed, watching as a boulder held overhead by chains was lifted over Henry Cavill. Ramy tensed.

"So, tomorrow?" Sophia supplied. "Can you start work tomorrow?"

"Mr. Cavill, though," Ramy argued, watching intently as the crew moved out of the way, preparing to run through the scene. "He'll need to replace me. I need to give my notice. It could take quite some time to find someone as devoted and attentive as me."

Sophia sighed, thinking of how annoyed Henry Cavill seemed when being doted on by Ramy. "I'm not sure that's the problem you think it is."

"The problem is not the problem. The problem is your attitude about the problem."

"Wow, you have that movie memorized," Sophia said, impressed.

"I helped Johnny Depp prepare for the role."

"Oh, you were his bodyguard too?"

Ramy shook his head. "No, but I got thrown off his property a lot during the filming of the first movie, and I'm pretty sure I offered him the inspiration he needed to be a fantastic pirate. You should have seen his eyes when I broke into his house and drank all his rum."

"So that's the memory he channeled when Elizabeth Swan drank his store of rum, huh?"

Ramy clapped a hand on Sophia's shoulder as the boulder dangling over Henry Cavil began to fall. The bodyguard sprinted forward, yelling, "Noooo!"

Everything after that happened in slow motion. Henry looked over as Ramy rushed at him, his hands reaching forward. The director yelled, "Cut!" Sophia simply remained frozen, as though being forced to watch a car crash happen.

Ramy dove into the actor, pushing him out of the way. Henry landed on his backside, sliding several feet away. The boulder continued to fall, and finding himself directly under it, Ramy froze and looked up, his face constricted with horror. Yet, he simply peered up at the boulder about to crash into him.

CHAPTER TWENTY-EIGHT

Sophia was about to rush forward and push Ramy out of the way of the falling boulder, the way he'd done for Henry Cavill. However, she spied something that kept her still.

The boulder was tethered to a steel rod above it by a chain. It unraveled as the boulder fell and when it was a few feet from the top of Ramy's head, the chain went taut, and the large rock bounced in the air for a little before merely swinging.

Ramy hadn't moved as the boulder plummeted toward him, his chin sticking straight into the air and eyes wide on the object of his demise.

"You idiot!" the director yelled, throwing his arms into the air. "You ruined the shot."

Visibly vibrating from fear, Ramy kept his eyes focused on the boulder. "I-I-I didn't know it was a stunt. I thought that Mr. Cavill was in danger, and my job is to protect him."

"Ramy, you're fired." Henry pushed up to his feet. "I've had enough of the mishaps you cause."

"I was going to quit anyway," Ramy said, his tone shaky as he stared at the swinging boulder.

"Well, good." Henry strode in the opposite direction. "I'll be in my trailer for the afternoon."

The director looked about to protest when the chain holding the boulder loosened suddenly, many of the links expanding.

"The rig!" someone yelled. "It's about to give way!"

"Clear the set," the director ordered.

Henry Cavill spun, his eyes wide. Sophia tensed. To everyone's surprise, Ramy simply stood beneath the boulder that was about to fall, not part of any stunt but rather a mistake by the rigging crew.

"Ramy, get out from under there!" Henry ordered.

The bodyguard shook his head. "I can't move...I'm too scared."

"How are you scared?" Sophia had to ask. "When you die, you come back. Plus, you don't feel any pain."

He shook his head. "The fear never goes away."

Everyone had scattered to the perimeter, most of them turning back to watch the show of Ramy standing in the middle of the stage, looking up at the boulder that had jumped down another inch, the chain wrapped around the beam loosening.

"Move!" the director ordered.

Ramy stayed frozen.

Sophia started forward, intent on pushing Ramy out of the way. The director held out an arm, pausing her.

"Don't," he warned. "I won't have any other's blood on my stage." Turning his attention back to Ramy, he shook his head. "Damn it! Get off that stage now!"

"I-I-I'm trying," Ramy nearly cried.

"Just run!" Sophia encouraged.

"Do it now!" Henry yelled.

Everyone around the sound stage began to holler, telling Ramy to get out of the way of danger.

More of the links expanded, almost giving way completely. The boulder slid down another couple of inches.

"I can do this. I can do this," Ramy chanted as though trying to encourage himself to move. He smiled up at the boulder swinging overhead. "Rock, this is the day you will always remember as the day you almost caught Ramy Van—"

Before he could finish his statement, the chain snapped and sent the boulder crashing down onto the man, crushing him instantly—ending him in a gross mess that everyone saw firsthand.

CHAPTER TWENTY-NINE

Sophia sharply spun away while covering her face from the grotesque sight of the large rock crushing the man's body. She'd seen some of it since it happened so fast but didn't want details of the image burned into her mind.

There were screams from around the sound stage. Gasps. Cries. Thankfully, those drowned out the grosser sounds of crushing bones and pulverizing flesh.

To Sophia's surprise, the sounds of frustration soon replaced those of grief.

"Damn that guy!" the director yelled. "That death was avoidable."

Sophia pulled her arm down to find the crew moving into action. Henry was beside the stage and shaking his head.

"If Ramy was waiting for the opportune moment, that was it."

"That's not very thoughtful," Sophia admonished. "A man has died."

The director shot her a scolding look. "That man has ruined my stage and put us back a day."

Sophia didn't look, but she saw the crew members rolling the boulder off Ramy's body in her peripheral vision. "He saved Henry from getting impaled. That boulder could have come down on anyone."

"No, it was probably meant for Ramy," the actor said. "The guy brings this stuff on himself all the time."

"Henry wasn't going to be under the boulder when it fell," the director stated. "He would have been out of the way well before that."

"Not to mention that Ramy stood there looking up at it when he could have gotten out of the way," Henry added.

"He was frightened," Sophia countered.

"Yeah, I was," Ramy said in a raspy voice.

Sophia dared to look, afraid he'd be covered in blood and guts. To her surprise, he looked the same. She rushed over, shocked and relieved.

"You're okay?"

He still lay on the ground, the boulder beside him. A few crew members rolled it backward out of the way. Ramy gave it a cursed expression and nodded. "Yeah, a bit shook, but that's normal."

"You're not...you know..." Sophia didn't know how to say what she was thinking.

"Bloody?" he supplied. "Yeah, I don't bleed. Or break. Or pretty much anything that would make my deaths super gross."

"So you really can't be killed," Sophia marveled.

"Easily," he added.

"Ramy," Henry began while striding over. "I realize that your heart was in the right place. I know things got heated, but I'm willing to give you another chance if—"

Ramy held up his hand, pausing the actor. "That's okay. I think our time spent together has come to an end. I'm ready to move on." He stood and looked at Sophia. "I have another opportunity, and something tells me that it will offer me the chance to do more than protect national treasures."

"Are you sure?" Henry asked. "I appreciate your protection."

Ramy nodded. "And I yours as the Witcher."

"You realize that I'm not really that person, right?" Henry Cavill asked. "That's a character, you know..."

Ramy pursed his lips and backed away. "Don't ruin it for me."

"But you know—"

Ramy held up a single finger toward Henry's mouth. "Shush now, my man of steel. I need you to be strong for me. Allow me to walk away, knowing that you might not ever see me walk back in your direction."

"Okay, well, see you later then," Henry said casually and waved.

"Goodbye, Mr. Cavill," Ramy stated. "May we meet in another life."

"Sure thing," he sang while heading back in the direction of the stage.

"Or I'll see you at the Oscars!" Ramy exclaimed as Sophia led him away, toward a portal to Roya Lane.

CHAPTER THIRTY

S ophia entered Heals Pills tentatively, unsure if she was more nervous about introducing Ramy to King Sweetwater or the other way around. The two would make an interesting pair. Hopefully, Rudolf wouldn't have gotten too far ahead in the interview process.

A long line of what she suspected were applicants holding resumes and vials of blood dashed those hopes when she entered the shop. She'd ask about the latter items later, if at all.

Sophia headed toward Rudolph, tugging Ramy with her as she moved around the applicants, who all shot her glares as though she was cutting in line.

"Okay, under references you have Ms. Lois Alst—" Rudolf glanced up, looking at the candidate, a fae who was dressed impeccably but also appeared slightly inebriated, as usual for the fae. "Lois…that's one of my ex-girlfriends. Did she mention me? Oh…this is her attempt to get me back, is it? She had me open a pill shop, knowing I'd one day need help, then offer to write a reference for you and all so she could get me back."

"She's a friend," the fae said flatly. "We used to work together. She can vouch for my skills."

"Who can vouch for your breath," Rudolf stated and threw the guy's resume over his shoulder. "Next!"

Before Sophia could move around the next applicant, a rather attractive elfin woman stepped forward and thrust her resumé into Rudolf's hand. Realizing that Sophia needed to be discreet in front of all these candidates for the position she'd filled, she held up a single finger at Ramy and mouthed, "Hold on."

He nodded and teetered back and forth, looking like he might fall over on one of the display cases.

"Lady of the Owls." Rudolf read the woman's name on the top of her resume. "You have quite the list of experience here. Don't you think that you're overqualified for this position? I mean, you've done some impressive stuff, and here, you'll be selling lifesaving elixirs. Not to mention that your boss is a real tightwad. She thinks she owns this place and although that's true, she flaunts it."

Deciding she'd had enough and was tired of being diplomatic, Sophia threw up her arms. "Okay, everyone out! Interviews are over! I've filled the position."

Sophia's declaration met with protests, most of them by the king of the fae. Then he recognized that it was Sophia making the statement and began ushering everyone out the door.

"You heard the very reasonable and modest boss," Rudolf stated. "Who hasn't heard all the mean things I've been saying about her."

"I heard the last one," Sophia said over the thundering of candidates filing through the door.

Rudolf fake-laughed. "I knew you were there the whole time, Sophia. I was simply playing that little game we love so much."

"Which one?" Sophia asked dryly.

"You know, the one where I pretend you're not there and say bad things about you, then we both laugh."

Sophia shook her head. "I'm not aware of that game and didn't know we played it."

He waved his hand. "Loads of times. You love it."

"Right." Sophia groaned.

Rudolf swatted Ramy on the shoulder. "Hey, didn't you hear? The interviews are over. She filled the position." Then, as if it finally registered for him, Rudolf swept back around to face Sophia. "Wait, it is? By who?"

Sophia held out a presenting arm to Ramy. "By this gentleman here."

Rudolf ran his eyes over the unsuspecting guy. "Him? Does he want to sell Heals Pills or drink all of it in hopes that it helps…"

Sophia tensed. To her relief, Ramy laughed. "I had a boulder hit my face. That's not to mention the Mack truck that hit me this afternoon. Or the vultures that chased me from my car."

Sophia shook her head at him. "Seriously, what is wrong with you? That all happened today?"

He nodded. "In the last few hours. This morning—"

She held up her hand and halted him. "I think I've heard enough."

"I still have the job though, right?" Ramy sounded worried.

"Yeah, it's simply that the less I know about the accidents that happen to you, the better," Sophia answered.

"So why did you hire this guy, who is apparently a magician who doesn't use magic?" Rudolf asked. "Not to mention he's wearing strange socks, and I'm pretty certain he's not wearing moisturizer." He said the last part in a loud whisper.

"My fairy godmother said he was the right guy for the job," Sophia answered.

"You left me the responsibility of filling the opening." Rudolf almost sounded hurt.

"My fairy godmother said your time was much too valuable to mind the shop or interview to fill the position," Sophia explained.

That seemed to raise Rudolf's spirits immediately. "What a bright and thoughtful and totally accurate woman your fairy godmother is." He paused and leaned forward, hesitation in his gaze. "I'm going to assume she is a woman, correct?"

"Good assumption," Sophia stated dryly.

Rudolf studied Ramy. "Well, if a fairy godmother said he's the right guy for the job, who am I to argue with her?" He walked around him, measuring him with his eyes, it seemed. "I guess I can work with this. Can you dress better?"

Ramy nodded. "I can add a sweater vest to this ensemble and a tweed hat."

"I said better," Rudolf scolded, peeling away. "Not can you dress like an old crusty college professor. Why don't you put on a jacket with elbow patches and burn this world down already?"

Sophia gave Ramy a commiserating expression. "I'm sorry, excuse me for not making introductions. King Rudolf Sweetwater, this is Ramy Vance. Ramy, this is a brick who masquerades as the king of a race of magical creatures. Ignore most things he says, never take offense to them, and if he asks you to smell something, always say no."

Ramy dutifully nodded.

"Why, thank you for the thoughtful introduction, Sophia," Rudolf stated humbly. "Now, Ramy-Cans. I can call you that, right? It seems fitting. Anyway, what are your qualifications?"

"I was the bodyguard to—"

"He can't die," Sophia interrupted. "My fairy godmother seems to think we need someone resilient to mind the shop because it could see multiple dangers."

Rudolf nodded while thinking. "That would explain all the threatening notes I've been getting and attempts on my life."

Sophia lowered her chin. "When were you going to tell me about this, Ru?"

"I did," he sang and pointed at the side of his head.

"Right," Sophia chirped. "Through the telepathic link."

"You have to remember to check your messages when you've been away or asleep," Rudolf lectured. "I leave them on the voicemail."

"Of my mind," Sophia added.

"Exactly!" Rudolf exclaimed.

"Anyway, Ramy, this is the shop," Sophia stated. "Rudolf can show you around and fill you in on the details and supply chain, which comes in from next door at the Rose Apothecary."

"Friday's lunch?" Ramy asked, his tone tentative.

"It's all taken care of," Sophia answered. "Tell us whatever you need. You have my number, and—"

A text interrupted her. Since her phone was on silent, Sophia knew it was something important.

She retrieved the device from her pocket and checked the message, her heart suddenly racing. The text was from Liv. It read:

I have something important to tell you. Meet me at the Fantastical Armory as soon as possible. Don't delay, please...

That didn't sound like a Liv message. Usually, they were full of jokes, and even if she was in a headlock with a troll, she was flippant about the matter. This sounded serious.

Sophia strode for the door at once. "I have to go now. Ramy, you're in..." She glanced over her shoulder at Rudolf. "You're in his hands now."

"Good hands," Rudolf added.

Sophia gave Ramy an uncertain look edged with an apology. "You're in hands...his. Anyway, good luck. Be careful. Try not to die."

"No promises," Ramy sang, waving at Sophia as she exited the shop and hurried for the Fantastical Armory.

CHAPTER THIRTY-ONE

Not only Liv but Papa Creola were pacing back and forth when she entered the Fantastical Armory. Sophia paused in the doorway, taking in the scene of the Warrior with her windswept hair striding back and forth between the back row of waist-high display cases. In the other row, closer to the door, was Papa Creola, his long hippie hair also unbrushed as he worried away, chewing on his lip.

Conversely, Subner sat behind the counter on his stool in his new elfin form with his black hair pulled back into a ponytail and an indifferent expression on his face as though the troubles plaguing the other two weren't problems of his.

"What is it?" Sophia asked, unsurprised to hear the worry in her voice. "What's wrong?"

Liv and Papa Creola both looked up, startled expressions on their faces.

"World hunger, political divide inside warring governments, seasonal allergies, fundamental economic issues, eczema, the list goes on and on," Subner stated dryly.

"You're a ray of sunshine since losing your hippie ways, aren't you?" Sophia jibed.

He shook his head, a serious expression on his face. "I hope never to think with that kind of mindset again. Too often I found myself focused on promoting peace or wondering how to unlock a higher creative level inside myself."

Sophia nearly burst out laughing. "So? What's wrong with that?"

"What's wrong with that," Subner began, "is that as the Protector of Weapons, I can't be obsessed with peace and creativity. I need to maintain an objective mindset and gravitating toward peace isn't the way to do that."

"I don't know, I think peace could be a good thing, but call me crazy," Sophia retorted, watching from the corner of her vision as Liv and Papa Creola continued to pace in opposite directions.

Subner, still unconcerned for their worried state, snapped his fingers at Sophia. "Then give me your sword."

Sophia's eyes swiveled to Inexorabilis. "No, I can't do that."

"Why?" Subner challenged. "If you believe in this peaceful world so much, then give me the instrument you carry that's related to violence."

"It's unrealistic to think that things are simply going to be peaceful." Sophia pointed out the door at Roya Lane but meant the world at large. "I can want peace, but if it doesn't happen out there, then I need to be prepared to defend myself."

Subner simply crossed his arms over his chest and leaned back with a satisfied expression that seemed to say, "You made my point."

Appreciatively, Sophia nodded. "Well played, Subner. Well played." She directed her gaze to Liv and Papa Creola, confused why one of them hadn't weighed in on the conversation, which usually would have caused one of them to chime in with their opinion. "What's going on with you two? Something is wrong." The last sentence was more of a statement, and neither one of them contradicted it.

Liv paused her pacing and gave Papa Creola a long look before glancing at Sophia.

"I have something to tell you." Liv drew in a steadying breath.

Sophia tensed and looked her sister over. She didn't appear hurt, but magic sometimes worked from the inside out. Liv could be cursed, or it could be Clark or Stefan or Rory…

"What is it?" Sophia asked in a rush, anxious to know. "Is every-thing okay?"

Liv nodded with an uncertain look in her eyes. "Yes, everything is fine."

"Then what is it?" Sophia questioned because she got a distinct impression that not everything was fine—at all.

"Soph, I'm pregnant." Liv's eyes cut to Papa Creola once more.

Sophia wanted to jump up and down. Run over to her sister and hug her. Squeal. Rejoice. Yet, she stayed frozen in place, her nerves humming in her chest.

"Why do I have the sense that this isn't the great news it should be?" Sophia looked between Liv and Papa Creola.

The Father of Time turned to face Sophia. "Because we highly suspect that the baby has demon blood."

CHAPTER THIRTY-TWO

"Because of Stefan?" Sophia guessed. All the excitement she'd felt moments prior evaporated.

Liv nodded. "Yes. Remember I told you a demon had bitten him, but we were able to get the cure and he recovered, making him have all the demon's powers like speed and longer life, but without all the wanting to steal souls part?"

Sophia nodded. "Yes, he's the best of all worlds, right? It makes him an excellent demon hunter, right?"

"That's right," Liv affirmed. "However, he still has the demon's blood coursing through him, even if it doesn't make him evil. We," she motioned between her and Papa Creola, "highly suspect there's a chance the baby could inherit the demon blood."

"Without having the antidote that keeps he or she from turning evil," Papa Creola added.

Sophia slumped. That was bad...not only bad, but it also was good news wrapped up in highly dangerous news, and that was what made it worse. A baby should be the greatest thing in the world for Liv and Stefan. For the Beaufonts. To know that the child might be part demon, well, it crushed the entire good spirit of the notion.

"So what do we do?" Sophia wanted to be proactive. However, she reasoned that if she found Papa Creola and Liv pacing around in the Fantastical Armory that there was a chance that they didn't know what the solution to their problem was yet.

"The genie's bottle?" Liv asked in a tentative tone, immediately earning a scolding expression from Papa Creola.

"I told you—"

Liv waved him off, interrupting him. "Yes, I know. It's dangerous."

"Because the genie will try and kill you after you use up your wishes," Sophia guessed, realizing now why Liv had been acting so strange and asked her to find out the location of the genie's bottle and enlist Evan's help. It was all starting to come together...sort of.

Papa Creola shook his head. "No, Liv won't use all the wishes so we won't have to worry about Stan murdering her. At this point, she has to worry about me doing that."

Liv laughed at him dryly. "I realize that using wish magic destroys the fabric of time, but you can sew it back together."

He grimaced at her. "What do you not understand about the word 'destroy?'"

"Fine." Liv waved him off, seeming more like her old self as she bantered with the old man. "We'll get you a new bolt of the fabric of time."

"Again, not how it works," he argued.

Liv stuck her hands on her hips. "We'll endure one little snag to avoid my child being born a demon, okay?"

He considered her for a moment, matching her defiant expression. "We won't resort to that option unless we know that it's necessary."

"You did get the location and also a means to get the genie's bottle, right?" Liv asked Sophia.

She nodded and pulled out the map that Rudolf had made for them, having kept it in her cloak since he gave it to her. "Yes, and Evan agreed to help. We need to pin down when."

"Or more importantly, if it's necessary," Papa Creola stated.

Sophia looked between him and Liv, confused. "What are we supposed to be doing, exactly?"

Liv sighed. "We have to determine if the baby has demon blood and therefore the potential to be one, first. According to Mr. Rules over here, anyway."

Papa Creola's eyes fluttered with annoyance. "Excuse me for not wanting to take unnecessary extremes if we don't have to."

"So how do we know if we need to use the genie's bottle to retrieve Stan?" Sophia asked, realizing that Liv had planned on using a wish to fix the baby.

"You need to enlist an expert," Papa Creola explained. "Someone who can help determine the child's status."

"Is there such a person?" Sophia asked. "Can we do that?"

Liv nodded. "Apparently."

Sophia scratched her head. "Wait. Papa Creola, can't you tell us what the baby will be? You often see the future and know what we'll become."

He shook his head. "I can't see the child. Probably because something skews its timeline. It's not fixed at this point."

"Maybe because he or she is a demon," Liv argued. "And we use the wish to reverse it."

"Maybe," Papa Creola stated. "It's as likely that it's because I'm too close to the situation. I'm losing my objectivity when it comes to you."

Liv playfully batted her eyes at him. "You like me…you really do."

"I'm your boss and need you back on cases," he argued, but Sophia could spy the twitch of his eyes that marked his lie. Papa Creola didn't want anything to happen to Liv, and giving birth to a demon was probably one of the worst things that could. It would kill her. The baby would go on to plague the Earth and have to be ended by its father. It was awful on all avenues. That much was clear.

"How do we find out about the baby?" Sophia asked, willing to drop everything at this point to devote her full attention to this. There was little else that was important at this point.

"His name is Renswick," Papa Creola stated.

"The elf who helped to heal Stefan," Sophia guessed.

Liv nodded. "Yeah, he's an expert on demons. Our best chance of testing the baby."

"Can't you tell us if Renswick will be able to help?" Sophia sensed Liv's and Papa Creaola's doubt.

"That's not how it works," Papa Creola answered. "I'm not an all-knowing creature. I can sometimes see the future. Sometimes I can't. Sometimes I know things. Sometimes I don't."

Liv grinned at Sophia. "Isn't he cute? He's sometimes helpful. Sometimes not. Sometimes a pain in the ass. Sometimes not..."

"Okay, so we need to go and see this Renswick." Sophia angled her head in the direction of the door. "Let's go."

"You're going?" Liv asked, surprised.

"Of course," Sophia replied. "We're in this together. I'm not letting you go through all this alone."

"It's fine, Soph. You're busy, and I don't need—"

"She needs your support," Papa Creola cut in. "Go with her, Sophia, and both of you hurry. You do have other cases that demand your attention separately."

Liv made for the door while shaking her head at the Father of Time. "It's always rush, rush, go, go with you, Papa. I swear, if I were in charge of time, I'd be a lot chiller about it than you are."

CHAPTER THIRTY-THREE

"That's Renswick's home?" Sophia stood on a grassy hill in a park directly across from an old Victorian house that stood out in the idyllic town of Ashland. Liv had warned Sophia that the small valley was home to many West Coast hippies, and that she shouldn't make eye contact with them unless she wanted to be told her bogus fortune and also food allergies that she didn't know were possible—like intolerance to beet juice or caraway seeds.

Liv nodded. "Yep. He doesn't ever leave it because although he's an elf, he can't stand hippies."

"Make sense." Sophia noticed a horde of long-haired hippies frolicking in the distance. They were like carefree children, dancing while holding hands and singing with their chins straight up to the sky. That would have been inspiring on its own, but their children were crawling toward the nearby road where VW Bugs drove by or other shaggin' wagon vehicles passed.

"Hey!" Liv yelled to the group, who were doing a lot more dancing than parenting. "Get your kid before she gets run over!"

A hippie playing the guitar looked up with a smile on his face. He glanced at the toddler crawling toward the road and back to Liv. "Daffodil is on her own journey. It's not our place to corral her."

Liv sighed, pointed, and flicked her finger in Daffodil's direction. A short baby gate-type fence popped up along the road as the child neared it, preventing her from getting in the street. "I'm the tour guide for Daffodil's journey, and I say she can't get run over today."

The guy shook his head and went back to playing the guitar, a look on his face that seemed to say, "You're not ready."

"I really think they all want me to kill them," Liv seethed.

"So, Renswick." Sophia indicated the Victorian, which was large and mostly black and white. The yard with the wrought iron fence and statues resembled a graveyard. "Something tells me he's not all chipper like the hippies here with long tangled hair and dirty clothes."

Liv shook her head. "Renswick is the anti-hippie. Thankfully, I had to get past his wards once, which means that we won't have to fight the gargoyles, or as it were, not fight them because that was the riddle."

Liv started forward, but Sophia held out a hand and stopped her sister.

Liv glanced up, looking around as if her sister had stopped her from getting hit by a passing car or hippie or something else crossing the road she hadn't seen.

"Hey, I know that it's probably hard to celebrate with all the unknowns, but congratulations on the baby." Sophia offered her sister a simple smile.

Liv released a heavy breath, seeming to relax a little. "It's hard to celebrate yet. For one, it doesn't seem real. I never really considered myself mother material."

Sophia pursed her lips. "If it weren't for you, I wouldn't be the person that I am. I wouldn't even be a dragonrider."

"Soph, I abandoned you for five years."

"You were a teenager," Sophia argued. "Someone murdered our parents, and you were the only one willing to notice that it had something to do with those inside the House of Fourteen, who we were supposed to trust. I don't think anyone faults you for leaving to maintain your sanity."

Liv sighed, not at all appearing convinced. "This baby will be born to two Warriors for the House of Fourteen. It seems a little unfair to bring someone into the world who will have so much danger around them all the time."

"Mom and Dad were Warriors and Councilors for the House of Fourteen," Sophia offered. "You were constantly around danger, but that was because they believed in what they did, like you and Stefan. Isn't that better than offering your child this safe existence where they don't witness their parents fighting for a better life?"

Liv lowered her chin and regarded Sophia with an intense expression. "When did you get to be so wise?"

Sophia smirked at her sister. "I learned it firsthand from you, so think how much you'll have to offer your child. They'll be very lucky to have two talented and loving parents."

Liv gulped, and Sophia spied the tension hiding behind the surface. "Yeah, I want to believe you're correct, but first I have to ensure I'm not giving birth to a demon. Then I'd be contributing to the world's problems."

"If that's the case, we'll get the genie's bottle and make everything right."

Liv nodded, not at all appearing convinced. "Yeah, I guess so."

Sophia grabbed her sister by the arm and tugged her across the road toward Renswick's house. "Come on. Stop worrying before we know what's going on. Even then, don't worry because we have options. You're going to have the best, most awesome baby in the world."

CHAPTER THIRTY-FOUR

The figure who opened the door almost reminded Sophia of a butler. Renswick wore an old-fashioned, tailored suit that was all black except for the starched white shirt under the jacket and vest and a single red rose in the lapel.

Sophia knew this was Renswick and not a butler because of his air of authority. It was subtle, but there was a dominance in his cold eyes that told her he owned this house. He opened his door because he was the only one there, or so Sophia guessed.

"Liv Beaufont, Warrior for the House of Fourteen." Renswick sounded like someone speaking from centuries prior with a dignified nature to his tone. "I hadn't expected the honor of your visit...or rather, the bad news that you could be bringing."

Liv feigned a smile. "I'm sorry to call on you without warning. I'm not here regarding any bad news. It's uncertain circumstances that I hope you can shine some light on."

Renswick nodded. "I'm happy to be of service to you and your...friend?"

"Sister," Sophia supplied and offered a hand to the elf. "I'm Sophia Beaufont."

He eyed the offered hand and raised an eyebrow at her. "A dragonrider as well."

"How do you know that?" Sophia asked, curious.

"The chi of the dragon simply radiates off you," he answered, standing back. "Won't you both come in, and we'll get down to your requests, Liv."

Dutifully, they both stepped into the house. No one had ever recognized Sophia as a dragonrider like that. This Renswick was already proving to be quite exceptional and observant.

He strode confidently down the hallway after shutting the door, seeming to expect them to follow him to a back room.

Sophia blinked at her surroundings, for a moment feeling like she'd stepped into a black and white movie. Almost everything in the house was varying shades of the two colors, and the objects she passed on the way to the sitting room were as curious as the color palette. There were all sorts of strange artifacts on display as well as interesting antiques. This definitely wasn't the home of a hippie. Renswick was a fascinating character for sure.

"Can I offer you a drink?" Renswick asked once he'd led them to the back room, which was full of elegant furniture, all of it either black or white. "Maybe a brandy or a whiskey?"

Liv shook her head at once. "No, and we won't take much of your time. It's just that Father Time thinks you're the only one who can determine something for me. You remember that when you healed Stefan of the demon bite that Sabatore's blood remained in him?"

"Yes." Renswick poured himself a glass of brownish liquid. "It will almost assuredly be to his benefit. Make him stronger, faster, have enhanced senses, and greater longevity." He paused and suddenly looked up. "Is this about how he's more sensitive to evil now? Is it controlling his impulses as I warned?"

"If by controlling, you mean that he hardly sleeps and hunts demons every chance he gets, then yes," Liv replied with a laugh. "He's learned how to corral the urges. We know his limitations and keep him away from situations that would be too overwhelming."

"Very good." Renswick sipped his drink. "Then what is it that brings you here today?"

"Stefan and I are married now," Liv began, her tone uncertain.

"Well, then congratulations are in order." Renswick held up his glass. "A toast to you and the demon hunter." He smiled, then his mouth twitched, and he lowered his drink once more, his expression shifting. "Ooooh...I think I understand..."

Liv nodded. "I thought you might."

"You've conceived then," he guessed.

"Correct."

"You're worried that the child could..."

"It's a possibility, isn't it?" Liv asked. "The baby could have Stefan's blood."

"They most assuredly do," Renswick answered. "What you need to determine is if it's his magician blood or that of the demon."

"If it was, would it be a problem?" Sophia dared to ask, gaining the attention of the other two in the room. She swallowed and collected herself. Sometimes she still felt like a child having discussions in an adult's world. "I mean, Stefan was given the antidote, which kept him from turning. So it goes to reason that the child, if it has the demon's blood, is also immune from the negative effect."

Renswick exhaled, his gaze off in thought for a moment. "It's possible, but it's a risky wager. I'd be more likely to assume that the child would gravitate toward shifting into a demon. You see, the antidote cured Stefan from shifting, but he retained the demon blood. That means the cure resides in him, stopping the blood from turning him into a monster. The child, well, the child would have gotten the blood, the demon's DNA, without the antidote."

"Could you administer a dose of the cure to the baby?" Sophia asked.

"I could," Renswick reasoned. "But first, that's risky to do to a young infant. Second, I simply don't have any more. I used it all to cure Stefan."

"I have a solution if we determine that the child has demon blood,"

Liv stated. "It's not something we want to employ unless we have to. That's why I need your help. Renswick, can you run tests or do something to figure out if the baby has demon blood?"

"Yes, but we must hurry," Renswick said in a rush, finishing his drink and setting it down, hurrying for a case sitting on a nearby bookshelf.

"I'm sorry to have dropped in on you," Liv stated apologetically. "I didn't want to pull you away from anything."

He shook his head, opened a briefcase, and withdrew a series of medical instruments. "I have little concern for my schedule or your interruption. You were right to come and see me. I simply believe we must hurry and determine the status of the child because if they have demon blood, then you'll have a small window of time to remedy the situation."

"I will?" Liv asked, her eyes wide. "Why?"

"There's little information on the subject," Renswick began. "However, demon babies grow fast. They, like the living, breathing form they would become, suck the life from around them."

Sophia gasped, realizing the full implications of what he was saying. "The baby would deplete Liv, wouldn't it?"

He nodded darkly. "I'm afraid so. We don't know how long we have. The tests I'll need to run will take some time to complete. I'll do them as fast as I can to get results but not compromise their integrity. Liv, every day that you're pregnant with that child, you could be at serious risk."

Liv nodded. "I realize that."

"Are you sure you simply want to determine the child's status?" he asked. "It might be easier—"

"No, I want the baby," she said adamantly, cutting him off. "I'm willing to take the risk. It's worth it."

Not needing to be convinced anymore, Renswick nodded and motioned Liv over. "Very well then. Let me get some samples, and I'll get to work on the tests. Do come over, would you?"

Sophia watched as Liv strode over to the elegantly dressed and undeniably competent man. She felt confident that he possessed the skills to help Liv. She now knew that even if Liv was nervous about becoming a parent, she wanted this for her and Stefan. What worried Sophia was if they'd all regret her taking this risk.

This child could be a blessing, or it very well could be the end of Liv Beaufont.

CHAPTER THIRTY-FIVE

The green dragon swooped through the air over the Expanse of the Gullington, flapping her wings and sailing effortlessly up to the clouds. Speeding behind her were two other dragons. Riders didn't accompany them, but the new dragons were getting stronger, better at flying. Soon, they'd be ready for their riders.

Sophia gazed across the Expanse where the new dragonriders also looked up at the sky, watching their dragons soar around the clouds, spiraling and speeding along. Sophia also read the tension on Cooper's face, and she imagined he wondered how he would hold onto his dragon when she barreled through the air, high off the ground.

"Remember when you were as petrified as him?" Lunis asked by her side.

She rolled her eyes. "I was never petrified," she argued. "If I remember correctly, I wanted to ride you, and you simply refused."

He snorted at her, smoke issuing from his nostrils. "I was testing you. You were asking for permission, and I wanted you to get to the point where you knew when to make demands and when you knew when not to because as much as I like you, at the end of the day, I can eat you."

"You know what else it is at the end of the day?" Sophia watched as

Evan urged the younger, less experienced dragonriders to join him for combat training on the other side of the lawn.

"What?" Lunis asked.

"Night," Sophia answered at once.

Lunis groaned, apparently not appreciating her joke. "Leave the comedy to me."

Sophia harrumphed. "If I remember correctly, you said during our time together that I'd make three requests of you that were essentially demands."

He nodded. "The first was the first ride."

"Which was so I could save the day and investigate Thad Reinhart's facility."

"Hey, I'm not chopped liver, and contributed on that case," Lunis stated. "I mean, I was your ride, wasn't I?"

"Yeah, my flying Uber," Sophia joked, earning an eye-roll from her dragon.

"Again, I could use a snack."

She giggled. "Then I requested for you to abandon me to get Mahkah to safety when he was harmed while we were getting the token."

"I remember."

"So that means I have one more blind request I get to make and you have to comply with regardless."

"Is this your way of hinting at wanting to make your final request?" Lunis asked. "Do you want me to roll over and do a trick for you? Play dead? Let you rub my belly? Or do you crave some frozen yogurt? I can take you for a run if you'd like. Maybe some white chocolate mousse ice cream with Reese's Pieces?"

"Why do most of those things sound like things you want to do?" Sophia questioned. "No, I'm not wasting my last request so easily. I'm going to make it something good. Something you wouldn't do otherwise."

He nodded. "Like tolerate Wilder?"

Sophia laughed. "No, I'm not asking for that."

"Good." Lunis sighed. "Because it's supposed to be a request, not a miracle."

"Oh, come on," Sophia complained while watching the new riders running through various training exercises under Evan's and Wilder's supervision. Mahkah was guiding the dragons in the sky close by. Sophia glanced over her shoulder at the Castle in the distance and pictured that Hiker was probably watching the whole thing from his office window.

"Everything is shifting here at the Gullington, isn't it?" she asked Lunis when they'd been quiet for a long moment.

He nodded, a peaceful look in his eyes. "It feels right though. Like the timing is good and will work in our favor. If we'd had new angel dragonriders before, it might not have worked, but we're ready. The dragons are ready."

Sophia sighed. "Let's hope when we leave here that the world will be ready."

"That's something that has less to do with us and more to do with the world," Lunis stated, taking on a sage-like tone. "We can only ever be in charge of our evolution and preparedness. When they're ready, the new riders will venture out into the world, and whether it's ready or not won't be up to us. Sometimes these things have to be forced though."

"I don't know," Sophia said with uncertainty.

"Those three new dragons," Lunis began, indicating the majestic creatures in the air, "when they first were reunited at the Gullington, there were small skirmishes. They'd grown, come into their skills and grown territorial."

Sophia shook her head. "I bet you're happier than ever to have your place right now."

"Don't you know it," Lunis agreed. "There were all sorts of problems, but the elder dragons or I didn't intervene because breaking them up wasn't up to us. Maybe they weren't ready to interact yet, but there was no way for us to delay it. So, trial by fire. There were fights and wounds and drama and now, look at them."

Sophia smiled up at the sky. "They're fine."

"They're better than fine. They needed to go through that rocky period to get to where they are now. It's part of the process. So the world may not be ready for dragonriders after everything that's happened, but it's going to get us regardless. We'll weather the challenges."

Sophia loved when Lunis joked and was silly. It made it all the more special when she knew he was capable of dipping into his wise persona, offering timeless wisdom.

"Hey, Little Bit!" Evan called in Sophia's direction.

She simply nodded in return.

"I need my ax from the weapons room in the Castle," he called to her and snapped his fingers.

Sophia smirked. "That sounds like a 'you' problem."

"I was making it your problem," Evan stated while striding over. "Since you and your puppy are hanging out, I thought you could go fetch it for me."

"I'm horrible at fetch, as far as puppies go," Lunis stated. "We can work on my skills, Evan. Run off over there, and I'll fetch you with my teeth."

"I thought Hiker wanted you on big-picture Rogue Rider stuff," Evan said to Sophia, ignoring Lunis.

She nodded. "No leads have come in. I'm waiting to hear from my contacts about criminals. I have eyes and ears keeping surveillance. I'm ready to spring into action."

Evan shrugged. "Seems like you could be doing more. Like getting my ax from the Castle."

"I could, but I need to conserve my energy for the important tasks."

Evan shook his head and glanced up at the Castle. "Speaking of the boss, looks like he's calling you. I bet you're in trouble for slacking off."

Sophia turned, striding in the Castle's direction where Hiker Wallace stood on the steps, his hands on his hips and his eyes watching the activity on the Expanse. "Maybe you're right. Maybe I'll get fired."

Evan's eyes lit up. "Oh, a man can dream. That would be the total best."

CHAPTER THIRTY-SIX

"Sir, if this is about Pink Princess' insubordinate nature then I agree that it's overdue that you discipline her," Evan sang as he strode up to the Castle beside Sophia.

"Evan, what are you doing here?" Hiker scolded, his meaty arms across his chest. "You're supposed to be training the new dragonriders."

"I realize that, sir." Evan slightly bowed as they approached. "I needed my lucky ax and Sophia, who was lolly-gagging with her dragon and not helping at all, refused to go up to the Castle to get it for me. So here I am."

"She's not your servant." Hiker looked down his nose at Evan. "And those who are your servant, you shouldn't take advantage of, if you know what I mean."

Evan nodded. "Coming from you, I know exactly what you mean. You're the person who's harbored feelings for our old housekeeper for centuries and have now moved her out of the position and given her special privileges that are mostly outside the Dragon Elite."

Hiker narrowed his eyes at the dragonrider. "Our situation is different. I'm simply saying, don't make Trin unhappy with your drama. I can't afford to replace her if you screw things up with her."

"What if I make her so happy that she's the best housekeeper this place has ever seen?" Evan challenged and shrugged. "Although the bar is set awfully low."

"Do you want me to punch him in the face, sir?" Sophia asked, quite seriously. "Or would you rather do it?"

Hiker shook his head. "I'll ignore his acting out. I'm certain the Castle will punish his bad behavior since it has a particular fondness for Ainsley."

"It also has a particular fondness for Trin," Evan argued. "I make her smile."

"You also make Quiet want to vomit, so I'm not as hopeful that the Castle won't punish you for your brazen statements," Sophia retorted.

He shrugged, strode past Hiker, and into the building. "Let the darn Castle do its worst to me. It's already locked me in my room, taken all my things and put them on the Expanse, and terrorized me in every possible way for the last hundred years. I'm certain it's out of tricks at this point. I mean, it is old and going senile by now."

Sophia shook her head at Evan as he disappeared into the Castle. "It's like he's asking for the punishment."

Hiker agreed with a nod. "I'm certain that he likes the abuse. It gives him attention and a reason to complain, without which he wouldn't have anything to talk about."

Sophia asked. "You needed me, sir? Is this about the Rogue Riders? I'm still researching leads. Nothing concrete yet, but hopefully soon."

"Very good. No, this is about something…" Uncertainty filled his eyes. "It's more of a personal thing I need help with."

"Oh?" Sophia asked, suddenly curious. She couldn't remember a time when Hiker asked her for anything personal. She'd assisted with giving him the reset point and learning about his history with Ainsley, but that had been different. Now it seemed he hoped for a favor.

"I don't want anyone to know about it," Hiker began. "Which is why I'm asking for your help and your discretion."

Sophia nodded. "Of course, sir. What can I do?"

"I need you to find something. The Castle is downright refusing to help me, and I know that it took it. I also know that for whatever reason, the Castle favors you."

"Because I'm nice to it and don't disrespect it," Sophia offered.

He rolled his eyes. "Give it another few decades of it taking your things and changing the layout of the hallways on you, and that will fade. Then you'll curse it the same as the rest of us."

"Well, this thing you need me to find," Sophia began tentatively. "What is it?"

"I can't tell you," he stated.

Sophia nodded as though this made perfect sense. "Great. I'll get right on it. So, I'm looking for something that I don't know what it is. Do you want to give me a hint of where to look or should I stumble around blindly?"

He sighed. "I really can't tell you what it is. However, it's in a small red velvet pouch that has orange tassels on the ties."

"Okay, that's marginally helpful," Sophia conceded and quickly added, "I promise not to look inside if I find it."

Hiker nodded, relief flickering in his eyes. "Thank you."

"Why do you think I'll be able to find it when you can't?"

"Because as I previously mentioned, the Castle likes you," Hiker explained. "Also, it's easier to find something if it belonged to you or at least someone in your family."

"Wait, what you're looking for belonged to a Beaufont?" Then a brief memory rose to the surface of when Sophia was in Adam Rivalry's room. There was an old picture of the dragonriders, and one of them was an Oscar Beaufont. So much had happened after that that she'd forgotten about it.

Hiker nodded. "Oscar gave it to me centuries ago. It was an heirloom, but he wanted me to have it. Anyway, it was right before the Great War broke out and everything went to hell with Thad Reinhart and the rest of the world."

"So it's yours?" Sophia asked.

He nodded. "I think you might have better luck finding it though. At least, I hope so."

"Okay, then I'll start looking." Sophia sensed this was of great importance to Hiker, for whatever reason. However, she would respect his privacy, although she was exploding with curiosity about what her ancestor gave Hiker and was lost somewhere in the Castle.

She had to hope that she found it and that in time, Hiker shared with her what it was. They had made progress after all, and she considered him a friend. Based on the trusting look he gave her with the task, she wanted to assume he thought of her in the same way.

CHAPTER THIRTY-SEVEN

"Where is my blasted ax?" Evan asked out loud with no one else around. He stopped outside his room, having already checked the weapons hall.

"You've done something with it, haven't you?" Evan looked around at the walls of the Castle, accusing it while holding up a fist. "You know, you might have some power over me, but I'm not letting it get to me. You can take my ax. I'll get another one. What you're mad about is that I'm so handsome, and you're just a pile of rocks. I'm dating the housekeeper, and all she does is mop your floors." He chuckled. "I guess if I were you and musty and old, I'd steal my ax too."

Evan turned the corner, thinking he was headed back for the entryway, but finding the corridor to look a little different than the last time he was there—which had been only a few minutes prior.

"Wait, what the what?" He spun and found a brick wall that cut him off, making a dead end.

Evan sighed. "Oh, very funny. This is your punishment, is it Castle? That's fine. Turn me all around and make this place into a maze. I'll find my way out eventually. Then I'll find my ax and hack into your walls. See who's laughing when you're all broken down to pieces. Oh, and wait until you see what I have in store for you at our next breakfast session."

Evan knew that his threats were pretty useless, but he'd played this game with the Castle enough to know that it liked it. If he pretended to ignore the Castle or Quiet, as it were, then it would act out more. For whatever masochistic reasons, the old gnome liked being picked on.

Second, Evan knew that the "punishments" never lasted too long. The Castle would try to confuse him. Hide his stuff. Trick him a little. Evan would act frustrated, and when the Castle felt satisfied with the job it had done, it would put everything back to normal, and they'd go back to how things were...well, until the next time.

Evan strode down the corridor on the second floor. It was unrecognizable from any other hallway he'd seen in the Castle. That wasn't unusual. After a hundred years, the Castle didn't really look the same from day to day. However, this time, Evan didn't recognize any part of it. There wasn't the usual suit of armor in what he guessed was the eastern hallway that led to the great staircase.

"Have you had a nap?" Evan asked the Castle, sensing that it had some pent-up energy after taking a snooze. It was such a strange beast and not totally the groundskeeper. Ainsley had tried to explain it to him once, and it made his head hurt. The Castle was apparently part of the gnome. It was like his heart or head or something. All Evan knew was that it was whacked-out crazy at the moment.

He strode down the hallway, blinking at the far end. It seemed to go on for miles.

"Stupid deceptive visuals," Evan muttered to himself. The Castle either did change, or it appeared it had changed, but for Evan's mind, it was two of the same.

He felt the entryway draft, with the fresh scent of the mountains wafting in from the Expanse. That meant the great staircase would be up ahead.

"Ha-ha," he triumphantly called to the Castle. "You can make it look like one thing, but you can't erase what's there."

Evan turned abruptly and put his hand to a seemingly solid wall and found that his hand went through it like it was indeed an illusion.

"Bam!" Evan exclaimed. "Found the great staircase even with your tricks. You're losing your edge, old shorty!"

Evan was about to feel around for the banister so he could safely step onto the great staircase and through the faux wall. However, he caught a strange statue in his peripheral vision that seemed to have appeared out of nowhere.

Turning to face it directly, Evan tilted his head, finding it incredibly curious. "What are you and where did you come from?"

The statue was an angel that matched his height. It was made of gray stone and wore a long flowing gown tied at the waist, and its wings spread behind it. It was unclear whether the angel was female or male because it had its face covered with both hands. Evan got the strange impression that it was weeping.

CHAPTER THIRTY-EIGHT

How was she supposed to find something when she didn't know what she was looking for? Sophia wondered while striding through the Castle. She searched everywhere for the pouch that Hiker described, half-expecting to find it lying on the floor when she turned various corners.

It was strange that whatever the object was had belonged to Oscar Beaufont. Why had Oscar given it to Hiker? And right before the Great War? The timing was odd. Sophia hadn't given much thought to her ancestor, who had been a dragonrider. Now she'd learned that Hiker knew him. She guessed that she would have assumed that since she found her ancestor's picture in Adam Rivalry's room with many other dragonriders.

Oscar had been alive right before the Great War. Sophia guessed that he became a war casualty like so many Dragon Elite when they faced Thad Reinhart's army.

The Castle was so overwhelmingly large that it could take some time to find the pouch. There were at least five stories and a basement and possibly more stories, depending on the Castle's mood and whether it had napped lately, which usually meant additions and renovations.

Before, when Quiet had required that Sophia find various parts of a key to "unlock" Lunis' Pad, she had enlisted Trin's help, knowing that the housekeeper got around the Castle more than anyone else. However, Sophia knew she couldn't do that this time. Hiker had asked her to keep things private on this matter, and she respected that. He trusted her not to look in the pouch, and she couldn't require that of Trin. Also, Sophia suspected that she needed to search for and find the bag. If it was easier for residents of the Castle to find something if it belonged to their family, that meant she was the one who had to look for it.

The possibilities of where it could be were overwhelming. Sophia found herself in a study of sorts, but it wasn't Hiker's. She didn't think there was another one in the Castle since she hadn't run across this particular room yet. That spoke to the reality of how hard it would be to find this mystery object.

Sophia opened the top drawer of the desk in the middle of the dusty room, finding various objects within like quills and ink wells and papers. No velvet pouch.

She sighed and closed the drawer. A poof of dust sprang into the air and made her cough. She covered her mouth and coughed again.

"Castle, do you think you can point me in the direction of this pouch Hiker needs?" Sophia asked. "We can play the hot and cold game. Or you could simply put the object in front of me. I won't tell Hiker. I'll make it sound like it was a complicated scavenger hunt, and I only won it due to my diligent efforts."

She waited for a response. When there wasn't one, Sophia ducked and went back to rummaging in the desk.

"Evan?" Trin called from the hallway. "Is that you?"

Sophia tilted her head, listening as the cyborg drew closer. "It's me, Trin."

She lifted from behind the desk as Trin poked her head through the open door. "You looking for Evan?"

Trin nodded, looking worried and confused. "I haven't seen this room before."

"I know." Sophia pushed to her feet. "I just found it myself. I guess it's not new since there's a fine layer of dust on everything."

"Whose office is it?" Trin looked around at the various maps on the walls.

Sophia glanced at the papers on the desk, looking for a name. She probably shouldn't have been surprised when she saw a familiar one at the bottom of a correspondence. It read,

Sincerely,

Oscar Beaufont

Sophia gulped, wondering what the implications of her stumbling across her ancestor's office were. Timing had to be a factor as well.

"It's one of my relatives'," Sophia answered.

"Oh, wow." Trin's eyes widened. "That's amazing that there have been two Beaufonts who were members of the Dragon Elite."

"Amazing," Sophia agreed, off in thought, trying to string together why something suddenly felt out of place. "Also perplexing." She shook off the confusion and pulled her chin up. "You were looking for Evan. He was downstairs looking for his ax in the weapons room."

Trin's brow creased in a frown. "That's the thing. I was in the weapons room organizing when I got the distinct impression that Evan is lost."

"Lost?" Sophia asked. "How could he be lost? He knows his way around pretty easily, although…" She looked around at the new-slash-old office they'd found. "I guess that doesn't really apply to the Castle."

Trin nodded. "I don't think I'll know my way around this place even after a century. I feel bad for the new riders."

Sophia perked up. "The new riders. When I first got to the Castle, Ainsley told me that someone should accompany me to and from my room until I got used to the place. Not only because it's big and changes on a whim, but because the Castle likes to play tricks on new residents. Maybe that's the feeling you had, that one of the new riders got lost in the Castle."

"Maybe." Trin didn't sound convinced as she strode over to a set of drapes and pulled them back.

The afternoon light streamed through, giving the room a whole new look. It was then that Sophia realized there had been lamps on in the office, as though the Castle expected them to enter it.

Trin peered out the window, craning her head to look around. "One, two, three," she counted and pointed out the window before turning to face Sophia. "All the new dragonriders are on the Expanse."

"And Evan?" Sophia asked. "Maybe he already got his ax and returned to the grounds before you went into the weapons room."

Trin looked around the grounds again and shook her head. "I don't see him, and there's Mahkah with the dragons and Wilder training the new riders."

Sophia pulled her mouth to the side, thinking. "That's weird. Well, I'm sure he'll show up. He probably got distracted by his reflection in a mirror and is lavishing himself with compliments."

Trin laughed, taking notice of Sophia behind the desk. "Are you looking for something?"

"Sort of," Sophia answered. "I mean, yes."

"Oh, can I help?" Trin asked. "Like I did with the key pieces?"

"Thanks," Sophia answered. "I don't think that's a good idea."

When a look of disappointment flickered over Trin's face, Sophia quickly added, "Well, and that's mostly because I don't know what I'm looking for. I have a feeling that the Castle has me on a detective mission, but I don't have any clues at this point."

Trin nodded, seemingly relieved. "I guess there would be all sorts of interesting things you'd find in your ancestor's office. Maybe there's a family secret…"

Sophia nodded. "I'm certain there are tons of family secrets." She looked around at the many cabinets and shelves. "Unearthing them will be the fun part."

Trin laughed. "I like that you use the word fun when most might be overwhelmed by such a task."

"Well, overwhelmed fits too," Sophia agreed, then thought of something. "Hey, Trin, I wondered if we could have a Thanksgiving dinner here. I know that most aren't Americans, but with the holiday coming up, I hoped we could bring it to the Gullington. I mean, we have a lot to be grateful for even if there are a lot of complications for the Dragon Elite out there in the world."

Trin thought about it for a moment. "I'm happy to do it, but it all depends on what ingredients the Castle offers me. I can't make a turkey dinner without a turkey."

Sophia nodded and giggled. "That's true. Well, maybe the Castle will comply. I think it would be nice to have a celebration. Something to welcome the new riders to the Gullington and make it feel festive. Christmas is coming up after all, so getting in the holiday spirit would be fun."

Trin returned the smile. "Okay, I'll see what I can do. What kind of pie would you prefer?"

"Chocolate," Sophia said at once, not having to think on it.

"Chocolate?" Trin asked. "That's not a very traditional flavor of pie for Thanksgiving. No apple or pumpkin or sweet potato?"

Sophia grimaced. "Can we keep the fruit and vegetables out of dessert, please?"

Trin winked at her. "Fair enough. You don't ask for much, and that seems like a reasonable request. Chocolate pie it is, then."

"Thanks," Sophia said as her phone rang in her pocket. She withdrew it, surprised to see who was calling her. Sophia sighed, preparing for the headache that would no doubt follow afterward. She accepted the call and put the phone to her ear.

"What's up, King Rudolf?"

CHAPTER THIRTY-NINE

Evan studied the angel statue for a long moment before deciding that he'd better get back to work on the Expanse training the new dragonriders. He spun to the faux wall and heard something move behind him.

Tensing, Evan turned back around to find the angel statue closer. "Did you just move?" he asked the object as if it would answer him back.

It didn't.

Shaking his head, Evan turned back around, realizing that the Castle was attempting to play games with him. "Lame attempt, Castle. Angel statues that sneak up on me." He waved his hands in the air. "Oh, I'm sooooo scared."

There was more movement at Evan's back as he neared the fake wall. Again he turned with a smirk. This time the angel statue was even closer, but now its hands weren't obscuring its face but instead held its arms as though it was blocking out bright sunlight.

"What the hell?" Evan asked. He studied the statue, trying to see around its hands to determine what its face looked like. Deciding this wasn't worth his time, Evan shrugged and spun back for the staircase.

There was a *swooshing* sound at his back and a rush of air. Evan, feeling like he was about to be run over, whipped around to find the angel almost right upon him. Now he got the glimpse he'd wanted.

The thing was scary as hell with its stone eyes wide and its teeth bared like a vampire's. Evan nearly stumbled back, trying to gain distance from the thing that was right on top of him.

"Whoa, man!" Evan exclaimed, catching himself on the real part of the wall that was solid and didn't lead to the edge of the stairs where he could have fallen to his death...or more likely, a really bad headache. "Dude, Castle, are you trying to make me break my neck with your creepy angel? There's playing around, and there's being plain mean, and I think you can guess what this is."

He waited, expecting the Castle to make another move. Maybe have its angel statue attack him or something.

Evan shook his head and scoffed at the statue. "I guess that's all you've got, Castle. You're such a coward, having an angel fight your battles. Well, a stone statue can't best me, and I think we both know that."

Daring to take his eyes off the angel statue again, Evan turned for the stairs, but this time he didn't find the faux wall. All he saw was blackness as he was transported through space and dropped into a new corridor that he recognized as belonging to the fifth floor. He landed hard on the stone floor with a little more force than he thought was necessary.

Evan stood and dusted himself off. "Seriously, now you're moving me around this place? That's your new game? Seems pretty dull, Castle. I guess that's all you've got."

He glanced out the window once he came to a bend in the hallway and found that the guys were still on the Expanse, training. "If I get in trouble for being late, you're going to pay, Castle," he threatened before turning the corner and halting at the sight of the figure at the far end of the corridor.

It was another one of those stone angel statues. This one like the other with its hands covering its weeping face.

CHAPTER FORTY

"What's up?" Sophia asked King Rudolf over the phone as Trin waved and trotted back down the corridor, probably continuing her search for Evan.

"4 Non Blondes," Rudolf answered randomly. "Okay, my turn to give you a song title and you name the band. *Fun and Games.*"

"What? What are you talking about?"

"Nope," Rudolf replied. "There are a few artists who have had songs with *Fun and Games* as the title. I would have accepted Kelsea Ballerini, The Connells, Tiahzzi Cherrelle, Chuck Mangione, Giulia, and Pennywise."

"Are you high right now?" Sophia asked, quite seriously.

"Probably," Rudolf replied. "Also, I don't get why *What's Up* is called that because the entire song, the 4 Non Blondes say, 'What's going on,' not 'What's up.'"

"This seems like a really good use of my time," Sophia testily responded. "Is this about Ramy? Is he working out okay? You haven't ordered him to make certain life choices, have you?"

"Ramy?" Rudolf questioned. "I don't know a Ramy."

Sophia sighed. "The guy I hired to man Heals Pills."

"Oh, Ramy-Cans!" Rudolf stated. "Sorry, that's my pet name for him. I didn't recognize the name before when you said it."

"I'm not going to explain why that defies logic," Sophia muttered.

"He's fine," Rudolf stated. "He's great with the customers and keeps things stocked. Totally took a load off me so I could return to my kingdom business. Although Ramy-Cans does try to sell our customers books that he's written. He likes to slip it into the conversation, seemingly casually."

"Good." Sophia sighed in relief. "That was the concern my fairy godmother had, as well as you having time for your project with Lee, I think."

"Lee?" Rudolf questioned. "I don't know a Lee."

"The assassin baker who you're going into business with to use her talents to fix water supplies worldwide," Sophia supplied.

"Oh, you mean Lee-Beans. You want to know what my nickname is for you?"

"Not really." Sophia looked around the office that belonged to Oscar Beaufont and wondered what she was searching for.

"Sophia-Duck," Rudolf said abruptly.

Instinctively, Sophia ducked. She spun when on the floor, looking for something that could have knocked into her. There wasn't anything.

"Why did you tell me to duck?" she asked into the phone still pressed to the side of her head.

"I didn't. That's your nickname from me. Sophia-Duck."

"That's weird," Sophia replied.

"Yeah, and Liv is Liv-Ace. Rory is Rory-Soary. Stefan is Stefan-the-Horrible."

"Although this is fascinating information, can we get to the reason you called?" Sophia stood from her crouched position.

"Sure thing," Rudolf stated casually. "Not a big deal at all, but I thought that you should know about something."

"If it's a weird rash you got from Serena, I don't need to know details. Use some of the Heals Pills ointment."

"Heavens no," Rudolf stated. "Those rashes cleared up ages ago."

"What a relief," Sophia said dryly.

"Anyway, I returned to my kingdom to find some mean guys circulating in Las Vegas," Rudolf explained.

Sophia tensed, remembering that there had been a spotting of dragons in Las Vegas. "Mean guys?"

"Yeah, and not the ones like usual who come in and question me about avoiding tax laws and ask if I'm abiding by gambling laws."

"You mean the Feds?" Sophia questioned.

"I call them a name I can't say," Rudolf retorted. "But yeah, this isn't them. They've been on the Strip, intimidating the tourists and roughing up the locals. I thought you might want to know about it."

"Why is that?" Sophia asked.

"Well, because I know how much you like animals and they're really mean to the ones they ride."

"Dragons?" Sophia's pulse beat wildly. "Are they riding dragons?"

"Big old lizards," Rudolf stated. "They're huge, have wings, blow fire from their mouths, and roar really loud."

"So dragons?" Sophia repeated.

Rudolf sighed. "Honestly, I couldn't say. I'm not a zoologist. All I know is that I sense these mean guys are going to keep making trouble in my city and I can't have that. Not when I'm trying to sell the city to Asian businessmen. It makes me look like I don't control this place. I think Mr. Matoshima will only buy that the giant flying lizards are a theatrical stunt for so long."

"I have so many questions for you on a variety of subjects that you've just mentioned, but we'll have to get to them later."

"Oh, do you have parkour lessons to get to too?" Rudolf asked.

Sophia shook her head. "No, but the Dragon Elite will be there soon. Stay on alert and let me know if anything changes. We're coming to defend your city for you."

"Great! If you're stopping by the store, will you bring me a bag of jelly beans? I always work up an appetite from my parkour practice."

"No, but I'll save your butt if it comes to that," Sophia confidently affirmed while making for the hallway, intent on rounding up the others.

"You know, and here I thought we were friends." Rudolf sounded offended. "All you can think about is my rear end and how nice it looks in slim fit jeans. If Serena finds out about this..."

Sophia shook her head. "We'll be there within the hour, Ru. Stay inside and safe. Things might escalate fast if this is the Rogue Riders and we have to defend Las Vegas from their attacks again."

"Sounds exciting. I'll roast some popcorn and pull up a front-row seat by my penthouse windows. Try to keep the action on the east side of the Cosmopolitan next to the Bellagio."

"Sure thing," Sophia said and added, "See you soon, Rudolf-Mins."

CHAPTER FORTY-ONE

"Where the hell is Evan?" Sophia strode across the Expanse toward Mahkah and Wilder, and their dragons lined up behind them, Lunis landing gracefully.

They both shook their heads. "We haven't seen him."

"Neither have Mama Jamba or Hiker." Sophia had questioned them as she suited up for what she expected to be a battle in Las Vegas. "Well, we'll have to go without him."

"He probably realized that the new dragonriders were already mastering skills he's struggled with for a century and is crying in his bed," Wilder remarked with a laugh.

"They're doing quite well," Mahkah affirmed in a serious tone.

"That joke fell as flat as your hair," Lunis blithely needled Wilder.

Reflexively, Wilder's hand went for his hair. "Hey, my hair isn't flat. It has tons of body."

"It looks fine." Sophia strode up to her dragon.

"See there," Wilder smugly retorted. "My girlfriend likes my hair." Like a child and not a two-hundred-year-old dragonrider, he stuck his tongue out at the blue dragon.

"Real mature." Sophia shook her head.

Wilder pointed at Lunis. "He started it. He's jealous that I have a girlfriend who is so supportive."

"Are you two going to do this again on this mission?" Sophia questioned, partly amused by Wilder's and Lunis' antics but hiding it.

"Probably," Mahkah interjected.

"I'm not jealous. I don't have a girlfriend," Lunis stated. "Although I do know a female dragon who'd be mad if she heard me say that."

"Good one." Wilder laughed.

"It was also a good line the first time that Mitch Hedberg said it." Sophia swung her leg over her dragon and prepared for takeoff. In the distance, the three new dragonriders watched them as they got ready to leave the Gullington.

"They know what they're supposed to do while we're gone?" Sophia indicated the three men.

Mahkah nodded. "Sharpen their swords. Sharpen their minds. Sharpen their skills."

"Also, I've sent them on a hunt," Wilder added while mounting his dragon, Simi.

"A hunt?" Sophia curiously questioned.

"To find their personalities," Wilder answered with a sly grin.

She tilted her head and gave him a look that said, "Oh, come on. Give them a break."

"He's right," Lunis stated. "Those three are about as dull as Simi and Tala and the other elders."

Simi huffed and nobly put her head in the air. Tala, like her rider Mahkah, didn't seem to care about the jab.

"They're nervous," Sophia defended and grabbed the reins. "Imagine how intimidating it has to be for them to join the ranks of the Dragon Elite."

"I think we're all in a position to do that," Wilder argued. "Although none of us knew how to do it when dragons were thought to be extinct, or there hadn't been a new rider in one hundred years or ever a female rider."

"That's true," Mahkah stated from atop Tala while taking a position next to the other two dragons and riders. "If anyone should have been reserved, it would have been Sophia."

Lunis laughed. "Fat chance of that ever happening."

Sophia rolled her eyes. "I was respectful of the Dragon Elite's traditions in the beginning. It's not like I came in here flaunting my ways and ignoring the dragonriders' ancient culture."

"You introduced electricity and gadgets to the Castle," Wilder argued.

"You let me sleep in your room even though Hiker was adamantly against it," Lunis added.

"Also, you, Sophia," Mahkah began, "went on missions although Hiker was against us intervening in the world's affairs at that time."

She shook her head at the stoic Native American. "Not you too? You're not joining these Laffy Taffies, are you?"

"Just recalling the facts," he stated simply.

"My point," Sophia began with a great inflection on the words, "is that the new dragonriders will take some time to adjust. I'm sure in time, they'll banter and joke along with the rest of us. They're trying to assimilate into an old world that's thought of hesitantly by the new world. It can't be easy for them."

Mahkah nodded. Wilder too.

Lunis, however, shook his head in the direction of the dragonriders watching them about to take off through the Barrier. "Learn some jokes, newbies! I want you to make me laugh, or I'm toasting you upon my return."

Sophia shook her head at Lunis as the three dragons started forward in a rush, their wings effortlessly moving as they picked up speed before they launched into the air in unison, a beautifully choreographed dance.

CHAPTER FORTY-TWO

"I've got a blonde joke for y'all," Lunis said through the howling wind as they soared through the air. They were gaining altitude as they rode toward the Barrier. Soon, there would only be the soft whistling of the clouds as they flew through them.

"I'm not a fan of those," Sophia declared.

"Can we make them mousy brunette jokes?" Wilder offered.

Lunis shook his head. "That won't work. We all know that blondes aren't dumb, Sophia. They're merely easy targets. I need you to be secure on these matters."

"Cool," Sophia replied. "After you tell your jokes, I have some about blue dragons."

"About how they're so ruggedly handsome and suave?" Lunis questioned.

"I'm not sure I'd see the joke there," Mahkah offered, adding to the conversation when he was normally a listener.

"There is a blonde, a redhead, and a brunette—"

Sophia coughed loudly, cutting off Lunis' joke.

"Oh, fine." He sighed. "There's a brilliant yet misunderstood blonde, a fiery redhead, and a meek brunette. Happy, now? You're ruining the joke."

"Only making it fair." Sophia smiled as she leaned forward, the chilly autumn air tangling her blonde hair and making her cheeks ruby red.

"Anyway, they're trapped on an island, and the nearest shore is fifty miles away," Lunis continued. "The weak redhead swims a few miles and drowns."

"Seems about right," Wilder scoffed.

Sophia giggled.

"The boring brunette drowns after ten miles," Lunis stated. "But the blonde swims twenty-five miles, at which point, she's exhausted so she turns and swims back."

Wilder howled with laughter.

Mahkah smirked slightly.

Sophia said, "Ha-ha. Very funny."

Lunis joined Wilder, laughing loudly, swallowing cold air. "Twenty-five miles! She could have kept going!"

"Did she make it back to the deserted island safely?" Wilder questioned.

"I think you're missing the point of the joke." Lunis shook his head.

The three dragons and their riders slipped through the Barrier and over the rolling hills of Scotland. They only had a brief moment to enjoy the way the terrain was absent of modern buildings and stretches of roads and industry before Sophia threw up a portal to Las Vegas in the distance.

They broke into formation, Sophia in the lead as they slipped through the portal and into a land much different from where they'd come from.

Las Vegas was the very opposite of Scotland with its concrete and skyscrapers and bright lights. Currently, it was much different than how Sophia had ever seen it with demon dragons and their riders on the ground, seeming to be attacking the locals and tourists.

CHAPTER FORTY-THREE

Sophia and the other Dragon Elite held their positions in the air, watching from high above instead of springing straight into action. It was difficult to determine what was going on below.

Sophia could see King Rudolf selling the visitor dragonriders as theatrical stunts. They sort of blended in with the huge Optimus Prime robot that the tourists were all lining up to get their photos with or the statue-like man on stilts who was doing a fantastic job of not laughing as a couple of guys mooned him.

However, she knew better than to think that the demon dragons and their riders on the ground were simply trying to entertain the public. There was something different in the way they interacted. There was an air of bullying about them, as though their show was for intimidation rather than amusement. It was because of that observation that Sophia knew that the demon dragonriders on the ground were the Rogue Riders.

She also recognized the redhead on the green dragon who she'd seen at the elfin island—the one Evan had run off a few times.

"Too bad Evan isn't here," Wilder said from beside Sophia as if he were in her thoughts. "I know he's wanted to hand that guy's butt to him ever since the last battle. His name is Nathaniel, and he's the second in command."

"To Versalee," Mahkah added.

Wilder nodded. "His dragon is aligned with lightning."

Sophia gulped. "Good to know. I wonder what Versalee's dragon's element is?"

Wilder shrugged. "I'm not sure, but it doesn't look like she's presently down there creating trouble."

Only a few dragonriders were on the ground. By the way they flew, most were poorly trained. They rode their dragons like one pushes a lawnmower rather than how it should have been, like riding on a magic carpet—being one with it.

Rudolf would be relieved that the display was going on next to the Bellagio Hotel and Casino right next to the Cosmopolitan, where he held his court and had his primary residence at the top.

A couple of the dragonriders spiraled through the air, cutting through the water from the fountain display. Usually, that show at the Bellagio Hotel and Casino stole the attention of a few hundred tourists who paused to watch the spigots of water cascading in different directions in a beautiful dance of choreography.

However, the demon dragonriders were cutting through the water, throwing it onto the tourists, and interrupting the show with one of their own.

Another demon dragonrider approached Optimus Prime. The dragon's wings were outstretched, and the rider held on as they neared the fake robot in an act of intimidation.

The other demon dragonriders, Nathaniel and his dragon included, sat in the middle of Las Vegas Boulevard as though they'd decided to set up camp there. Behind them, cars were at a standstill from the blocked road. Drivers were getting out of their vehicles to view the strange sight of the two large dragons casually mock-fighting in the street.

They were seated but now and then, threw their claws through the air. The one attacked would duck and spit fire in the other's direction, usually missing them but creating damage to the road.

Wilder glanced at Sophia, where the three of the Dragon Elite hovered out of sight—cloaked. "What do you say, boss?"

Sophia thought for a moment. In combat and in the field, she had the leadership role, and she didn't take that lightly. Swallowing, she made a decision, hoping it was the right one.

"Let's try the civil approach." Sophia pointed at the Strip where the two demon dragons and their riders were causing the biggest disturbance. "We'll try talking to them and working things out rationally."

"And when they react like the monsters they are?" Wilder asked with a sideways grin.

"Then we boot them out of this city and show them their acts of disturbance aren't welcome here or anywhere else," Sophia answered with confidence.

Wilder nodded in confirmation. "We'll keep doing it as long as it takes."

CHAPTER FORTY-FOUR

Sophia and Lunis dove toward Las Vegas Boulevard and removed the cloak from the three of them. She didn't want to intimidate those on the ground into thinking they were getting ambushed by more rude and destructive dragonriders. However, she didn't know how to communicate to the mortals that they were the peaceful solution-oriented society of dragonriders. She hoped that their demeanors did that for them since they were approaching with the intent of discussing things civilly and not fighting.

A blonde, a redhead, and a brunette dragon were lost in the desert, Lunis began in Sophia's head.

She laughed, not having expected it to be joke time with everything they had going on. However, she really should've at this point.

It doesn't help that you made them dragons, Sophia replied. *I'm still offended that blondes are the butt of your jokes.*

That's a "you" problem, Lunis stated. *Anyway, they find a lamp and a genie comes out and states he'll grant each one a wish.*

The ground was quickly approaching, and they'd gotten attention from those on the street, the Rogue Riders included.

The redhead wishes to go back home, Lunis continued. *And just like that, the dragon is transported to the hovel where they live.*

I like the details you add to these jokes, Sophia teased while steering Lunis to an open patch of road between the Rogue Riders and the cars, hoping to serve as a protective barrier. That was going to be tricky because there were so many people around that if a fight broke out, she worried that there would be a lot of collateral damage and innocent mortals harmed.

The brunette dragon wished to go home to be with her boring family, Lunis stated as though they were casually flying through the sky and not nearing what was increasingly looking like a very tense situation on the ground.

And the blonde dragon? Sophia had to ask, wanting the punch line before the drama started.

The blonde was suddenly lonely, Lunis answered. *So she asked that her dragon friends join her.*

Sophia groaned. *That was bad, really bad.*

So bad it was good, right?

Not really. Sophia landed her dragon exactly where she intended, putting a protective barrier between the line of cars at their back and the Rogue Riders. Wilder and Mahkah landed beside her, their faces full of confidence and protective edge.

It was time to talk, Sophia thought while facing off against Nathaniel on the ground, looking down at him from high atop her dragon.

CHAPTER FORTY-FIVE

The redhead rolled his eyes and looked at the other demon dragonrider a few yards away. "Oh, look. The Boring Elite are here to bore us all to death with their holy agendas."

Sophia narrowed her gaze. "We're here to find out why you're causing problems in Las Vegas. I got a call from the king of the fae. He doesn't like that you're creating a disturbance in his city."

Nathaniel laughed and threw his hand up in the direction of the Cosmopolitan where King Rudolf no doubt watched from the safety of his penthouse. "Well, tell the little fairy to come down here and tell me to my face!"

"I think it's better if we deal with this between each other, dragonriders to dragonriders." Sophia watched as the crowd around them pushed back, apparently sensing the tension building. She didn't want to fight the Rogue Riders. Not here or anywhere, but they hadn't left her many choices on the matter in the past.

"I don't see what the problem is," Nathaniel said casually as his green dragon rose on his back legs and hooked his claws around the traffic light, bending it down using brute force as it made an awful screeching noise. The dragon broke the piece off, stuck it in his mouth, and began chewing on the end as a dog does with a bone.

Sophia cringed and tried to corral her anger. They were goading her. She couldn't afford to react too quickly. There were too many innocent fae, mortals, and magicians around. She hadn't noticed the latter until they started to pour through the crowd, pushing to the front. Whereas the mortals and fae appeared interested in the scene on the Strip, the magicians seemed downright angry, as if this was a personal encounter and they were ready to spring into action.

She sensed Wilder tense beside her as well. Mahkah stayed watching, nothing changing about his posture.

"You have to realize that you can't take up residence in the middle of the street here and destroy this city," Sophia began, careful to keep her tone even. "The world is happy to welcome the Rogue Riders, the Dragon Elite will see to that, but you have to abide by the same laws as everyone else. No one is above them!"

That got a reaction from the crowd. If there had been any confusion on who was who, this ought to settle it. Those witnessing and recording the events unfolding on their mobile devices knew that Sophia and the two dragons and riders flanking her were trying to protect and uphold justice. In contrast, the two in front of them were about promoting chaos and their own agenda.

Although Sophia didn't like that the education had to come out this way with so many dangerous aspects in proximity, she was grateful for the opportunity to inform the public. The videos would hopefully go viral and many across the world would know that there were the Rogue Riders and the Dragon Elite, and they weren't the same. One could be trusted and the other...well, they were a loose wire, and no one knew what to expect from them.

Nathaniel grinned up at his dragon as sparks rained down from the traffic light it had just destroyed. "Aw, we're only having some fun. What's wrong with that? It is a free country, isn't it?"

Sophia's jaw tensed. He was trying to get under her skin. Trying to make her do something rash. She couldn't allow the Rogue Riders to get the best of them. "It's free for all, which means you can't block the roads and disrupt traffic." She pointed at the Bellagio fountains. "You can't ruin a show that many enjoy."

Nathaniel stuck his hands on his hips. "What can we do, Princess? You kicked us off the stupid elves' island that they weren't using."

"They were living there," Sophia argued through gritted teeth, watching as the dragon messing with the person in the Optimus Prime suit whipped his tail in the robot's direction, coming dangerously close to knocking it over.

Nathaniel scoffed. "Whatever. We got off that stupid island as you wanted. Now we're here, drifting and bringing the charm of our dragons for all to see, but you're still not happy because the Dragon Elite have to control everything. Hanging out isn't against the law."

"What do you care about the law?" Sophia argued. "You steal what you want. Destroy without concern. You have no respect for what the rest of us value."

With a cocky smile on his face, Nathaniel nodded. "Here I thought that you didn't understand the Rogue Riders at all. What a relief. That's right. We don't operate above the law like you all. We don't pretend to be the law. Instead, we govern all that are breaking the laws." He looked out at the scene all around them. "What better place for such ventures than in the city of sin?"

"Do as you please in regard to governing criminals," Sophia began carefully. "I'm not trying to stop you there. If you're doing it right, I don't have any problems with that. What we have a problem with is creating disturbances, endangering the public, and thinking that you own a city that belongs to the fae."

There were cheers from the crowd all around them. Most of those expressing their support were magicians, who had come forward in large numbers and gave the Rogue Riders impatient glares.

Nathaniel narrowed his eyes at the crowd's reaction. He threw his arms wide at those supporting the Dragon Elite. "You think you know who you're messing with? We own the criminal world. Want to feel safe in your beds at night? Then you better bow at our feet, not those of the Dragon Elite who only make the criminals hide while still doing their deeds."

"You're thieves!" a magician yelled, his fist in the air.

"You ruined my house!" another exclaimed.

"You have to be stopped!" someone else screamed from the road.

Sophia felt the crowd growing more hostile. Suddenly, tensions were high, and everything escalated faster than she had expected. She needed to quell tempers.

Nathaniel turned, reached for the reins to his dragon, and yanked hard on them, making the dragon's head jerk to the side as it tried to resist being mistreated. "Who of you will stop the Rogue Riders? Line up, and we'll pick you off, one by one. Then you'll see who deserves your allegiance and not the Dragon Elite."

Sophia glanced at Wilder and Mahkah. They both followed her line of vision, first to the fountains, then to the area of the Strip where the other demon dragonrider had finally knocked down Optimus Prime. Angry magicians tired of the bullying now surrounded him. They weren't wrong, but they needed to handle the Rogue Riders the right way. Sophia reminded herself that if they didn't, they'd repeat history and there would be no more dragons or riders left.

CHAPTER FORTY-SIX

S ophia's eyes connected with Wilder and to the two dragons making a mockery of the Bellagio fountains. He nodded curtly, obviously following her silent direction.

Her gaze went to Mahkah, then to the dragon bullying the character of Optimus Prime. He understood the subtle gesture.

The pair lifted off on their dragons without having to pull on the reins or make demands, gracefully flying in different directions.

Nathaniel's eyes skirted up, following Wilder as he took off after the other demon dragonriders, then Mahkah barreling in the other direction. He swung his leg around, not at all gracefully climbing onto his dragon, who resisted the rider getting into place.

"You can't let us have anything, can you?" he fired at Sophia. Spit flew from his mouth.

"I'm prepared to help you." Sophia sensed magicians moving in closer, some of them brandishing staffs or other things that could be considered weapons. "If you're not careful, you'll make enemies that I can't defend you from."

"We don't need your help!" Nathaniel exclaimed. The other rider next to him also crawled onto his dragon's back.

Then many of the magicians around the street decided not to hold back and charged forward, their fists and weapons up, their mouths open and screams and complaints flying from them.

Sophia didn't have to worry about herself because one thing was clear—they were going after the Rogue Riders. Still, the way that Nathaniel's dragon bowed up and swung around, his tail knocking over a nearby car, Sophia knew that everyone was in danger if things got out of control.

Yes, the Rogue Riders needed to learn their boundaries. Yes, magicians had every right to be mad. However, the disagreement between the two couldn't happen right then. Sophia's chief job now was to stop a fight rather than start or finish one. If she did her job, hopefully no one would get hurt, and it would humble the Rogue Riders in the process.

One could hope, she thought as she sprang into action.

CHAPTER FORTY-SEVEN

E ver since the Rogue Riders had captured and tortured Wilder, he'd longed to get his hands on them. He'd had to witness as they abused their dragons and each other, not at all working together as a team like he was used to with the Dragon Elite. The Rogue Riders were out for themselves and only formed a team for selfish self-preservation reasons.

Before, when Wilder worked with the Dragon Elite to get the Rogue Riders off the elves' homeland, he'd been trying not to cause any unnecessary damage. That was the right thing to do, and Hiker had ordered it.

Wilder respected the Dragon Elite's leader and would do whatever he ordered, as he respected Sophia as a leader and would dutifully go after these two clown Rogue Riders ruining the Bellagio fountains in Las Vegas. However, she hadn't said anything about not harming these riders, and Wilder didn't know how he could stop them without breaking a few bones. He wouldn't kill them. He'd ensure they understood what was right and wrong and when they broke the rules, they got broken too—at least a little bit.

Speeding over the crowd on Simi, Wilder stayed hunched over.

The tourists he flew over could have reached out a hand and nearly touched the white dragon's belly they were so low.

Wilder smiled when the crowd *oohed* and *ahhed* at the sight of the Dragon Elite member flying close overhead toward the disobedient Rogue Riders in the fountain. They all seemed to know that he was there to defend them from getting splashed and their tourist experience ruined.

Wilder grinned over the side of Simi as mortals took pictures and videos of him flying past, hopefully creating social media that would speak of the Dragon Elite's good name. They hadn't planned this public relations campaign, but it probably couldn't have worked out any better for them. Hiker had worked on some positive propaganda and promotions for the Dragon Elite to recover their reputation after everything the Rogue Riders had been doing. *Still, this organic approach was leagues better,* Wilder thought as he neared the other dragonriders.

They caught sight of him from the other side of the fountain, all of the spigots going straight up at that moment. If Evan were there, he could use Coral's water magic to mess with these guys by turning the fountain into a gnarly weapon. Who knew where he was though? *Probably sleeping in the basement, or flirting with Trin, or eating a bag of mega-stuffed Oreos in his bedroom.*

The demon dragonriders cackled as Wilder neared, maybe recognizing him as the guy they captured and beat with his arms restrained because they were cowards. Or perhaps they thought because there were two of them and one of him that this fight would be decisive. One thing was clear—they knew a skirmish was coming. It had to be evident based on Wilder's expression and how he'd poised for an assault.

The other dragons were smaller than Simi, not yet fully grown. One was gray like the color of stone and looked about as ugly as a rock wall battered by wind and dust. The other was brown, the color of dirt.

"Man, you guys have ugly dragons," Wilder observed, sure that they could hear him even with the sounds of the fountains and music and crowd at his back. The chi of the dragon would make it so that they had enhanced hearing and other senses. One thing the chi of the dragon couldn't do was make them skilled. That took practice, training, and expertise, and something told Wilder they didn't have that.

The gray dragon heard the insult and jerked its tail so it hit the wall of water and sent it straight at Wilder like a blast of bullets. Easily, using only his intention, he pulled his dragon up a few feet to avoid getting hit by the spray.

Wilder studied the area around them. He needed to stop these guys. He wanted to teach them a lesson. He also knew he didn't want any innocent people harmed. Now, damage to the area was less avoidable. He simply hoped that King Rudolf wouldn't mind making the repairs, knowing it was for a worthy cause. Teaching demon dragonriders how to behave was a valuable lesson.

CHAPTER FORTY-EIGHT

The strange sights around Las Vegas made Mahkah feel like he was on a different planet. A lot had changed in the last few hundred years that he'd been locked away at the Gullington. The world before that was a simpler place, and where Mahkah grew up was basic and natural.

There was no concrete or buildings or dazzling lights in the world that Mahkah came from. However, he'd spent enough time in the modern world recently so that the sights around him weren't totally foreign although they still took some getting used to. Mahkah's best approach to keep himself from getting disoriented by all the strange newness was to expect to see things he didn't understand and come at it from a place of acceptance.

That's how he viewed the strange large robotic creature that currently lay on the ground and suffered from the abuse of the demon dragonrider who bullied it. Mahkah didn't know if the robot was a strange magitech, a real robot or a fake one, or a person in a suit. It didn't matter. No matter what it was, it was evident that it was in distress and needed help.

No one deserved bullying—no matter what. Some needed to be stopped. Some needed to learn a lesson. Others needed punishment.

Still, even bullies shouldn't be bullied. That was an eye for an eye, and that didn't work for Mahkah. He had to be better than his enemies.

The demon dragonrider harassing the strange robot caught sight of Mahkah as he flew in their direction on Tala. The new dragon was one that Mahkah recognized from when it hatched at the Gullington months ago. It was a shimmering silver and quite attractive, but not full-grown and hadn't come into all of its powers yet, Mahkah observed. If it had, then it wouldn't need to run to take off for flight, but when it circled the robot as Mahkah and his dragon neared, it did just that, nearly knocking over a group of tourists standing too close and taking pictures like this was all a show put on for their amusement.

The demon dragon and rider circled low, struggling to maintain a slow speed as they flew. It was true that it was easier to fly fast than slow and in a small, deliberate movement. That was the case for most things, Mahkah had often noted. It was easier to sprint than to stroll. It was easier to charge than it was to retreat. It was easier to soar than it was to hover. Still, it was the latter in all these instances when real changes could occur.

Peaceful negotiations didn't usually happen from fighting. They resulted when people listened, one of the hardest of all skills.

Slowing Tala, Mahkah nearly came to a halt in the air directly across from the demon dragonrider. His dragon hardly had to move her wings to keep them aloft. Mahkah simply looked across the space at the other rider, hoping that it wouldn't come to violence. The Rogue Rider would know that Mahkah was there to stop his bullying. He would understand that Mahkah was the more skilled rider and if provoked, the demon dragonrider would suffer from his attacks. The question was, would the Rogue Rider have the good sense to retreat or make amends for his misdeeds?

The silver dragon opened his mouth and shot a stream of fire straight at Tala.

It appeared a peaceful end to this situation wasn't in store.

CHAPTER FORTY-NINE

Everything happened so fast.

The magicians charged forward at once. The demon dragons struck defensive stances, rose on their hind legs, and spread their wings, taking up way more space on the road. The Rogue Riders pulled out their weapons and brandished them at the aggressive magicians.

Sophia and Lunis sprang into action, not needing to communicate to know what they were doing next. The blue dragon swung around and put himself between the Rogue Riders and the approaching magicians. Sophia held up her hands, encouraging her fellow magicians to halt.

"Get out of the way, Dragon Elite," a magician with a long white beard and a lazy eye said, holding a sword in his hands. "Our beef isn't with you. We heard you trying to talk sense into the maniacs!"

"Yeah, get out the way so I can rearrange these guys' faces!" Nathaniel yelled, but he hadn't come forward. Instead, he was enjoying the safety behind Lunis like the coward that he was. The blue dragon was almost as long as the street and created a sufficient barrier between the magicians and the Rogue Riders.

"You all have to listen to reason," Sophia urged in a rush, watching as a magician in the crowd held up his hand.

"This has gone too far!" the man yelled.

"No!" Sophia yelled, but it was too late to stop him from releasing the spell.

A red light shot through the air like a laser beam. Lunis ducked, but the attack wasn't on him. It hit the dragon belonging to the other rider in the side and knocked him down at once. His legs shot out straight as if paralyzed and he teetered back and forth on his side like a board wobbling.

"No!" the Rogue Rider yelled and charged forward, trying to make it around Lunis and to the magician who had sent the attack.

Everything was escalating too fast. No one would listen to reason when violence was an option. That left Sophia with no choice but to use her reserves to create a visible shield in the shape of a dome that covered the Rogue Riders and stopped the charging demon dragonrider from leaving the protected area while also deflecting the magicians' attacks.

That didn't stop them right away, and a few magicians joined the first, sending their stunning spells at the barrier, but it worked as Sophia designed and the attacks bounced off.

The Rogue Riders were caged. They were also protected. The magicians were at a standstill.

Now, hopefully both sides will listen to reason, Sophia thought and sighed in relief.

CHAPTER FIFTY

Gray and Brown, as Wilder had taken to calling the dragons ridden by the Rogue Riders challenging him, zipped back and forth on the other side of the wall of water like it was an impenetrable barrier. Wilder thought he knew what was going on. These guys were making a show of intimidating, but neither wanted to make the next move, knowing that they would be the one Wilder attacked first.

Doesn't matter, Wilder thought to himself. *You're both going down anyway.*

He heard the song playing on the speakers near its end, which meant the water display would too. That would be Wilder's opportunity—when the Rogue Riders were disoriented and without the water barrier between them and the Dragon Elite member.

Right on cue, the wall of water fell at the song's conclusion, making Brown and Gray completely visible.

Wilder shot after them on Simi. As he suspected, the rider farther away retreated, probably not wanting to get the punishment he knew he deserved. That left his mate vulnerable, and they both knew it.

"Where you going?" the guy on Gray yelled.

"I'm out of here!" the man on Brown replied.

"He thinks he is," Wilder sang and shot his hand in the direction of Brown, who was quickly retreating.

Combined with the speed of the fleeing dragon and rider and the shot of wind that Wilder sent at them, the momentum carried them fast across the waters where they collided with the corner of the Bellagio Hotel and Casino. There was no one in that vicinity since it was on the far side of the water. Those inside the building felt the impact when Brown slammed into it and cracked the wall before falling and landing on the pavement below.

Rider and dragon fell in a heap but were on their feet immediately, startled and disoriented from the assault. They didn't waste any time, and the rider was soon back on the brown dragon, this time running for safety around the side of the building.

Wilder caught all this as he closed in on Gray, who was distracted by watching his mate being thrown against the side of the building by a gust of wind. That's why he didn't know when Simi was right on top of him.

She slowed in front of the gray dragon, lifted her front feet, and grabbed the dragon around the neck. Using incredible strength, she lifted the dragon and slammed it down toward the fountain. The pair fell like a stone and created a huge splash when they plummeted into the water.

The tourists all covered their faces from the wave that splattered out of the fountain. There was a great flapping of wings below as the gray dragon pulled itself up out of the water, its rider barely hanging on as it took flight, staying low and landing when it made it to the pavement where, like the other Rogue Rider, it chose to run rather than fly—and fled the scene at once.

CHAPTER FIFTY-ONE

Tala opened her mouth and as quick as lightning shot out a stream of fire that was faster, hotter, larger, and more forceful than what the silver dragon had sent in their direction.

The two assaults met and like two stones, stopped each other in midair. The fire rained down on the ground below and made the crowd disperse.

A few people helped the robot to its feet, and they hurried off. Mahkah hoped they'd stay out of the way. The last thing he needed was to have to worry about defending mortals when stopping this Rogue Rider. He suspected the silver dragon and rider would use the mortals to their advantage, making them barriers and hostages of sorts.

"We don't have to fight," Mahkah said over the space, Tala hardly beating her wings to keep them aloft.

Conversely, the silver dragon struggled to stay in place. That was so much more difficult than flying. That's probably why the silver dragon lowered to the now-clear ground and looked up at Mahkah with menace in his eyes. The demon dragon would know that fighting the Dragon Elite member was futile. They wouldn't want to admit it, but dragons were logical, and if they went into a real fight, it would be decisive and over quickly.

The Rogue Rider held up his fist. He obviously didn't have the same sense as his dragon and probably wasn't listening to it. "You don't want to fight because you're scared. The Dragon Elite don't know how to fight because all they do is sit on their hands and avoid conflict. Come down here and get what you deserve!"

Mahkah sighed, wishing it hadn't come to this. At least the silver dragon had made it easy for him, putting itself and its rider straight down on the element that Mahkah controlled—the earth.

He held his arm out straight, his fist closed.

The Rogue Rider frowned up at him, confusion evident on his face.

Mahkah twisted his fist upward in a swift movement, and a second later, the ground buckled under the silver dragon and rider. The concrete fractured severely in multiple places. The cracks spraying out resembled a spider's web.

The rider stumbled and fell on his backside. The dragon flapped its wings to avoid falling into the chasm opening up in the ground. Its wings hit the rider in the head and knocked him back several yards.

The silver dragon recovered once in the air and hovering above the mini earthquake. Realizing that he'd knocked out his rider, the silver dragon swooped down and picked up the guy by the shoulders and one leg a little clumsily. They slumped, and for a moment it appeared that they'd both crash back down onto the pavement. However, the silver dragon beat its wings extra hard a few times, and they lifted into the air, gaining height as they retreated the opposite way, leaving Mahkah and Tala staring after them.

CHAPTER FIFTY-TWO

"Stop!" Sophia yelled, making the ground under the Rogue Riders and magicians shake, or so she imagined the earthquake created by her voice.

Everyone started, suddenly fearful of the dragonrider whose voice could make the ground vibrate.

They all tensed and gave Sophia their attention.

"The magicians have every right to be angry with you Rogue Riders," Sophia began, all eyes on her. "You show no respect to the race you come from or the community that serves us. You take and take and pillage and destroy. It has to stop. Otherwise, you'll find yourself with a war on your hands. That's the last thing the Dragon Elite wants. If we battle, there will be casualties. There could be no end in sight, and the result will repeat history where we destroyed each other until there was nothing left."

"Destroy the Rogue Riders!" a magician in the crowd yelled. "They deserve the Dragon Elite's wrath."

Sophia turned her attention to the crowd of her fellow magicians and fae and mortals. "Our wrath will come at a price. Dragons aren't meant to fight each other. Riders should be able to coexist. The magical races must stop fighting us as well. We're here to create peace, but as long as we meet with resistance, there will only be more battles."

Sophia sat tall on her dragon, looking out at the crowd before glancing over her shoulder at the Rogue Riders trapped in the protective dome. "Hear this final warning. Respect each other. Respect the Dragon Elite. We are your friends. However, if you or anyone challenges us, there will be hell to pay. We are the supreme governing body on this planet, and we make this declaration. If the Rogue Riders don't find a place that stops causing problems for the world, they will pay. That is our job to do and not magicians'."

She glanced out at the crowd. "Is that clear?"

There was a collective murmur of yeses from the group along with reluctant nods, but no one fought her authority. She looked directly at Nathaniel and the other Rogue Rider.

"Get out of here and don't cause problems in this city or any other, or you will have hell to pay. I promise that."

At the conclusion, Sophia dropped the protective shield.

Nathaniel narrowed his eyes at her. He didn't move, and for a moment she was sure he'd try and fight her. The other dragonrider broke the stare-off by running and jumping on his dragon's back and taking off, flying to the east.

Nathaniel's fingers flexed by his side.

Sophia tilted her head and gave him a challenging look that said, "Don't do something you'll regret."

He seemed to understand the meaning in her expression, or he knew that today wasn't his to challenge her. For whatever reason, he unhurriedly strode over to his green dragon and swung his leg over its back. The pair took off, flying overhead in a circle before speeding away, Nathaniel looking over his shoulder at Sophia the entire time— menace strong in his eyes as he fled.

CHAPTER FIFTY-THREE

"Why did the blonde put lipstick on her forehead?" Lunis asked Cooper, one of the new dragonriders.

He and his rider exchanged confused expressions as though looking at each other for the right answer. Tension marked the spot between Cooper's eyes when he shrugged, seemingly afraid he'd be in trouble for not getting the correct answer.

"She was trying to make up her mind," Lunis said and howled with laughter.

Sophia shook her head at her dragon and offered the new rider and dragon a look of apology. "You'll get used to his humor...or, well, you'll come to tolerate it."

"Or if you're Bell, Hiker's dragon, then you'll get a sour expression on your face anytime anything amusing is said," Lunis offered and grinned at the red dragon not too far away on the Expanse.

Bell swooshed her tail and tossed her head in the air with a look of superiority.

"You made my point," Lunis called to the older dragon.

All the riders were on the Expanse, training per Hiker's orders. Well, all but Evan. He was still strangely missing, although Trin and Ainsley said that he was somewhere in the Castle, according to the messages they'd "felt" from the sentient building. As usual, Quiet didn't offer any information on the subject.

Hiker had been satisfied with how the three Dragon Elite had handled the situation in Las Vegas, minimizing damages and keeping the public safe. Things were still tense with the magician community, but thankfully, they knew that the Dragon Elite weren't to blame for all the bullying and theft done by riders. The situation had worked to fix the Dragon Elite's reputation, and for that, Hiker was even more relieved.

"We need to find you all weapons that suit your skills and strengths," Wilder said to the three new dragonriders, who all stood stoically at attention, hardly blinking as they faced the weapons expert.

"Then why do you carry a sword?" Lunis asked Wilder, his expression quite serious. "Why not carry a scythe like the Grim Reaper?"

Wilder lowered his chin, a slight grin on his face as he waited for the punch line.

"Well, you know," Lunis continued, "because your skill is killing all the fun in life."

The newbie dragonriders all appeared to be covering their laughter, afraid that it would offend Wilder. However, he was the first one to chuckle at the joke and the loudest.

"At least he's moved off blonde jokes," Sophia offered to her boyfriend.

"For Scottish Thanksgiving, I'm only telling Mitch Hedberg lines," Lunis stated proudly.

Sophia twisted her mouth to the side, an apology on her face. "I don't think the dragons are invited to the Thanksgiving celebration."

Lunis sat back on his hind legs and folded his front across his chest, looking like an annoyed teenager. "Why not? I'm American and demand to be part of the festivities."

"You're a dragon," Sophia argued. "I don't think you have a nationality."

"That's highly offensive." Lunis stuck his snout in the air and pretended to be insulted. "How dare you take away who I am?"

Sophia ignored him but giggled still. "The Scottish Thanksgiving is in the Castle where dragons aren't allowed, so you'll have to do your own thing. Why don't you host something for the dragons in the Pad?"

"Because I like my space and don't want it to smell like old cheese," Lunis stated and looked at Simi. "Hint, hint. A bath wouldn't kill you —or maybe it would."

The white dragon rolled her eyes and returned to snoozing with the other elder dragons who were lying on the grass nearby, soaking up the autumn sun.

Wilder laughed and returned his attention to the three new riders. "We can have you all explore weapons in the Castle. We have a large inventory, and there should be a suitable option for you."

Cooper pointed at the elfin-made sword on Sophia's hip. "Is that where you got that weapon?"

Wilder shook his head and answered before Sophia could. "Oh, no. The mysterious Sophia showed up with that and few details about where she got it from."

Sophia pulled Inexorabilis from its sheath and brandished it proudly, admiring the curved blade and craftsmanship. "My sister recovered it for me. It belonged to my mother, who was a Warrior for the House of Fourteen. The famous elfin sword-maker Hawaiki created it."

"Mysterious and boring with hardly any interesting family history," Wilder teased.

Sophia shot him a mock look of offense. "You're one to talk. You're so boring with that rare skill of being able to access all the memories of a weapon."

Lunis yawned loudly. "He's dull. Not a single redeeming quality that I can find and I've really, really tried to find a single one."

Wilder nodded in agreement. "I'm the total worst. The only one who beats me on that is Evan, wherever he is."

"I'm sure he'll show up right before Scottish Thanksgiving when he smells the turkey and gravy," Sophia offered.

"Probably," Wilder answered while striding for the Castle. "Well, how about we go explore the weapons before dinner?"

Mahkah, Sophia, and the three new dragonriders followed him, heading for the Castle.

"Don't worry about me," Lunis called. "I'll be here listening to Tala snore."

"We're not worried," Wilder sang over his shoulder.

"If anyone wants to bring me some mashed potatoes, I won't stop them," Lunis said in a rush.

"We'll see," Sophia called over her shoulder and winked at her dragon.

"With extra gravy," Lunis added. "Like, I want those potatoes swimming."

CHAPTER FIFTY-FOUR

Evan was breathless, sweat running down his brow, his hands gripping the corner of the hallway in what he guessed was a distant corner of the dungeon far under the Castle.

The weeping angels had "transported" him over two dozen times to various places in the building. None of the locations were remotely close to others, his room, the kitchen, or the exit.

Evan was starting to think that he'd be "lost" in the Castle for the rest of his life. Or until he starved, which felt like it wouldn't be that long.

He pressed his head into the corner of the cold stone wall and muttered to himself, "Please don't be there. Please. Please. Please."

Drawing in a breath, Evan straightened, knowing that he couldn't put this off anymore. He thought that he'd figured out the trick to getting past the stone angels, but it wasn't easy. The last time he'd tried it, they'd blotted out the torches, cast him in darkness, and ruined his chances. Then they'd transported him to another part of the dungeon. The torches lining the wall were still lit, but that might not last. He only had to make it to a part of the Castle with windows, then that little trick of the mean angels wouldn't work anymore.

He prepared himself and released the breath he'd been holding. He then stepped around the corner and faced the long dark hallway lined with torches.

Stiffening, he found exactly what he'd expected—at the far end of the narrow corridor was another stone angel with their face covered with their hands.

Wide-eyed, Evan stepped forward and approached the angel that divided him from the dungeon's exit on the other side.

"Don't blink," he told himself, thinking that was the answer to the riddle of the stone angels. When he took his eyes off them, they moved. If they got close to him, they transported him.

"Don't blink," he repeated and took another step.

The torch closest to him snuffed out.

"Oh, damn it," he seethed. If there was no light, then the point went to the angels, and they transported Evan yet again.

His stomach rumbled. He could swear he smelled fresh bread and other savory aromas wafting down from the Castle's kitchen.

I must be losing my mind. Another torch extinguished ahead. "Oh, hell no."

Evan didn't have much magical reserve left after playing this game with the Castle for what felt like days. However, he would drain the very last of his magic to get to the feast happening upstairs.

Holding out his palm, Evan created a light orb. It bobbed above his palm, glowing brightly.

All of the torches in the hallway extinguished at once, but the light orb did its job. Evan could still see the stone statue not too far ahead.

He kept his eyes wide, feeling them start to burn from not blinking. As quickly as he dared, Evan strode forward while keeping his gaze on the weeping angel.

When he was to it, he stepped around it, walking backward to ensure he kept his eyes on the angel. He was almost there…

Evan's heel found a step, and he nearly fell back on the stairs behind him. Then the light orb would have gone out, and he would have found himself transported once more.

Carefully, Evan climbed the stairs backward, keeping his burning eyes focused on the back of the stone angel. Light began to stream in from the space up ahead. He was almost to the first floor and the entrance to the dungeon off the Castle's entryway.

He'd almost defeated the weeping angel. He only needed not to blink for a little longer—a few more steps. Freedom was right ahead. Evan could taste it.

CHAPTER FIFTY-FIVE

"I haven't slept for ten days," Lunis said casually.

"Oh, really?" Mahkah fell for the joke.

"Yeah, that would be too long," Lunis replied and howled with laughter. The others at the dining room table joined him, the new dragonriders giggling conservatively. It had been weird for them at first when Lunis poked his head through the Castle's open window to join them for Scottish Thanksgiving. Then the Castle created a bank of larger windows, and many of the other dragons joined, their long necks poking through as they regarded the spread of food on the dining table.

However, the blue dragon was the only one eating a large vat of potatoes drowning in gravy.

"That was another Mitch Hedberg line," Sophia confessed to the table while taking the green beans Wilder handed to her.

Lunis sighed. "You don't have to inform everyone every time I quote the great Mitch Hedberg."

She spooned a pile of green beans on her plate, next to the "chips" that Trin had insisted on serving with the Thanksgiving meal, although it wasn't traditional. She said it was because French fries were Evan's favorite, a bit of longing in her tone. The housekeeper still got the impression from the Castle that Evan was somewhere inside the building, but no one had seen him and it was starting to become worrisome.

"Everything is delicious, Trin." Ainsley smiled across the table at the housekeeper, who had finally taken a seat after serving the turkey —well, what was supposed to be the turkey. That was the one thing the Castle hadn't supplied. Instead, it had offered a huge haggis. The new dragonriders were eyeing the gray sheep's stomach stuffed with various other organs and grains with trepidation.

Wilder leaned over and whispered to Cooper, "It tastes as bad as it looks."

"It does not," Mama Jamba scolded and pursed her lips at the dragonrider.

Wilder indicated her short stack of pumpkin pancakes with his fork. "Then why aren't you eating any of it?"

"I don't eat any of my creatures," Mama Jamba stated smugly, then cut into a pancake and took a bite. "Especially sheep because they're so cute."

"You know, if you can't sleep, count sheep," Lunis began, quoting another Mitch Hedberg line. "Don't count endangered animals. You'll run out."

Most at the table laughed.

Mama Jamba nodded, like this was a perfectly good idea and not a joke. "Sheep are good for many things. Dumb as rocks, but cute. I did pretty good with those creations."

"Dumb as Wilder," Lunis corrected. "That's how the expression goes. I'm pretty sure."

The other dragons with their heads inside the dining hall regarded Lunis with keen interest. Sophia was pretty sure the new dragons didn't know how to respond to his flippant and playful style while also being under the elder dragons' influence. It would take time before their real personalities came out and the dragons acted naturally. The same was true for the new riders as well.

"Well, thanks for making this happen, Trin." Hiker took a roll from the basket and buttered it.

"It was all Sophia's idea," the cyborg stated.

"You did all the work," Sophia replied. "Hopefully, we can do something festive for Christmas too. I think it's good to take breaks and celebrate with each other."

Ainsley nodded. "I agree. Now we have new faces, and the table is filling up, which is nice."

Hiker glanced down the table where the three new riders sat on the other side of Mahkah. Quiet was across from them and the chair beside him where Evan usually sat, empty. "Yes, I envision that this table will be full not too long from now."

"Oh, can we hang stockings from the mantle?" Lunis asked, having finished his vat of potatoes. "I want one with my name on it."

"What do you want for Christmas?" Wilder asked the blue dragon, looking over his shoulder at him.

"Peace and cheer," Lunis answered at once and quickly added, "So, for you to off yourself."

Wilder laughed. "I should have seen that coming."

"You really should have," Sophia replied.

"What is the ultimate stocking stuffer?" Lunis asked quite seriously.

"What?" Mahkah took the bait.

"A severed foot," Lunis answered, and the whole table laughed at another of his Mitch Hedberg lines.

The laughter seemed to be infectious, or maybe it was the flowing wine, but it went on as though it would never stop.

Running feet made everyone pause and tense, although most still wore gleeful expressions.

A moment later, Evan sped into the dining hall, looking awful. His brow dripped sweat, and it drenched his shirt. His face was long and his eyes wide as he whipped his head over his shoulder as if something followed him. His chest dramatically heaved as he bent over to collect himself.

Trin jumped up from her seat. "Evan! Where have you been? No one has seen you for ages."

"Hey mate," Wilder chirped. "I didn't realize you'd been gone."

Evan rose and narrowed his eyes at Quiet, who hadn't turned to look at the commotion and was simply digging into the haggis. Evan pointed with an accusatory expression on his face. "You!" he seethed. "It was you behind that trick with the angels."

"Angels?" Hiker questioned. "What about angels?"

"Stone statues of angels that if I looked away from them transported me to distant places in the Castle," Evan replied. "I've been lost all this time."

Wilder shook his head. "After a hundred years, you'd think you'd know your way around this place better."

"Are you all right?" Trin looked Evan up and down.

He nodded and eyed the spread on the table. "I'm starving."

"I was about to eat the last of the chips." Wilder picked up the platter. "Since I guess no one else wants them."

Evan grabbed them and delivered a challenging look as he sat in his usual place. "Not a chance, mate. Those are all mine. Everything here is mine. I'll even eat the haggis at this point."

Trin also returned to her seat and gave Quiet a speculative look. "Did you really play that game on Evan?"

The gnome mumbled something and stuffed a bite in his mouth.

Mama Jamba nodded. "We all have to be humbled sometimes, especially the mouthier we are."

Evan rolled his eyes. "There's no winning with that short guy. He's going to torture me no matter what I do."

"Maybe don't give him so many reasons to punish you," Sophia offered.

"That could be impossible," Wilder stated.

Hiker shook his head. "Well, I'm glad you're back. I was starting to wonder."

"I'm grateful that you were worried about me, sir." Evan crammed a handful of french fries into his mouth.

"I didn't say worried," Hiker corrected. "It's good to have everyone at the table for this celebration though."

"Including me," Lunis added.

"Everyone," Hiker repeated and held up his goblet of wine. "I think this calls for a toast. We've had a small victory, and I'd like to acknowledge that."

"We have?" Evan asked, confused.

"We did." Wilder indicated himself, Sophia, and Mahkah. "You were fooled by stone statues."

"They moved, man," Evan said in a convincing voice. "Like, came after me."

"You also suffered from hallucinations," Wilder added.

Hiker cleared his throat, still holding his goblet high in the air. "Anyway, as I was saying, we have much to be grateful for. We've pushed the Rogue Riders back yet again. We've earned back our reputations as defenders of good. We've welcomed new members to our ranks. Cheers."

There was a collective chorus of cheers around the table as they all clinked glasses. Sophia smiled, thinking that things were coming together for the Dragon Elite. Hiker was right. One day, the table would fill with riders. One day, the world would fully rely on them as the supreme source of adjudication.

First, well, they needed to refill their reserves and take this opportunity to enjoy each other. There would be time to save the world tomorrow, and the next day, and the next.

Today, it was time for them to preserve their spirit, and there was no better way to do that than to be with the ones they loved.

CHAPTER FIFTY-SIX

"Hold her still," Nathaniel ordered the two Rogue Riders needed to restrain the Warrior for the House of Fourteen.

They'd used a few restraining and stunning spells on her, but she seemed to tolerate them like hard liquor.

The large woman thrashed back and forth, nearly knocking one of the dragonriders holding her against the nearby wall. Her eyes were red with vengeance, and her cheeks puffed out from her efforts, fighting the others as they restrained her hands.

Nathaniel had tried to avoid what he was forced to do next. If he was going to get information out of the Warrior, then it was best to have her conscious, but it appeared he needed to deplete her first. Weaken her and try it again.

Raising an eyebrow, he gave a pointed look at the dragonrider on the other side of the Warrior, who wasn't struggling as much once restrained. "Do it," Nathaniel ordered, knowing that the other man knew what he had to do at this point, per their earlier discussion.

The large dragonrider nodded and picked up a stick leaning against the wall. Before the woman could push back in her chair and complicate matters more, the Rogue Rider brought the weapon swiftly across the Warrior's head, sending her chin straight down at once. She went still immediately, passed out.

Nathaniel sighed. Thankfully Trudy DeVries had been knocked out and hopefully would give them less trouble when she awoke, no doubt bleary-eyed, with a giant headache.

CHAPTER FIFTY-SEVEN

"What was she doing when you found her?" Nathaniel asked the Rogue Rider who had snuck up on Trudy DeVries, a known Warrior for the House of Fourteen.

She'd busted Nathaniel more than a few times for selling illegal magi-tech and various other business dealings she deemed "amoral." That had made it harder not to beat the woman senseless upon learning that she'd been spying on the Rogue Riders. However, Nathaniel needed information.

Versalee had recently cut him off for whatever reason. She'd left on a secret mission to secure "something or another that will be important for the Rogue Rider's future," and she wasn't answering any of his messages. He knew she got them. Knew she was okay, for the most part. However, her clipped replies made him think the leader of the Rogue Riders might be double-crossing him.

What if she'd made a deal with the House of Fourteen behind his back? Offered him and the dragonriders in Las Vegas in exchange for immunity or something? That had been his first thought when they'd found the Warrior for the House of Fourteen prowling around. The Rogue Riders were the Dragon Elite's problem, as evidenced by them trying to make a mockery of them recently on Las Vegas Boulevard.

A mob of angry magicians had overrun Nathaniel and his men, enforced by the Dragon Elite. One day, they'd get their reckoning. One day he'd make them pay for trying to make him look bad. First, he had to find out why a Warrior was in his territory or at least the area he was trying to secure.

Las Vegas had proven harder than he imagined to get reins on. The fae weren't the problem. They were dumb as bricks and didn't seem to mind that the Rogue Riders were infiltrating the city. The magicians had been the bigger issue, which further fed Nathaniel's suspicions about the Warrior for the House of Fourteen since they were part of their domain.

The Rogue Rider who had knocked Trudy DeVries over the head and made her pass out had also caught her spying. He combed his hands through his greasy brown hair. "She followed me down here, into the underground city."

Nathaniel slapped the guy on the side of the head. "I told you to be more careful. We can't have anyone knowing this is where we're setting up our operations."

The guy flashed Nathaniel a seething look when he recovered from the assault, but he didn't dare return the attack. There weren't many Rogue Riders at Nathaniel's disposal, but the ones under his authority didn't cross him. That was the other thing. Versalee had taken the bulk of the dragonriders with her, saying that she'd need them and also spoke of recruiting more.

However, Nathaniel didn't know how many more were out there. Only the Dragon Elite would know that apparently since they had access to the globe that showed the demon dragons. But still, there couldn't be too many out there.

"I caught her following me, boss," the guy replied. "My dragon snuck up on her and knocked her out with his tail when I told him what was going on. So I think it's okay that she followed me. Otherwise, we wouldn't have her."

Nathaniel narrowed his eyes. "I don't accept your rationale for being incompetent, but at least you've finally mastered telepathy with your dragon. It's about time."

The guy shrugged. "It only works half the time, but it's better than it was before."

Nathaniel shook his head and glanced at the other guy stationed beside Trudy DeVries. "Keep an eye on her and let me know when she wakes up. I need to find out who sent her here and how she knew to follow a Rogue Rider."

He nodded dutifully in reply as Nathaniel made for the aluminum door and beckoned the first one to follow. It smelled like garbage in the underground tunnel outside the small concrete room where they held the Warrior, and darkness blanketed the graffiti-covered conduit.

The passageways that ran under the city of Las Vegas were wide enough to accommodate the dragons, but some of the larger ones had to duck inside them. The tunnels used to be home to the city's bums and low-lives, but Nathaniel and the Rogue Riders had run them out pretty quickly. Now it was their domain, and although it wasn't open, light, or pleasant, it was a place for them to grow stronger and take over Las Vegas.

Versalee knew that they had taken up residence in the underground warren, which was another thing that made Nathaniel suspicious of the Rogue Riders' leader. The Warrior for the House of Fourteen might have simply followed someone down there, but it was also possible that she knew exactly where to look.

"When you were up there, leading a Warrior down here," Nathaniel began, nodding up to the ceiling where the city was humming above them, "did you find any more recruits?"

The guy nodded. "Sure did boss. Word is spreading. The criminals in this city seem keen to have our protection from the authorities in exchange for a cut of their profits. I think people are starting to like what the Rogue Riders can do for them."

Nathaniel grinned. "It was only a matter of time. We keep them out of jail, and they keep our pockets full."

"What about regulating their crimes though, boss?" the guy asked as they strode down the darkened tunnel in the direction of the main room. There were dragons up ahead, lounging against the spray-painted walls and chewing on various bones. "Isn't that part of it?"

Nathaniel grimaced as a dragon slung a half-eaten dead rat at his feet. He lifted his boot and stepped over it. "Yeah, we're not doing that. Versalee had talked about it, but we've decided we don't care how criminals operate. Our game will be protecting them from the police in exchange for their profits. Who cares how they conduct their business, as long as we get paid?"

"Copy that, boss," the guy replied. "What do you want me to do now?"

"Go figure out how to fly your dragon already," Nathaniel growled and turned into the main room. It was a large concrete space filled with the various things they'd stolen, and where most of the Rogue Riders hung out, played cards, fought, or slept off their hangovers.

"Yeah, about that," the guy began. "I hoped that someone could help me...maybe you?"

Nathaniel kicked the makeshift table where one of the dragonriders was giving another a tattoo. All the equipment slid across the floor and both guys tensed, the needle nearly stabbing the one getting the tattoo in his arm. "Is that the best use of your time, you idiots? Why don't you make yourselves useful and prowl the city for criminals? We're not going to build a reputation decorating our arms with pig's faces."

The tattooist stood, his eyes shifting with fear. "It's a dragon, boss."

Nathaniel shook his head. "Seriously, you're a horrible artist. Go up to the city and find some drug dealers and prostitutes."

"Yes, sir." The guy gathered up the tattoo equipment. The other man rubbed his arm where his unfinished tattoo was located and frowned at the bad artwork.

Nathaniel turned to the other guy. "No, I can't help you learn how to ride your dragon. Figure it out on your own, like the rest of us."

The guy combed his hands through his hair again. "I just thought there has to be some training of sorts. Or a book or something..."

"We're dragon-freaking-riders," Nathaniel spat. "Not stupid nerds. Now get out of my sight and don't return until you can ride your dragon."

The guy didn't hesitate before speeding off. Many of the Rogue

Riders in the main area followed him out, probably not wanting to suffer Nathaniel's wrath.

That's how it should be, the redhead thought proudly. He didn't know who he could trust anymore, but he held authority over his men. So if Versalee double-crossed him, he'd take her down. Regardless of what happened, he would take over the city—one criminal at a time. Soon, he and the Rogue Riders would own Las Vegas.

CHAPTER FIFTY-EIGHT

"Hey, will one of you lame-os hand me the bacon?" Evan pointed at the silver platter on the far side of the table, sitting right in front of Cooper.

Sophia shook her head and held out her hand to the newbie drag-onrider before he could comply with the request. She narrowed her eyes at Evan. "Why don't you try that again? This time, with no name-calling."

Evan rolled his eyes, pinned both his elbows on the table in the dining hall of the Castle in the Gullington, and leaned in Cooper's direction. "Would you, person who acts in ways that are lame, hardly says anything, and acts like we're going to cut you for showing a personality, hand over the bacon?" He flashed a wide smile at Sophia and added, "Pretty please..."

Wilder laughed and took a bite of bagel. "You're so charming that it hurts sometimes."

Evan leveled his gaze at him. "That's because you're a wuss who has a low pain threshold."

"It's true," Wilder chirped. "That's why I've wanted you to cover your face. Looking at it pains me."

"Because I'm so handsome and it pains you that you have to live in my shadow for many more centuries to come," Evan boasted.

"The idea that I have to stand you for any amount of time, let alone centuries, is the excruciating part." Wilder turned to Sophia. "If it gets too much to bear, will you put me out of my misery?"

She shook her head, unamused by the guys' usual antics. Something had her worried...well, a lot of things. "You both have to figure out how to live with each other for the rest of your days."

"I might kill you if you don't get out of my chair," Hiker boomed as he strode into the dining hall and pointed at Wilder, who had taken up residence in the leader of the Dragon Elite's chair.

"Oh, sorry, sir," Wilder stated. "Cooper was in my usual chair next to Sophia, and I didn't know if you'd show up for breakfast."

The newbie dragonrider jumped to his feet. "I-I-I'm sorry. I didn't know we had certain seats." He scrambled for one of the empty chairs on the other side of the two other new men. There were at least twenty open seats on the far side of the table that stretched the room's length.

"We don't," Hiker growled, his chin low as he stared down at Wilder, taking the now empty chair next to Sophia.

"Then how was Wilder in your seat?" Ainsley strode into the dining hall and entered the conversation like she'd been there all along. She took the seat next to Hiker, which was still open and right next to Evan, as usual. Mahkah sat next to him. Mama Jamba and Quiet hadn't yet joined them for breakfast.

"This is my Castle, and these are my Dragon Elite," Hiker argued, still not having taken a seat but now his furious gaze pinned on Ainsley. "I'm the head of this place, and I sit at the head of the table."

"What if I start sitting at the opposite end?" Evan proposed. "At the other head? Does that diminish your role?"

Hiker shot him a murderous look, his fists clenched.

Evan quickly added, "I'm asking for a friend, sir. I'd never do anything that would diminish your role." He indicated Wilder with a subtle nod. "Someone wanted to know."

"Why are you still talking?" Hiker asked him quite seriously.

"It's a good question and one I find myself asking Evan all the time," Wilder stated, taking a bite of his bagel.

"Where are Mama Jamba and Quiet?" Ainsley peered down the table.

Hiker sighed. "Mama was on the phone with a travel agent when I left my office and who knows about Quiet. Probably tending to the herd."

"Probably coming up with a diabolical plan to try and ruin me." Evan took two pastries from the tray.

"Why that woman needs a travel agent stumps me." Wilder shook his head.

"That and simple math," Evan stated. "Those two things stump you."

Trin strode out of the kitchen, carrying another plate of pastries. When she went to put them on the table, Evan stopped her. "I think we're good on pastries, my darling."

The cyborg raised an eyebrow at him. "Are you saying you don't want me to provide you with extra pastries when you're usually complaining that there aren't enough?"

He held up the two glazed pastries in his hands and smiled. "I'm good, but thanks for thinking of me. I wouldn't want any of those to go to waste."

She gave him a skeptical glare before turning and striding off for the kitchen.

Evan whipped around and leaned forward in the direction of the three new dragonriders. "You want to get on Quiet's good side, right?"

They all nodded.

"Well, he can't stand the sight of pastries, so if you don't want to see him mad and therefore have a chance of getting into his good graces, then you better make all those disappear." Evan pointed at the silver platter with three remaining flaky dough pastries.

The three new dragonriders didn't hesitate before taking one each and stuffing it in their mouth like they were doing a charitable act.

Evan sat back, taking a bite of one of the pastries in his hand and looking satisfied. The others simply shook their head at him, knowing that it was too late to say anything. This would play out how it always did between the groundskeeper and Evan—with one of them madder than hell and the other laughing.

"I agree," Mama Jamba sang as she entered the dining hall beside Quiet. "Travel by boat is my favorite."

The old woman found her usual spot, smiling around at the table. "Good morning, y'all."

Everyone greeted her. Well, not the new dragonriders. They didn't look capable of speech as Mother Nature slid the short stack of pancakes in her direction.

"Why is it that you need a travel agent?" Wilder asked, curious.

"Because," Mama Jamba said simply, pouring the maple syrup onto her pancakes.

Quiet hadn't taken his seat. Instead his eyes slid to the empty platter of crumbs and then to the two pastries in Evan's hands.

Taking note of this, Evan took a bite out of the other pastry he hadn't yet sunk his teeth into and smiled. "Something got you down, little guy? Is it the sheep again? Are the lambs taller than you already?"

The gnome mumbled something inaudible, his hands on his hips.

The three newbies all looked between Evan and Quiet, nervousness in their eyes.

Wilder leaned over and whispered to them, "You see, they have a long-running feud. Evan has been stealing all the pastries before Quiet can get to breakfast for the better part of a century. Then Soph showed up, and he almost got a knife to the face. Now that you three are here, it seems he's playing the game again." He clapped Cooper, the closest dragonrider to him, on the shoulder. "Now I think you're all caught up."

Evan threw both the partially uneaten pastries on his plate, wiping his hands. "Man, I'm stuffed."

Quiet narrowed his eyes, and Evan's chair disappeared, sending him straight down on his tailbone on the floor. He yelped from surprise and probably also pain.

"Trin," Ainsley called over her shoulder. "We'll take those pastries after all."

The cyborg housekeeper strode back from the kitchen carrying the tray piled high with pastries. She glanced down at Evan, who was rubbing his backside and looking quite offended. At once, she laughed at the sight.

Evan jumped to his feet and pointed at Quiet, who helped himself to the pastries that Trin had set down. "That little runt did this to me, and you're laughing?"

Trin shrugged. "You seem to be okay, and if you weren't, I'd be questioning your strength. This ongoing feud is between you and Quiet. I'm not getting involved."

"Why not?" Evan crossed his arms over his chest.

Trin pursed her lips at him, then smiled. "Because there's no way to win there. Picking sides between you is certain death."

"If you're quite done with your drama, Evan," Hiker began. "I'd like to discuss actual business."

Evan yanked another chair out and dragged it around to his spot. "Business, yes. Let us discuss. What life-saving mission would you like me to go on?"

"None," Hiker answered. "Continue to train the new guys." He turned his attention to Sophia. "What do you have going on since the others are training?"

Sophia thought for a moment. "Not a whole lot. I'm still inquiring with the Brownies about a list of criminals so I can track down Versalee and the Rogue Riders. I'm waiting on results to find out if my sister is having a demon baby and if so, we need to uncover a genie's lamp. In my spare time, I'm running Heals Pills. Oh, and I have a dentist appointment."

"Seems like you could be taking on more," Evan quipped.

Sophia narrowed her eyes at the other rider.

"I agree," Hiker added, to her surprise.

"You what?" Sophia asked.

"Well, none of that is immediate, and I'm sure you can slide in another task or two," Hiker explained, but Sophia's phone ringing in her pocket cut him off.

Since it was supposed to be silenced, she knew it was urgent. Realized it was from someone important.

Hiker tilted his head and gave her a stern expression that said, "Don't you dare take that call."

He had a strict policy of no phones at the dinner table. Normally, she'd listen, but something told Sophia that she shouldn't ignore this. It could be Mae Ling or Father Time or—

Sophia's eyes widened as she looked at the caller ID.

"Put your phone away," Hiker ordered.

She didn't listen and answered it, putting it straight to her ear. "Yes, Liv? Have you heard about the baby?"

"Oh, man, sir," Evan stated. "That was bold and rude, and I think you need to punish her."

"I might," Hiker seethed, glaring at Sophia as Liv spoke on the other side of the line.

She spoke fast, and within a minute she'd heard everything Liv had to say and turned off the phone.

"Well, that better have been important, or you've lost your phone for good," Hiker threatened.

"Sir, really there isn't a good enough reason for total insubordination," Evan urged. "Just fire her. She'll never learn, and she's teaching the new guys bad behavior."

Sophia ignored him and looked straight at Hiker. "It appears I do have something more immediate to add to my schedule. The Rogue Riders have abducted one of the Warriors for the House of Fourteen."

CHAPTER FIFTY-NINE

On the one hand, Sophia was grateful that Liv and the baby were okay. Or that at least there was no bad news—yet. Really, no news yet...

On the other, to know that the Rogue Riders had abducted Trudy DeVries, a Warrior for the House of Fourteen that Sophia had known all her life, felt personal. First, it had been Wilder, and that was incredibly difficult for Sophia. Now Trudy was suffering under the demon dragonriders' cruelty.

Few knew that Trudy DeVries was a seer and there was no way that Sophia would volunteer that information. Hiker and the others didn't need to know. In the magical world, most didn't respect or tolerate seers. It was probably because they were too powerful or the certainty of a future coming to pass was scary. Still, seers' visions weren't one hundred percent reliable. Some of their prophecies had come to pass, and others hadn't.

Moreover, they were limited in what they could see, which was why Trudy wouldn't have known to avoid the abduction. A common misconception was that because someone could see the future, they could see all of it. Even Papa Creola and Mama Jamba were limited in what they knew and saw because there were too many variables that changed things second by second. The future was never fixed.

After learning about Trudy's abduction, Hiker thundered straight for his office. Sophia hadn't finished her sausage roll but knew that didn't matter. Without him saying it, Hiker wanted her to follow him so they could start planning how they'd get the Warrior for the House of Fourteen back.

Scooping up the sausage roll, Sophia hurried after Hiker.

"We eat at the table, young lady!" Evan called after her, a teasing quality in his voice. At her back, Sophia heard him continue mouthing off for the newbie dragonriders' entertainment or more likely to cause them even more confusion about how things ran at the Castle. "You'll discover that the Pink Princess pretty much does whatever she likes, whenever she likes. Hiker can hardly stand her, so don't get attached. It's only a matter of time before she's booted out of here yet again."

For as large as Hiker was, he moved relatively fast and gracefully. He was already to his office by the time Sophia made it to the stairs. When she found him in his office, he was regarding the Elite globe with sincere frustration.

"It won't tell me a damn thing that I need to know," Hiker grumbled as Sophia entered the office. To her surprise, Mama Jamba was already seated in her usual place on the chesterfield sofa although she'd been at the dining table when Sophia left.

The old woman sifted through the contents of a box sitting on her lap. She sighed and looked up at Hiker. "That's because it's to tell you about your riders, the Dragon Elite. Not the Rogue Riders. They aren't yours, remember?"

"You know I can't stand rhetorical questions," he muttered and gripped his beard with annoyance.

"Yet, I still ask them," Mama Jamba sang with a smile. "How do you like that?"

"Tell me everything your sister told you about this," Hiker ordered, putting his back to the two women and looking out the bank of windows that faced the Pond. The morning sunlight shimmered off the placid body of water.

Sophia eyed her sausage roll that she was seconds away from taking a bite of moments prior. Her stomach was growling something awful all of sudden as if it knew that if it didn't get food now, it might lose its opportunity. "She didn't have much information. The Council sent Trudy to Las Vegas to look into the skirmishes between magicians and the Rogue Riders. She hasn't returned and isn't responding to messages, so they assume she's been caught. Her light in the Chamber of the Tree is still on, so they don't believe she's dead."

Hiker punched his thigh, obviously having trouble quelling his temper, which was known to have a short fuse anyway. "Damn it! Why would they do that when they know that taking care of the Rogue Riders is our responsibility? That falls under our domain since they're one of us."

"Possibly because they don't think you're doing a good enough job," Mama Jamba matter-of-factly stated while tossing a passport onto the coffee table and continuing to sort through the box's contents.

"That's not appreciated," Hiker snapped.

Mother Nature shrugged. "I didn't say that was my opinion. I think you're doing a fine job, son. I simply said that could be what the Council thinks."

"Well, it's a fragile matter, and I've had to act conservatively," Hiker explained, strangely sounding like he was defending himself. "I hoped to give Versalee and the Rogue Riders enough rope to hang themselves. Then they'd come groveling to us, realizing that as new dragonriders, they don't know a damn thing."

"I think that was an excellent plan, son." Mama Jamba tossed another passport on the table.

"But..." Hiker's voice trailed off.

"It sounds like it's time for a different approach," Mama Jamba continued and tossed another passport onto the coffee table.

Sophia eyed them and took a bite of her sausage roll.

Hiker spun to face them. "Sophia, you should have destroyed the Rogue Riders in Las Vegas."

She furiously chewed, covering her mouth. "Sir, you told me to send a strong message. A warning, and not to cause any unnecessary damage and avoid violence if possible."

He threw up his hands. "You see where that got us. I learned this the hard way with Thad. I thought I was giving him a chance to change his ways, but we can't expect demon dragonriders to act in a civilized way."

"I don't know," Mama Jamba said in a sing-song voice.

He whipped around to face her, his eyes connecting with the stack of passports and her. "What's that mean?"

"Well, in my experience—"

"Which is as vast as the history of this planet," Hiker interrupted.

Mama Jamba batted her eyes at him. "Well, I don't like to brag, but yes. Anyway, in my experience, it all comes down to leadership. Think of a naughty child. Under the direction of a neglectful parent, they act out even more and cause all sorts of mischief. Under the guidance of a thoughtful and caring parental figure, they learn to curb their urges."

"Although the lecture on parenting is fascinating, I'm dealing with real problems here," Hiker complained.

"Under Versalee's leadership," Mama Jamba continued subtly, "the Rogue Riders are indulging everyone's whims. They're untrained, unwilling to learn, boastful, and downright bullies."

"Of course," Hiker said, as though all of this suddenly made sense to him. "It always comes down to leadership. Cut off the head of the monster. Versalee is an obvious problem, but so is that demon dragonrider you met in Las Vegas. What was his name?" Hiker glanced at Sophia, who had attempted to take another bite.

Through a mouthful, she said, "Nathaniel."

He nodded. "Yes, he's obviously running the show there, and it sounds like he didn't heed your warnings if there were still issues happening with magicians. I can't say I blame the Council for being concerned, but they really should have consulted with us first.

Sending one of their Warriors in there only complicates matters more."

"Or maybe it's exactly what you needed to happen," Mama Jamba offered and put another passport from the box on the stack on the table.

Hiker arched a curious eyebrow at her. "Go on, then."

"Well, things sometimes have to accelerate before they can come to a swift halt," Mama Jamba explained while opening one of the passports and looking through it. "Sophia and the others intervened in Las Vegas, but it appears that the Rogue Riders didn't listen. Otherwise, they wouldn't have taken a Warrior. Who knows what else they're up to?"

"I've been trying to track them down," Sophia interrupted.

Mama Jamba nodded. "Now you have more motivation. Before, you suspected they were up to something. Now you know. Plus, they've given you a reason to take more decisive action. A villain who simply looks at you wrong is tempting you. One who throws a punch is asking for you to put them down."

Hiker blinked at Mama Jamba with surprise. "I've never heard you talk like this. Are you encouraging us to kill other dragonriders? I thought we were trying to stop history from repeating itself."

Mama Jamba thumbed through another passport casually. "I'm telling you that you might have to cut off the head of this monster so that a new one can grow. Sometimes evolution requires a death or two. Your job will be to create that evolution while also not repeating history. Take out the leadership. That's my advice. Try not to take out their army, or I'm certain they'll take out yours too."

Hiker glanced at Sophia, a solemn look on his face. Mama Jamba hardly ever gave advice, and they both knew it. Her words had been pretty clear. If they took out the demon dragonriders, they'd lose the new ones they'd acquired. Their mission had to be to get rid of the leadership and restart the Rogue Riders. That was the only way to keep the peace between the dragonriders and therefore the world.

"Do you think you can track down this Warrior and rescue her?" Hiker asked Sophia.

She eyed her last bite of the sausage roll and nodded. "Yes. Then we can work on reorganizing the structure of the Rogue Riders. I'll find out what I can about what's happening in Las Vegas."

"If you find yourself in that city again, don't drink the water," Mama Jamba offered out of the blue. "It isn't right there."

Hiker glanced sideways at the old woman. "What's with all the passports? Are those all yours?"

"Who else would they belong to?" Mama Jamba asked him.

"If you don't mind me asking," Sophia began. "Why do you need those? You're...well, Mother Nature."

She laughed good-naturally. "You try telling a TSA agent that. I've spent more than a few nights detained by the authorities, foolishly thinking that my children would simply recognize me and grant me access."

CHAPTER SIXTY

"Mooooo!" Lunis called over his shoulder as Sophia approached on the Expanse.

"Are you mooing at me?" she asked her dragon, a mock look of offense on her face.

He shook his head and indicated behind her. "No, I'm mooing at Bell and implying that she's a big fat cow."

Sophia glanced over her shoulder to find the red dragon lounging in the distance, her eyes closed, but Sophia suspected she was only pretending to sleep.

"I think you're more than implying at this point." Sophia turned back.

"Well, I'm only trying to motivate her to take care of herself," Lunis explained. "It's because I care and don't like seeing her let herself go. That's what real friends do. The elders are enabling you, Fatty!" He said the last part loudly in Bell's direction.

"I think she's fine," Sophia stated.

"She doesn't move," Lunis argued. "I saw a sheep outrun her yesterday."

Sophia couldn't help but laugh. "Well, she doesn't get out as much as you and the other dragons since Hiker sticks around here."

"Not an excuse," Lunis said smugly. "She could fly around the Gullington or play with the dragonettes. That way they'd leave me alone!" Lunis said the last part in Bell's direction again.

"Where are all the dragonettes?" Sophia looked around.

Lunis shrugged. "Someone might have told them that the first one to bring me a black sheep from the northern hills of the Gullington got a prize."

Sophia arched an eyebrow at him. "I didn't think there were any black sheep here. I've never seen any if there are."

A sly grin spread on Lunis' face. "There are none in the northern hills because there's a magnetic field up there that causes disorientation. Mahkah advised me early on not to fly there because I'd get lost."

"Oh, but he hasn't told the dragonettes that yet?"

Lunis lowered his head, a guilty expression in his eyes that he tried to hide. "He left that job up to me."

"You..." Sophia shook her head at her dragon. "So you're tricking the dragonettes. Making fun of the oldest dragon on Earth. Anything else you're doing to avoid contributing to the Dragon Elite?"

"I drank a bottle of whisky that Evan thought he'd successfully stashed in the Nest," Lunis stated.

Sophia pursed her lips. "I think you helped us out there. Yeah, I knew he snuck away there to drink when we're supposed to be 'training.'"

Lunis stretched before lying down on the grass. "Now I'm going to take a nap and enjoy my buzz before the angel dragons return with newbie riders."

Sophia glanced out to the edge of the Expanse where the Barrier was. "Do you expect them to return soon?"

He nodded. "I suspect as much. So get ready for some freshmen."

"Things are quickly changing, aren't they?" Sophia asked, excited for new riders and nervous. It was good that their numbers were growing for many reasons, but the most important one was that she suspected they would need more riders to defeat Versalee and Nathaniel swiftly. Hopefully, it wouldn't come to that, but she didn't have a lot of hope at this point. Not with the Trudy situation.

"They are, but that's life. It's the way of life. Those who resist die. Those who avoid it find pain." Lunis slipped into his sage-like voice, then lifted his head and glared at Bell. "And those who lay on their butts get fat."

Sophia covered her giggle. "Isn't that what you're doing?"

He nodded. "I'm going to get up after a while and run around Bell so that she remembers what the movement looks like." Lunis grinned at the elder dragon, who had one eye peeked open now. "I'll even reteach you how to fly. It's like riding a bike. But if you fall it hurts a whole lot more."

"Well, good luck with that," Sophia stated. "Rest up. I think I'm going to need your help soon on a mission to rescue a Warrior for the House of Fourteen."

"Oh, good!" Lunis chirped. "Liv got herself abducted. Dreams do come true. I can't help. I'm real, real busy."

Sophia shook her head. "It's not Liv. It's Trudy DeVries."

Lunis looked at his wrist as if he wore a watch. "Oh, look at that. My schedule has cleared up, and I can help."

"I'm going to try not to be offended at your insensitivity that my sister could have been in danger."

He shrugged, stretching out. "It would be better if you did get offended. Get those feathers ruffled a little, you know. It's good for you."

Sophia shook her head and ambled back toward the Castle. "See you later, Lun. Try and behave yourself."

"No," he spat at once. "Also…"

Sophia glanced over her shoulder at him. "What?"

"I knew it wasn't Liv," he stated. "She's way too skilled to get herself abducted. Yes, I'll be ready to help."

CHAPTER SIXTY-ONE

S ophia knew it wasn't that Trudy DeVries wasn't skilled. She had been a Warrior for much longer than Liv. However, the Rogue Riders shouldn't be underestimated. They were dragonriders after all, even if they were new and untrained. Dragons only magnetized to highly skilled magicians. The Dragon Elite already knew that the Rogue Riders didn't fight fair and there were a lot of them and only one of Trudy. Somehow they caught her. Hopefully, the Dragon Elite could rescue her before something happened to her.

First, Sophia needed more information. That's why she had gone to Roya Lane after planning a meeting with Liv.

When Sophia entered the Fantastical Armory the smell of corned beef and sauerkraut was strong in the air. Subner sat in his usual spot, opening his mouth wide to stuff a Reuben sandwich into it.

Liv grimaced, looking green as she waved her hand in front of her on the far side of the shop. "Do you have to eat that in here?"

Subner took his time chewing and finally replied, "Well, it's my shop, so yes."

Liv's eyes fluttered with annoyance as she glanced at Papa Creola, who was right next to her. "I've never seen that man eat in this shop, but he finds out that I have morning sickness and brings in the smelliest food he can find."

"I could have brought in something smellier," Subner retorted. "I happened to be in the mood for a Reuben with extra sauerkraut."

"What's on the menu tomorrow?" Liv narrowed her eyes at the Protector of Weapons. "Anchovies? Maybe some durian? Or surstromming?"

"Why not all three?" Subner took another bite.

Papa Creola gave Liv a sympathetic expression. "The morning sickness will hopefully pass soon, and you'll feel better."

Subner dropped the sandwich on the wrapper it came in and rolled his eyes. "Maybe. Or maybe you'll be one of those pregnant people who is sick through to the third trimester. It might get worse."

Liv shot him a murderous glare. "Why are you so cheerful all the time? Your optimism is overwhelming."

Shaking his head, Papa Creola patted Liv's hand resting on the counter. She seemed to be bracing herself, as though she might run to the restroom at any moment. "I'm sure this will pass. Let's see if Bep can make you a potion that helps."

Subner's face pinched with evident frustration. He wrapped up the sandwich, but only loosely, and dropped it into the waste bin next to him, glaring at Liv the entire time.

"Oh, so you craved a Rueben, did you?" she fired. "That's why you took two bites and now will let it stink up the place for the remainder of my visit?"

"Again, my shop, my rules," Subner replied. "If you don't like it, you can leave."

"I would, but I was waiting for Sophia." Liv finally directed her attention to the door where Sophia stood, quietly watching the strange exchange. The tension between Liv and Subner was palpable.

"Well, she's here so you can leave, can't you?" Subner unraveled a mint and popped it into his mouth.

Unhurried, Liv brought her chin around to look at Papa Creola. "Do you have anything else for me before I go? We're going to try and find information on what's happening in Las Vegas."

"That's the chief priority," Papa Creola stated. "As soon as you hear from Renswick, I want to know about the status of the baby, whether it's a demon or not."

"Either way it's going to be insufferable," Subner mumbled.

Liv shot him another angry look. "Well, maybe you can give him or her lessons on how to cope then."

"I don't like people and don't care if they like me," Subner fired back, shooting dagger-like looks at her.

"Oh good," Liv said with mock relief. "Here I was worried that you didn't know we all can't stand you."

"I messaged Rudolf on my way over," Sophia interrupted, trying to interject extra positivity into her tone. "He's at the Crying Cat Bakery. You want to head over now, Liv?"

Without taking her gaze off Subner, she grabbed her cloak off the counter and slipped it on. "Yeah, let's go. I could use a cookie."

"Try not to become fat," Subner called as she headed for the door. "As a magician, you're not immune to gestational diabetes."

"Try not to die of a heart attack from eating that Reuben," Liv sang back, ushering Sophia out the door. "As a pain in the ass, you're not immune from death."

"Actually, as the Protector of Weapons, I am." Subner had to have the last word in the argument. "Don't worry. I won't attend your funeral."

CHAPTER SIXTY-TWO

"What the fork was that about?" Sophia asked when they were out on Roya Lane, the skies gray and the air brisk.

Liv shook her head, sighing. "Methinks that Subner is a little jealous. He's had Papa Creola's attention since the beginning. Then I came along and started working for him. He's never liked me much, but he doesn't like anyone, as he admitted. Then I made it that much worse by being awesome and whittling down Papa's tough exterior, making him sort of like me."

"Now there's a baby to add to the mix," Sophia guessed.

"Yep." Liv popped her lips. "Poor little Subner probably thinks the baby will come along and steal his attention away even more."

"That will never happen," Sophia stated. "He's Papa Creola's assistant and always has been."

Liv grinned. "The baby is totally going to steal attention away from that grumpy old man. He or she or demon or whatever is already."

Sophia nodded. "Yeah, I've never seen Papa Creola dote on you the way he was a minute ago."

"Exactly," Liv chirped. "I think a new baby is making him a little sentimental. Nothing like new life to remind the oldest being of why they created time in the first place."

"I'm sure that's a fascinating story," Sophia mused.

Liv nodded. "It involved a really strange conversation with Mother Nature and stardust that has hallucinatory effects. Bam, that's how babies are made."

Sophia laughed. "I don't think so. Hopefully, poor Subner will come around eventually."

"Subner has never come around," Liv argued as they turned the corner, heading toward the Crying Cat Bakery. "I think it's safe to assume that he'll be as consistent as time with his stubborn crankiness."

"Are you feeling better?" Sophia noticed that some of Liv's color had returned.

She nodded and lifted her chin. "The fresh air helps. A cookie will too."

"I don't think you should eat anything from this bakery when you're pregnant, or otherwise either," Sophia advised. "I know all too well that the ingredients are suspect and never what you'd expect."

"Sounds like Clark's cooking."

Sophia laughed while pulling open the door to the bakery and holding it for Liv. Her sister lowered her chin and gave her an irritated expression.

"Don't you start doting too."

Sophia shook her head. "I want you to go in first to deal with whatever charades are happening in there. The last time I came in here, I had a knife thrown at my head."

Liv proudly nodded. "I respect your reasoning. I throw knives when guests enter my place too."

CHAPTER SIXTY-THREE

Lee was shaking her head at King Rudolf when they entered the bakery. She leaned back and crossed her arms over her chest. "Nope. Nope. Nope. I refuse to help hippie elves."

Rudolf sighed. "It doesn't matter who they are. They're paying customers and have an algae problem on one of the South Pacific islands."

"Well, then they should try showering regularly," Lee stated. "That's what they get for being dirty hippies."

Rudolf scratched his head, the confused expression he wore so often springing to his face. "I don't think the algae grew because they don't shower enough. It's their drinking water. Apparently, it has strange effects on them and makes them more docile."

"Now I'm really not doing it," Lee affirmed. "Docile hippies are an improvement. They'll be less likely to go on about their essential oils and crystals."

The king of the fae grew slightly more irritated. "You can't turn away business because you don't like someone. If that were the case, I wouldn't sell Heals Pills to half the ugly magicians who come into the store, but I hope they take the elixir and it fixes their bad attitude as well as their homely faces."

"I agree with Lee on not helping the hippie elves," Liv stated, gaining both their attentions. "Maybe we poison their water some more instead of fixing it."

Rudolf sighed and looked at Sophia. "Help me out. Your boyfriend is a hippie. You have some sympathy for them."

Sophia shook her head. "He's not a hippie. He's a dragonrider."

"He's a hippie," Liv argued.

Sophia swung around to face her sister. "No, he's not."

"His name is Wilder," Rudolf argued.

"He's a vegan," Liv added.

"I bet he prefers living away from people, knows all the latest music, suffers from wanderlust, and he walks around barefoot all the time."

Sophia grunted in frustration. "Wilder doesn't walk around barefoot."

"But he does all the other things," Rudolf said victoriously.

"I'm staying out of this discussion anyway," Sophia stated. "We're here to get information on what's going on in Las Vegas."

"I'm happy to help you, but first I have to take a phone call." Rudolf pulled out his phone and stuck it to his ear.

"It's not ringing, King Dork-Face," Liv pointed out, indicating the phone.

"No, it isn't, but my spidey senses tell me that it will be." Rudolf held up the device. As he predicted, the phone rang a second later.

"Were you expecting a call?" Liv asked.

He shook his head. "No, but recently I had some dental work done, and the filling in my molar vibrates when my phone is about to ring."

"What kind of dentist did you go to?" Sophia asked.

He frowned at her. "Dentist? I didn't go to one. I used a spell when I was at the Apple store."

Liv rolled her eyes. "Well, there you go, Mr. Dimwit."

Rudolf held up his finger as the phone rang in his hands. "No, no, no. That's King Dimwit, remember?"

Before Liv could reply, he answered the phone while striding for the opposite corner of the bakery.

"Why do I ask that man questions?" Liv shook her head.

"Why does he get cavities?" Lee questioned. "He's a fae with access to a magical elixir."

"I've never brushed my teeth," Rudolf called from the other side of the bakery, obviously have overhead them. "Ever," he added.

Sophia shivered. "Gross."

Liv shrugged. "Not really. For as repulsive as that man is, the fae always smell great. They don't have bad breath, bad hair days, or bad body odor. It appears their luck does run out and they can get a cavity."

"After six hundred years," Rudolf added, still on the phone.

"Speaking of getting cavities," Sophia began, speaking to Lee. "I need you to make a cake."

"What's it for?" Lee questioned with a skeptical expression.

"Christmas," Sophia answered.

"What flavor?" Lee asked.

"Oreo."

Lee nodded. "Who's it for?"

"My dragon."

Lee pulled a piece of paper from a stack on the table where she sat and sketched something. Sophia thought it was a design for the cake, but then the assassin baker turned the note around and in bubbly letters was the word, "Nope."

"What do you mean, nope?" Sophia asked.

"None of those things exist," Lee answered. "So there's no way I'm making that cake."

"Ummm, Christmas, Oreos, and dragons are all real things," Sophia argued.

Liv tapped her boot, looking amused. "I'm with Lee on the dragon thing. I think Phillip is a big dog in a suit."

"His name is Lunis," Sophia muttered, irritated. "He's a real dragon."

"Christmas was invented by the gnomes when they tried to pull off a hoax that they worked for that bogus Santa character," Lee explained matter-of-factly. "They were trying to make us all believe that they could take most of the year off to make toys, but we figured them out. They were sleeping in their dumb caves and living off government subsidies."

"Makes sense," Liv stated. "And Oreos?"

"Those are real cookies," Lee argued. "There was this whole thing with fairies. They were supposed to be trying to help the gnomes make fake snow for their pretend Santa's Village, and they made an overabundance of that cream filling. Once the gnomes were caught, the fake snow had to be cleared out so some smarty decided to put it between two chocolate wafers and sell it as cookies since it's sweet."

"So then it's a cookie?" Sophia questioned.

"Sure," Lee answered. "But it's also fairy-made fake snow that used to cover a mountaintop, so eat it at your own risk."

"I wasn't going to," Sophia stated. "I wanted you to make an Oreo cake for Lunis for Christmas. Something huge that has to be delivered on a forklift. I know him well enough to know he wants something he can smash and eat for Christmas."

"He and I aren't so different," Liv observed.

"Yeah, I guess I can make that for you," Lee stated. "You want it by when?"

"Christmas," Sophia answered flatly.

"Which is…" Lee began sketching on the pad of paper again.

"December twenty-fifth," Sophia stated, her tone growing irritated.

"Of what year?" Lee continued to draw on the pad.

"This one," Sophia quipped.

"Every year, I'm thinking," Liv added.

"One final question." Lee looked up with a serious expression. "Do you think chainsaws can cut through bone?"

"What does that have to do with my cake?" Sophia asked.

"I would think they could," Liv mused, answering the question thoughtfully. "I mean, they can cut through a tree, so why not bones?"

Lee nodded. "Yeah, but some races' bones tend to be a little denser."

"True," Liv chirped. "Like, I'd assume that a fae's head is mostly skull with a very, very tiny brain."

"Speaking of tiny brains," Rudolf sang, striding back over. "I'm back and ready to help. Where were we?"

"You were going to give us an update on what's happening in Las Vegas," Sophia answered.

Rudolf nodded, rocked back on his heels, then forward. "Right. I'm happy to help. The update is that I have zero ideas what's happening in Las Vegas because I don't live there anymore."

CHAPTER SIXTY-FOUR

"You what?" Liv asked, shocked. "Las Vegas is where the fae kingdom is."

"It was," Rudolf corrected. "This is the twenty-first century. We don't need a physical location anymore. The overhead is astronomical, and it gives all my citizens a way to find me."

Liv lowered her chin. "You're their king."

He nodded. "I know, but they always have so many problems, and I think I'm enabling them. 'King Rudolf Sweetwater, I lost all my money on blackjack. Help me.' 'King Rudolf Sweetwater, I have a drinking problem.' 'King Rudolf Sweetwater, the schools are awful.'"

"Those sound like real problems that you should help the fae with," Sophia argued.

"Fae?" Rudolf questioned. "Oh, no. Those are the Captains. They complain incessantly. Captain Morgan drinks juice all day and then has to pee-pee all night. Captain Kirk doesn't get how blackjack works. I think that is because Captain Silver is correct and the schools are awful."

"Your children are strangely advanced for being so young," Liv observed and added, "well, and also for being yours."

"Well, the fae part of them is advanced," Rudolf stated. "We mature quickly and abruptly plateau."

"And immediately regress," Liv stated.

"Why, thank you." Rudolf grinned broadly. "Anyway, the fae always complain too. Stuff about the gambling, prostitution, and drugs that are so rampant in Las Vegas. It got me thinking."

"That you should clean up the city and put some restrictions in place?" Lee guessed.

Rudolf gave her a look of surprise. "Heavens no. It made me realize that it was a horrible place to raise children. So I moved Serena and the Captains up to Canada where everyone is nice, and they never do anything because it's too cold to go outside. Oh, and healthcare is free, but we don't use it."

"Because you have Heals Pills," Liv suggested.

Sophia shook her head. "No, because he does his dentistry in the Apple store."

"Exactly," Rudolf stated. "So, as you can see, I don't know what's happening in Las Vegas. It really is full of the very worst."

"It's mostly fae," Liv imparted.

"We're the worst," Rudolf agreed. "I decided to leave the life I used to know and love behind and pursue other efforts. I have Heals Pills and the water purification business with Lee. Oh, and Rory and I are going to work on a literacy program to help teach impoverished societies how to read."

"Wow," Liv said, impressed and surprised. "You're becoming a good person."

He nodded arrogantly. "I am. I'm one of the best people ever to live."

"And so very humble too," Sophia said dryly.

"Regardless, I'm proud of you, Ru," Liv stated. "You're making the world a better place despite all the horrible things you've done for centuries."

"It's true," he agreed. "I'm making magicians not so repugnant-looking. I'm making tons of money off communities desperate to have clean water and willing to pay any price for it. And I'm undercutting

Lee on the whole thing because she's not smart enough to look at the bookkeeping."

"Standing right here," Lee said absentmindedly, still sketching on the pad of paper.

"The book that is the basis for our literary program is my autobiography, *Somehow I Rule the World*," Rudolf explained. "It's six hundred and twenty pages of fun facts about all the awesome things I've done."

"I sort of want to read this," Liv stated.

"Me too," Sophia agreed. "The problem remains that we don't know what's happening in Las Vegas now."

"I will tell you," Rudolf began. "Those awful jerks on giant lizards were running a lot of underground operations when I left. The city had gone to hell so I was happy to leave it behind. Who knows who is running the place now?"

Sophia lowered her chin and regarded the king of the fae with hooded eyes. "The Rogue Riders are running it."

"Good!" Rudolf exclaimed. "Let them drink the stale water in that place, and their children suffer from all the bad influences. Not I though. Nor Serena or the Captains."

"They're going to take over and turn it into the debauchery headquarters," Sophia said, irritation heavy in her voice.

Liv nodded. "This does us little to figure out where to look for Trudy."

"I think I can research another lead on that one." Sophia chewed on her lip.

"Good," Liv stated with relief as Rory the giant entered the Crying Cat Bakery, having to duck to clear the door.

"Oh, good." Rudolf clapped. "You're here for our meeting."

Rory nodded and pushed his curly brown hair out of his face. He nodded politely to the others, the usual no-nonsense expression on his face. When his eyes connected with Liv, his gaze dropped to her midsection. His mouth popped open. Eyes widened.

"What?" He sounded surprised. "Why didn't you tell me that you're pregnant?"

CHAPTER SIXTY-FIVE

"Pregnant?" Rudolf exclaimed.

Lee straightened.

Liv slumped.

Sophia simply watched.

"Well, now the secret's out," Liv muttered.

"How could you tell?" Rudolf looked between Rory and Liv. "Is it because she's looking chubby?"

Liv's eyes widened in horror. "I haven't gained a pound yet. If anything, I'm losing weight from the morning sickness."

Rudolf tilted his head to the side. "Are you sure? You're looking kind of bloated."

"Thanks," Liv said dryly.

"I can tell because it's obvious," Rory stated matter-of-factly.

"For weird giants who can see things the rest of us can't," Liv mumbled.

"So who's the father?" Rudolf asked quite seriously.

Liv rolled her eyes. "My husband. Stefan."

Giving her a look of disbelief, Rudolf said, "Oh, are you two still together? I thought he dumped you for a fat gnome when he fell off the bandwagon from his drug addiction."

"None of that happened," Liv stated dryly.

"Oh, well, that's my prediction anyway," Rudolf sang happily. "Anyway, congrats. I'm so excited I'm going to be a godfather."

"You aren't," Liv said flatly.

"I want my godchild named Skye or Blue or..." Rudolf gasped. "We're naming it Blue Skye. That will be a remarkable name for the child, even if it's as ugly as its parents."

Liv nodded. "I don't even know where to begin with you, so let's just go with sure. That all sounds great. You're the godfather. The child's name is Blue Skye, and you're the smartest person in the world. All of those statements are facts, or none of them are."

"Okay, I'll draw up the documents for you to sign," Rudolf said cheerfully, striding for the door. He turned once he'd swung it open and grinned. "I'm going to include a clause about how I get to cut the umbilical cord. Oh, and Serena has a breast pump you can borrow. The Captains can babysit when we go on dates with your new husband."

"No, no, and what the hell?" Liv shook her head. "Stefan is my only husband."

Rudolf shook his head, clicking his tongue. He looked directly at Sophia. "Will you please help your sister realize that she can do better than a womanizing drunk who thieves and gambles nonstop?"

"He's a brave Warrior for the House of Fourteen who keeps the magical world safe," Sophia argued.

Rudolf shook his head, looking disappointed. "He's put his little spell on you too. Don't worry. I'll take you both in when you finally wake up to reality. You can live with us in Canada. We do nothing all day because...well, there's nothing to do. It's boring. Please move in."

"Please leave." Liv glanced at Rory, who grew increasingly stressed, his eyes teeming with tension.

"Okay, I'll go draft a contract for you to sign," Rudolf sang.

"I won't," Liv replied as he left.

"Well, congrats. That's wonderful that you're breeding. Hope your offspring is healthy, happy, blah, blah, blah." Lee strode forward and pushed on Liv's shoulder as the door swung shut.

"Looks like it's time for you to leave and not come back for nine months."

Liv gave the baker assassin a quizzical expression. "What's the deal, Lee?"

She exhaled. "It's bad for business to have pregnant women in the bakery. You all tend to buy a ton of baked goods, especially the No-Nausea Nutella Crepes."

"Those sound like exactly what I need," Liv said excitedly. "I'll take a half- dozen."

Lee's hands reached into the air. "Noooo. That's what I'm saying. Pregnant women are the bane of my existence."

"Because?" Sophia asked.

"Because they buy all the pastries. Then I have to bake more, and that's annoying," Lee answered.

"You run a bakery. Don't you want to sell out of your inventory each day?" Liv asked.

"She doesn't," Sophia answered for her, having had this conversation with the assassin baker before. "She wants to do the bare minimum of work. The bakery is more of a cover than a real business."

"For?" Liv pretended not to know.

"For money laundering," Lee said, an edge of doubt in her voice as though she was pretty sure that wasn't going to fly.

Liv tilted her head. "Try again."

"It's a tax write-off," Lee stated. "I've been defrauding the government on taxes for decades. I owe bazillions."

Liv shook her head. "Nope. Try one more time."

"I murder people," Lee admitted. "Horrible, awful, waste-of-space people, and I put them in the baked goods. Only the best parts and I ensure they provide magical advantages."

Liv smiled victoriously. "Now, was that so hard?"

"Not really," Lee admitted. "It felt good. Now get out." She pointed at the door.

"I won't buy all your pastries." Liv held up her hands in surrender. "I do want some of those crepes."

"You did hear the part about how there are dead people in the baked goods, right?" Rory whispered to Liv.

She nodded. "Bad people. I'll eat a villain all day. At least then they go to good use."

"Fine." Lee trotted toward the back of the bakery. "You can have a few crepes, but nothing else after that. I don't want to restock the case today...or tomorrow...well, really anytime this week. I have plans."

"By plans, do you mean you're killing people?" Liv asked.

"Yes...I mean no..." Lee shook her head. "This honesty thing is weird."

When Lee had disappeared in the back, Rory swung around to face Liv, a super-serious expression on his face. "You're in danger. If you're pregnant, there's a chance the baby has Stefan's demon blood."

Sophia drew in a breath. So Rory knew about Stefan. It wasn't common knowledge since it would make many leery of the Warrior. There weren't any other magicians who had survived a demon's bite, and most would worry that he'd turn, but Renswick had been able to create the antidote.

"I know," Liv said in a hushed voice. "I'm working on it though. We're going to find out if the baby has demon blood. If he or she does, then we're going to recover a genie lamp from the bottom of the ocean. Make a wish. Toss the lamp back in the water, then have a baby shower...well, after a real shower, of course. I hear genies are disgusting."

"How?" Rory growled.

"How am I showering?" Liv asked. "That's a bit personal. I don't ask you how you floss with those huge hands. Really, how do you get into all those hard to reach places? Your knuckles are gigantic."

"How are you going to get the genie's lamp?" Rory asked.

"Oh." Liv blinked. "Well, Sophia has a method."

She nodded. "Yeah, I know a dragon that can dive deep in the ocean. The rider has agreed to help."

"I have a better method," Rory stated matter-of-factly. "My mum has a magical creature that will be easy and possibly more efficient."

"The only drawback is that I have to talk to Bermuda Laurens, who hates my guts," Liv said with a sigh.

"She doesn't hate you," Rory argued.

"Strongly prefers not to look at my face," Liv corrected.

He shook his head. "She's not good at showing her affections."

"Yet you learned how to stop that family trait," Liv teased.

The giant rolled his eyes. "When you find out about the baby, if you need to recover the genie's lamp, go see mum. She'll help."

"Well, hopefully, we don't have to, and everything is fine." Liv interjected fake positivity in her voice.

Rory nodded. "I hope so, but prepare for the worst and hope for the best."

"That's pretty much my motto in life," Liv imparted. "That and make all the bad guys die painfully slow."

"You're not still working are you?" Rory said in a rush.

"Of course I am." Liv looked offended.

"You can't," Rory argued. "You're pregnant. What if you get hit or several other things? The villains you face won't know, and they might not take it easy on you."

Liv laughed. "Tell me about it. The troll I fought this morning didn't seem to care that I was hella nauseous."

"Liv…" Rory said, a warning in his tone.

"Rory," she replied, a similar edge in her voice. "I'm not going to put on a bathrobe and not do anything for the next nine months. I'm pregnant. So what? The baby will be fine, whether it's a demon or not. Same goes for whether I work." She indicated Sophia and her. "Our mother worked as a Warrior through all of her pregnancies."

"Your mother is dead," Rory argued, shaking his head.

"Because of her, the world is better," Liv stated with determination. "Mortals can see magic again because of what she started. The magical world is healing. Yes, our family suffered, but I won't forget that she sacrificed her safety for a reason. I get why. She couldn't simply sit and watch the world suffer. She knew that she risked everything by working, but if she didn't, her children wouldn't have a future. My child won't either unless I get up every morning and fight, the way I have since I started as a Warrior for the House of Fourteen."

He considered this and finally nodded. "Promise me that you'll be careful."

"I promise," Liv said with a wide smile. "Now will you tell me the easiest way to subdue a rabid magical anaconda that's loose in the sewers under New York?"

Rory's eyes closed for a half-beat. "Please tell me you're joking."

Liv winked at Sophia. "Of course I am. The anaconda is loose in the Hudson River."

CHAPTER SIXTY-SIX

Sophia smiled at Pricilla after crawling through the small door into the Official Brownie headquarters. She was the receptionist for the office, a mother, and Mortimer's wife. It appeared her talents weren't limited to that. The Brownie was currently wrapping up chocolate truffles covered in cocoa powder and expertly decorated with little holly leaves and snowflakes.

There were thousands of truffles all over the office. So many that the surface of Pricilla's desk was unseen. Bits of colorful papers were stacked all around the space, and the Brownie's head was barely visible over the boxes filled with wrapped candies.

"Hey there." Sophia stood, but not all the way, or else she'd hit her head. "You look busy."

The receptionist smiled, her fingers working double-time to cover a truffle, tie it with a bow, and toss it in a nearby box. "I'm on break."

Sophia blinked at the small elf, expecting her to say, "Just kidding." When she didn't, she eyed the stack of chocolate that filled the air with a sweet aroma. "Well, I see that you know how to relax about as well as I do."

Pricilla laughed. "These are the Christmas treats for mortals who have been especially good this year. Wrapping them up is a real privilege. Well, and…" she leaned forward and whispered, "a perk of being married to the boss."

"Oh, well, what a fun surprise for them." Sophia giggled at the notion that doing more work was considered a privilege. Brownies were the best creatures on the planet. "Where do they think the candy came from?"

Pricilla giggled. "They always make up a reasonable explanation, such as an anonymous friend left it, or they bought it and forgot. Something innocent that they believe without a second thought."

Sophia nodded. "I guess these same people are used to waking up to a clean house and chores done that they didn't do, so maybe they aren't in the habit of questioning things."

"They are excellent mortals, and in being so, they work extremely hard," Pricilla explained. "Most pass out at the end of the day after working nonstop, tucking in their children, and helping a friend. Usually in the morning, upon finding the laundry pressed and folded and the dishes cleaned and put away, they imagine that they did it and simply forgot in their tiredness."

"Wow, it seems you all take care of the best mortals."

Pricilla smiled wide, showing her large square teeth. "We do. They're very deserving."

"I'm sure they'd be grateful for your help, if only they knew about it." Sophia winked.

The Brownie blushed. "Well, we do it because they should be rewarded and for no other reason." She pointed at the back. "Now, on the other hand, there are the not-so-well-behaved mortals, and I believe Mortimer was working on that list for you."

Sophia nodded. "Thank you. I'll go and visit him now."

Pricilla held up a little trinket of chocolate. "First, you must take one of these."

"Oh, I can't do that." Sophia shook her head. "I'm not a well-behaved mortal."

"You're better in my opinion," Pricilla whispered, leaning forward again. "Because of what you do selflessly and usually without credit, those mortals we reward can go about their lives, safe on a happy planet. If anyone deserves our help and treats, it's you. That's why Mortimer and I are always happy to assist."

How could Sophia argue with that? The truth was that she couldn't. She was hungry, not having gotten a cookie at the Crying Cat Bakery because...well, it was probably poisoned. She took the offered treat and smiled. "Well, thank you. I'm sure this will be delicious."

"I made them last night," Pricilla said proudly.

"If the Brownies take care of the hardworking mortals, I want to know who takes care of you all." Sophia winked.

As Mortimer told Sophia during their last conversation, Pricilla said, "We all take care of each other. That's the way it should be."

Sophia smiled, not adding anything because she couldn't agree more. In the ideal world, the magical races and mortals would all look out for one another—a perfectly reciprocal process.

CHAPTER SIXTY-SEVEN

"Sophia Beaufont, rider for the Dragon Elite," Mortimer said when she entered his office. The Brownie was leaning back in his chair, his hands behind his head.

Sitting on the desk in front of him was a large stack of paper. Like the chocolates and wrapping and boxes in the receptionist area in front of Pricilla, it nearly obstructed Mortimer.

She smiled at him and nodded. "How are you? Are things better with the union?"

He toggled his head back and forth. "They go back and forth. Again, you do your job and let me help you. In time, we'll win this battle."

Sophia nodded. "I hope you're right."

"It's what my instinct advises me," Mortimer stated. "Now, you asked for a list of all the criminals so you could stop bad guys and therefore make good guys' lives better. Or at least, that's how I'll position it when I give the full report to the union—after you save the day." He patted the stack of paper. "Here we have a list of every mortal that's regularly breaking the law. I used a complex equation that's different than our usual one."

Sophia tensed, guilt prickling her throat. She had to make a separate request of Mortimer based on new information, and that instantly filled her with remorse. "Oh, I hope it wasn't too much work."

"Not at all." He shook his head. "For Sophia Beaufont, rider for the Dragon Elite, it is never too much work."

"That's a relief." Sophia sighed.

"I simply had to throw out the qualifying criteria I use for finding good mortals," Mortimer began. "I didn't want to home in on those who sometimes break the law. We don't cater to those types, but they also didn't seem like the ones you were looking for. From what I understand, you needed criminals who regularly broke laws and profited from their dealings."

Sophia nodded. "Correct. Not people who speed or skimp on their taxes or take too many napkins at a restaurant."

He pursed his lips. "Yes, not mortals we'd serve, but also not bad ones either. Merely the middle range. So I therefore put my attention on finding mortals who were always breaking laws—ones who had their business centered around illegal activity." Mortimer slapped the stack of paper and grinned. "I've come up with a list here."

Sophia tilted her head, unsure if the stack was too small or too large, considering how many mortals she expected regularly broke the law. "That's it?"

"Yes," Mortimer chirped. "There are six thousand pages here, and the names are in eight-point font, single-spaced with four columns per sheet."

Sophia gulped.

"Oh, and the pages are double-sided," Mortimer added.

Sophia closed her eyes for a half-beat, feeling overwhelmed. "Maybe my job should be to go after every person on that list and knock them upside the head."

"I thought your job was to stop the Rogue Riders," Mortimer said, confused.

"It is," Sophia related. "I didn't realize how many criminals were out there in the mortal world. No wonder my job is never done."

Mortimer nodded, a sympathetic expression on his face. "In this instance, I get why you're focusing on criminals. However, I'll go back to my original point the last time we spoke. You can punish every bad guy, or you can reward every good guy. We Brownies prefer to do the latter. Also, you're very talented, Sophia Beaufont. I don't think your job should be to go around slapping thieves on the hand. Let the police officers do that. You're cut out for bigger things."

"Thanks." Sophia swallowed the tension in her throat. "I guess you're right. I needed this list so I can stop a big bad guy whose actions are trickling over and creating huge issues worldwide."

"Exactly!" Mortimer stuck his finger triumphantly in the air and almost immediately deflated, his eyes shrinking suddenly. "Of course, this is a large list, and tracking down all of these criminals to see if they have dealings with the Rogue Riders will take you some time. I wish there were more I could have done to help."

Sophia brightened, the guilt she'd felt moments prior receding. "Actually, there is something. I've determined where the Rogue Riders are and think if we focus on criminals in that area, I'll have an easier job."

"Oh, that is good news!" Mortimer exclaimed.

"So not too much work for you?" Sophia asked.

He shook his head. "It shouldn't be, depending on the area. Is it like before? Are they on an island in the South Pacific or some other remote location where they're keeping their dragons?"

Sophia twisted her mouth to the side. "No, they're in Las Vegas."

"Oh." Mortimer drew out the word. The lightness fell from his face.

"Is that a problem?"

He shook his head at once, his ears knocking him in the head. "No, not at all, Sophia Beaufont, rider for the Dragon Elite. Don't you worry. I can get you a list of repeat offenders in Las Vegas. It will take a little more time."

Sophia smiled, grateful. "Can you also have your Brownies look around Las Vegas for suspicious activity? While they're doing their day-to-day jobs?"

Mortimer's eyes shifted to the side. "I can, but I have to admit that we don't serve many mortals in Las Vegas. Only a few families, to be honest." He leaned forward, cupping his mouth. "If I'm honest, there aren't a lot of well-behaving mortals there. There's also a ton of very badly behaving fae."

Sophia nodded. "I figured as much. If you don't mind, that will help."

"I don't mind at all!" he yelped excitedly. "Again, helping you helps me, and that helps the world."

"Well, specifically, I'd like the Brownies to look for any prisoner who could be held by criminals or the Rogue Riders," Sophia explained. "It's a Warrior for the House of Fourteen."

"Not Liv Beaufont though?" Mortimer asked, worry springing to his tone.

She shook her head. "No, but we still need to rescue this Warrior fast so any clues you can give us for a location will be helpful."

"Of course," Mortimer said with confidence. "I'll narrow down the list of criminals in Las Vegas and assign some Brownies to do some investigating."

Sophia smiled broadly. "You really are the best, Mortimer. I don't know what I'd do without you."

He returned the gesture. "I say the same about you and your lovely sister."

CHAPTER SIXTY-EIGHT

"Here's the case of Heals Pills you asked for." Ramy, the new shopkeeper for Rudolf and Sophia, put a large box in the middle of the table at the Forever Vegan Café. He looked like he was going to pass out from the effort. He pointed over his shoulder. "There are also two more boxes, but I left them at the shop."

Sophia smiled. "Thanks. Since I have to stop by the shop anyway, you could have left this there, and I could have gotten it when I stopped by to get the rest."

Ramy waved her off, his eyes skirting to Wilder beside her with curiosity. The other dragonrider had decided to meet Sophia for a quick meal and because she'd need help carting all the Heals Pills back. Sophia had the business for many reasons, but the chief one wasn't to make money. It was to help the world. A village in Africa was suffering from a plague and Sophia thought that one of the newbie dragonriders and Evan or Mahkah or Wilder could deliver the supply. It would be good training and also a positive mission.

"I wanted to be helpful, so I brought one of the boxes," Ramy stated, sliding into the booth opposite them.

"That's not helpful because we have to cart this back," Sophia observed.

"I realized that halfway here, but turning back seemed silly especially since I hadn't had any cardio today." Ramy pulled off the backpack attached to his shoulders.

"Well, thanks for the thought and for meeting me," Sophia offered, smiling politely. She still hadn't figured out why he was the person to run Heals Pills, but she didn't doubt the advice that Mae Ling had given her. She was merely unsure about it all. "I wanted to check in with you about the shop. See how you like the job and if King Rudolf Sweetwater is treating you okay. And if there are any concerns."

Ramy looked around the place speculatively. "I don't see any movie stars daily at the shop."

Sophia nodded. "I wouldn't expect you to."

"I once thought I saw ET on Roya Lane," Wilder offered. "Then I realized it was a really ugly gnome."

Ramy grinned. "I sold that guy some of the elixir. I hope it fixes his face—and the rest of him." He offered a hand to Wilder. "I'm Ramy. And you'd be?"

"Wilder Thomson, a member of the Dragon Elite."

"You look like you could be famous. You have movie star hair," Ramy stated. "Have you been in any films?"

Wilder laughed. "Not that I'm aware of."

Ramy nodded. "Well, where do you all want to eat?"

Sophia batted her eyes at him. "Here. That's why I asked you to meet us here."

"Ohhhhh," Ramy said, obviously disappointed as he took in the bong in the corner and the many hippies chanting in the corner or discussing each other's past lives. "A vegan restaurant. I was under the impression that you made good decisions, Sophia."

She couldn't help but laugh. "I do, but Wilder here is a vegan, so I figured we could eat here. There's a variety of food."

Sophia handed Ramy a menu, which he didn't look at.

"Yeah, no thanks." He opened his backpack and pulled out several containers. "I bring my food in the event of dining with such bad decision-makers. It happens more than you'd think when hanging out with celebrities."

Wilder laughed at this. "Well, I can't stand myself, so what can I say."

"How are you doing with the shop?" Sophia glanced at the menu and found zero options that intrigued her.

"It's fun." Ramy opened a full container of various cheeses. Most of them gave off a pungent aroma. "The customers aren't prettier than me, which is nice. They all need my help instead of telling me to back up and give them space. They ask for my advice instead of asking me why I'm standing outside their showers."

Sophia nodded. "Wow, the bodyguard business is really strange."

Ramy nodded and picked up a piece of cheese.

"And that is?" Wilder pointed at the hunk of cheese.

"It's ten-thousand-year-old goat's cheese," Ramy answered. "I've been carting it around for a while, looking for the right time to eat it. This seems like the one."

"Because?" Wilder questioned, amusement bouncing around in his eyes.

"Because I haven't died in almost a week," Ramy stated.

Wilder blinked in confusion, looked at Sophia, and showed her an expression that said, "It's probably about time you explain this to me."

She smiled politely. "Right. Well, you see, Ramy can't really die."

"Easily," Ramy interrupted.

"Exactly," she continued. "He can sort of die, but he'll come back to life based on some incident he had where he fell in a fountain, one we're guessing is linked to the fountain of youth. The flip side to never being able to die, or rather, always come back from death, is that he's sort of accident-prone."

"Which isn't the case when I'm on Roya Lane." Ramy gobbled down a piece of cheese and wiped his mouth. "This has been the longest stretch I've had in a while."

"I wonder why that is," Sophia mused.

He shrugged. "Probably because I don't leave the shop much. Things remain pretty normal. I work in the store. Go home, then do it again. There aren't movie sets and crazed fans and Los Angeles traffic. It's normal stuff."

SARAH NOFFKE & MICHAEL ANDERLE

"Well, that's a relief," Sophia said. "That was going to be my next question. The person who suggested I hire you seemed to think that the shop would be in danger of sorts and therefore you were the right person for the job."

"Because I'm so very brave, right?" Ramy asked.

Sophia shook her head. "I think it was because you can't die, and that's the potential."

"I want to believe it's because I'm so brave," Ramy countered as the waitress approached.

Wilder patted the table. "No one is stopping you from believing that."

Ramy rolled his eyes with dread as the waitress wearing lots of colors and flowing fabrics approached. "It's about time, missy. We've been waiting for a while for our order to be taken."

The woman, who was probably named Rainbow or Summertime or Cosmic, simply blinked at him. "My inner child was busy exploring feel-good exercises. If you needed me, then you should have sent your inner child to tag mine, and we would have played chase until I arrived here to take your order."

Ramy's eyes widened as he turned to face Sophia. "Where have you taken me? Is this hell?"

She laughed and nodded. "Pretty much. It's a vegan restaurant. It's full of hippies, and their mission in life is to make us all suffer indirectly."

"We're all on the same mission, man," the waitress said in an airy tone. "It's to love one another."

Ramy let out a long breath, looking directly at Sophia. "Is this about my performance at the shop? Is this your way of firing me?"

She shook her head. "No, it's a place that has lots of options for Wilder, and since I didn't care and figured you didn't either, I allowed it."

"So what are you going to have?" Rainbow Sparkle asked.

"I'll have this piece of chocolate." Sophia held up the candy that Pricilla had given her.

"I brought cheese," Ramy stated proudly.

"I'll have the protein power goddess bowl," Wilder said.

"Do you want that with extra empowerment essence?" Palm Tree questioned.

"No, I'm good," Wilder stated.

"I'll bring your order when it's ready or when my inner child finishes napping," Coconut said and danced back toward the kitchen.

"Wow, this place is nuts." Wilder shook his head.

"It's the worst," Sophia stated. "Thought you'd get a kick out of how most vegans are a pain in the ass. Thanks for not being one."

He nodded. "I'm vegan to piss off Evan, mostly. And because animal products are poison. We should get rid of all of the animals on the planet. They're foul creatures."

Ramy took a bite of his cheese. "So you're not vegan because you're holier than thou and want to pass along your agenda?"

"No, that would be a lot of work," Wilder answered.

"It's some sort of anti-animal thing?" Ramy continued.

"Yeah, but unfortunately I get lumped in with all these damn hippies who are doing it because they like eating hemp powder." Wilder leaned forward. "It's gross. Don't eat it."

"Don't worry." Ramy shook his head. "So what would it take to eat a burger, you think?"

"Why?" Wilder questioned.

"Well, because everyone has a price for doing something they don't want to do," he answered. "Like, I didn't want to tell Val Kilmer a thing or two, but Keanu made me a promise. So I did it. That was my price. Totally worth it."

"I don't think I have a price," Wilder stated as the waitress brought a bowl of bright greens sprinkled with other colors to the table.

"Do you want any blessings or are you trying to shape your world today?" Lily Pad asked.

Wilder shook his head. "I think I'm good."

Ramy crammed a bunch more goat cheese in his mouth. "So, your price. What will it take to eat a steak?"

"I simply won't." Wilder dug into his salad.

"You two seem close." Ramy indicated Sophia and Wilder. "What if she was going to die if you didn't eat an entire ribeye? Would you do it?"

Wilder took another bite. "I mean, that seems sort of extreme. I guess, but I'm not sure what sort of circumstances would call for such things. What sort of ridiculous circumstances anyway."

"That's beside the point," Ramy stated, cheese bits spurting from his mouth onto the table in front of him, landing dangerously close to Wilder's food.

"So the shop," Sophia said, redirecting the conversation. "Everything okay there? King Rudolf okay?"

"He tells me how ugly I am daily," Ramy answered.

Sophia nodded. "Join the club. You haven't noticed any dangers? Nothing strange?"

Ramy thought for a moment. Then his face constricted oddly. He gripped his throat.

Sophia leaned forward suddenly, looking him over, noticing how in a matter of seconds, he was sweating profusely. His face flushed red. "Ramy, are you okay? What's happening?"

He began shaking violently. His eyes bulged. Around the restaurant some looked over, most not concerned. There were a few who remarked that he was having an "out of body experience" and that it happened to them when they had the beet soup.

Ramy's hand moved to his stomach as he began to convulse. Wilder shoved his food away.

"What can I do?" Sophia asked in a rush. "Are you okay?"

Erratically, Ramy shook his head. "N-N-No, I remember about the cheese now and why I hadn't had it in so long…"

Sophia sank back. "Because it's poison."

He nodded and fell face-first on the table, dying straight away from the ten-thousand-year-old goat cheese.

Sophia shook her head. "Damn that guy! That death totally could have been avoided."

"What do we do with him?" Wilder asked, pushing his food away, obviously losing his appetite after watching a guy die at the dinner table.

Sophia stood, taking the box of Heals Pills. "We leave him here. He'll wake up in a few. He can pay the tab since he ruined your meal."

Wilder nodded. "Sounds good to me."

The waitress sauntered over. "Is your friend all right? Did he overdose on peyote too? There's a place at the back where we keep those who do. Do you want me to have someone put him back there?"

"Sure," Sophia answered. "That will make his journey back that much more interesting."

CHAPTER SIXTY-NINE

Two dragons soared through the air at each other, racing with their claws extended, trepidation the most dominant expression on their faces.

Sophia held her breath, waiting for the collision. She bit her lip, hoping neither dragon got injured. Before impact, the smaller of the two dragons swerved, diving quickly for the grounds of the Expanse, the larger dragon zooming overhead.

Evan shook his head. "That was a good example of how not to win a fight!"

Mahkah stood in the distance, surrounded by the newbie riders and their dragons. He nodded over his shoulder at that before turning back. Sophia figured he was telling the new riders and their dragons something sage, like when he first taught Sophia how to fly and Lunis how to fight in the air. It was probably something like, "There's a time to avoid a fight, and there's a time to collide." The key was in how you did it because you couldn't always avoid battles.

Evan sighed at Sophia's side. "Man, these new guys are the worst. When I tell them to do stuff, they do it. When I tell them they suck, they simply nod."

"And that's a problem because..." Wilder asked, amusement

written on his face. The sharp winds on the Gullington knocked his hair around, making it into various arrangements.

"Because it's boring," Evan huffed.

Sophia had to agree with Evan on this one. "Yeah, they pose no real challenges. I can see where they're each individually talented, but they don't have any zest."

"Oh, I get it." Wilder laughed. "They need to tell Hiker how he's not doing his job right after five hundred years of doing it and waltz into the Castle and shake things up, do they?"

"That would be nice." Evan picked up one of the boxes filled with Heals Pills and secured it on Coral's back. Since Sophia didn't need him on call if Liv needed the genie's lamp recovered, he had volunteered to run the supplies to the village in Africa.

"That would be what Sophia did," Wilder added.

Evan gave him a sideways look. "Yeah, but something tells me the newbies won't be as bold as Pink Princess. Even when we get other new riders."

"Why is that?" Sophia planted her hands on her hips.

"Because Dragon Elite aren't like you," Wilder answered plainly, picking up another box of Heals Pills and handing it to Evan.

She pursed her lips. "That's inherently false since I'm a Dragon Elite."

Wilder gave her a sympathetic look, as if she misunderstood a great truth. "You're a Dragon Elite, but from what I know of our history, they aren't usually like you. Think about it." He indicated himself, Evan, and Mahkah in the distance. "The three of us hung around the Gullington for decades doing whatever Hiker told us to do, never really questioning his orders for us to train and stay inside the Barrier."

"Well, I questioned it a time or two," Evan argued.

"Then you passed out from drinking too much whiskey," Wilder remarked. "Adam questioned it, but he was different from the others too. As you've heard before, Soph, Adam was more like you, which was why Hiker made you his number two. He's smart enough to know he needs someone who doesn't think like him by his side. As great as we are." He nodded at Evan and himself.

"And I'm pretty damn great," Evan cut in with a smug grin.

"He's okay," Wilder teased. "Anyway, for as great as we are, we don't question things like you and Adam. The Dragon Elite before us didn't either if I know my history well enough."

Sophia nodded, having picked up on this theme when reading the *Complete History of Dragonriders*. The Dragon Elite tended to have strong followers who did as told, carrying out missions that helped the Earth. A leader rose through the ranks every few centuries, but even they were more like Hiker, playing it carefully and following Mama Jamba's direction.

"Well, why do you think that Adam and I are so different from the rest?" Sophia asked.

"Because you're an awful human being," Evan stated matter-of-factly, picking up the last crate and loading it on his dragon. "I mean, not Adam. He was totally cool, and I have mad respect for the dude. May he rest in peace. But you, Little Bit, are winning the award for being the absolute worst."

Sophia nodded, unaffected by the jab. "Thanks."

Wilder shrugged. "Who knows? Maybe it's because you were the first female dragonrider and meant to spawn the second batch of eggs. Adam, well, if it wasn't for him, then there might not have been a stop to the Rogue Riders. He was the only one who would stand up to them, really stand up to them. I think there's a reason that a rebellious Dragon Elite comes along every few centuries, but to be honest, I don't know what that reason could be."

A shiver of fear ran down Sophia's back, but she worked to hide her sudden nervousness. What if she was what caused the Rogue Riders and Dragon Elite to war again because she didn't handle things right? Hiker counted on her and had said as much. She was in charge of finding Trudy DeVries and controlling the Rogue Riders. Mama Jamba had hinted at taking out the leadership, but what if it didn't stop there? What if later history told that all dragonriders were gone and they'd wiped each other out and it was all Sophia's fault?

Wilder placed a hand on Sophia's shoulder, looking down at her with a comforting expression. "Being different from us is a good thing. You're a change agent. If it weren't for you, then we'd still be stuck in the Gullington, waiting for the right time to resurface. You forced Hiker to see that it was our time to reign again."

She gulped. Nodded. Tried to pull in a relieved breath. "Yeah, maybe you're right."

"I'm right," he said with a crooked smile. "I do believe that the Dragon Elite need to be complacent and model soldiers for the most part, like the new riders we have. We can think for ourselves, and we're devilishly smart—"

"And handsome," Evan interrupted.

Wilder agreed with a nod. "But at the end of the day, we need someone like you telling us what to do."

Sophia didn't know what to say. It had been weird for her from the beginning to be selected as Hiker's second in command. She was the youngest dragonrider at that point and so new, but she had to admit that she was like how they described Adam and did give it to Hiker straight instead of simply accepting everything he said as gospel.

"But still, it wouldn't kill the new guys to have a little personality," Evan stated, swinging his leg around and mounting Coral. "I mean, I do what I'm told, but with a little pizzazz."

"What you're trying to say is, pain in the ass," Wilder corrected. "You do what you're told but as a pain in the ass."

"Not all of us can be as insufferable as you, but I aspire to try." Evan winked.

"I'll teach you one day," Wilder remarked, backing up simultaneously with Sophia and giving Coral room to take off.

Evan gripped the reins, setting his sights on the Expanse and the Barrier in the distance. "Okay, well, I'm off to save the day and probably the world while you dorks sit around looking at each other."

"Thank the angels that you're here, or we'd all be doomed," Wilder joked.

"We'd all have fewer headaches," Sophia remarked.

"Whatever." Evan shook his head. "Speaking of headaches. I'm out of here before Quiet, the second-worst person at the Gullington, gives me one."

He nodded at the Castle where the groundskeeper stood, looking rather ominous, his gaze directed at them—or rather Sophia. In his hands and held up in the air was a small object. It glinted in the sunlight, giving away its metallic appearance.

It was a key…

CHAPTER SEVENTY

Sophia left Wilder with the new riders, dragons, and Mahkah, and strode in Quiet's direction. There was something about the gnome's expression that put her on guard. Maybe it was because, like a statue, he simply held a skeleton key straight up in the air with an intense look on his face.

She didn't know if the key was for her or if Quiet wanted Sophia to stride over instead of Wilder or both of them. But for some reason, she got a distinct impression that she was the one Quiet wished to have the object.

Tentatively, Sophia approached the groundskeeper, her head to the side as she studied the strange key. Its silver finish glinted in the sunlight cascading down on the Gullington.

"Hey, Quiet," Sophia said cautiously. "What do you have there?"

He mouthed two words: "For you."

When she was close enough, Sophia took the key, and the gnome finally lowered his short arm. She looked at it and wondered what it would open. "What's this for?" she asked and knew at once that the question would go unanswered.

As she suspected, Quiet spun and marched in the opposite direction, out toward the Cave, Nest, and Pad.

Sophia shot an irritated look at the gnome's back, half-tempted to make an Evan-type comment, but didn't want to incur the groundskeeper's wrath. He could make her life hell, as he often did to the other dragonrider.

Returning her focus to the strange key, Sophia wondered what it could open. No doubt it was something important, and most likely in the Castle. She started for the entrance, knowing that she was on yet another exciting and confusing scavenger hunt.

CHAPTER SEVENTY-ONE

The Castle's second floor felt colder than it had earlier, Sophia thought, pulling her cloak tighter. The winter winds whistled through the cracks of the windows, sending cold air drafting through the corridors.

Sophia held the silver object tightly in her hands, wanting to laugh that she had a key that she didn't know what it went to. That was ironic since Quiet had sent her on an earlier mission to recover parts of a key from the Castle to unlock Lunis' Pad.

"What does this open?" Sophia asked aloud, knowing that the Castle could hear her. She didn't expect it to show her, but she did believe it would lead her if she were looking for clues. Sophia thought that Castle behaved similarly to the library in the House of Fourteen. One couldn't simply look for a book in that place. No, the searcher had to think about the book they wanted, really focusing on the subject and not getting the least bit distracted.

However, much like Hiker's quest for her to find the mystery pouch that belonged to her ancestor, Oscar Beaufont, Sophia didn't know what she was looking for. How could she focus on finding something when she didn't know what it was?

She eyed every piece of furniture she passed, looking for a keyhole.

Racking her brain, Sophia tried to remember all the places in the Castle where she'd seen locks, but suddenly none came to mind.

"What am I looking for?" she asked, remembering the pouch that she needed to recover for Hiker. Sophia hadn't wanted to think about the task since it seemed so important and she had no idea where to look. There had been Oscar Beaufont's office that Sophia had strangely stumbled upon recently. However, she'd searched the space and hadn't found anything that resembled the small pouch that Hiker described.

Feeling defeated before barely starting on the search, Sophia halted in the corridor. She closed her eyes, overwhelmed by both of her mystery tasks. Why was she supposedly able to recover the item from her ancestor? That plagued her more than what the actual object was. Things operated so strangely in the Castle—as though by a set of its own laws.

Opening her eyes, Sophia blinked, realizing she wasn't where she'd been when she closed them. She shouldn't be surprised about being teleported in the Castle, yet she sucked in a breath, shocked by the sight in front of her.

Much like the library in the House of Fourteen, the Castle had brought Sophia to the place her thoughts had focused on moments prior. That part shouldn't have been a shock. Finding herself standing right in front of Oscar Beaufont's old study also shouldn't have come as much of a surprise. However, it all did because the key in her hand warmed and she knew, just knew, that it had to open something in the office. But what? And why?

So many questions plagued her now as she stepped forward into Oscar Beaufont's study.

CHAPTER SEVENTY-TWO

The lanterns in the office flickered to life when Sophia stepped over the threshold into her ancestor's study.

She spun in a slow circle as she took in the room, searching for something that required a key. The office was the same as the first time that Sophia had been there, with a large desk, a few cabinets, a bookshelf, some artwork on the walls, and an armchair in the corner. That was it. There wasn't a locked armoire or drawer that she could see.

Coming around the desk, Sophia continued to search, looking for anything that required a key, like a small box or something. She'd already gone through the office pretty thoroughly the first time and hadn't seen anything that was locked.

Sophia slumped against the wall and sighed, wishing that things could be easy for once. That someone would give her the answers to the many riddles that so often challenged her.

Her shoulder knocked against the painting on the wall next to her, sliding it to the side. She didn't think much of it, but worried she'd displace the artwork, Sophia straightened it. That's when she noticed there was more than a bare wall under the now-crooked painting. There was metal.

Curious, Sophia slid the painting to the side, finding that it moved like it was on a hinge. Sophia gasped when she spied what it had concealed. Behind the oil painting was a small metal box built into a wall—a safe. In the center was a lock, the keyhole the exact size as the key she held.

CHAPTER SEVENTY-THREE

Lifting the key to the lock, Sophia held her breath. She wouldn't allow herself to think that this was the actual key to unlock the safe. Not yet. Not until it had worked. She didn't want to get her hopes up in case this had all been misdirection and what the key opened wasn't in Oscar Beaufont's office. Maybe the key didn't open something in the Castle. Perhaps she was completely off base.

Letting out a heavy breath, Sophia slid the key into the lock. So far, it fit. She bit her lip and turned it. The lock's tumblers stuck in several places, probably from disuse. With a bit of coercing, the key finally completed the rotation and *clicked* into place. The door to the metal safe opened slightly. It was the right key.

Sophia pulled the door wider, unsure what she'd find, or even what she was looking for. She peered into the small black box, squinting to see its contents.

There wasn't much there. Only two items.

Sitting in the middle of the space was a leather-bound journal, tied shut. On top of it was something Sophia had been looking for but hadn't known where to find: the small red velvet pouch with orange tassels on the ties that Hiker had asked her to retrieve.

CHAPTER SEVENTY-FOUR

"You found it." Hiker stood at once when Sophia dangled the small pouch in front of him.

He strode around the desk, disbelief on this face. "Where was it?"

"In the Castle," she remarked, the book pressed to her chest with her other hand.

Mama Jamba chuckled at her back.

Hiker rolled his eyes while taking the dangling red velvet pouch from her. "Very funny. I knew it was in the Castle. I was inquiring as to where you found it specifically."

"That's the curious part," Sophia began. "Didn't you say that Oscar Beaufont had given it to you?"

Hiker opened the pouch using the drawstrings and peered inside.

"Is it there?" Mama Jamba asked absentmindedly, thumbing through a Rick Steve's travel book on *Naples: the Amalfi Coast*.

He sighed in relief and nodded. "Yeah, it's here."

"What's there?" Sophia dared to peer forward.

Hiker snatched the pouch away and shook his head. "None of your business."

"Cool," Sophia said casually. "I'll remember that the next time you want me to go on a treasure hunt."

"Good," he growled. "Do that. I'll throw you out of the Castle the next time you mouth off to me."

"Are you back to making that threat after all this time?" Mama Jamba asked, grabbing a sticky note from beside her and marking a page.

He nodded. "I never quit. It's only that this lot quit taking me seriously when I'd try to fire them and throw them out on their butts."

Sophia couldn't help but laugh. She remembered the first time that Hiker had told her she wasn't with the Dragon Elite anymore and told her to leave the Gullington. She'd thought he was serious and almost left. Then she learned that he fired Ainsley regularly and was always tossing Evan out of the Castle. Everyone always returned because it was an empty threat.

"Back to my question." Sophia decided she didn't need to know what was in the pouch. She simply felt relieved and proud that she'd found it—and also a handwritten journal, supposedly written by her ancestor, Oscar Beaufont. Sophia hadn't had a chance to read anything in it. She'd peeled it open a tiny bit with the binding still around it to check that it was what she thought it was—a journal. "You said that Oscar Beaufont gave you that pouch, right?"

Hiker closed the red velvet sack and slid it carefully into his pocket. He nodded. "Yes, that's correct."

"Yet, you couldn't find it, right?" Sophia continued to question.

"Yeah, it had been in my office the last time I had it," Hiker answered. "Where did you find it?"

"That's the curious part," Sophia began. "It was in a locked safe inside Oscar Beaufont's study."

Hiker's eyes registered his surprise. "Oscar's study? I haven't seen that room in ages...not for centuries, I'd say. I didn't know it still existed."

"I was surprised when I stumbled upon it too," Sophia stated. "It was right after you asked me to look for the pouch."

"You said it was in his safe?" Hiker questioned.

"Yes, which means the Castle must have put it there," Sophia reasoned. "I mean, if the last place you had the pouch was in your office."

Hiker nodded. "Yeah, I figured the bloody Castle was behind taking it, but who knows why? I never know why it does half the stuff it does, but I'm relieved you found the...well, the thing I was looking for."

Sophia was sure that Hiker was about to slip and reveal the object in the pouch accidentally, but he'd caught himself. "I think I might know why it took the pouch and put it in Oscar Beaufont's safe."

Hiker simply glared at her, an expression that seemed to say, "Go on," written on his face.

"The Castle must have assumed that you'd ask me to find the watch when you couldn't," Sophia said slyly.

He shook his head. "Nice try. It's not a watch. I'm not following you."

"Well, I think the Castle wanted me to find this." Sophia held up the leather-bound journal.

Hiker blinked at the book in confusion. "What is that?"

"I think it's Oscar Beaufont's journal," Sophia answered. "It was the only other thing in the safe. Quiet gave me the key earlier. It goes to reason that he knew I'd be looking for the pouch and wanted me to find this."

Hiker reached for the journal, but Sophia pulled it back. He gave her a punishing look.

"Let me see it," he demanded.

"I think the Castle wanted me to find it and read the contents," Sophia argued.

"That was an order," Hiker stated angrily.

"She's right, son." Mama Jamba put another sticky note on a page in the travel book.

"Stay out of this," he argued.

"I won't," she said stubbornly. "I think your reasoning is sound, Sophia. The Castle wanted you to find the journal but didn't have another way for you to search. So it took Hiker's object that it knew he'd want soon and hid it in the safe with the thing you were to find. Great detective skills."

Sophia pressed her lips together. "The question is why."

"If you'd let me see the journal, I might be able to help," Hiker seethed.

"If you let me see what's in the velvet bag, I'll let you see the journal," Sophia offered.

Hiker cut his gaze to Mama Jamba, who was giggling again. "No deal."

"Well, then there's your answer," Sophia said firmly.

Striding back around his desk, Hiker shook his head. "Fine. Let me know if you learn anything of interest."

"I will," Sophia stated, not moving. "Let me know how the compass works."

He lifted his head and gave her an annoyed look. "It's not a compass."

Sophia tapped the journal. "Well, maybe at least you'll tell me a little about Oscar Beaufont."

Hiker sighed and relented a little. "He was a dragonrider."

Sophia laughed. "Okay, I guess I deserved that."

"For the Dragon Elite," Hiker added.

"Incredibly helpful, sir."

Hiker's beard twitched from the subtle smile on his face. "Adam was my second in command, but Oscar Beaufont was my third. Incredibly dependable and brave. Also a very good friend."

"Were you ever going to tell me that my ancestor was a friend of yours and dragonrider?" Sophia questioned.

He shrugged and sat. "Not really. It didn't pertain to you. Then I lost the...thing and realized you might be able to help."

"Yes, the mysterious thing." Sophia pretended to be annoyed, but she was more amused at that point.

Hiker nodded. "Anyway, Oscar was many things, but what he was most valuable for, well, it wasn't something most knew about him..." He let the sentence die, hesitation on his face.

"Are you going to tell me or should I ask the Castle to steal the pouch back from your pocket?" Sophia threatened.

Reflexively, Hiker's hand went protectively to his pocket. "You wouldn't dare."

"I would," Sophia fired back.

"The Castle can take something out of your pocket or pretty much anywhere it likes," Mama Jamba added, continuing to page through Rick Steve's book on the Amalfi Coast.

"I know that," Hiker said through clenched teeth. He let out a long breath and sat back in his seat. "Fine. I'll tell you. I'm not sure it matters at this point. Your ancestor, my friend Oscar Beaufont, was a seer."

Sophia tensed. She hadn't realized there were any seers in her family. Many times it was genetic and showed up every few generations, but because most regarded it as such a taboo and disgraceful ability, they often hid it.

"Based on your expression, I guess you didn't know you had a seer in the family," Hiker observed.

Sophia nodded and pressed the journal more firmly to her chest.

"Anyway, I don't know what's in the contents of Oscar's journal," Hiker admitted, indicating the book. "I'd guess that it includes a few prophecies. He didn't often tell me of the visions he saw, but he did a couple of times, and they always came to pass."

"And the Castle wanted me to find this book," Sophia said, mostly to herself.

"There's probably a prophecy in there that pertains to the Beaufonts," Hiker stated. "Or maybe something to do with the Rogue Riders." He shrugged. "Or it could be a family history. Do let me know when you find something of interest, although I'm getting tired of the Castle giving you books that really should belong to me."

"He was my ancestor," Sophia argued.

"I realize that, but he was my dragonrider," Hiker countered. "And my friend."

"Well, if I come across a book from one of your relatives, I'll be sure to hand it over." Sophia winked.

A sliver of a smile danced in Hiker's eyes. "Thanks, but I doubt that will happen." He pulled himself closer to his desk and indicated the door. "That journal isn't going to read itself. Go on then."

Sophia shook her head at the leader of the Dragon Elite. "Yeah, okay."

"Thanks for finding the thing I was looking for," Hiker said as she turned to the door.

"Well, I know how important those cufflinks were to you," Sophia teased, winking at Mama Jamba.

Hiker didn't reply, only huffed with annoyance.

When Sophia was at the office door, she paused and regarded Mother Nature. "Those travel books are written by a mortal. Why would you use them for reference when... Well, you know?"

Mama Jamba pressed the book open to keep her place as she glanced up at Sophia. "It's all about perspective. I might have created a place, but I want to know how others view it to shape my adventures. I thought that Antarctica was a beautiful place, but after reading about others' perspectives of it, I realize that it might not be everyone's favorite."

Sophia pursed her lips and nodded. "That makes sense."

"Oh, and also, I want to know the best places to eat and drink," Mama Jamba stated. "The travel experts know that. You can create the planet, but that doesn't mean you know where the best pasta places are."

CHAPTER SEVENTY-FIVE

Although Sophia looked forward to diving into Oscar Beaufont's journal, she didn't have an opportunity to open it. As soon as she left Hiker's office, her phone began vibrating, stealing her attention. The call was much more of a priority than learning about an ancestor's prophecy or discovering any family history.

"Hey," Sophia said, knowing that Liv was on the other side of the line. "What's going on?"

"Not a whole lot," Liv replied over the phone. "I ate Indian food for every single meal for the last few days, and I'm pretty sure I'm sweating out curry at this point."

"How do you feel?" Sophia didn't want to ask about her obvious concern.

"I have an awful headache, but I'm sure that will pass."

"Oh, probably from hormones," Sophia guessed, striding for her room.

"Maybe," Liv replied. "But also could be from an orc that tried to take me out today. That guy had horrible aim, which was to my advantage, but dude, could he scream. My eardrums are still ringing."

Sophia tossed Oscar Beaufont's journal on her desk upon entering her room and immediately started to pace from worry. "Are you sure that you should be working cases for the House of Fourteen? Maybe Rory was right."

"Rory isn't right," Liv stated. "He never is. I remind him of that regularly. Besides, this wasn't connected to a case for the House of Fourteen. It was some creep I caught breaking into the pawnshop down the street from John's electronic repair store."

"Wow, that's crazy," Sophia offered, continuing to pace.

"Total cray-cray," Liv answered. "That just goes to show you that I should keep working for the House of Fourteen because trouble will follow me around regardless of whether I'm conducting my Warrior duties or not. So I might as well be doing something to make the magical world a better place."

Sophia nodded, not saying anything.

"Don't worry, Soph. I'm careful, and everything is going to be fine."

Slumping into her chair, Sophia let out a long breath. "Yeah, I suppose you're right. I hope your headache goes away."

"I hope the orc problem goes away," Liv related. "Otherwise, the headaches will keep coming back."

"I'm sure it was a rogue orc and it won't be a continuous problem."

Liv didn't sound so sure. "I don't know. There are a few things out of whack around town and by that, I mean the planet."

Sophia sat forward. "Oh yeah?"

"Yeah," Liv answered. "Some want to believe it's because the criminals in the mortal world are overrunning cities."

"I'm working on stopping the Rogue Riders," Sophia argued.

"I know," Liv said with confidence. "I didn't say that's what I believe. The Rogue Riders are only part of the problem. Criminals are getting cocky, acting like they own things because they think they're invincible. There's also the fact that we're down a Warrior for the House of Fourteen."

"Which is also my problem," Sophia said heavily.

"Our problem," Liv corrected. "We'll fix it together. First, I need your help with something."

"Sure." Sophia wondered if she needed to quell the Council's fears again. Or maybe this was about Clark and how she and Liv usually went in on a Christmas present for him. "What is it?"

"I need to locate Stan." Liv suddenly sounded serious.

Sophia rose to her feet, automatically feeling outside herself. "Your..."

The breath Liv released riffed over the phone. "Yeah, Renswick just gave me the results. It appears that the baby has a predominance of demon blood. The antidote didn't cross from Stefan so the blood was passed on and has taken over. If we don't make a wish using the genie's lamp, I'll give birth to a demon."

CHAPTER SEVENTY-SIX

L iv hadn't wanted Sophia's apologies and sympathies. She knew that about her sister. What Liv wanted was a solution. There was no point wasting energy on regret when they needed to focus on changing the future. That's why Sophia worked to keep the remorse on her face corralled when she met Liv outside the circus where Bermuda Laurens still kept her magical creatures—educating the mortal world about the strange and exotic animals.

"You know, in my next life, I'm going to run away with the circus." Liv looked very much out of place as she and Sophia strolled through the magical circus' straw-covered grounds. Performers dressed in bright colors and practicing their various acts stopped to stare at the sisters as they made their way to the big top at the back.

In contrast to the jugglers wearing orange spandex and tossing bowling pins in the air, Liv and Sophia wore long black traveling cloaks, their swords strapped to their sides.

"Oh, really?" Sophia questioned. "I never took you for a circus person."

Liv shot her a look of offense. "I heart the circus. Where else can you go and be dazzled by amazing acts and reminded about the fun of magic?"

Sophia gave her sister a surprised look. "You're sort of sounding dreamy and romantic."

The Warrior slumped. "I know. It's the hormones. I cried last night."

Wanting to hug her sister, Sophia pressed her lips together. "That's understandable. You've got a lot going on, and this news is a big deal."

Liv laughed. "Oh, I didn't cry because I've got a demon baby. That's a point of honor at this point. How many people can say that they're carrying a demon around? I'm probably the first. I cried because Clark finished the Oreo cheesecake and didn't leave me any."

"That was so rude of him," Sophia said, shocked by her brother's behavior when he was usually so thoughtful.

"Well," Liv drew out the word. "I had told him that he could when he asked because I'd already eaten half of it for lunch and most of the rest of it for dinner. So I figured he could have the last piece. But he should have known when I said, 'You can have the rest' that I was lying." She stopped and looked at Sophia quite seriously. "I hadn't even had dessert."

Sophia giggled. "You poor thing. I can see why that made you cry."

Liv joined her, chuckling as they continued. "You should have seen Clark's face when I cried. I thought he was going to make another Oreo cheesecake to make things better."

"Poor guy," Sophia said. "I can appreciate your thoughts on the circus. It's such a great place. I'm glad to see a small traveling one like this still operating. I thought it was sort of a dying art form."

Liv nodded. "Thanks to YouTube and millennials, it sort of is. People can't be bothered to leave their house to watch acts when they can get fat on their couch and watch it on a screen. And what's cool about a woman flying through the air when you can watch funny cat videos?"

Sophia smiled at her sister. "I realize now you have strong feelings on this subject."

Liv waved at two pairs of acrobats who were standing on each other's shoulders. They glanced at the magicians like they were the freaks and didn't return the gesture. "I mean, these art forms have been passed down through families for centuries. These guys have a lifestyle that most can't fathom, living on the road and traveling from city to city all to bring entertainment to people. Most of them don't even have healthcare. They settle for less to do what they love. I wish people like that were better rewarded."

Sophia shot her sister another look of surprise. "Wow, I had no idea you harbored this kind of passion for these things."

"I didn't either." Liv shook her head. "Stefan thinks my emotions are going to the extreme opposite of evil to preserve my wellbeing and make up for what the demon baby would be doing to me otherwise."

"That makes sense," Sophia offered, not having thought about the actual physical and emotional implications of having a demon baby inside a person. "It's pretty impressive that your body and mind seem to know how to react to preserve you."

Liv nodded. "The thing is, I don't think I can keep it up much longer. I'm a ticking time bomb, and that bomb is a demon baby. When it goes off, I think I'll be insane and who knows what I could do or be capable of doing."

Sophia shivered but did her best to cover it. She also hadn't thought about how carrying a demon baby could make Liv crazy or dangerous. Liv filled with evil would probably be one of the most deadly things since she was the most powerful Warrior for the House of Fourteen. No wonder Papa Creola was so concerned.

They had to get Stan's lamp or bottle or whatever it was and fix things. One wish. That's all they needed, then Liv and Stefan could have the healthy, happy baby they so deserved.

They were almost to the big top where Bermuda Laurens kept her magical creatures when something flew by them and landed beside the tent. It was large. Too big to fit in the big top since it was almost the size of it. The animal had wings like an eagle. It was also a wolf. It was by far the strangest animal Sophia had ever seen, and that was saying an awful lot.

The sisters halted, staring up at the creature. Liv shook her head, not at all appearing unnerved by looking into the eyes of a giant wolf-bird, and smiled. "Aren't you a cute little fella?"

CHAPTER SEVENTY-SEVEN

The creature growled, drool rolling down its chin and landing on the ground at Liv's and Sophia's feet. Neither sister backed up or struck a defensive pose although the beast bared its teeth, its black eyes narrowed, and large wings expanded.

It was quite the beautiful animal, Sophia observed, taking in its thick black and white coat and majestic build. However, even pretty creatures could be dangerous. All the wolf-eagle had to do was reach down and take a single bite, and one of the Beaufonts would be gone.

"I don't have any puppy treats," Liv said from the corner of her mouth to Sophia. "Did you bring any of Larry's snacks?"

"If you mean Lunis, then no," Sophia answered in a hushed voice, hardly audible over the beast's loud growl.

"Well, maybe if we stand here and stare it down, it will get bored and return to licking its butt, or whatever else it does," Liv said, careful to keep her focus on the animal.

She was right. Sophia knew from experience. Turning your back on predators such as this was the way to invite an attack. Keeping one's eyes on a potential aggressor was one way to get them to back down.

The wolf-eagle snapped in their direction, its mouth nearly a foot from Liv's face. The rush of hot air from its breath knocked into both sisters. Neither moved. They continued to stare up at the animal. They didn't budge even when it started to beat its wings in a show of intimidation.

Sophia's hand tensed by her side. She was certain that Liv's was doing the same thing. Although the last thing that Sophia wanted to do was fight one of Bermuda Lauren's magical creatures, she was starting to think she wouldn't have a choice. This one was obviously deranged.

The wolf-eagle backed up several feet but kept up the air of intimidation, which was why Sophia wasn't surprised when it lunged forward again and halted when only a few feet away. It knelt low on its front legs, its wings angled down to the ground and its hind legs high in the air. The creature hadn't attacked, but Sophia and Liv also hadn't moved. It was waiting for them to pull a weapon or to make a move. Then it would make them into puppy chow.

Looking up into the wolf-eagle's black eyes, Sophia got the impression that it was as ancient as some of the oldest dragons. Deep within the creature, Sophia sensed pure wisdom, as if it had the world's history locked away in its consciousness. That was one of the many reasons that killing the beast would be heartbreaking, but it wasn't leaving them any choice. The monster would attack them soon, and both sisters knew it instinctively. The animal simply couldn't hold itself back any longer.

The magical creature threw its head into the air and howled loud and deep, making the ground under them shake, and the various structures around the circus vibrate, creating more noise.

It was a cacophony that went on even when the wolf-eagle stopped howling, jerked its head to the side, and gave the Beaufonts a murderous look, its snout pinched and sharp teeth showing.

"Get your sword ready," Liv whispered. "It's about to get ugly."

CHAPTER SEVENTY-EIGHT

Three things happened in quick succession.

Sophia yanked Inexorabilis from its sheath.

Liv did the same with Bellator.

The beast lunged forward before freezing in midair, its mouth open and ready to attack.

"What is going on here?" Bermuda Laurens yelled at the tent's entrance. The giantess' face was beet red, and her large hand was high in the air.

Sophia immediately realized that Bermuda had put a paralyzing spell on the wolf-eagle, which based on its size would take an incredible amount of power. That was the only explanation for why the creature was suspended in midair, seeming like it was floating on its extended wings.

Sophia and Liv both backed up several feet, giving them much-needed space from the beast's open mouth. They both kept their swords high in the air and stayed tense and ready should the paralyzing spell fail.

"Your dog-bird was about to attack us," Liv stated and glanced at the giantess.

Bermuda lowered her hand, and the creature drifted to the ground where it rested although still frozen. Her scrutinizing gaze ran over Liv, and she shook her head. "No, Luminous was about to attack you, Liv. He wanted nothing to do with Sophia. I'm certain of it."

Liv pursed her lips and lowered her sword a little. "Well, that's fine. I'm more of a cat person anyway. He probably sensed that or saw Plato's hair on my cloak."

Bermuda shook her head of curly brown hair. "No, he sensed the evil inside you. Chamrosh can't stand evil and will destroy it at all costs. Otherwise, they're the most peaceful magical creatures and very gentle. You were seconds away from being destroyed."

Liv sheathed Bellator and put her hands on her hips. "Seriously, I've defeated Medusa and vampires, saved the magical world, and taken down the God Magician, and your money was on the winged puppy?"

Bermuda returned the defiant expression. "It's a chamrosh, and I wouldn't underestimate it. They destroy evil at all costs."

"You mentioned that," Liv muttered dryly.

Sensing that Bermuda held the paralyzing spell firm, Sophia sheathed her sword too. "So this creature—"

"Luminous," Bermuda interrupted.

"Luminous," Sophia continued. "It can sense the demon inside Liv?"

Bermuda smirked. "Or maybe it's her bad attitude."

Liv laughed in response. "Oh, look at Mrs. Laurens throwing down a joke. Now I've seen everything."

The giantess narrowed her eyes, but a smile hid underneath it. Sophia knew that Bermuda was cold and no-nonsense most of the time. She hadn't seemed to like Liv very much from the beginning, but Sophia also sensed that she had a great fondness for the Warrior for the House of Fourteen. It was just that showing it would be impossible for her.

"Yes, Sophia," Bermuda said. "Luminous sensed the demon inside Liv." Returning her attention to the Warrior, the giantess softened but only slightly. "I'm sorry about your child. Rory told me, and I hope I can help you to recover the genie's lamp. It's the best option, although I can't tell you that it will work."

"Papa Creola says the same thing." Liv sounded heavy-hearted for the first time. "I realize it's a gamble. The child's timeline could be fixed, and if that's the case, then a thousand wishes wouldn't change that. Still, I have to try."

"What if you can't change the baby?" Bermuda asked.

"I'll deal with that when I get to it," Liv replied.

"You can't bring a demon into this world," Bermuda stated coldly.

An angry look flashed across Liv's face, and Sophia thought she would yell her next words at the giantess. Instead, a smile broke through the grimace. "You brought Rory into this world."

Bermuda, unamused, shook her head and stepped back, lifting her arm and welcoming them into the tent. "Follow me in here. I think I have a magical creature that can help you. Sophia, I also have one for you."

Sophia blinked in surprise, wondering why she'd need an animal when she already had Lunis.

CHAPTER SEVENTY-NINE

Apparently as confused as Sophia, Liv shot Bermuda a bewildered expression as they entered the big top. "Why does Sophia get a magical creature? She has Geoff."

Bermuda blinked at her, obviously not getting the running joke. "Who is Geoff?"

"Liv likes to call Lunis by other names that aren't his," Sophia explained, amused.

However, the giantess wasn't at all entertained as she stuck her nose in the air. "Disrespecting a dragon is incredibly immature."

Liv laughed at this. "We're talking about a dragon who eats cheese puffs and is always watering my plants on Animal Crossing. You realize that, right?"

"You two are friends on Animal Crossing?" Sophia asked her sister, surprised.

"We are for now," Liv replied.

"I don't know what this Animal Crossing is that you speak of." Bermuda looked between the two sisters.

"And you call yourself an animal expert," Liv teased.

Bermuda harrumphed. "I'll have to look into this."

"You really must." Liv winked at Sophia.

Finding it nearly impossible to cover her laughter, Sophia looked around the big tent, which was dimmer than usual and much darker than when they were outside—her eyes took some time to adjust. In the center of the large big top was an above ground pool that appeared to be about five feet deep. There was other equipment besides that, which was rare. Usually, Bermuda's tent was filled with things that contained the animals. Even stranger, there didn't appear to be any magical creatures.

"The animal that I have for Sophia isn't for her," Bermuda stated smugly, continuing the conversation from before.

Liv grinned. "Well, I don't know if you're struggling with the English language, but if the animal that you have for Sophia isn't for her, then it's not for her."

Seeming to have trouble containing her irritation, Bermuda let out a long breath. "I'm giving Sophia a magical creature that I'd like her to deliver to the Great Librarian since he is new to the position, and I think he could use the help. Not only that, but it's a nice gesture, and I think that Paul deserves recognition for taking the crucial role."

Liv turned to face Sophia. "You're a courier service now because you didn't have enough going on."

"She has direct access to the Great Library," Bermuda stated, annoyance flaring in her voice. "It's much easier for her to get there than the rest of us, so that's why I'm asking for her help."

"I'm happy to do it," Sophia stated. "It will be good to check in on Paul and see how he's doing."

"Your sister could learn some manners from you," the giantess said to her.

"No, I couldn't," Liv argued. "I've tried. I'm unteachable. A total lost cause."

"I honestly suspected as much." Bermuda nodded and held out her arm.

From somewhere at the top of the tent, there was a flapping noise. It grew closer, then a creature flew down and landed on Bermuda's outstretched arm. The animal wasn't a bird, and it wasn't *not* a bird.

"It's a gryphowl," Bermuda stated, having read the quizzical expressions on Sophia and Liv's faces.

The magical creature was quite large even resting on the giantess' arm where it folded its snowy-like wings into its body and regarded them with majestic eyes. The gryphowl appeared to be a cross between an owl and a large cat. It had the wise face of an owl with brown and white feathers. Under its large wings were four sets of legs that resembled those of a jungle cat. It also had the large pointy ears and striped tail of the large jungle cat.

"It's beautiful," Sophia said, in awe of the creature.

"Do you like to be referred to as an 'it'?" Bermuda asked, offense jumping to her face.

Liv leaned over and whispered loudly, "It's a trick question. There's no right answer."

"The right thing to say is 'I apologize,'" Bermuda said arrogantly. "Her name is Beatrix."

"She's the gift for Paul?" Sophia indicated the gryphowl, which hadn't taken much note of the two magicians.

"That's correct," Bermuda answered. "She'll make a nice companion for him. I know the role of the Great Librarian is a lonely one even with the many visitors I'm sure he'll get over time."

"Man, I should have taken that position," Liv joked. "I could use some alone time." She looked at Sophia and shook her head. "Not from you. Or from Stefan. Mostly from Clark, who acts like I'm a wilting flower, and Rudolf, who portals to my location if I don't take his calls—no matter where I am. Then there's Rory, who's having a hissy fit over this demon baby."

"As he should," Bermuda scolded. "Although my son never has and will never have a hissy fit, as you call it."

Liv chuckled. "Then you haven't seen him when I track mud into his house."

"If you're wearing shoes inside a home, you have much to learn," Bermuda stated.

"We've already covered that and that I'm unteachable, remember?"

Liv elbowed Sophia and leaned closer again. "I think Bermuda's losing her memory. That conversation was like, a second ago."

"It was over a minute," Bermuda corrected.

"She hasn't lost her need to be specific and literal about everything," Liv said to Sophia, as though she wasn't talking out loud about the giantess right in front of them.

"I'm sure that Paul will be honored to receive the gift." Sophia tried to steer the conversation back on track, remembering that Liv was a ticking time bomb.

"He will," Bermuda stated with confidence. "Not only will she serve as a loyal companion, but she's incredibly intelligent and will be a great assistant to him too."

"So you want me to deliver her to him right away then?" Sophia wondered if she had to carry the gryphowl the way Bermuda was doing, her arm still extended. She was pretty sure that the magical creature was too large for her to hold.

"That's correct," Bermuda stated. "But helping Liv to find the genie's lamp is the top priority. Beatrix will accompany you on that mission and then if you will, please take her to Paul."

"Okay," Sophia said tentatively. "Does she fly along beside me or what?"

Based on the look on Bermuda's face, that was a dumb question. "Of course. You aren't expected to carry her around. She will only land on her master's arm, and currently, I'm that. Once you give her to Paul, he will become her forever master. The gryphowl are incredibly loyal creatures and bond only to one person at a time."

"What do they do?" Liv asked.

Bermuda's eyelids fluttered with annoyance. "What do you mean, what do they do?"

"Well, it's—"

"Beatrix," Bermuda corrected again.

"Unteachable, remember," Liv sang with a smile. "As I was saying, she's a bird, but she's also a cat, right? And you said the doggy-bird—"

"Luminous," Bermuda interrupted.

"Bad breath Lumos," Liv went on. "You said that he was good at sniffing out evil and getting rid of it, whatever the cost." She said the last part while impersonating the giantess' tone. "So what does Beatrix do?"

"Sometimes creatures just are," Bermuda stated regally. "She flies, and that should be enough. She also has the agility of a wild cat, is incredible at hunting instincts, has a wisdom that is unmatched by smaller winged animals and the ability to find most hidden things with relative ease."

"That will come in handy at the Great Library," Sophia related, impressed.

Bermuda nodded. "I thought so as well."

"Great, well, I'll take Beatrix to the library as soon as I can," Sophia stated.

"Now that leaves the matter of the creature you have for me to recover the genie's lamp." Liv looked around the giantess, to the large pool in the center of the big top. "Is he or she in there?"

Bermuda pursed her lips, seeming to recognize that Liv tried to use the right pronouns. That seemed to annoy the giantess as though it deprived her of the opportunity to correct her. "Yes, and his name is Heathcliff."

"Cool," Liv stated. "A magical swimming creature is perfect for recovering the genie's lamp from the bottom of the ocean. Should we stroll on over and meet the animal that's quite literally going to help save my unborn child?"

"No need." Bermuda snapped the fingers of her other hand, making a sharp sound that echoed around the big top.

A great splashing came from the large pool, and another strange winged creature emerged from it. It soared through the air, diving straight in their direction before landing at Bermuda's feet. The magical creature was maybe one of the cutest animals that Sophia had ever seen.

CHAPTER EIGHTY

S taring up at them with big brown eyes and a seeming smile on its face was a sea otter of sorts. It had the body and visage of an adorable otter, but on its back were two large brown wings that resembled those of a hawk.

Heathcliff folded the wings into its body and looked up dutifully to Bermuda.

"Very good," the giantess said proudly. "Heathcliff will be your assistant for this mission. He's excellent at diving and with few clues can find the object you're looking for at the bottom of the ocean."

"Rudolf made us a pretty detailed map," Sophia explained, remembering the very interactive map that the fae had given her to find Stan's lamp.

"King Rudolf," Bermuda corrected, obviously very much about names that day. "Regardless, the bottom of the ocean is a very dark and confusing place. Heathcliff will have no problem finding what you're seeking. If you take him to the spot, all you must do is wait until he retrieves it. Then simply send him back to me, and he will fly in this direction."

"Great," Liv said with relief. "Is the theme of this week's circus winged creatures?"

"No, why?" Bermuda asked, quite seriously.

Liv tilted her head and gave the giantess a speculative glare. "Seriously, you're not sensing the theme here?"

"No," the giantess answered. "What am I missing?"

"Every punch line I've ever told, ever." Liv knelt and looked at the adorable otter. "So you're going to be my little pal and help me find the genie's lamp, right?"

Heathcliff waddled forward, his body low to the ground, and his head affectionately brushed Liv's side. He was so cute it kind of hurt.

Liv looked up, obviously overwhelmed by his adorableness, and grinned. "Maybe I can keep him when we finish," she said, her tone expectant.

"You can send him straight back here," Bermuda answered at once. "He's part of the show. You know how the phrase goes."

"The show must go on," Liv guessed.

The giantess narrowed her eyes. "I've never heard that one."

"How is that possible?" Liv asked.

Bermuda sighed. "I meant the phrase, 'there is no show without a winged otter.'"

Liv gave Sophia a look of surprise. "I think I missed that one..."

CHAPTER EIGHTY-ONE

King Rudolf Sweetwater had loaned his boat for the expedition as he did when Liv and Stefan used it to sail to the elves' homeland in the South Pacific.

He'd offered to be their captain, but they declined, Liv stating that she wanted to get there without a migraine. The king of the fae had also delivered the map which gave them so many details about the coordinates, where the genie's lamp was located at the bottom of the ocean and even places of interest to stop along the way. Most didn't seem that interesting to Sophia, but she realized that she and Rudolf had different definitions of entertaining. To her, a rock shaped like a naked woman wasn't worth a detour.

The *Serena* sailed through the choppy Arctic waters toward their destination. Heathcliff and Beatrix both flew above the ship in the frigid air. Rudolf had thrown Stan's lamp into the nearly freezing waters off Greenland. He'd mentioned that if sinking it to the bottom of the ocean didn't work then maybe he could freeze the genie, thereby keeping him from killing him.

That was the concern with becoming a genie's master. When in someone's service, they had to fulfill the three wishes. However, once the master made their last wish, the genie would then do whatever they could to off the person so that they were no longer a slave and finally had their freedom.

That's why people usually put the genie in the lamp and "lost" it, getting as far from it as possible after the last wish. The trapped genie couldn't kill them and had to wait until some unsuspecting person happened across the lamp again, restarting the entire process. Successfully killing their master freed them, but that rarely happened.

Sophia and Liv weren't going to take a chance. Once they'd "fixed" the baby, they'd toss the genie's lamp back into the frigid Arctic depths and sail away. That was another reason Liv used for why Rudolf couldn't accompany them. He was Stan's last master, and if they were reunited, the genie would go after the fae and try to kill him for his freedom.

"It's sort of sad that they're slaves," Sophia said, referring to Stan and other genies, as the ship sailed itself on course for the location of the genie's lamp.

"Again, having a lot of alone time doesn't sound like such a bad idea," Liv muttered while pulling up her cloak against the cutting wind.

"You okay?" Sophia gave her sister a sideways look. "You seem a little more distant and like you want space from the world."

"I would usually answer that with 'I'm fine,' but I'm not, and it's you asking," Liv replied. "The truth is, I'm having such a hard time processing this baby thing. I've not gotten the chance to celebrate or feel excited because from the beginning we suspected it would have demon blood. Then I found out that it did and that's been a whole other set of problems. Like, oh no, I'm going to bring a demon into this world. Then I was like, oh and the demon could turn me into a monster." She shook her head, looking overwhelmed. "The whole thing has been very frustrating."

Sophia offered her sister a sympathetic look. "I don't think frustrating covers it, but that's my perspective."

"The thing is," Liv went on, looking out at the gray ocean waters and icebergs in the distance, making it all feel even colder. "When I get past this whole demon aspect, I feel like the real hurdle begins. I never saw myself as a mother. I've always been such a loner and to think that someone is going to rely on me for…well, just about everything is such a weird notion. Like, what if I don't love my child or I don't know how to take care of him or her? What if I do put this baby in danger by being a Warrior? I have so many doubts about my abilities to be a good parent that I'm almost glad that all I can think about is whether the baby will be a demon or not."

Sophia took a long moment to consider what her sister had said, also looking out at the choppy waters but not really seeing them. She hadn't considered all these concerns, but they made perfect sense to her now. Finally, she reached out and put a comforting hand on her sister's arm and smiled. "You never saw yourself as a Warrior for the House of Fourteen, and you're by far the best one it has ever had. You're like a mother to me, whether you know it or not. You're the most loving person anyone in your life knows. It's just that you're not packaged like one would expect that kind of person to be. You don't smile when you mean to frown. You don't compliment unless it's genuine. You always say things like they are. More than anything, you make everyone and everything better by being a part of our lives. I understand you have doubts about being a mother. I think that's totally understandable. I think all new mothers face that. But I have zero doubts because you're the Unstoppable Liv Beaufont and there's no way that you're not going to be the best mother to your baby. You'll love it as you love Stefan and me and everyone in your life and it will come as naturally as slaying a bad-tempered troll."

Liv laughed, seemingly grateful for the joke thrown in at the end. "I appreciate the vote of confidence. I wish I felt that for myself. You're probably right. I have to let it happen, and it will all unfold as it did with my Warrior role for the House of Fourteen."

Liv didn't look confident or sure about this, but she did seem to be trying to convince herself. Sophia would have offered her more words of motivation, but right then the boat slowed and the anchor magically rattled over *The Serena's* side. They'd reached their destination. They were right on top of Stan's genie lamp.

CHAPTER EIGHTY-TWO

"Well, Heathcliff," Liv called, looking up at where the winged sea otter hovered in the sky. "Looks like it's time for you to do your job. You know what to do?"

Heathcliff had seen the map that Rudolf had created, showing where Stan's lamp was on the ocean floor. Sand, rock, and shells covered it, so getting to it would be a challenge. However, Bermuda had reassured the sisters that Heathcliff was right for the job. Evan could have also done it with Coral, but in the frigid water, it would be much more difficult for them. Heathcliff, the winged otter, made much more sense.

Something sparked in the magical creature's eyes before it dove for the surface of the water like a missile, entering the Arctic Ocean without hesitation.

Liv shivered. "Man, I'm glad I don't have to go in that water. Of course, Ru had to toss the genie's lamp in the Arctic."

Sophia laughed and agreed with a nod, looking over the side of the anchored boat. "Now what do we do?"

Liv looked around as Beatrix landed on the mainmast, folding her wings in and bracing herself against the gust of icy winds.

"I've meant to watch the latest season of the *Great British Baking*

Show," Liv offered, pulling out her phone. "I should be able to get reception out here."

"Because you can create a hot spot?" Sophia questioned, impressed that Liv would have WiFi in the middle of the Arctic Ocean.

"Because my phone has so much magitech in it that it can get reception in the middle of the planet if I want it to," Liv answered with a laugh.

"I can't remember the last time that I could sit back and relax and watch a show," Sophia said, getting excited. "But I think we should stay on the main deck for when Heathcliff returns."

"I agree," Liv stated, creating a fireball in her hand with ease. She'd been given fire magic by Papa Creola, making it easy for her to create a flame when it would normally tax another magician. Not Sophia, because she had the chi of the dragon. The fire instantly made the sisters warmer.

Liv pulled the show up on her phone while leaning on the ship's railing. A moment later, something heavy landed on the deck behind them. It made *The Serena* tilt dangerously to the side before righting itself.

Both sisters whipped around, pulling their swords in a flash. Instantly, Sophia relaxed and took in the unexpected guest.

"Lunis, what are you doing here?" Sophia laughed at the blue dragon now taking up a majority of the ship's deck.

He lifted his head regally and glared down at the two magicians. "You were seriously going to watch the new season of the *Great British Baking Show* without me? I've been waiting for you for ages to watch that."

Sophia continued to chuckle. "Sorry. I would've watched it with you too. How did you get here so quickly?"

He harrumphed. "When I heard about this treachery brought on by that booger-face, I had Wilder open a portal for me outside the Barrier so I could get here pronto."

"Wow, that was fast," Sophia admitted, impressed by the timing.

"It's important," Lunis replied.

"Did a supposed know-it-all majestic dragon just call me a booger-face?" Liv asked, amused.

"In my head, I called you something much worse," Lunis stated.

Sophia glanced at her sister, amused. "Don't worry. He treats Wilder equally bad."

"He must like the abuse if he diligently made you a portal so quickly," Liv offered.

"Okay, well, let's watch the latest season," Lunis ordered and settled down, making the ship rock again. "I hope you brought snacks, Soph."

"I didn't," she said with a laugh.

"I was told there would be snacks at this viewing party," the blue dragon complained.

Liv pursed her lips. "You weren't invited to this viewing party, Bruce."

Lunis ignored her. "Use a projector spell to make the screen bigger. I want to see every pore on host Noel's face. Whatever that guy uses for his skincare, I need to know."

Liv gave Sophia a sideways look. "Wow, your dragon is so very strange."

"So is your face," Lunis quipped. "Now, more show and less talk. The secret of good writing."

"That's not how that phrase goes," Liv joked and pulled her phone back up. She didn't get too far before Beatrix hooted loudly overhead, her call carrying a warning of sorts. Then, a second later, something large knocked into the side of the ship.

CHAPTER EIGHTY-THREE

"Liv, did you fart?" Lunis asked as the sisters whipped around, looking over *The Serena's* side where the commotion came from.

Sophia expected to see something to do with Heathcliff, although whatever was knocking into the ship's side was much larger than the winged otter. The choppy waters of the Arctic Ocean made it hard to see what was causing the disturbance. The sea bubbled and splashed, but something large was causing the uproar and making the ship tip dangerously back and forth.

"What is it?" Sophia squinted to see what was under the water's surface.

Lunis' head lowered right next to hers, and he also studied the scene. "It's a whale."

"That can't be good." Liv straightened with sudden enhanced tension.

"Settle down, Sally," Lunis commented. "It's not a huge blue whale. It's a tiny little narwhal."

Sophia leaned further over the side of the ship, as Lunis was able to do thanks to his long neck, granting him a better view of what was happening. When she began to slip over the side, the blue dragon secured her in place with his arm. "Watch it there, missy. If you fall in, I'm going to have to take an ice bath and me no likey the cold."

Sophia nodded, catching her breath from the sudden excitement. It *was* a narwhal. She realized that as she finally spied what was knocking into the ship.

"They aren't usually aggressive whales," Sophia related, having read about them in Bermuda's *Magical Creatures* book. Most didn't know that narwhals were magical animals with a few unique properties. They were always ninety-eight degrees no matter the temperature, and the male's tusk could transmit a telepathic signal across great distances, serving as a communication device. For those reasons, evil poachers wanting their hide and tusks often hunted the narwhal.

"I think she's simply trying to get our attention," Lunis offered as the narwhal swam away from the ship several yards and turned around, looking at them intently from the surface of the water.

"How do you know it's a girl?" Liv asked.

"Because she's wearing an apron and looks peeved about something small and trivial," Lunis joked.

"Because she doesn't have a tusk," Sophia answered with a laugh.

Liv nodded. "Oh, yeah, that unicorn horn that the funny whales often have."

"The males do," Lunis corrected. "They aren't unicorn horns, genius."

"I think she wants us to follow her," Sophia observed, watching as the narwhal swam off several more yards and turned, looking at them with an intense expression of fear in her eyes.

"Well, we're sort of waiting for Heathcliff to arrive, but I guess he'll find us." Liv twirled her finger and brought up the anchor. *The Serena* sailed through the waters and followed the narwhal, who swam in the opposite direction at great speed.

When they neared a beautiful bluish-white glacier that rose out of the Arctic waters, the whale turned and paused, her snout indicating the block of ice.

Liv leaned over the side of the ship, then stated, "There's something down there."

Thankfully, the waters were so clean next to the glacier that it was easier to see through them. When the ship had anchored again, the water's surface became still once more, and they could make out what was causing the narwhal so much stress.

Trapped with his tusk firmly embedded in the glacier was another narwhal. He was stuck, and it seemed the only way he would be freed was if someone, or somebodies, helped him.

CHAPTER EIGHTY-FOUR

"Oh, that poor whale," Sophia exclaimed, seeing the stress on the stuck narwhal as he tried to maneuver out of the predicament.

"It's like the time that Liv licked a frosty telephone pole," Lunis teased.

Liv shook her head. "Not the time for jokes, Carl. This is serious."

He grimaced. "It's always time for jokes. That's how I keep Sophia calm in high-intensity situations."

Sophia nodded. "It's true."

"Plus, it's not like I'm not going to swoop in and save the day," Lunis stated with a huff. He backed up several feet as he unfolded his wings.

Nimbly and without rocking the boat, the blue dragon sprang into the air, flapping his wings and sending icy wind onto the magicians below.

"Wow, that was quite the takeoff," Liv said, sounding impressed.

"I heard that," Lunis called from the air. "You complimented me. That's going in the scrapbook."

"You're reading into it," Liv teased as Lunis dove for the waters where the narwhal was trapped. He plummeted neatly into the ocean, disappearing as the waters swelled from his displacement.

Sophia and Liv couldn't make out what was happening due to the bubbling water and waves. However, Sophia could see from Lunis' mind and spied as he gently but firmly secured his grasp around the narwhal. Then he yanked the whale in the opposite direction, pulling him back. The stuck tusk popped free of the ice, and as soon as he'd untangled the narwhal, Lunis released him and swam up from the waters, flying at once. He landed on the deck of the ship, shaking. Even the short stint in the water was almost too much for the blue dragon. Temperatures like those in the Arctic Ocean were too much for a dragon whose element wasn't water.

While his teeth chattered, Sophia and Liv went to work using a warming spell to thaw the icy dragon. The process was swift with both magicians working on it, and Sophia was grateful when relief flooded Lunis' eyes.

"Thank you," he said, returning to his previous relaxed appearance.

"You made quick work of that situation," Liv said, again sounding impressed.

The light expression dropped from Lunis' face. "That was only the beginning. I saw why the narwhal was stuck, and we have a major ordeal on our hands."

CHAPTER EIGHTY-FIVE

"Poachers," Liv seethed after Lunis explained what he thought was going on.

"Yeah, from what I could tell," Lunis began, "they've created a narrow opening in the glacier that's big enough for a baby narwhal to get through but not a grown-up. It's constructed so the narwhals can get in but not out of the container area. It looks like they've carved out the glacier to create a cage of sorts. It's thin enough that I could see dozens of baby narwhals trapped on the other side."

"That's despicable." Sophia looked over the side of the ship and spied the momma and papa narwhal swimming around in distress, obviously trying to get to their baby.

"I could use my fire to melt the glacier," Lunis offered. "That would release the narwhals."

Sophia thought for a moment. "That's a pretty straightforward plan, but there's a problem with it."

"That you didn't come up with it?" Lunis quipped.

She shook her head. "No, that glacier is probably a hundred thousand years old. The oldest ones in the world are in Greenland. We can't in good conscience melt it, thereby creating problems for the planet and destroying something so old."

Liv nodded. "Soph is right."

"Guys, we're talking about a few dozen baby narwhals that are trapped and going to be slaughtered by poachers," Lunis argued. "We can wait around for those jerks to show up and take them out, or we can melt the glacier they've already partially destroyed and be on our way."

"We're going to do both," Liv said, her eyes sparkling with sudden excitement. "Then we're going to fix the damage they've done."

"How are we going to do that?" Sophia asked, confused, and also intrigued.

Liv sighed, looking slightly disappointed. "We have to call someone I hoped not to because he has ice magic."

Sophia groaned. "Oh, but I hoped we got to accomplish this mission without him…"

Liv returned the defeated expression. "Yeah, I know, but it appears we'll have to rely on King Rudolf after all."

CHAPTER EIGHTY-SIX

The plan made the most sense, although summoning King Rudolf Sweetwater wasn't something anyone wanted to do. However, as a fae, he had ice magic. This meant that Lunis could melt the glacier to release the baby narwhals, and the fae could resurrect it after, repairing what the poachers had done. Then Liv planned to follow the clues and go after the poachers, taking them out before they could do any more harm to magical creatures or the planet.

Pulling a small crystal out of her pocket, Liv gave Sophia a tired look. "Are you ready to be thoroughly annoyed?"

Sophia laughed. "Yeah. Once again, Rudolf is strangely going to save the day. I still don't get how he's so helpful when he has to wear loafers because he hasn't figured out how to tie his shoes."

"After six hundred years," Liv added.

"Maybe when he turns seven hundred," Lunis stated.

Liv held the crystal in her hand and rolled her eyes. "Please ignore what I'm about to say. It's the only way the summoning crystal that Rudolf gave me for emergencies will work."

Sophia nodded, having heard about this stone that would pull Rudolf from anywhere on the globe and instantly bring him straight to Liv. It was a pretty incredible magical artifact.

"Let's hope that he's decent." Liv closed her eyes and released a breath. "Rudolf, I need you."

The words were hardly out of her mouth when King Rudolf Sweetwater appeared beside them on the ship, his face covered in a charcoal face mask, his blond hair wrapped in foil rolls and dressed in a thick bathrobe—surprise evident on his face.

CHAPTER EIGHTY-SEVEN

"Holy bananas!" Rudolf exclaimed, cinching the bathrobe tighter around his body. "It's freaking cold here in this spa."

Liv sighed and glanced at Sophia. "At least he's decent."

"Sort of," Lunis muttered. "I don't think he has anything on under that robe. Nice leg, Rudolf."

"Why thank you," Rudolf sang with a smile that looked very strange with the thick charcoal face mask. "No, I don't have anything on under this robe. Anyone want to see my birthday suit?"

"Not unless you want me to poke out my eyes," Liv replied.

Sophia twirled her finger and magicked a thick parka around the fae, covering his bathrobe.

"This isn't real fur, is it?" Rudolf asked, apparently the more burning question rather than why he was suddenly on his ship in the middle of the Arctic Ocean.

Sophia shook her head. "No, and this isn't a spa."

Rudolf looked around, taking in the sights. "Are you sure? I've heard that the thermal pools in Iceland are amazing. I'd take one of those baths about now."

Liv rolled her eyes. "No, King Dorkface. This is the Arctic, and we were trying to recover the genie's lamp you had to throw in these waters instead of the ones off the coast of…I don't know, anyplace else that's warm."

"Oh, you need my help after all as the ship's captain?" Rudolf snapped his fingers, making the face mask and hair foil disappear.

"Nope," Liv replied.

"You need help finding the genie's lamp?" Rudolf questioned.

"Nah," Liv answered.

"Then you simply missed me," Rudolf stated triumphantly.

"I'd need a few hundred years away from you for that to happen," Liv remarked.

"Then why would you interrupt my daily spa appointment? You know that if I don't have daily massages and facials that I get grumpy and start to look as bad as you," Rudolf remarked.

"Because…" Liv seemed to have trouble getting the words out. "We maybe, kind of, sort of need your help."

"Oh, well, I'm happy to do that." Rudolf snapped his fingers again and added clothes under the thick fur-lined parka. He looked at her sideways and nodded. "Yes, you're right, that cloak makes you look fat. What else would you like me to advise you on? Your hair is probably beyond help at this point."

"Strangely, I didn't summon you here so you could advise me on fashion and hair," Liv muttered.

"We need your ice magic," Sophia cut in.

Rudolf glanced around. "Oh, silly girl. Isn't this enough ice for you? There's a whole block of it right there." He indicated the glacier in front of the boat.

"That's the thing," Liv stated. "We're going to melt that glacier."

Rudolf's eyes widened. "But melting glaciers is wrong according to the news."

"Exactly," Lunis chirped.

"Which is why we need you to put it back together," Liv added.

"Oh…that's a big job." Rudolf suddenly looked overwhelmed. "I'm glad I ate that entire pan of brownies for breakfast."

CHAPTER EIGHTY-EIGHT

"I had an entire pan of brownies for breakfast too," Lunis stated.

"Me too," Liv muttered.

"Then you had an Oreo cheesecake for lunch and dinner?" Sophia questioned her sister.

"That was yesterday. Keep up," Liv answered.

"Okay, so how is this going to work?" Sophia felt like she needed to keep everyone focused or they'd all exchange brownie recipes instead of attending to the narwhal situation.

"You and Chip need to fly over the glacier and melt it to pieces," Liv began. "Then you can usher the baby narwhals to freedom."

Everyone nodded except for Rudolf. "I don't know who Chip is, but I think it would be easier if Sophia rode Lunis and he melted the glacier."

"Great idea," Sophia stated.

"For me to put the glacier back together, I'll need to be directly over it," Rudolf stated.

Liv frowned. "Well, we have a boat and Sophia is using her dragon. Did you bring a hot air balloon?"

He felt around in his pockets as though one might be in there. "I don't think so, but I do have this."

Rudolf pulled out a small scrap of fabric from the parka that Sophia had manifested for him, which was entirely too perplexing for her brain to understand.

"Oh, great," Liv said with mock excitement. "You brought fabric samples. That will be incredibly helpful as we try and rescue a bunch of baby narwhals from poachers. I'm so glad that against all my better instincts, I decided to summon you."

"I know, right?" Rudolf agreed, not at all catching the sarcasm in Liv's voice. "You're going to forever be in my debt after this one."

He laid the small piece of fabric on the ship's deck and tapped his finger on his chin. "Now, what was the incantation to make this work?"

"I'm a dumb idiot, oh why does anyone like me?" Liv sing-songed.

Rudolf shook his head, quite seriously. "I don't think so." His face brightened with realization. "That's right! It's open sesame."

Nothing happened.

Rudolf continued to drum his fingers on his chin. "Hmmmm... maybe it's shazam."

"I'm certain that it's not," Liv muttered dryly.

Again nothing happened to the piece of fabric.

"Oh!" Rudolf exclaimed, throwing his finger straight into the air. "It's abracadabra!"

"Right," Liv drew out the word. "The magical phrase to transform that piece of fabric into something useful is abracadabra..."

The king of the fae nodded at her with confidence, as though she was serious. Liv ate her doubt when the piece of seemingly useless fabric rose into the air with a poof of smoke, expanded in every direction, then scrunched up on itself. It appeared to be a large wad of fabric for a moment before it unrolled to reveal a lovely Persian rug hovering in the air.

Rudolf had done it again, surprising them all by creating a magic flying carpet.

CHAPTER EIGHTY-NINE

E veryone was silent.

Liv scratched her head, looked at Sophia with total surprise, then at the magic flying carpet, and back at Sophia.

Finally, she threw up her hands in surrender. "Is the joke really on us? Rudolf, are you a genius and you've made us all believe you're an idiot? Or are you brain-dead as I've suspected all along and accidentally do things that are incredibly skillful and well, sometimes unintended?"

Rudolf held up his finger and wagged it back and forth. "I'm never going to tell you and therefore keep you guessing."

"So, you regularly carry a magic carpet in the coat that someone else magicked for you then?" Lunis sounded amused.

The fae nodded. "Usually. It depends on what side of the equator I'm on. Oh, and the season. Oh! And if I've had beans recently."

Sophia glanced at Lunis and shook her head at the confusion writing itself on his face. "Don't ask. It's better if you don't ask."

The blue dragon nodded. "You have more dealings with this genius looney-toon than I do, so I'll take your word for it."

"You..." Liv began and pointed at Rudolf, her voice fading, seeming lost for words. "You...you...created a magic flying carpet..."

"Well, I need to fly over where the glacier needs to be," Rudolf explained. "Since we're also retrieving a genie's lamp from these waters, it only seemed fitting. Which reminds me, when Stan gets here, I need to skedaddle. I don't want him to kill me and all."

"Good point," Liv stated. "I'd like to be his new master, so don't worry. I'll intervene."

"Okay, then it sounds like we're ready to rescue some baby narwhals." Sophia strode over to Lunis and stepped up onto his wing to get into the saddle.

Rudolf jumped quite nimbly onto the floating carpet, then spun and offered a hand to Liv. "Will you accompany me on my mission, my lady?"

Liv pursed her lips, but a smile hid behind her eyes. Finally, she climbed onto the flying rug without taking the king's hand. "Do you know how to steer this thing?"

"Yeah, it's like Mario Kart," Rudolf answered.

"You need a game controller?" Lunis questioned.

"The fact that you get that reference is weird, Greg," Liv imparted.

"No, it's like Mario Kart in that if you get hit by a turtle's shell, you'll get thrown off course," Rudolf explained as if that made perfect sense.

Liv gave Sophia a tentative look. "I guess we're avoiding flying turtle shells then..."

"Well, those are the metaphor, Liv," Rudolf reasoned. "They represent sharp winds and clouds. As long as we don't get hit by either, we should be fine."

"Oh good," Liv said sarcastically. "Because neither of those exists here in the frigid Arctic..."

Sophia looked up to where white puffy clouds rolled by, spurred on by the constant winds sailing over the Arctic Ocean. "Let's make this fast. Then we can recover the genie's lamp."

Rudolf nodded as Lunis took off into the blue skies, the magic carpet following behind the dragon and rider. "Then we can all go and get some ice cream."

"Think I'll have my fill of ice after this," Liv stated, crouching low to secure her balance on the moving carpet as it soared higher into the sky.

CHAPTER NINETY

The winds were stronger as Lunis and Sophia gained altitude. She looked over her shoulder, staying low, and worried how Liv and Rudolf were faring. She realized that she probably should be worried. Not only because the winds were cutting but because it looked like he was a little rusty at steering the magic flying carpet.

Liv held onto the sides of the Persian rug while looking over the side like she was thinking of jumping back onto the boat before it was too late. The carpet swung to one side and the next like a leaf being thrown around by the wind.

"Maybe we should go back and get Liv," Sophia related to her dragon.

"She'll be fine," he stated with confidence. "They have their job, and we have ours. Have some confidence in the king of the fae."

"But…"

"Have some faith, Sophia. They're two of the most powerful magical people on this planet," Lunis argued. "Sometimes you have to face forward and believe that the people you've put stock in will come through. Otherwise, you'll be the one to let them down when you fail from being overly concerned about their wellbeing."

Sophia couldn't believe it, but Lunis had done it again. He'd gone from talking about Mario Kart to giving her sage advice.

Turning fully back to face forward, Sophia focused on the glacier as they approached. She didn't have to do much at this point. Navigating was part of her job, but it was Lunis who would scorch the iceberg. Still, her dragon was right. If Sophia didn't stay focused, she would ruin this for everyone.

After steering Lunis to the floe's center, Sophia was careful to position him in exactly the right place. He could spend all day blasting fire to melt it like a blow torch dissolving an ice cube. Or he could hit a critical area and break the glacier at a pivotal part, sending it into pieces and thereby freeing the baby narwhals. That would be the most efficient strategy. Not only that, but it would make Rudolf's reconstruction job easier.

When they were in place, Lunis hovered in front of the berg, close but not too close. They both knew that the potential of his fire rebounding off the thick ice was very likely. This wasn't a straightforward job. It would take speed and resourcefulness.

"Are you ready?" Sophia leaned low on her dragon.

"Are you?" he asked. "A one-hundred-thousand-year-old glacier falling into the ocean won't go unnoticed by those in the sea or the sky."

Sophia nodded. "We've got this, Lunis. Soon this will be all over, and we'll be warm once more."

CHAPTER NINETY-ONE

L iv was pretty sure she was going to kill King Rudolf Sweetwater after this. He laughed with glee like they were joyriding on the magic carpet, which had zero shocks and jerked violently with every wind. She felt like she was riding on...well, a Persian rug over the Arctic Ocean. There wasn't a better description. She'd once flown on a tiny single-engine plane and thought that was rough. That experience seemed like a luxury as the freezing wind blasted her in the face and she clung to the side of the magic rug, wishing there was a seat belt or an airbag or a puke bag.

The things I do to save the world, Liv bitterly thought as they swerved from side to side for no apparent reason. It seemed to her that they could have taken a straight course like Lunis and Sophia, who flew ahead of them, but instead, they were on an invisible obstacle course.

A massive gust of wind hit the carpet's front, sending it up, and the rug nearly went vertical. Liv held on for dear life, wondering why she decided to accompany Rudolf when she could be safe and much warmer on the ship below. The fae didn't at all seem unnerved by the ride. Instead, he hollered and slammed his fist down on the front of the rug, and it snapped back to a horizontal position.

I'm definitely going to kill him. Liv almost rolled off the side from the momentum. She caught herself with the front of her boot on the edge of the rug, which was much stiffer than she would have expected. Her gaze fell over the carpet's side to the waters below, and Liv tensed, not wanting to know what the sea felt like. She didn't think she'd survive a plunge into those waters. The baby definitely wouldn't.

The magic carpet felt more like a roller coaster than a romantic ride that Aladdin and Jasmine would have taken. When Liv thought she was about to throw up over the side, it slowed. Stilled. Rose like an elevator, taking a position right next to the blue dragon.

Sophia looked so confident sitting on her dragon. She glanced at Liv, nodded, and turned her attention forward to the glacier in front of them.

It was time to free the captured narwhals.

CHAPTER NINETY-TWO

Sophia knew that Lunis was right. She needed to focus on her mission with her dragon and lend him her support. Liv might look a little green on the magic carpet beside them, but she was safe. She'd be okay, Sophia told herself.

"Time to melt some hundred-thousand-year-old ice," Lunis said casually.

"Just a regular Tuesday," Sophia joked as her dragon opened his mouth and shot a massive spout of flame at the bluish glacier.

The fire was hot and fast, with an intensity that could knock over a steel-reinforced bank vault door. It hit the colossal ice floe and rebounded off it as they'd expected, but not so much that it hit them.

Lunis shot all his fire in one hot and fast blast. It wasn't long, but it was all that he had, having concentrated his efforts. When he closed his mouth, the blue dragon sank a few inches, having lost a considerable amount of energy. At first, nothing happened. The glacier hadn't melted immediately, turning into water. It hadn't done anything. It was almost like it hadn't worked at all, which meant they needed to figure out another plan.

Then there was a huge *crack* that echoed all around them like thunder in the sky. It created another set of cracks like an avalanche.

The front of the iceberg broke off, falling into the sea and sending frigid water into the air, but thankfully not high enough to reach them.

The floe didn't melt all at once. It didn't sink into the ocean as they'd expected. Instead, it split in half like a door opening, and it parted neatly, creating an exit.

Like an opened flood gate, the baby narwhals instantly started swimming through the gap, excitement in their every movement. Sophia glanced down, watching reunions happening all around them.

Adult narwhals surfaced all over the Arctic Ocean, splashing and making noises she could only characterize as ones of relief and joy.

The two halves of the glacier continued to move farther apart as the last of the baby narwhals spilled through the opening. It was time to put things back together.

Sophia looked at Liv and Rudolf with an expression that said, "Now it's your turn."

Liv nodded, standing confidently and sturdily on the floating magic carpet. It was up to the unlikely pair to fix the ancient and irreplaceable glacier.

CHAPTER NINETY-THREE

Without Rudolf having to say it, Liv knew what her part of this job was. She needed to guide the pieces back together after the last baby narwhal had left. Then it would be up to Rudolf to seal it into a whole.

Standing firmly beside the king of the fae, Liv looked at the two halves drifting in opposite directions. She held up both hands and focused with all her being, knowing that it would take a huge amount of magic to pull the two structures back together.

She gritted her teeth, trying with all her might to stop the glaciers from sailing in opposite directions. Beside her, she felt Rudolf's attention on her. He knew what she had to do and just like she couldn't help him with his job, he couldn't do anything. Only watch and wait.

The ice floes halted with an enormous lurch, sending water splashing sharply over the sides from the stopped momentum.

Liv had done it.

Well, she'd done half of her job. She'd stopped their progress. The next part was even more critical and challenging, and Liv didn't know if she had the strength to draw the vast glaciers back together.

Her knees felt weak. Her breath was short. The cold was quickly draining her.

She needed help.

CHAPTER NINETY-FOUR

There was being confident in your friends and family, and there was recognizing when they needed help.

Liv had been through so much. The baby was taking her reserves. Sophia knew that if she didn't step in, they would fail. It was too big a job for one pregnant magician who needed her reserves.

Holding out both her hands, copying Liv's movements, Sophia focused on drawing one side of the glacier to the other. It had stopped drifting the other way, but now it needed to come back together.

At first, it didn't move. Then, as though it was trying to make up for lost progress, it sailed back the direction it had come like it wanted to reunite with its other half. The work was draining. Sophia at her full strength couldn't have imagined Liv drawing both halves together.

Yet, Sophia knew that once the half she was responsible for was in place, she wasn't going to be able to do much more. Her reserves would be low, especially after lending so much to Lunis so that he could use his fire magic.

When her half of the glacier was back where it had been, Sophia lowered her hands and slumped, not even having the energy to look at

Liv to see if she knew that she had to take over for a moment. Sophia was so drained. She closed her eyes, knowing that she needed a moment to recharge. Otherwise, she'd be worthless.

CHAPTER NINETY-FIVE

Tears prickled in Liv's eyes. Her little sister had come to her rescue and just in time. If she hadn't pulled the other half of the iceberg back into place, then all would have been lost. It was simply too much for Liv.

But Sophia had done it. Now it was up to Liv to do the rest.

She directed all her focus on the glacier, finding a motivation deep inside her to complete this challenge. It was a new one and connected to her fear. Liv realized at that moment that it was also becoming her strength.

She'd worried about having a child. She was still. However, she was no longer worried about being a mother. She'd watched the narwhals trying to rescue their baby and knew that feeling instinctively. Liv might not know how to parent, but she knew how to protect. Taking care of her child would come as easily as her job as a Warrior. She'd *know* how to be a mother. Somehow...some way...

With a shaking hand, Liv sent a huge force of magic at the other half of the glacier. It didn't drift back in the direction in which it came. It soared across the gap and attached to its other half straight away, like the narwhal babies that had reunited with their parents.

Once the two halves were up against each other, Liv lowered her hand, feeling light even after the considerable feat. Now the next and final part was up to King Rudolf Sweetwater.

CHAPTER NINETY-SIX

The look of concentration on Rudolf's face was so different from his normal jovial expression. Sophia watched as he lifted his hands, but not focusing as she and Liv had done. He looked like he was the conductor of a symphony, about to start a show.

A great *cracking* sound filled the air.

The air suddenly grew thicker as if the water molecules in it had all turned to ice, making it harder to breathe.

Sophia felt frost forming on her face and looked down to see ice growing like fungus on her cloak. She stiffened but realized that she was simply experiencing a byproduct of Rudolf's extensive use of magic.

The two parts of the glacier were sewing back together, becoming one again. Even more impressive was that the hole the poachers had dug in the center to cage the narwhals was refilling. The glacier was becoming anew.

The fae was repairing all the damage. It wasn't an easy feat, but with the help of three other incredibly strong magical beings and some impressive teamwork, it was happening.

It didn't take as long as Sophia would have expected for a single man to repair a one-hundred-thousand-year-old glacier. When he finished, there was no evidence that it had ever been damaged.

Rudolf casually lowered his hands and let out a breath that looked like a cloud of mist. He turned and smiled at Liv and Sophia, relief flooding his eyes.

That instance reminded Sophia of how a few people could save the world. It didn't take much. It only took the concerted effort of a small group who would rather lose a little of themselves to save the greater good.

The world might not know what they'd done that day, but Sophia knew, and it reminded her of why she regularly risked her life. It was worth it. The world would always be worth saving—no matter what.

CHAPTER NINETY-SEVEN

"I need nachos," Liv said when she stepped off the magic flying carpet back onto the ship. She was so happy to be on a more stable surface that she looked ready to kiss the deck.

"I need a hot fudge sundae," Sophia added, sliding off Lunis after also landing on *The Serena*.

"I'll take a chili cheese hotdog," Lunis supplied, shaking out his wings before folding them against his body.

"I could really go for some green beans," Rudolf stated.

All eyes turned to him, regarding him with disbelief.

"Seriously?" Liv questioned. "We're all zapped of our magic after that ordeal and need a substantial amount of calories to refill reserves, and you want green beans?"

"Or edamame," Rudolf answered.

"Good thing he's good-looking," Lunis muttered loudly to Sophia.

Liv shook her head. "I wonder if Uber Eats delivers out here?"

Rudolf scratched his head. "If so the food would probably be cold by the time we got it."

"I was joking, you Cracker Jack," Liv retorted.

Sophia pulled a protein bar from her cloak. "You want this, Liv?"

Her sister eyed the chocolate chip protein bar like it was a steak dinner, then shook her head, seeming to shake off the longing. "No, you have it."

Sophia opened the bar and broke it in half, handing it over to Liv.

Reluctantly, her sister took it, knowing that she was no good to anyone if she passed out from low magical reserves. "Thanks."

"Hey, can I have some of that?" Rudolf asked.

Sophia nodded, breaking her half in half and handing it over to the king of the fae. They all ate their cold protein bar pieces in silence.

"I think I'll go eat a penguin." Lunis scanned the area, trying to decide which was the best direction to take off to find such a thing.

"This isn't that bad," Rudolf said in between bites. "I mean, it's probably not as good as one of the meals that the five-star Michelin chef on the lower deck of this ship could make us."

Liv slowly lowered the rest of her protein bar. Sophia stopped chewing. Lunis' mouth dropped open.

"Are you freaking kidding me?" Liv nearly yelled. "You have a personal chef on this ship?"

Rudolf continued to eat his part of the protein bar. "Yeah, Sergio. He makes the best...well, I don't know what they are, but they're like little clouds of heaven dripping in a sauce made of angels."

"He's here now?" Sophia asked in disbelief.

Rudolf nodded. "Yeah, he's always on *The Serena*. I make him live here. I can't stand having to make my own grilled cheeses when we take boat rides."

Liv glanced at Sophia and back at Rudolf and once more at her sister. "Should I kill him or do you want to?"

"I'd actually like that honor." Lunis bared his teeth at the fae.

"Oh, do you guys want Sergio to make us some food?" Rudolf asked, confused.

Liv rolled her eyes. "No, after melting ancient ice, freeing a bunch of narwhal babies, and fusing a glacier back together, we'd like a stale protein bar."

"Me too!" Rudolf exclaimed. "I never get to eat commoner food. You guys all have handy food that's easy on the go." He sighed. "I'm always forced to eat at candlelit tables with the finest linens and choke down filet mignons and saffron-infused potatoes with truffle sauce. It's so annoying."

"Sounds horrible," Liv stated dryly.

"Seriously, I could eat him, and no one would know," Lunis offered.

Sophia shook her head. "We would know." She glanced at Liv. "You want to head to the lower deck and get some braised lamb and roasted duck?"

"I'll race you." Liv started for the main hatch that led to the lower deck of *The Serena*.

Sophia gave Lunis a pleading expression. "Will you stay up here and keep an eye out for when Heathcliff returns? I'll bring you a rack of lamb."

"And some chocolate mousse," he added. "Of course. You two get some food. I'll ensure that King One Brain Cell steers the ship back in the right direction."

"Thanks, Lun." Sophia smiled over her shoulder at her dragon. Her stomach rumbled something awful. She hoped there was bread with warm butter—a crusty baguette. If so, she would eat all of it and still have plenty of room for some dinner, dessert, and more dessert.

CHAPTER NINETY-EIGHT

Feeling a thousand percent better, Liv and Sophia made their way back up to the main deck after filling up on cheesy tartiflette, rich phyllo-wrapped beef Wellington, lobster fra Diavolo, chocolate truffle layer cake, and lots and lots of bread.

Sophia had one of the waiters bring up a rack of lamb for Lunis, only lightly seared—the way he liked it. Liv told the waiter to pass along a few insults from her to Rudolf when he was on the upper deck.

Based on the broad grin on the fae's face when the sisters met him and Lunis up top, the waiter hadn't complied. Or, as was more likely was the case, Rudolf had taken the insults as compliments.

Lunis licked his chops as Sophia arrived beside him, looking much more content than when she left him.

"Feeling better?" He looked her over.

"I feel like I ate an entire cow." She held her stomach but was grateful for the fullness. It would fuel her for whatever she had to do next, which was always a surprise.

"I've eaten an entire cow before, and if you did, you'd be asleep right now," Lunis offered with a laugh.

Liv patted her stomach while smiling wide. "It wasn't nachos, but it was delicious."

"Sergio could have made you nachos," Rudolf stated. "He makes these spa nachos for Serena. Instead of chips, he uses slices of cauliflower, and instead of cheese he uses a nut paste, and instead of jalapenos he uses—"

"Stop murdering my soul," Liv interrupted.

"They're delicious and good for you," Rudolf argued, looking offended.

"Instead of joy, does he use pain and torment?" Lunis questioned quite seriously.

Liv laughed. "Good one, Thomas."

"I don't know if this is of interest to any of you," Rudolf began, squinting in the distance, his hand over his eyes. "A flying monkey carrying a shiny gravy dish is headed our way."

Liv and Sophia both jerked their heads up to find the winged otter flying in their direction, a golden genie lamp in his front paws.

"That's not a flying monkey, you special needs chimp," Liv said in a rush. "That's Heathcliff."

"That's not a gravy dish," Sophia corrected. "That's Stan's genie lamp."

Rudolf deflated, looking disappointed. "Oh, so no gravy then, huh?"

"There's a five-star Michelin chef below deck," Liv stated blankly.

"Yeah, but he makes it all fancy, and I like it like the stuff they make at KFC," Rudolf whined.

Sophia shook her head. "Hey, that genie's lamp will have Stan in it," she said to the fae.

His face transformed. "It will be nice to hear how he's been. I wonder what he's been doing?"

Liv lowered her chin and regarded him with hooded eyes. "He's been locked in a lamp at the bottom of the Arctic Ocean."

"Oh," Rudolf groaned. "That sounds boring."

"He's been at the bottom of the sea because that's where you put him," Sophia added because the fae didn't seem to be putting two and two together.

"Right!" Rudolf exclaimed, fear springing to his face. "Well, I better be off then. Don't want to be murdered today. Or any other day. Bye ladies. Bye silly guy." He waved at Lunis. "I love your costume."

Then the fae opened a portal and disappeared as Heathcliff landed on the deck and dutifully handed the genie's lamp to Liv.

It was finally time to make the wish and hope that it saved her and Stefan's baby.

CHAPTER NINETY-NINE

Sophia spied the nervousness in Liv's every movement as she reached down and took the lamp from Heathcliff. Having completed his job, the winged otter flew up to the mainmast and perched next to Beatrix.

"Remember that wording is key," Sophia urged.

Liv nodded, holding the golden lamp that was encrusted with turquoise and red jewels. She gripped it by the handle and looked it over. After bringing her other hand to the shiny surface, Liv hesitated. Sophia knew that so much was riding on what happened next. If this didn't work, who knew what would happen to Liv's and Stefan's baby?

"I think that you might as well not throw away two wishes," Lunis interrupted, making both Beaufonts suddenly look up at the blue dragon.

"You don't, do you?" Liv asked. A smile whisked to her face, taking over from the tension.

"Well, I know you can't risk it and shouldn't make three wishes," Lunis continued.

"Because of that whole not wanting to be murdered by the genie thing?" Liv teased.

"Yeah, that," he answered. "But there's no reason to waste a perfectly good wish before you chuck the genie's lamp back in the ocean."

Liv considered him for a moment. "Well, I have everything I want. A fantastic family, a gorgeous husband, my dream job. Sure, I'd love world peace, but according to the genie handbook, you can't wish for that."

"World peace would put you out of a job, anyway," Lunis replied.

"I'd wish for Trudy to be returned safely," Liv stated.

"Or the Rogue Riders' treachery to stop," Sophia added.

Lunis shook his head. "Neither of those can be wished for, not with confidence. There are too many variables that can go wrong depending on how the genie fulfills the requests. It could backfire. Fixing an unborn child isn't as risky because you have nothing left to lose. However, Trudy could be freed and put on a deserted island where we still can't find her. The Rogue Riders might be stopped by a worse evil we then have to fight."

Sophia and Liv exchanged nervous glances. That was the risk of genie magic. It wasn't as straightforward as most thought. One could wish for a million dollars and get it, only to find out that it's in an offshore account they can't get to. Or one might wish to get a mansion, only to discover that it's made out of marshmallow. Genies were cruel and mischievous creatures, probably because they'd been enslaved for so long. Time alone in a lamp allowed them to craft all sorts of diabolical ways to mess with their would-be masters.

Being specific with making the wish did help, but still, genies usually found loopholes. If someone said, "I wish for a million dollars put into my Chase account," they might learn that since they didn't dictate a timeframe, it would happen the moment after their death.

"Lunis is right," Sophia stated with a sigh. "It's too risky to ask the genie to help us with the Rogue Riders or Trudy. Those are problems that the Dragon Elite have to resolve on our own."

Liv nodded, looking sideways at the blue dragon. "Why do I get the impression that you have an idea for how I can use the second wish?"

A coy expression took over Lunis' face. "Oh, well, I mean, if you have an extra wish and nothing you'd like to ask for, I thought I could help you out."

Sophia stuck her hands on her hips and glared at her dragon. "What is it that you want? If it's unlimited leaf tickets on Animal Crossing or tons of Robux on Roblox, the answer is no. I'm tired of you wasting your money and energy on virtual dollars to buy furniture that doesn't exist."

He returned the glare. "I don't judge you for how you spend your money with your Amazon addiction."

"So what if I buy something from Instant Amazon every single day? It's all stuff I need," Sophia argued, crossing her arms in front of her chest defiantly.

"You bought a bunch of yarn the other day," Lunis replied.

"So?" Sophia challenged.

"So, you don't knit or crochet," he countered.

She narrowed her eyes at him. "I'm thinking of taking up the hobby."

"When?" he questioned. "In all your free time?"

"I might get a break at some point," Sophia answered. "With the new dragonriders joining us, things could ease up."

Lunis shook his head. "Yeah, because as second in command of the Dragon Elite and the lead in the field, you're not going to have way more to manage."

"I need a scarf," Sophia argued, not backing down.

"You already bought a dozen off Amazon."

"They aren't the right colors."

"Although this is highly entertaining," Liv cut in, an amused expression on her face, having watched Sophia and Lunis argue back and forth, "I think we should probably make the most of our time." She pointed at her midsection. "Demon baby, remember?"

Sophia and Lunis both nodded.

"So, Cyrus, what is it that you want me to wish for?" Liv asked.

He slid his gaze to the side, a sly expression on his face. "A hedgehog."

"Are you serious?" Sophia nearly yelled, throwing her hands in the air. "What do you want with a hedgehog? Have you heard they're good snacks or something?"

He shot her a look of offense. "Absolutely not. I want it as a pet."

"Why do you think you get a pet?" Sophia questioned.

"Well, the Great Librarian gets that owl-cat thing." Lunis indicated where Beatrix was still perched, glaring down at them with indifference. "Liv has that cat—"

"Lynx," Liv corrected. "And I wouldn't call Plato a pet since he pretty much owns me and is the most powerful being on this planet, save for Papa Creola and Mama Jamba."

"Wilder has Evan," Lunis continued as though he hadn't heard her.

"They're friends," Sophia argued. "Evan isn't Wilder's pet."

Lunis shook his head. "That's not how I view it. Then Evan has NO10JO, and it seems like I should have a pet. I promise to take care of it and feed it, and you won't even know that I have one."

"Why a hedgehog?" Liv asked, highly entertained by this conversation.

"Have you seen YouTube videos of them?" Lunis questioned. "They're so flipping cute. You can put little socks on them, and they lay on their backs and have the cutest little bellies and—"

"If you want a hedgehog, then go and get one," Sophia interrupted. "We shouldn't waste a wish on one."

Lunis shook his head. "Liv was going to throw it away anyway. And I might have already tried that…" His words trailed off as a look of shame covered his face.

"What happened to the hedgehog you snuck into your Pad?" Sophia asked, narrowing her eyes at the dragon.

"Well, they're tiny, and I'm big and—"

Liv laughed. "You sat on your hedgehog and killed it, didn't you?"

Embarrassed, Lunis nodded.

"So now you want me to wish for a hedgehog that can't be crushed, don't you?"

Another nod.

"Sounds good to me," Liv sang, holding up the golden lamp again.

"Wait, you're going to give him what he wants?" Sophia questioned in disbelief.

Liv shrugged. "Why not? He's right that I wasn't going to use the wish. You don't seem to want anything. So give Herald what he wants, and maybe he'll start being nicer to me."

"Doubt it," Lunis muttered.

"Well, either way," Liv continued. "How badly can a genie sabotage a wish for an indestructible hedgehog? That one can't backfire on us too badly, but any other wish could carry serious consequences."

Sophia sighed with resignation. "Fine then. You get what you want, Lun."

The blue dragon grinned.

Holding the lamp with a renewed sense of nervousness, Liv let out a breath. They'd put it off for long enough. Now it was time to summon the genie known as Stan.

CHAPTER ONE HUNDRED

Sophia knew that Liv had battled vampires, werewolves, dogs with three heads, faced down the God Magician, and defeated armies of zombies and other monsters. However, she had never seen her as nervous as when she rubbed the surface of the genie's lamp. Her hands shook, and she chewed furiously on her lip.

Almost immediately, thick bright turquoise smoke began to pour from the spout of the lamp. It continued to flow as it rose, taking shape and creating a figure of a man. The genie stayed connected to his vessel as he bobbed in the air towering high above Liv and Sophia and as tall as Lunis.

Stan was semi-transparent for only a moment before taking solid form, the smoke whisking from his bottom portion swirling but still somewhat translucent. His skin was the color of the turquoise smoke.

He had a mostly bare barrel chest. Around his neck, he wore a large gold necklace encrusted with many different colored gems. A similar belt wrapped around his waist as well as red fabric that would cover his bottom if he had one instead of a trail of smoke for legs and feet.

On the genie's head was a turquoise turban with a red feather and more gems. A long braid that looked possessed danced in the air at his back, like a snake. Long golden hoops hung from his ears, and he wore a forked goatee. He looked madder than hell about being summoned as he regarded the two magicians in front of him.

Stan's red eyes narrowed at them as he crossed his arms over his chest.

"Who dares to wake me?" he boomed in a deep voice.

"Hey, Stan," Liv began, shaking off her prior nervousness. "Sorry, but we're going to skip introductions since they're pretty much irrelevant and time is of the essence."

"Stan?" he questioned, his mouth pinching for a moment as anger flared across his face. "How dare you call me by that name?"

"They dare to do a lot of things you don't like," Lunis teased, appearing amused by all this.

"My name is not Stan," the genie complained. "That's what the horrid last master I had called me before sinking my lamp to the bottom of the Arctic Ocean."

"Yeah, Rudolf rarely gets names right," Liv mumbled.

"So is your name Kevin?" Lunis asked. "Or Kurt? Or Kiran? Or Karl? Inquiring minds want to know."

Liv's eyelids fluttered with annoyance because no one wanted to know and they didn't have the time for all that, but they also didn't have the time to discuss hedgehogs, and that had happened.

"No, none of those are my names," the genie replied bitterly, holding his thick, muscular arms wide. "I am the great, the powerful, the incredibly majestic Bob!"

A snort followed by a laugh popped out of Lunis' mouth. "Bob? Like, short for Robert?"

"No, like Bob," the genie corrected.

"So it doesn't stand for anything?" Liv asked. "Like, 'billowing ominous body?'"

"You dare to insult the great, the powerful—"

"Are we running through that again?" Lunis interrupted, obviously amused by this whole show.

"I refuse to be insulted by a dragon," Bob said, offended.

"Are you okay with being insulted by a magician?" Lunis indicated Liv. "Because she's a lot worse than me."

"This is cute and all, but regardless of whether you're Kyle or Bob or Byle or Kob, I don't care," Liv began. "I rubbed your lamp, and now I'd like to make my wish."

"Very well," Bob stated while undulating up and down. "You can have three. Make them now, and I will grant them."

"I'll take two, Bob," Liv replied.

"But you have three," he argued.

"Got it," Liv stated. "I'm pretty good at math despite what my accountants say. They're awful people who keep using my money to pay taxes. They're obsessed with giving money away."

"You must make all your wishes," Bob demanded, heat flaring in his words.

"Nice try, Not-Kyle," Liv sang. "I know my rights. I can order a whole burrito that I don't have to finish. I'm an adult and get to do what I like."

"If you don't make all your wishes—"

"Then you can't murder me because you're only allowed to do that once you've fulfilled your duty to your master and therefore, you won't get your freedom," Liv interrupted. "I'm really sorry, Bud. I don't know who enslaved all your kind. It sucks badly for you, but I've sort of got other problems."

"Yeah, like, she needs a hedgehog," Lunis cut in.

Liv rolled her eyes at the blue dragon. "I don't. I'm going to make my first wish. Then I'll get you a pet." She drew in a breath and closed her eyes for a half-beat. When she opened them again, she looked determined. "I wish that the baby I'm currently carrying is healed of its demonism."

Sophia held her breath. At first, she wished that Liv had said more, like that the baby was born healthy or normal, but that could have caused complications. Then the child could have been born a mortal, which was considered normal. Magicians weren't. They were rare and powerful. It was smart that Liv had been so brief with her wish.

Supplying pertinent details when making a wish was important, but adding too many could cause different problems.

Bob nodded briefly. "Your wish is my command."

Liv glanced down at her midsection as though expecting it to look different somehow. "Is that it? Is it done?"

"It is," Bob stated. "Now for your second wish?"

They'd have to have Renswick test Liv again before they knew if the wish had worked. Sophia understood the tension written on her sister's face. That had felt too easy. She'd probably expected for there to be this big show of magic or to have felt a jolt or something. The whole thing had been a bit lackluster.

Liv gulped, seeming to be trying to compose herself after the letdown. "Okay, then I'd also wish for an indestructible hedgehog."

If this wish was a surprise to Bob, his face didn't show it. Again he simply nodded. "Your wish is my command."

At Liv's feet appeared the cutest little spiny creature that Sophia had ever seen. The hedgehog had a pointy face and small black eyes framed by round ears.

"Oh my gosh!" Lunis squealed, putting his head low and nearly putting his snout against the hedgehog's nose. He could easily have squashed the little guy if he hadn't been more careful, but thankfully that wouldn't matter. The hedgehog would be indestructible with hopefully no other drawbacks—having been created by the genie. "I'm going to call him Sir Alexander Connery MacDonald the Second. We're going to do everything together."

"What about me?" Sophia asked, slightly offended.

"You can't do anything with him." Lunis scooped up the little animal and snuggled him to his chest. "You didn't want me to have him."

"Are you not doing anything with me now?" Sophia questioned.

Lunis lifted the hedgehog to his ear and listened as if the creature was whispering to him. "Sir Alexander Connery MacDonald says that we'll see. He's not sure if he likes you."

Sophia sighed. "Fine. Play your little games, Lun."

"I'm ready to grant your last wish." Bob looked straight at Liv.

SARAH NOFFKE & MICHAEL ANDERLE

She nodded and pulled back her arm as though about to throw a football. "I'm sure you are Bob, but unfortunately, it's time to go swimming again. Sorry."

"No!" the genie yelled, but it was too late.

Liv launched her arm through the air, and the lamp flew over the railing. Bob's floating form automatically sucked back into the vessel where he disappeared at once.

The golden lamp hit the surface of the Arctic Ocean and immediately sank, plummeting to the bottom of the sea where Bob would stay in solitary until some unsuspecting person might find him one day.

CHAPTER ONE HUNDRED ONE

"Well, we all got what we wanted." Lunis looked fondly at the tiny hedgehog.

"I didn't get anything," Sophia argued, her hands on her hips.

"You get to pout," Lunis stated. "That's what you wanted, right? If you got something good, you'd have nothing to complain about. I got my hedgehog, and Liv got her new car or whatever else it was she wished for."

"My child not to be a demon," Liv corrected.

Lunis waved her off, enamored by the little hedgehog. "Like I was paying attention."

"Obviously you weren't," Liv muttered. "Now I need to find out if Bob delivered on his wish." She turned to Sophia. "I'm going to pay Renswick a visit, then look for clues about these poachers who trapped all the baby narwhals."

Sophia nodded. "That's a good idea. I can accompany you to see Renswick again if you'd like."

Liv shook her head. "Thanks, but that's not necessary, and you have a pet to deliver." She pointed up at the mainmast where Beatrix was still perched, patiently looking out at the rolling sea.

"Okay, well, let me know as soon as you hear from Renswick about the test results," Sophia ordered.

"Of course," Liv stated, looking at Sophia fondly all of a sudden. "That's for coming with me to get the genie's lamp and, well, pretty much everything else. I'm not sure how I would have done it if you hadn't been with me."

"You would have been fine because you're Liv-freaking-Beaufont."

"That's not my middle name." Liv laughed. "But thank you. I'm grateful that you were here for me."

Sophia smiled. "Of course. I'll always be here for you. Familia est sempiternum."

CHAPTER ONE HUNDRED TWO

S ophia was relieved that she could bring Beatrix into the Gullington so that she could take the gryphowl to the Great Library through the portal connected to the Castle. Quiet seemed to allow access to this kind of stuff more and more. Maybe it was because the Dragon Elite was expanding so much and more needed to be allowed in to see if they qualified. Or perhaps it was because the days of the Barrier being firmly in place were behind them since they were less vulnerable as they grew stronger. Sophia hoped it was the latter.

"I'm going to take Beatrix to the Great Librarian," Sophia said to Lunis, who didn't seem to notice her as they crossed the Expanse, too focused on Sir Alexander Connery MacDonald.

"Yeah, I'll give him a bath first probably," Lunis stated absentmindedly. "Then I'm making him a bed, and we're going to watch *Sabrina the Teenage Witch* and play Top Trumps for hours."

"You didn't hear a word I said, did you?"

He glanced up, blinking at her. "Yeah, you said, 'I'm going to go read Beatrix Potter books in the library.'"

She shook her head. "Have fun, Lunis. Don't stay up too late. You never know when I'll need your help."

"Yeah, I do," he argued. "Why do you think I came to the Arctic Ocean with hardly a moment's notice?"

"You didn't want me to watch the *Great British Baking Show* without you," she countered.

"No, I knew you'd need backup," Lunis stated.

"You wanted to use one of Liv's wishes to get an indestructible pet."

He paused, lowered his chin, and gave her a meaningful look. "Sophia, I knew the whole situation was going to be very emotional for you and Liv. Mostly for Liv and you'd need the extra moral support to lend her strength. I knew that fixing an unborn child with wish magic was risky and scary and as much as I pretend to loathe your sister, I can hardly find a thing wrong with her. She's second-best to you, but if you ever, ever tell her that, I will eat you. Slowly."

Sophia giggled, feeling the affection rebounding off her dragon. "That's very sweet of you to say."

He smugly held his head in the air. "I didn't say it to be sweet. I said it because it's true. And I hold allegiance to Liv, whether she knows it or not."

"Especially now that she got you a hedgehog you can't squash," Sophia joked.

He nodded. "Especially now. But I was planning on joining you before I heard about you cheating on me to watch the newest season of the *Great British Baking Show*. I knew you'd need me."

"Thanks, Lun. That's really thoughtful of you."

He held up the tiny hedgehog. "And look, my awesome thoughtfulness was rewarded. We're going to go and play in the Pad."

Sophia giggled and waved at her dragon, Beatrix flying overhead and circling them. "Have fun. Thanks. You're the best."

CHAPTER ONE HUNDRED THREE

The Great Library was unsurprisingly quiet when Sophia stepped through the portal door with Beatrix flying behind her. The gryphowl hadn't wanted to perch on her arm as she had with Bermuda, as the giantess had predicted. She would only do that with her true master, and that would never be Sophia. She had Lunis—and he had a hedgehog.

Sophia laughed, thinking of the ridiculousness of it all. Of course, her dragon wanted a hedgehog, and now he had one. Good thing that hadn't been what she was getting him for Christmas or she would have to come up with a different option.

What did surprise her upon entering the Great Library was that Paul wasn't anywhere in sight. Usually, when she visited the Great Library, he materialized almost immediately. On this occasion, she'd been strolling the aisles for over twenty minutes and not seen a trace of him.

Sophia glanced up at the gryphowl flapping its wings beside her. "Aren't you supposed to be good at finding things? Well, people in this case?"

The gryphowl hooted beside her.

"I'll take that as a yes, then." Sophia laughed. "Can you help me find the Great Librarian? He's, like, this tall." She held her hand up as high as she could. "And he has dark hair and is wise and, well, he's most likely the only other person in this place."

Beatrix hooted again and set off, flying down the long central aisle of the Great Library before disappearing down a row.

Sophia ambled forward. "Maybe she can help me find where I left my sanity." She laughed, her voice echoing strangely in the extensive library. Something was off about the space, and she instinctively knew it. Felt it.

Tensing, Sophia's hand went to her sword as though she feared danger hid around the next row of books. Or that some villain had taken Paul. The Rogue Riders could technically get into the Great Library since they were dragonriders, but why would they when they'd shown no interest in learning and training so far? All they wanted was to exploit their power for their gains.

The Great Library represented growth and learning because it was all about taking the works of others and using them to get better. To learn from past mistakes and do good. To fix the things that had gone wrong. The Rogue Riders, it seemed to Sophia, didn't care about any of that. Only themselves and benefiting from the criminal world.

Sophia strode forward on alert, whipping her head back and forth as she passed each aisle, searching it for dangers. She was about to call for Paul when Beatrix hooted from up ahead. Sophia glanced up but didn't see the gryphowl so instead, she hurried forward, following the sounds of its call.

It was a good distance ahead, it seemed. Sophia sprinted, passing the rows in a blur, not daring to look at what she passed. Beatrix hooted again.

She must have found something—hopefully, Paul. However, something was wrong if he hadn't come out and the gryphowl was calling her, it seemed. The next hoot sounded so close.

Sophia rounded the corner to where she thought it came from and halted. Lying in the middle of a seemingly ordinary row of books was a normal-looking tome on the Great Library's floor. Beatrix perched next to it, looking between Sophia and the hardback.

She pointed at the book. "Is that where Paul is?"

The gryphowl hooted once more, and the sound seemed to overwhelmingly say, "yes."

CHAPTER ONE HUNDRED FOUR

W ith her heart pounding in her chest, Sophia peered at the cover of the book, careful not to get too close.

It was entitled *The Lost Forest*.

Perplexed, Sophia peered sideways at the book, trying to understand how Paul could be in there. He wasn't large, but he was much bigger than the small volume. Magic was definitely at play.

"Long ago," a voice began beside Sophia, nearly making her jump out of her skin. She whipped around to find Plato standing behind her.

Clapping a hand to her chest, she panted through the ragged breaths. "Can you announce your arrival in the future instead of sneaking up on people?"

"No," he chirped with defiance. "As I was saying, long ago, there was a forest made of trees imbued with dark magic. If someone went into the forest, no matter the time of day or year, they would get lost for ages. Usually, no one saw them again."

"That's awful," Sophia remarked while studying the strange lynx.

"It was," he agreed. "And so it was decided that a special task force would go in using protective spells to guard them and cut all the trees down. Some of those who volunteered were lost, but in the end, they were successful and clear-cut the awful forest so that it couldn't steal any more people."

"So this place, this forest," Sophia began slowly, working it out, pointing at the book lying on the floor. "That's what this book is about, isn't it? It's about the forest that loses people?"

To her surprise, Plato shook his head. "No, it's made from one of the trees."

"Say what?" Sophia questioned, shocked.

"There was an evil magician on the task force, and he thought it would be fun to create a book using the pulp from one of the trees," Plato explained. "Who knows why. Who knows why any evil person does anything. The point remains that he created a book with the pages made of a tree from the Lost Forest."

Sophia gasped, putting it all together. "So just like with the forest, Paul has gotten lost inside this book. How do I get him out? How did anyone ever get found in that place?"

"They didn't," Plato answered simply. "Paul's situation is slightly different because he is actually in the book. It contains him whereas with the forest, there were tons of trees and it was impossible to find a missing person."

"So how do I get him out?" Sophia questioned.

"That's the easy part," Plato stated. "The hard part is not getting lost yourself. Those who went into the Lost Forest to find someone usually became lost themselves. Those who didn't go into the Lost Forest were never lost."

Sophia scratched her head, perplexed. "Can you be a little more helpful here?"

"I've told you everything you need to know," Plato said flatly and disappeared.

Sophia groaned, wanting to strangle the lynx but also grateful for as much as he supplied. "Fine. So if you go into the Lost Forest, you'll get lost. Don't go and you won't. If I don't read the book, maybe I won't get lost."

The gryphowl hooted beside the tome.

As though that spoke to Sophia, she nodded. "Good idea," she stated, pulling her sword from its sheath. "I'll not chance anything. No reading the book. No touching it. I'll simply open it and hope that releases Paul."

Holding Inexorabilis at an angle, Sophia used the tip to open the cover. She averted her eyes at once, not daring to read the title page. Carefully using the tip and her peripheral vision, she continued to flip the pages until she found what looked like chapter one. She didn't dare look directly at it, which was why she was surprised and nearly bowled over when a figure sprang up from the pages and materialized right beside her.

CHAPTER ONE HUNDRED FIVE

"Paul!" Sophia exclaimed when the magician took his usual form in front of her. He'd shot out of the pages of the Lost Forest book as a morphed figure and quickly grown into his usual size.

Obviously in a daze from his experience, he looked around as though trying to figure out where he was and if he was in danger.

"I-I-I'm back," he said, seeming to recognize the Great Library.

Sophia nodded. "Yeah, I'm sorry. It appears you got lost in the pages of that book, but I was able to get you out." She pointed at the open volume sitting on the floor.

He turned to look. Sophia realized her mistake at once and used magic to shut it before he could reread it and get trapped and lost. The hardcover slammed shut, and for good measure, Sophia summoned a padlock and placed it on the outside of *The Lost Forest*.

Paul blinked in confusion and brought his gaze to Sophia. "I remember now. I had pulled the book out to read it and wasn't to the first sentence when I got sucked in. Then I was…well, so lost in the strangest dream."

Sophia nodded. "The book is made from a tree in a forest that makes people lost. It's a trick created by an evil magician."

"I would have no doubt been lost for ages if you hadn't rescued me." He looked relieved and grateful.

Sophia shook her head and pointed at Beatrix, still dutifully standing beside the locked book. "It was Beatrix who found you."

Paul, obviously having been dazed from the whole ordeal, glanced at the gryphowl and blinked. "Oh, my. What is this?"

"She's your new companion and a gift from Bermuda Laurens."

His eyes widened in shock. "*The* Bermuda Laurens? The creator of *Magical Creatures*? The utmost expert on magical creatures?"

Sophia smiled. "Yes, the very one. She thought you deserved a gift for taking the Great Librarian position and that Beatrix would make an excellent assistant. I think she's right since without her, I'm not sure how long or if I would have found you."

Paul turned to the gryphowl and knelt. "It's a pleasure to meet you, Beatrix. That's a lovely name, and you're a wonderful gryphowl. Thank you so much for rescuing me. I'm forever in your debt."

The creature hooted again, looking at peace and happy.

Paul smiled and extended an arm to the owl-like animal. She flew to it at once, perching there calmly. As if this was the most natural meeting ever, Paul rose and turned back to Sophia.

"I thank you for delivering her to me. And for helping me out of the book."

"You're welcome. I think it's best to keep the padlock on the Lost Forest book. We can't chance it taking anyone else."

He nodded while looking at Beatrix, a fondness in his eyes as he regarded her as if they'd always known each other. "I think you're right. We will guard it as well as all the rest of the books in this library. Some can make you lost. Others can make you lose your mind. Some are lost parts of a bigger picture, but they're all part of my responsibility."

Sophia smiled, thinking that they couldn't have found a better librarian for the Great Library. "Thanks, Paul. I feel much better knowing that you're guarding this place."

He nodded and returned the smile, looking at the gryphowl. "Now I feel much better since I felt that I was missing something."

CHAPTER ONE HUNDRED SIX

Sophia hadn't been back at the Castle for long when her phone buzzed with a message. It was from Mortimer. She hurried to Hiker's office, knowing that immediate action had to happen.

He thundered back and forth across his study, his head down after hearing the news she'd gotten from the Brownie.

"We have to go in and take them out," Hiker stated, referring to the Rogue Riders in Las Vegas.

She nodded.

"It sounds like there's a lot of them," Hiker continued.

"Yeah, and they're in the underground tunnels," Sophia added, reviewing the message she'd received from Mortimer.

"Getting Trudy DeVries out safely is our top priority," Hiker went on.

"Which will be tricky because we're not only facing the Rogue Riders," Sophia stated. "They have mortal criminals helping to guard their underground fortress."

"I'd expect no less from the scum," Hiker said bitterly.

"To get into such a small place with so many to fight will be tough," Sophia reasoned.

SARAH NOFFKE & MICHAEL ANDERLE

He nodded. "And yet, you're going to have to do it and pretty much on your own. You, Evan, and Wilder."

Sophia's mouth fell open. "You can't be serious, sir? There are at least four times as many of them, and this is their territory. Who knows what we're walking into?"

"I get it, Sophia. The new riders aren't ready," Hiker stated. "Mahkah is training them, and he should continue. I'm up to my eyeballs in adjudication cases. More importantly, we can't send brand new untrained riders into enemy territory yet. They'll be slaughtered. They haven't even found the Great Library yet."

"But you sent me after zombie horses before I finished training," she argued, referring to the ranch not far from the Gullington that Hiker had ordered her to go to when she was brand new. It had all been a trick too.

He halted his pacing and regarded her with hooded eyes. "You were a pain in the ass who wouldn't take no for an answer and wanted to save the world on your first day."

"So?" Sophia argued.

"So, I thought I could teach you a lesson," he answered.

"You thought you could break my spirit."

Hiker nodded. "It didn't work because as I've learned, you're resilient and that's probably your single best and worst quality."

Sophia laughed. "That doesn't make sense."

"You don't know when to stop," he explained. "Which is why you're usually successful. But you also don't know when to stop, and it's why you always find trouble."

"I guess I can't argue with you there. But three of us against all of them? It was bad enough when we had to face them on the streets of Las Vegas. Now we're going into their territory outnumbered."

"You're trained and much better than them," he said with confidence. "You use strategy. They'll respond with brute force. Once you get Trudy free, she'll be able to help you. Then you can take out the leadership, which as Mama Jamba explained is the problem with the Rogue Riders. Get rid of Nathaniel and Versalee, and maybe the

Rogue Riders can serve a real purpose instead of creating more problems for us."

Sophia looked around Hiker's office, realizing what—or rather, who—was missing. She'd been so excited by getting Mortimer's message about the Rogue Riders that she hadn't noticed until then. "Where is Mama Jamba? She's always in your office."

He pursed his lips. "She said something about getting fitted for a ski suit. I don't know. That batty woman is losing her mind."

Sophia studied the leader of the Dragon Elite and didn't buy his annoyance. He was scared. Fearful that Mother Nature was leaving them again. Afraid of not having her around. Apprehensive about what things would be like if he had to do it alone again.

"You know, sir," Sophia began in a calming voice. "Things have changed. You don't have to worry about leading alone anymore. You have your seasoned riders, Mahkah, Evan, Wilder, and me. You're getting a new army of dragonriders. Even if Mama Jamba disappears again, we're going to help you keep the world safe. Things aren't like they were before. Mortals can see magic again. The House of Fourteen wants our help. Once we cut off the evil heads of the Rogue Riders' leadership, hopefully, they can be our allies too."

He considered her words for a moment, his expression changing a few times from hesitation to frustration. Finally, he nodded, a spark of a smile in his eyes. "Thanks. I needed to hear that. I think you're right. I just like having her around."

Sophia smiled at him. "How could you not? We all do. But she has her life to live too."

"I know."

They were quiet for a long moment, the ticking of the old grandfather clock the only noise.

"I get it," Hiker said, finally breaking the silence. "We can't remain in the same place forever. I know that. I think I'm starting to understand that better than ever before."

Sophia eyed the man before her, not knowing what his ominous statement meant but feeling like there was great significance wrapped up in it. Something major that would apply to him, and therefore indirectly to her. She couldn't fathom what all that could mean or its implications for the future, but soon she'd do nothing else but obsess about it.

For now, Sophia needed to turn her attention to the impending battle with the Rogue Riders and rescuing a Warrior for the House of Fourteen from their clutches.

CHAPTER ONE HUNDRED SEVEN

Sophia hadn't been looking forward to returning to Las Vegas, and not only because she would have to face the Rogue Riders again. This time they weren't going to get a warning. She'd given them a chance, told Nathaniel the parameters, even protected him and the other demon dragonriders from the angry magicians who wanted to tear them in two. She sort of wished that she'd let them and saved herself and the Dragon Elite the trouble of having to return.

Sophia sighed, knowing that wasn't true. She wasn't going to stoop to the Rogue Riders' levels of fighting unfairly. A parent didn't simply throw down a punishment the first time a child unknowingly did something wrong. Yes, the Rogue Riders were children and should have known better.

Sophia reasoned that the young and inexperienced demon dragonriders had let the power go to their head. She could excuse that once or twice. But now, like children, they'd been told the limits and the consequences for breaking them again. It was up to the Dragon Elite to enforce these rules.

Although Sophia wasn't looking forward to making a fellow dragonrider pay or potentially intervene with magicians, she also didn't want to return to Las Vegas because, well, it was the city of sin.

Many loved Las Vegas. She understood that, but to her, it was the exact opposite of everything she cherished about Scotland. The latter was clean and green and full of nature. Conversely, Las Vegas was a concrete jungle with artificial lights and manmade structures, and neon colors. There was nothing that appealed to her about the loud city in the desert on the West Coast.

Maybe that was why the Rogue Riders had chosen it as their new headquarters, she reasoned. The demon riders were the opposite of the Dragon Elite by definition. It stood to reason that they'd call home a place that felt like the opposite of the Gullington.

CHAPTER ONE HUNDRED EIGHT

W hen Sophia, Evan, and Wilder flew through the portal on their dragons into the city of Las Vegas, they realized how bad things had gotten.

"The absence of the fae kingdom must have had an immediate impact on the city," Sophia said, pulling Lunis to a halt in the air and looking down on the Las Vegas Strip.

On either side of her, Wilder and Evan paused on their dragons.

"Who would have thought that the king of the fae had been holding things together here?" Wilder shook his head.

Sophia nodded. "You'd be surprised how strangely competent King Rudolf is."

On the ground, pandemonium was happening. It appeared that mortal criminals were looting in several areas. Fights amongst magicians and mortals were spreading.

The demon dragonriders seemed to be purely entertained by this, a couple of them sitting on the top of Caesar's Palace, looking down at the various conflicts going on below.

"Should we go and give those newbie riders something to really watch?" Evan asked. "Like a close-up of my knuckles?"

Wilder laughed.

Sophia shook her head. "Those are lemmings, hanging around because they want the entertainment. We need to focus on taking down Nathaniel and Versalee. We also don't want to spoil our cover until after we have Trudy DeVries back safely."

Evan deflated but agreed that was for the best.

Currently, the three Dragon Elite were cloaked in the sky—unseen by anyone in the city. Last time, they'd made their presence known when confronting the Rogue Riders who were bullying and pillaging in Las Vegas. That had been a goodwill mission of sorts. This was anything but.

The Dragon Elite needed to sneak into the city's underground system where Mortimer had informed Sophia that Trudy DeVries was being held. A network of tunnels ran under the city.

In the past, it had served many different purposes. Most recently, it was filled with many homeless who had nowhere left to go. From the sight on the ground, it appeared that they didn't have the underground anymore either. Lining many parts of the Las Vegas Strip with signs and grocery carts full of all their possessions were hundreds of homeless.

The Rogue Riders, according to Mortimer's Brownies, had kicked them out of the underground when they took it over. There was layer upon layer of problems, Sophia realized, her heart aching as she studied the displaced homeless, looting mortals, and fighting magicians. Also watching it while throwing back forties on the rooftop of Caesar's Palace were the demon dragonriders.

She narrowed her eyes at them, angry that they thought any of this was entertaining. However, they took a page out of the leader's book that encouraged it, so the demon dragonriders thought it was okay. Hopefully once Nathaniel and Versalee were gone, a more worthy leader would rise to the challenge. Sophia had to believe that under the right direction, the Rogue Riders could serve a purpose. Believing otherwise wasn't something she wanted to consider because that would mean the Rogue Riders would have to be taken out, thereby contributing to another possible extinction of dragonriders.

"What's the plan, boss?" Evan glanced sideways at Sophia.

She pointed at the underground entrance that Mortimer indicated was the closest to the Rogue Riders' headquarters. "We enter through there. There are at least a dozen demon dragonriders total. Not all will be down there, but they definitely outnumber us. There are also mortals serving them. I want Trudy DeVries found and returned safely. I want any demon dragonrider who gets in our way restrained. But I want to avoid any unnecessary lethal force to either them or mortals."

"Copy that, boss." Wilder saluted her with a crooked smile.

"One more thing," Sophia said, gripping the reins.

Both of the other dragonriders regarded her intently, hanging on her every word. "That last part doesn't apply to Nathaniel or Versalee. If you see them, take them down. We warned them. Now it's time to punish them."

CHAPTER ONE HUNDRED NINE

"Good thing that fatty Bell isn't here," Lunis commented as they landed outside the entrance to the underground.

"That's rude," Sophia admonished. "You're probably hurting her feelings."

Lunis grinned. "She doesn't have any feelings. She knows that I'm just being a boy, pulling her pigtails and looking to get a reaction out of her. If she'd give me one, I'd move on."

"Seriously, you need a hobby," Sophia stated.

"I have a hedgehog," Lunis bragged proudly.

"Which is food for most dragons," Simi imparted smugly.

Lunis leveled his gaze at the white dragon. "Eat Sir Alexander Connery MacDonald, and I'll tell all the angel dragonettes that you want them to start following you around."

"You wouldn't," she seethed.

Lunis nodded. "You know I would."

Sophia slid off her dragon, as did Wilder and Evan, and regarded the narrow entrance. It resembled a subway entry with a few dozen steps down to a dark opening. It was roughly the size of a garage door, but the Brownies had informed her that there were some narrow passages in the underground system.

"I realize that the dragons can use a compartment spell to navigate down there," Sophia mused. "I'm not sure if they should."

Wilder nodded at her side. "Yeah, it might not be the best use of their magic."

"That's my thought," Sophia mumbled while chewing on her lip. "I think we need at least one dragon down there. The Brownies say the demon riders have theirs in the underground."

Lunis shivered. "That's not the place for dragons. They can't be able to stretch out their wings or properly...I don't know, that thing we're meant to do."

"Fly," Coral supplied.

The blue dragon grinned in reply. "Wow, you should go on a game show. You're excellent with guessing."

Sophia and Wilder exchanged amused expressions. "It's sad to think that they're keeping dragons in confined areas," she admitted.

"Since Lunis thinks he's such a hotshot skinny-pants," Evan began. "Why doesn't he go down there with us?"

"I think that's fair." Sophia nodded.

Lunis' mouth popped open with surprise. "But there's a place called Nacho Daddy that I was going to check out while you all were playing cowboys and Indians."

"Who is who in that scenario?" Wilder questioned, hiding a laugh.

"Doesn't matter," Lunis chirped. "I'll go and get us all nachos. Simi can accompany you since all you have to do is graffiti her, and she'll blend right in. Coral can keep a lookout since she never likes to do anything fun ever."

Sophia laughed. She saw Lunis' point because spray paint covered the walls leading down to the underground. She could only imagine what they'd find down there. Based on the smell wafting up from there, it seemed like it wouldn't be pleasant.

"Great idea on the disguising," Sophia stated with confidence. "A dragon will blow our cover pretty quickly even if you're using a compartmentalizing spell to negotiate the narrow tunnels."

"Why thank you," Lunis sang. "What does everyone want on their nachos? Extra jalapeños for Sophia, I'm guessing. A side of sadness for Vegan Boy—"

"Vegan Man," Wilder corrected with a laugh.

"And double meat for Evan, right?" Lunis asked the other dragonrider.

"The nacho run will have to wait," Sophia interrupted. "You're right that the dragon who goes down should be in disguise. I'm pretty good with those spells, but it's easier for me to camouflage my dragon than someone else's."

Lunis sighed melodramatically. "Seriously, please don't tell me that means what I think it means…"

"Lun, you're going down with us in disguise," Sophia stated. "Coral and Simi, you two should stay up here and keep watch. Communicate with Evan and Wilder if you see anything suspicious or if things get any further out of hand." She indicated the chaos that was happening a few blocks away.

Both of the elder dragons nodded dutifully. Lunis, conversely, looked like he was close to throwing a full-on tantrum.

Sophia turned her attention to her dragon while tapping her chin. "Now the question is, what would be the best disguise for you so that you can get around and will go unnoticed?"

CHAPTER ONE HUNDRED TEN

"A rat!" Lunis exclaimed, his voice squeaky in his gray rodent form. He'd shrunk considerably and looked up at Sophia like he was about to bite her, infecting her with a plague.

Evan and Wilder weren't hiding their laughter, nearly doubling over after Sophia used the disguising spell on her dragon. Their dragons were marginally better at showing decorum, but even Coral and Simi appeared amused by seeing the blue dragon in the form of a mangy sewer rat.

"I can't keep the cloak on us anymore," Sophia explained, indicating herself and the other two dragonriders. "Disguising you is the most important priority because we can sneak around, but even with a compartment spell, they'll notice you, Lun. As a rat, you can sneak ahead for us and tell me what's going on."

"I can also sneak ahead and inform the enemy that you're coming so they take you down," he threatened bitterly, his voice high-pitched.

The guys continued to laugh, wholly entertained by Lunis' rat form.

Sophia shook her head, knowing that his threats were empty. "It's a good plan. Since I'm the one who spelled you, you can break free of it at any point and fight or shoot fire or whatever you need to do to help us. That wouldn't be the case if I used the disguising spells on Coral or Simi."

"That's fine." Lunis stuck his pointy nose in the air. "I'm secure enough to be a rat for this mission."

Sophia smiled proudly at her dragon, grateful he was willing to be a team player. "Good. I think this is the best plan." Turning her attention to Evan and Wilder, she gave them both sturdy expressions. "Are you two ready to confront the Rogue Riders?"

Both pulled out their weapons, Evan holding his ax and Wilder his sword. They nodded in unison.

Sophia pulled Inexorabilis. "Okay, remember the plan. No unnecessary lethal force unless it's Nathaniel or Versalee."

Evan's top lip curled up with a vengeance. "I don't ask for much, but if there's an option, I'd like the opportunity to take down Nathaniel. That guy's been asking for a bruising from me."

Wilder laughed. "You ask for way more than your fair share, but that's fine with me."

Sophia nodded. "It's more important that we rescue Trudy DeVries than anything else, so let's be off before her safety is further compromised."

CHAPTER ONE HUNDRED ELEVEN

Mortimer had stated that as of his latest report from a field Brownie, Warrior Trudy DeVries was alive and well, although not in the best condition. However, that didn't make it any easier for Sophia to delay. She knew that could quickly change when it came to the Warrior for the House of Fourteen being held by diabolical demon dragonriders.

That's why they didn't waste any more time talking and planning and instead hurried down into the underground, all the while on high alert for any mortals or dragonriders hiding in the shadows.

As Sophia suspected, the darkness of the tunnels smelled like a sewage system. There was trash everywhere and not one spot on the concrete walls that wasn't covered in spray paint. It was hard to see much in the distance since it was mostly lit by burning barrels of rubbish or spaced out floodlights.

With a single hand movement, she encouraged Evan and Wilder to cling to the walls and hide in the shadows should they approach anything as they progressed.

She made out a few competing noises in the distance. There seemed to be a loud eruption of voices up ahead and what she suspected was dragons fighting—the sounds of claws and flapping wings very familiar to her.

She really couldn't understand how dragons could stand tall and fight in this place. The corridors were wide, but the ceiling was no more than twelve feet high. Lunis would have to duck in his usual form, but she reasoned that he was much larger than any of the demon dragons.

The three and rat-Lunis strode quietly in silence, listening to the uproar ahead and the sounds of trickling water somewhere in the distance and watching for clues.

So far they hadn't seen any signs of mortals or dragonriders, but that did little to fill Sophia with confidence. She figured that they were probably more concentrated down there. However, one of her main concerns was about getting lost in the networks under the city. Mortimer had warned that the tunnels were numerous and navigating them would be a challenge. She could understand why because they probably all looked the same in the shadows.

As soon as she had that thought, they came to a fork in the corridors. One set of tunnels led straight. Two others split to the right and left.

Sophia halted and looked at Wilder, then Evan. "I think it's time we parted ways."

"Girl, I've been trying to get away from you for ages," Evan joked with a wink.

Sophia laughed. "I second that sentiment."

Wilder pointed straight ahead to where the uproar was coming from. It sounded like a party...or a wrestling match...or both. "I'll go that way."

"Are you sure?" Sophia asked. "I have Lunis, and he has to stay with me to keep up the disguise. I can go that way."

He shook his head. "You need to find Trudy DeVries, and she most likely won't be where there's a huge concentration of dragonriders having a party or whatever they're doing."

Sophia nodded. "That makes sense."

"I'll take this one." Evan gestured at the tunnel to the left. "I have a weird feeling I'll find my nemesis."

Sophia studied the corridor he was indicating and sort of understood his decision. The flood lamps in the distance flickered with strange electricity as if they'd been tampered with by someone who had electrical magic.

She spun to face the opposite corridor, which was dark and nondescript. "Well, then I'll take this one." Sophia took a step forward before looking over her shoulder.

Wilder gave her a serious look. "Be careful, Soph."

She nodded before setting off down the darkened tunnel with her rat-dragon at her feet.

CHAPTER ONE HUNDRED TWELVE

Something definitely wasn't right with the electricity in this part of the underground, Evan thought as he progressed, sliding down the tunnels, his back as close to the disgusting concrete wall as he dared to have it.

Ahead, his enhanced hearing picked up two men talking. They seemed to be arguing about something, their words terse.

"Dude, it's your turn to do the patrols," a man said from the shadows far down the tunnel.

Evan snapped his fingers, making the light ahead extinguish, hopefully hiding his approach.

"What was that?" a different man asked.

"The bulb blew out," the first guy said.

"I'm fueling it," a voice that Evan had heard before stated angrily from farther up ahead.

"C-C-Can you turn it back on, boss?" one of the men asked.

"I just tried," the demon dragonrider that Evan recognized replied. "Something is going on. You two go check it out."

"It should be him," the first guy said, his voice vibrating with worry. "I went last."

"He didn't either!" the other man complained.

"You'll both go!" the demon dragonrider boomed, his voice echoing down the long corridor.

"Okay, boss!"

A moment later, footsteps made splashing sounds as the two men reluctantly trudged down the tunnel.

Evan found a well-placed alcove that led to a utility closet. He slid into it, perfectly hidden out of the way, the dark making it harder for anyone to see him. He pointed at his face and put a night-vision spell on himself. It wouldn't last for long, but hopefully, he wouldn't need it much longer.

While peering around the alcove's corner, he noticed the two men approaching in the distance. Mortals, he realized right away. They wore tattered clothes and battered expressions. Criminals, he guessed. Evan had gotten pretty good at recognizing the sort. They had a way about them.

He lifted his hand and pulled in a deep breath, remembering Sophia's orders. His instinct told him to take out criminals. As a Dragon Elite, that's what he felt was right, ridding their evil from the world. However, he had to respect Sophia's orders. If she had said not to injure them fatally, then that's what he'd do, hoping she was right and they somehow served a purpose.

When the two men approached, ready to spring into the air from any sudden fright, Evan stepped out of his hiding spot. He shot a finger at the first man, who had just recognized that something had moved from the shadows and exclaimed loudly.

However, it was too late. Evan zapped the mortal with a paralyzing spell, sending him rocking back on his heels until he toppled over, lying completely still on the ground. He did the same thing to the next mortal, knocking him out with ease. They'd have a nice, long nap and wake up with a horrible headache that would last for days. Still, they were alive and would go on to commit more crimes.

Evan carefully stepped over the stretched-out figures and strode in the direction of the man ahead, who he was certain was a demon dragonrider. His night vision told him that he neared some stairs that led up. His instinct told him that he approached a person.

Evan tensed when a floodlight lit up the tunnel all around him. He squinted from the sudden brightness combined with his night vision and immediately pulled down the spell, willing his vision to clear.

With watering eyes, he blinked at the set of stairs in the distance as he registered footsteps. Ahead, a figure stepped out of the shadows. One he recognized.

The redhead named Nathaniel narrowed his eyes at Evan, taking in his appearance and no doubt recognizing him too. He halted on the first stair and shook his head, his hand resting on the corner of the long hallway leading up.

"It's you," the demon dragonrider seethed.

"It's me," Evan affirmed. "Ready to joust?"

Apparently, the answer was no because Nathaniel, the coward, spun at once and sprinted for the stairs that led back up to the city streets of Las Vegas. Evan didn't hesitate before springing forward after him.

CHAPTER ONE HUNDRED THIRTEEN

The commotion up ahead didn't fill Wilder with confidence that he was simply going to be breaking up a house party. It seemed more likely that he would be breaking into a riot of unruly demon dragonriders who were jeering at dogfights or dragon fights or mortal fights.

Sophia's orders to not use lethal force made the possibilities that much more difficult. It was always easier to stop an enemy with brute force. Disbanding people and only restraining them was much harder. It took precision and care, and that was probably one of the reasons that the Rogue Riders didn't bother with it.

Wilder spied a doorway ahead that seemed connected to all the loud noises since various voices echoed from the opening. Light also spilled out into the dark tunnel.

He had no idea what he was walking into, but he knew that he was outnumbered. However, he had a few things to his advantage. One was that he was at least a hundred years older than any of the magician dragonriders he was approaching. He was confident of that. That meant he had experience and training on his side.

The other thing was that as a weapons expert, elected by the Protector of Weapons—Subner—he could feel an arsenal of swords and other weaponry in the room ahead. His gift gave him a few advantages in battle and otherwise. One was that he could feel and see a weapon's memories, knowing all the fights that it had experienced.

In this case, Wilder knew that the weapons in the room he approached weren't that old. They didn't have very many memories. They were also cowards' weapons. Regardless, whatever magical powers Subner had imbued in Wilder gave him a special dominance over these weapons that was different from his power with swords and axes and other things with blades.

He tensed outside the room with all the noise and light, which he suspected was large, based on the information he was getting from the many weapons he felt on the other side of the wall.

He drew in a breath, braced himself, then turned into the door-frame, facing a room full of demon dragonriders and mortals. They all looked up at him at once, menace springing to their faces at the sight of him. These men likely felt no intimidation about a single Dragon Elite member walking up on them because guns and ammunition surrounded them.

Wilder smiled to himself, realizing how wrongly they'd placed their confidence.

CHAPTER ONE HUNDRED FOURTEEN

The rat feet scuttling next to Sophia nearly made her laugh, knowing that they belonged to Lunis. She wasn't trying to make fun of the blue dragon by turning him into a rat. It seemed like the best option, but she knew he was angry about the whole thing.

"I'm sorry," she whispered in the darkened corridor as they made their way to an unknown destination ahead.

He squeaked his indignation.

She sighed. "You're not talking to me now. I wasn't trying to humiliate you or anything."

Another squeak.

"Oh, good," she remarked. "You're acting real mature about this whole thing."

The scuttling beside her halted. Sophia took a few steps before she realized that Lunis wasn't right beside her. She paused and looked back, barely making out his beady eyes reflecting the ambient light ahead. His rat nose sniffed.

Sophia tensed. Something was wrong...well, more wrong than being in the tunnels under Las Vegas with a bunch of demon drag-onriders.

She blinked at her dragon. Rather, the rat that was her dragon presently. "What is it?" she hissed.

His nose twitched back and forth like he was picking up a scent on the putrid breeze. Lunis' eyes focused behind her.

Sophia glanced over her shoulder. There was minimal light ahead to make out the tunnel in the distance. She could see a bend in the corridor and a lot of trash and junk ahead, but that was basically it.

Turning back, she shrugged at Lunis. "Is it a mortal? A demon dragonrider? Versalee?"

The rat form of Lunis shook his head and mouthed, "It's a dragon."

Fear shivered down Sophia's spine. She froze. The only part of her able to move was her neck, and she looked over her shoulder as a dragon lumbered into the corridor from around the bend. It had to duck to move in the narrow space, but there it was, straight in front of her, its dark eyes narrowing on her as it opened its mouth, ready to shoot fire straight down the concrete corridor.

CHAPTER ONE HUNDRED FIFTEEN

E van took off after Nathaniel immediately, not sure where the Rogue Rider was heading, but also not caring. Ever since he'd met that demon dragonrider in the air over the elves' homeland island, he'd wanted to give him a proper punishment. Now was his chance. Sophia had stated that Nathaniel and Versalee could meet their end. It was time that redhead got what was coming to him.

Evan followed Sophia because he believed her instinct in battle was right. In this instance, he was confident she was right. The other Rogue Riders were like those lemmings at the Gullington. They'd do what they were told. But Nathaniel...he was pure evil, doing things because he was greedy and corrupt and had no desire to make the world a better place.

That was the thing. Evan believed the Rogue Riders could be selfish and dabble in the criminal world, but as dragonriders also want the overarching good for the world. That's why the angels and Mama Jamba had created the dragonriders in the first place, right?

He couldn't believe that the angel riders were created only to protect and the demon riders solely to destroy. That seemed counterintuitive. They had to be about balance and in achieving that, it meant some fat had to be trimmed.

Speeding up the stairs, Evan watched as Nathaniel exited a door at the top, continuing to flee.

Coward. Of course, the demon dragonrider was running. That was what the weak did, and Nathaniel knew that if he came face-to-face with the Dragon Elite member that he would be swiftly defeated.

Spilling out of the door, Evan found himself back on the streets of Las Vegas, sirens echoing all around. There was still chaos on the Strip. They'd have to deal with that later. For now, he needed to put an end to this so-called leader who was too wimpy to face him directly.

Evan spun back and forth in the darkening streets trying to locate Nathaniel. The sun had set fast, and the bright lights from the casinos were taking over, casting a strange glow on the pavement.

Catching sight of the green dragon, Evan watched as Nathaniel jumped onto its back and yanked hard on the reins, urging the majestic creature into the air as if he was a racehorse and not his partner.

The dragon's head jerked from side to side, but the creature finally took off, launching into the air, green wings beating against the wind as the rider and dragon gained altitude over Las Vegas.

Evan wasn't worried they'd get away. This was his fight, this time.

He snapped his fingers, unhurried, and a moment later, Coral arrived beside him almost silently.

"Right on time, lovely," he said sweetly to his lifelong companion while gracefully climbing on her back. Without a word or a movement, the purple dragon sprang into the air, quickly going after the Rogue Rider. This fight might not be easy or fair, but for Evan, there was only one way it could end.

CHAPTER ONE HUNDRED SIXTEEN

"Hey, guys!" Wilder said with a broad smile.

Everyone in the room bolted upright. Many grabbed the weapons besides them. That included everything from machetes to swords to guns, all of them pointed at Wilder.

The smile on his face not faltering, Wilder held up his hands. "Oh, hey. Calm down. I'm lost and wondering if you can point me in the direction of the closest Jamba Juice."

"He's one of those Dragon Elite," a burly Rogue Rider said. "I saw him out on the Strip when they were fighting us."

Wilder kept his hands up. "Actually, guys, we weren't trying to fight you at all. I believe we saved you from getting your butts handed to you from a mob of angry magicians."

There were laughs from all around. "They're lucky they didn't bring our wrath down on them."

Wilder shook his head and clicked his tongue. "I think you misunderstand how it works."

A few of the mortals narrowed their eyes and reached for guns. Wilder arched an eyebrow at them, not deterred, the look on his face saying, "Are you sure you want to do that?"

"We don't, Goody-Two-Shoes," a Rogue Rider said and strode

forward carrying a long knife. "We're dragonriders and magicians are just—"

"What you are and always have been but without the dragon?" Wilder supplied, cutting him off.

"Don't mouth off to me," the guy snarled. "You're alone and outnumbered." He laughed, a booming sound. "You should have known better than to come here by yourself."

Wilder pretended to hang his head like he felt defeated, stomaching the smell of sweat and garbage from the large room. "Yeah, I'm such a ditz. I thought I could come down here and convince you all to stop being dumb faces and fighting the Dragon Elite. I thought I could convince you that we're the stronger of the two organizations, and we could all benefit if you simply bowed to our jurisdiction since we're the more powerful entity."

Laughter erupted around the large concrete room.

"Yeah, that was your mistake," the guy in front of Wilder stated. "Simply naïve. Now you're going to pay the price." His eyes flickered down to the sword in Wilder's hand. "That's all you brought to stop us? Nice try."

Wilder shrugged and sheathed the sword. "Yeah, I wasn't thinking. There's all of you and one of me. I have one weapon, and you have all those guns."

Another chorus of laughter. "Yeah, you're a real idiot. What were you thinking?"

Wilder held his hands up, not in surrender this time, but rather as if he was about to throw a huge, magical spell at the room of magicians, mortals, and weapons in front of him. "I guess I thought that even if I'm alone, I still control every single weapon in this room, so brace yourselves."

CHAPTER ONE HUNDRED
SEVENTEEN

The demon dragon opened its mouth. Before Sophia could react, fire shot from it. Locked in the long concrete tunnel, she had no options. Running would only put her a short distance from the flames. Teleporting under those circumstances would be impossible. There was nowhere to go. No magic that could save her.

She spied the red and orange of the flames as they shot from the dragon's mouth. They flew at her and were seconds from scorching her to bits. Then a black wall suddenly blotted them out, and all Sophia saw was black. Wait, not just black...there was more.

She blinked, cleared her vision, and took in the different information from her senses. She spied blue and eyes and a wall of...Lunis.

Sophia's eyes adjusted and she noticed that the blue dragon had morphed into his usual form and was standing right in front of her, his wing extended and his face looking directly at her. Lunis had sacrificed himself to block the attack, protecting her.

Sophia ran forward, hugging her dragon. "Lunis, are you okay?"

He nodded while holding her in tightly with one arm. The other stayed extended, the wing shielding them, blocking the corridor where the other dragon stood a short distance away. "Remember that fire from another dragon doesn't easily penetrate our hide. If this runt keeps it up, yeah it will sting, but I'm okay for now."

"Thank you," Sophia said, her throat tight from emotion, realizing what her dragon had done to save her by springing into action.

Lunis hugged her tightly before releasing her. "No problem. Now I have to blast this fly before he realizes what's happening. Currently, he's probably trying to figure out where the magical wall came from."

Sophia looked up at her dragon from his clutches. "Do you have to hurt him? He belongs to a demon dragonrider, and you know we don't want to hurt them if we can avoid it."

Lunis considered this. "Yeah, fine. Can you disguise me as something that we all know dragons fear intensely, especially a newborn?"

Sophia grinned, knowing exactly what he meant. She stood back and aimed her finger at her dragon. He transformed instantly, shrinking down and taking away the wall that was him guarding and hiding her. She simultaneously shrank into the shadows out of the dragon's view.

From her hiding place, she spied the smaller dragon catch sight of Lunis. He at first looked confused. Then surprised. Then completely scared.

Lunis in the form of a mortal toddler with sticky hands and large eyes reached forward. "Dragon! Want to touch! Want to lick!" Then with his short stumpy legs, Lunis ran for the dragon, hands reaching.

The demon dragon's eyes widened with horror. The creature spun and ran off in the direction it had come, retreating from the tiny mortal child.

Sophia laughed. Dragons were majestic. They were brave. Neither did they want to kill tiny mortals nor be clobbered by them.

"You're a genius, Lunis," Sophia muttered to herself, setting off once more down the darkened corridor, alone.

CHAPTER ONE HUNDRED
EIGHTEEN

Coral and Evan took off into the night sky over Las Vegas, soaring higher and faster than Nathaniel and his green dragon not far in the distance.

Evan felt sorry for the redhead, but not that sorry. He'd been warned. Had been told to change his ways or there would be repercussions. The first two times, Evan and Coral had taken it easy on the Rogue Rider. Now there would be no lenient measures and for a cocky new demon dragonrider that would come as a shock when he was defeated so swiftly.

Don't be too self-assured, Coral urged Evan over the telepathic link they shared.

He patted his dragon and smiled as the cityscape took shape below them. *I can often be too confident, but I assure you, in this instance, I am not. A brand-new dragonrider who thinks he owns the world and fails to realize the Dragon Elite were created to protect it deserves my wrath. I have every confidence I'll give it to him.*

Almost as though sharing Evan's confidence, Nathaniel whipped around on his dragon when on the other side of the Eiffel Tower over the Paris Hotel and Casino, hovering in the air as the pair approached.

The redhead had a smug look on his face as he gripped the reins connected to his dragon. "You ready to go down?"

Evan laughed, having heard the dragonrider just fine thanks to the chi of the dragon. "If you mean down to that place that serves killer nachos, then yes. Are you ready to go down after I kill you?"

"You can try," Nathaniel said, and because he was full of no new tricks, Evan thought, he held up his hand and shot a bolt of lightning at them.

Evan and Coral easily swerved out of its trajectory. Unfortunately, it hit the Bellagio behind them. Evan shook his head, leaned low on his dragon, and chased after the Rogue Rider. "The damn Bellagio can't catch a break lately. Last time the fountains and structural damage and now this."

Nathaniel and his dragon weren't bad fliers, he observed, watching as they snaked around Planet Hollywood and shot in the opposite direction. Still, there was one thing they misunderstood on a fundamental level.

When a dragon and its rider truly fly together, there is no beginning or end, he thought to himself, taking off around a crane over a spot of new development. *There's no reason to plan or overthink. The two fuse and simply know. Nathaniel keeps trying to run, to outmaneuver, but when you're one, it just happens.*

Evan looked over his shoulder as he came to the other side of the crane, not knowing exactly why he and Coral had chosen that spot, but knowing it was right. They hovered on the opposite side of the enormous structure meant to pick up large objects and transport them onto buildings not yet erected. It resembled a large see-saw.

Nathaniel sped in their direction on the green dragon. When he was right on the other side of the crane, he slowed, his dragon flapping its wings furiously to stay in the air.

Evan drew in a breath, knowing what was coming next. He felt as if there was a television audience that they'd know what was coming next too. But would they know how it ended?

Nathaniel held up his hand.

Evan didn't react. Not yet. There was no reason, although he knew what his very uncreative opponent would do next.

In a no-show of surprises, Nathaniel shot another bolt of lightning at Coral and Evan. It streaked through the air.

Evan calmly held up his hand but didn't block the electricity. Instead, he directed the crane to swing around, the larger side rotating and catching the bolt of lightning and ricocheting it back at its maker. Usually the crane would have absorbed the shock, but Evan's quick thinking had fixed that with a spell.

The electricity raced through the air, and there was no time for Nathaniel or his dragon to react. It hit them squarely. The voltage covered them immediately, shocking them all over and sending them plummeting to the ground, where they cracked the pavement—dead immediately.

CHAPTER ONE HUNDRED
NINETEEN

If Wilder had faced a room full of dragonriders holding swords, the advantage he held over them would be different. He'd have information—knowledge connected to the weapon. That could be helpful, but usually in a long-term game.

However, Wilder's power as a weapons expert gave him different advantages when facing a bunch of coward demon dragonriders holding guns. He couldn't control missiles or cannons or other large weaponry. Guns on this scale? Well, this was his game.

He grinned as all the guys who thought they were about to blast him to hell released the safety on their guns in unison and pulled the trigger.

Wilder brought his arms down just in time, and a blast of smoke hit those firing in their faces. It didn't kill them. Sophia had been clear about that. It blasted them backward, and all of them hit the wall on the far side, their cowardly weapons falling from their hands and plunging the room into disarray.

Wilder knew that things would go from bad to worse fast, so he decided to cut it off.

He brought his hands up and pulled down the beam that held the doorframe in place in the surrounding concrete. It collapsed at once, pinning the demon dragonriders and the criminal mortals they'd taken control of in the adjoining space.

Wilder put his ear to the rubble that had fallen before him after waving away the dust that billowed up. He listened to the commotion on the other side as they all scrambled, trying to figure out what had happened.

When things started to settle down, Wilder cleared his throat. "Now, demon dragonriders, the next time we meet—the next time you're face-to-face with any Dragon Elite member—please remember, you're young. You're new. We are your authority, and you will respect us. In return, we'll ensure you aren't erased from this planet. Cool?"

When there was no answer, Wilder turned and hurried back the way he'd come. He knew the Rogue Riders would claw their way out, but not before Sophia found Trudy DeVries and they were out of there.

CHAPTER ONE HUNDRED TWENTY

S ophia heard something at her back and tensed, thinking another Rogue Rider approached. With Inexorabilis in her hand, she spun and nearly sliced the love of her life. The blade halted inches from Wilder's face.

Sophia tensed, held her breath, and took in his shocked expression and rapid breathing.

Then they both broke into quiet laughter, realizing that they'd nearly offed each other. They nearly embraced with relief that they were both okay, but instead, turned to the passage ahead.

Wilder gave her a sturdy look. They both knew that reunions and moments of relief were better saved for later when they could celebrate bigger victories.

"She has to be up ahead," Sophia stated.

He nodded and pulled his sword.

They ambled through the dark, listening to the trickling of water and taking each step soundlessly.

Ahead, they heard chatter. Two men were conversing—arguing. That seemed to be all the Rogue Riders currently did, besides exploit criminals.

Sophia laid a hand on Wilder's chest, keeping him from spilling around the corner and assaulting the men. She peered around the bend and saw that it was two demon dragonriders guarding a large woman in combat clothing. Warrior Trudy DeVries.

Her hands were pinned behind her back, and she was tied to a chair, her chin down as if she was asleep.

The guys were stationed on opposite sides of a doorframe, propped up as they both ate corn dogs.

For a moment, Sophia thought about assaulting them for their food but realized that wasn't the reason to knock them out, and she really wouldn't want their leftovers. She wanted her own food.

To her surprise, Trudy looked up. There seemed to be a flicker of a smile on her face, as though the Warrior saw her, but that seemed impossible from that distance and in the dark.

"All I'm saying is that with Tanner gone, I'm next in line for third in command," one of the guys said, then took a bite of his corndog and chewed with his mouth open. "Why do you think Nathaniel put me in charge of watching this one?"

The other guy shook his head. "I'm in charge of watching this woman too."

"Guys," Trudy said in a sing-song tone.

"How many times have we told you not to talk?" the first guy said.

"A few times," Trudy replied. "That's been fine and all, but now I'm ready to be done with this whole hostage thing."

The other guy laughed. "Well, thing is, sweetheart, that's always been up for us to decide when it's over. You're our prisoner, you see."

Trudy DeVries looked up, and Sophia knew at once that her gaze connected with hers. "No, the thing is, that's always been up to me."

She snapped her head to one side, and the guy closest to her eating the corndog fell to the floor instantly as if he'd passed out, his food rolling away. Before the other guy could react, Trudy snapped her neck to the other side as though rolling out an especially stubborn kink. Like the other guy, the demon dragonrider fell to the floor too, totally passed out.

Sophia and Wilder jumped out from behind the corner at once, looking around for other guards. There were none. Trudy DeVries smiled broadly at them.

"Well, hello, Rider Sophia Beaufont," Trudy DeVries stated proudly, looking strong. "I've been waiting for you to show up so I could do that."

CHAPTER ONE HUNDRED TWENTY-ONE

Sophia rushed forward and worked to release the Warrior from her bonds. "Wait, I don't understand. You were waiting for me to show up so you could free yourself? Because that's what I watched happen."

Trudy worked out her wrists when she was released, letting out the tension as she rolled them around. She nodded. "Yeah, that's right."

Wilder tilted his head and regarded the Warrior with confusion. "I'm not sure I understand."

"Nor I." Sophia stood back, wondering if this was a trick. Maybe it wasn't the real Trudy DeVries. Maybe this was a trap. Perhaps they'd been set up.

Trudy stood and smiled down at Sophia while clapping a hand on her shoulder. "You did good. You got to me. And you wouldn't have found the Rogue Riders if I hadn't been captured. My visions told me that much, so I allowed it to happen."

Sophia nearly choked on her gasp. "You what?"

"She's a seer?" Wilder asked in disbelief.

"Shush," Sophia urged. "She's good and helpful, and my family has kept the DeVries family secret for generations."

Trudy turned to Wilder with confidence and smiled. "You will too. I've seen it." She winked.

Wilder shook his head and shivered. "Okay, that's just creepy."

"And cool too," Trudy stated, seeming excited to be free.

"Wait, I need to back up." Sophia shook her head. "It seems like you could have gotten out of here at any point based on how you knocked these guys out." She indicated the guys on the floor.

Trudy nodded. "They have about as much experience as a college freshman."

"You got captured," Wilder argued.

"And you were here just now," Sophia stated. Then it dawned on her. "You needed me to find the Rogue Riders based on some weird vision you've had. You allowed all this to happen, knowing that it all needed to. You endured being captured because..."

Trudy simply stared at her, waiting for her to work it out.

"Something that happened tonight is crucial to the future, isn't it?" Sophia questioned.

Trudy pulled in a breath. "I dare say it's all crucial. What Evan did. What Wilder did. What you did. It all sets up the Dragon Elite, and without it, well, you all didn't stand a chance. So yes, I allowed an uncomfortable reality to happen for me so that you all could have the potential to succeed, but please note, that's all it is. It's potential. It's up to the Dragon Elite to make the most of the playing field that you've leveled."

Sophia couldn't help but grin, although she was a little angry that the Warrior put her and everyone else in danger for this. But then, Trudy had this confidence, and it seemed to be to create a better future so how could she be angry? "Wow, I can't believe all this."

"I know," Wilder said, a similar look of disbelief on his face. "You have the weirdest friends."

Sophia and Trudy both laughed.

Finally, Sophia shook off all the strangeness and looked the Warrior for the House of Fourteen over. "Are you really okay? You're not hurt, are you?"

Trudy glanced at her arms and nodded. "I'm stiff and need a proper meal, but I feel fine."

"That was pretty impressive when you knocked those guys out," Wilder commended.

Trudy smiled, looking down at Sophia. "You didn't really believe these kids could take me hostage?"

Now that Sophia thought about it, the whole thing seemed silly. "It was weird, but you knew I'd come and get you."

"I knew that, even without seeing the vision," Trudy stated. "Also, there's something else I need to tell you."

Sophia tensed and prepared herself for what came next.

"Call Liv and tell her to meet us," Trudy stated. "I need to tell her something, and you should be there."

CHAPTER ONE HUNDRED
TWENTY-TWO

"How did you know that I've wanted to try this place?" Liv pulled the mound of nachos to her, her eyes wide as she took in the hugeness.

"I didn't," Sophia admitted, excited by her pile of nachos at Nacho Daddy. "It was Lunis who mentioned it."

The blue dragon was back in toddler form, cleaning up a pile of nachos from his side of the table. It was a very strange sight. He pointed a chubby finger at Warrior Trudy DeVries. "It was her. She came to me in a dream and told me about this place. I will say no more."

The Warrior glanced at the sisters and nodded. "I have to admit that I knew the Rogue Riders would take me and that they had to. I can't tell you why or what happens from it, but I can say that if things go right, it sets things into motion that are important for setting up the future."

Sophia nearly shivered from the implications. This felt so important and also so risky. "What do I do?"

"Push forward." Trudy watched as Evan downed a beer. "I know it's weird for most when they know about the future, but that almost messes it up. So just proceed and know you're on track."

"That's some wicked stuff, seer." Evan wiped his mouth with the back of his hand.

"Hey, not a word about this, dragonrider," Liv warned and pointed at Evan.

He immediately held up his hands in surrender. "No worries. I'm much obliged to the Warrior who gave me the opportunity to take out that dirt weed."

Sophia nodded. "Nathaniel was no good. You did good."

"I agree," Trudy said with a nod. "As did Wilder, setting the foundation for a better future for the Rogue Riders."

Wilder held up his mug of beer and grinned. "Why, thank you. I love it when they pull out the big guns. I'm always like, you made it easy for me."

"You all performed beautifully," Sophia commended, holding up her glass of beer. "Great job, everyone. I'm grateful that Trudy is safe, even if it was a ruse all along."

They all clinked glasses. Well, all but Liv.

"Yeah, you sneaky future seers are always setting us up, aren't you?" Liv asked, digging back into her nachos.

Trudy nodded. "Unfortunately so. We can only tell you all so much to achieve the desired results. Too much and we'll undo the vision. Too little and it might not happen. Avoiding potential realities is even more tricky, which is why I didn't tell you anything about the baby so that you sought your own solution."

Liv dropped the chip in her hand. "The baby...you saw something about the baby?"

Trudy nodded. "And in every vision I saw, if I intervened, I made it worse. So I didn't say a word and let you sisters work it out together." She indicated Liv and Sophia. "Again, you've proven to be a perfect team and created the perfect outcome."

Liv's eyes widened. "Are you saying..." She looked at Sophia, then at Trudy, and back at Sophia.

The other Warrior smiled. "I am. Your baby is fine. The vision I see tells me that your child isn't a demon."

"Oh, my angels!" Liv exclaimed, nearly jumping up from her seat. "I have a normal baby."

Trudy's light expression dropped. "No, I said you don't have a demon. Your baby will be anything but normal. Yours and Stefan's baby will go on to rule empires but at many costs."

Sophia sat back in her seat, suddenly feeling very heavy.

Liv did the same.

"Much like all the Beaufont children," Trudy went on, "your child will be healthy and happy and extremely talented. They also happen to have inherited your great burden of having to save the world. No surprise there, right?"

The group all exchanged foreboding expressions before everyone laughed, knowing that was all of their fates. Grateful that the baby wasn't a demon and Trudy was safe and that they'd put the Rogue Riders in their place for a little while, Sophia laid her head on her sister's shoulder feeling victorious. Liv patted her shoulder, laying her head on hers.

"Well, we did it, didn't we?" Evan said proudly.

"We sure did." Wilder smiled at Sophia as she had a moment with her sister.

She straightened, suddenly thinking about something. "Evan took out Nathaniel. We met most of the other Rogue Riders. Where was Versalee? None of us saw her. What happened to her?"

They all exchanged foreboding expressions, unable to shake the feeling that they'd been successful, but the true evil was still out there in the world.

CHAPTER ONE HUNDRED TWENTY-THREE

From the rooftop of the Cosmopolitan Hotel and Casino in Las Vegas, Versalee glared down at the scene below on the Strip. There were ambulances and magical rescue operations, but none could save Nathaniel and his dragon, Bolt.

They were dead.

She smirked and shook her head. It was messy, but everything had gone to plan.

Nathaniel had never been her real second in command. She'd only told him that to get him to follow her deception.

Versalee glanced at Ash, her dragon, and smiled fondly. There had only ever been one second in command, and that was her dragon. Tanner and Nathaniel had simply been her attempts to keep the Dragon Elite's attention off her while she planned, worked, and figured things out.

And it *had* worked.

While Nathaniel had created problems in Las Vegas at her orders, she'd secured the Rogue Riders' real headquarters. She'd recruited real followers, not caring what happened to the ones in Las Vegas. Versalee had been planning, and it had all worked.

Now she had a headquarters that wouldn't just be perfect and protect the Rogue Riders, but it would make her and Ash stronger. It would make them the force they needed to be to defeat the Dragon Elite.

She laughed out loud, unheard over the city's noises. Soon she'd be so powerful that the Dragon Elite wouldn't know how to face her and her dragon. Things had all worked out perfectly, and soon the do-gooders would meet their end. That's when she'd take her throne as the reigning dragonrider, ruling over the world.

CHAPTER ONE HUNDRED
TWENTY-FOUR

The Castle had never looked so beautiful. Sophia strode down the great staircase to find the area lit with many twinkling lights. The Christmas tree was so large that it didn't seem real, but the evergreen scent wafting off it told her it was authentic and fresh-cut.

The tree towered to the top of the high rafters in the sitting area outside the Castle's entryway. There were decorations in every possible place. Last year had been beautiful with lights and bows and wreaths, the first time in a long while that there had been Christmas decorations or a celebration. Now it seemed that Trin had outdone herself.

The cyborg strode in from the dining hall carrying a silver tray with frosted cookies and chocolate-covered pretzels.

"Fantastic job," Sophia said as the housekeeper set the tray down in front of Mama Jamba and Mahkah lounging on the sofa. The stoic Native American was simply sitting, a slight smile of contentedness on his face as though the decorations brought him a new level of peace. Mother Nature was flipping through a monthly planning calendar. The three newbie dragonriders sat on the other side of the room, not looking as relaxed as the others.

Trin glanced up, confusion on her face. "Me? You think I did all this? It wasn't me."

"Oh," Sophia said with surprise. "I guess Quiet outdid himself yet again."

"Aren't you festive," Mama Jamba observed, looking Sophia over. She wore a red and black tartan dress with a large sash.

She smiled and curtsied. "I figured it would be nice to dress up for the occasion."

"What occasion?" Evan strode into the room, his shirt untucked and NO10JO on his heels.

"It's Christmas," Trin stated. "Did you just roll out of bed?"

He nodded. "Yeah, I sort of saved the world recently so I figured I'd sleep in. Sue me."

"I might," she sang, winking fondly at him and turning on her heels and heading back for the kitchen.

Evan's eyes widened at the sight of the tray of cookies. He bolted over and reached for one with each hand.

"Save some for the others," Sophia warned.

He stuck two cookies in his mouth at once and mumbled. "You mean, save one for Quiet."

"I do," she stated as the groundskeeper strode in from the outside, the sharp cold wind sneaking into the Castle through the stained glass front door.

"Quiet, you don't want any cookies, do you?" Evan asked through a mouthful.

The gnome mumbled something inaudible and strode over, taking a cookie.

Some things never change, Sophia observed, slightly amused by the pair's constant antics.

Quiet pointed at the tree and muttered something else.

Evan turned and looked where the gnome indicated. It was the angel on the top of the tree. It wasn't an ordinary Christmas angel. Instead, it was made of gray stone and wore a long flowing gown. That wasn't the strange part though. It was that the angel had its face covered with its hand.

"Oh hell nah!" Evan exclaimed, his eyes wide and keeping his gaze pinned on the angel. "Was that there before?"

Mama Jamba glanced up casually from her planner and shook her head. "No, I believe it just appeared. Must have been in your honor."

"Damn it. Now I can't look away from it," Evan complained. "This ruins everything."

"It's not particularly pretty," Ainsley observed as she entered the room wearing a shimmering blue gown that was snug on the top and flowing on the bottom. "Why can't you look away?"

"Because then I'll disappear," Evan stated through clenched teeth. "That's how that short fart made me lost for all that time."

"I thought you were drunk," Trin retorted as she returned with a tray of tea, joining the conversation like Ainsley, as though she'd been there the entire time.

"I told you," Evan seethed. "It was that man who played his tricks on me." He pointed in Quiet's general direction, but the gnome had already taken a seat in the opposite corner next to where Sophia had settled.

"Do we all have to stay looking at it?" Sophia questioned.

"I think only one of us," Mahkah commented in his usual tone full of wisdom.

NO10JO barked at Evan's side, looking up at the angel the same as his master.

"I think your best mate has you covered so you can enjoy your cookies." Trin pointed at the cyborg dog.

Evan sighed and looked down at the animal covered in metal and bolts, like his girlfriend, Trin. "Thanks, pal. You're the best canine ever. I'll relieve you after the festivities when I chuck Quiet in the snow."

Beside Sophia, the gnome mumbled something that sounded like, "I'd like to see you try."

A humming alerted everyone to Wilder's presence before he materialized from the staircase. He wore a broad smile at the sight of the decorations.

Evan, freed from having to stare at the angel on the tree, doubled over laughing. "Are you and Pink Princess wearing matching tartans?"

Wilder glanced down at his red and black sweater, which matched Sophia's dress although they hadn't planned it. She didn't even know he had that sweater.

"Why, yes, I guess we are," he stated proudly. "Don't we look dashing?"

She smiled at him. "I agree."

"If by dashing you mean like a bunch of gross dummies, then okay," Evan quipped.

Wilder nodded when he passed Evan on his way to Sophia. "Then a gross dummy I will be." He took a seat on the other side of her and grinned at Quiet. "Thanks for the jumper. I found it in my closet but didn't know you had this planned." He indicated Sophia and himself.

Quiet nodded and muttered something inaudible.

"You look very nice." Sophia took Wilder's hand.

"You all look very nice," Mama Jamba said while marking days in her planner. "Especially you, Ainsley."

The elf blushed and smoothed her blue gown self-consciously. "Thank you. I also found this in my closet and hadn't seen it before. I thought I had Quiet to thank for it." She nodded appreciatively in his direction. Ainsley did look especially lovely with her hair braided back in rows and a sapphire necklace around her neck, contrasting nicely with her hair.

Hiker's boots thundering across the floor told everyone of his arrival. However, this time, Evan didn't laugh when he entered the room, as he had with Wilder. Everyone was speechless.

The leader of the Dragon Elite wore a traditional kilt, but he hadn't stopped there. He also had the sporran and matching socks and shoes. If he had a set of bagpipes, he'd look just like a piper.

Finally, it was Ainsley who spoke while blinking at him with surprise. "Hiker, you…you…you look so handsome."

He nodded and pressed his hand to the side of his hair, which he'd slicked back. His beard was trimmed and combed.

"I didn't know you liked Christmas so much, sir," Wilder observed.

Hiker glanced at him. "I don't. I didn't even…well, I sort of knew, but that's not why I dressed up."

"It's not?" Sophia questioned. "Is it because we rescued Trudy DeVries and we're that much closer to controlling the Rogue Riders?"

"That's worth celebrating," he agreed. "But no, and I didn't realize you lot would be down here."

"It's Christmas, sir," Evan argued. "Do you want us to go and train? Or can we have a single hour off?"

Hiker rolled his eyes. "You can have an hour, but I want you all out on the Expanse straight after tea."

Wilder glanced out the window where white covered the green of the Gullington. Snow fluttered down harder now. "Great. I'll build a snowman and Evan can try and spar it. My money is on the snowman."

Hiker shook his head and chewed on his lip. Sophia spied a nervousness in the man. It was palpable. "Ainsley, can I see you in my office?"

"Oh, son." Mama Jamba put her calendar aside and sat up. "Not there. Do it here."

He glanced at the old woman. "But everyone is here."

"And it's because of everyone in this room that you learned to stop being a stupid idiot and have a heart," Mama Jamba argued.

"I don't think the new guys can take any credit." Evan pointed at the three who were like statues, simply watching.

"I don't think you can either," Hiker retorted.

Ainsley lowered her chin and studied Hiker. "You want to tell me something? What is it?"

He cleared his throat. "I do." Indecision rolled around on his face. "Truth be told, I knew it was Christmas and had something I wanted to give you." Hiker withdrew the red pouch with orange tassels that Sophia had recovered for him. The one that had come from her ancestor, Oscar Beaufont. She tensed at the sight, her heart suddenly pounding, although she wasn't sure exactly why.

Ainsley's eyes darted to the pouch. "A present? For me?"

Hiker nodded while holding out the pouch. "You don't have to take it, but I got it for you many centuries ago. I meant to give it to you, but then the Great War happened, and you lost your memory, and, well, you know the history."

Ainsley forced a nervous smile. "I do remember the history." Tentatively she reached out and took the pouch. "May I?"

Hiker glanced at Mama Jamba, who nodded encouragingly to him.

He handed Ainsley the pouch, and she nimbly opened the tassels and glanced down into the bag. Her mouth popped open. Her eyes widened. A gasp escaped her.

Before she could say a word, Hiker knelt on one knee and clasped her hands. "I know I haven't always made the best decisions. I've made a lot of mistakes. But I've always known that I was meant to spend my life with you. That would be the best decision of my entire life. Ainsley Carter, will you please do me the honor of being my wife for eternity? There is nothing I want more."

Tears slipped down the elf's cheeks as she nodded, not looking capable of anything more. She pulled on Hiker's hands to encourage him up off the floor, and the two embraced. The union was followed immediately by applause and cheers from around the room.

"Yes, yes, yes," Ainsley said through tears, holding on tightly to the man before her. "Of course I'll marry you."

Hiker pulled away slightly, taking the pouch from Ainsley. His thick fingers had trouble getting into the bag, so he knocked the engagement ring out into his palm and held it up. The large sapphire and diamonds on the band sparkled in the room's candlelight. It was breathtaking—Oscar Beaufont's ring.

With a shaking hand, Hiker slipped it onto Ainsley's finger and then kissed it with a twinkle in his eyes. Everyone in the room might have been watching, but for the pair, it was like they were the only two people in the world—the way they looked at each other.

When they kissed, the room erupted in cheers and applause again. Sophia felt so happy for her friends as she laid her head on Wilder's shoulder, loving that the Castle was so full of love.

He kissed her forehead and held her close. "Congrats, sir."

"Yes, congrats," Evan echoed. "It only took you five hundred years to put a ring on it."

CHAPTER ONE HUNDRED
TWENTY-FIVE

Sophia laid on the sofa in Lunis' Pad, flipping through the pages of Oscar Beaufont's diary. It was full of so many strange visions. Some had already come to pass. Some were scratched out like they never would. There were a few that were in the distant future. Sophia felt nervous reading through the book, as though spying the future was somehow going to jinx her.

"You mean so much to me," Lunis said fondly, lying next to her on the polar bear rug.

Sophia glanced up from her book. "You're talking to the hedgehog, aren't you?"

"Yes. Haven't you learned anything from Bermuda Laurens?" Lunis questioned smugly.

"The Beaufonts all have horrible manners, and we can't learn anything," she guessed.

"He's not simply a hedgehog," he corrected. "He has a name."

She flipped a page in Oscar's diary. "I apologize, Sir Alexander Connery MacDonald."

"The Second," he added.

"Who was the first?" she wondered.

"Doesn't matter."

Sophia laughed. "Well, I'm glad you like your indestructible hedgehog."

Lunis nodded while playing with Sir Alexander Connery MacDonald the Second. "Yes, it appears that everyone is coupling up at the Gullington. Hiker and Ainsley, Evan and Trin, you and what's-his-face."

"Wilder." Sophia laughed. "Yeah, but what about Quiet and Mahkah? I hope they find love."

Lunis eyed her speculatively, then shook his head. "You know, sometimes finding love isn't what someone needs. For you, it makes sense, but you shouldn't expect that what makes you happy will work for another. Sometimes being alone is a part of someone's destiny to find happiness." He shrugged. "Who knows? Maybe there's a gnome out there for Quiet or someone for Mahkah."

Sophia thought about this for a moment. "You're right. Maybe they're happy all on their own. Who am I to judge?"

"We all have our journeys," Lunis continued, dipping into his sage-like tone. "Like you, for instance. Your journey won't be the same as the other dragonriders. What fits you won't fit them."

"What's that supposed to mean?" she questioned at once.

"It means that you're cut out for something different," he answered. "I'd dare say, something more."

"Why would you say that?"

"Because you've already taken a leadership role and mastered it and I suspect that's only the beginning," Lunis stated.

"Why?" She felt like her dragon knew something he wasn't telling her.

"Because I know things." He winked.

"Tell me," she urged.

He picked up his hedgehog and looked at him fondly. "Read your book, Soph."

She sighed and turned the page, thinking she was going to punch her dragon. *Maybe she'd cancel his Christmas present,* she thought, turning the page. At the sight of the words on the next page, Sophia tensed. Looked up at Lunis. Glanced back down with alarm. "Did you know I was about to find that?"

Lunis gave her a coy smile. "Maybe. Or I'm just that good."

"How?" she asked, drawing out the word.

"I read the book when you were on a mission," he admitted.

"So you knew all this time?" she asked. "Maybe this prophecy isn't referring to me."

"Maybe," he sang. "But it seems uncanny if not."

Sophia glanced down at Oscar Beaufont's handwriting. The prediction was so strange, and she couldn't fathom what it really meant. It was perplexing, and yet, it had to mean her. Or maybe in the distant future, other Beaufonts joined the Dragon Elite.

Sophia gulped, rereading the words. The prophecy read: "One day, a Beaufont will be a leader among the Dragon Elite as well as another powerful organization—bringing order and peace to the dragonriders once more, preserving their race for all of history."

CHAPTER ONE HUNDRED TWENTY-SIX

"I t's my favorite Christmas present ever!" the blue dragon exclaimed, racing around the giant Oreo cake that Lee and Cat had made for him.

It had been delivered outside the Gullington as the sun was setting and the stars were starting to twinkle on Christmas night. Still, it was easy to see since the Castle and trees were dazzling with festive lights. *There had to be a million of them,* Sophia thought, amazed by how beautiful the Gullington looked with the snow and decorations.

The cake was the size of a house with at least twenty tiers. There was no mistaking that it was Oreo since the cookies lined every single layer. On the top was a giant chocolate-covered Oreo. It also smelled so sweet that it made Sophia's mouth water.

"I'm glad you like it," Sophia said proudly, watching as her dragon continued to race around the cake. "You don't have to share it with anyone, although maybe you'll give me a slice."

He halted and raised an eyebrow at her. "Maybe..."

Sophia laughed and pulled her thick coat tighter. Everyone was at the Castle, and she could see figures moving around in the dining hall. It was time for the big feast.

"Do you want to join me for dinner?" Sophia indicated the Castle.

"We can open a window although Evan will complain bitterly about the cold air wafting through, so let's do it."

Lunis shook his head. "Are you kidding me? I'm going to lick every square inch of this."

"On second thought, I don't want a piece of your cake," Sophia joked.

He nodded. "I wasn't sharing anyway." Giving her a fond look, he smiled. "Thank you, Soph. This is perfect. You know me so well."

"You're welcome," she replied. "No one knows us better than each other."

"For all our lives," the dragon agreed and came around beside her, unfolded his wing, and wrapped it around her, hugging her tightly.

She looked up at Lunis, regarding him with a deep fondness before looking out at the massive Oreo cake and the Castle and the Expanse, feeling so grateful for it all. Sophia didn't know what the prophecy meant. She was already a leader in the Dragon Elite but didn't know how she could lead another organization.

That couldn't mean the House of Fourteen, she hoped. That was Liv's place, and everything seemed to be working out for her sister. Only time would reveal what other places the world would need Sophia. And she'd be there. If the prophecy did refer to her, then she'd be honored to be a part of whatever it took to preserve the dragonriders for all of history. They were Mother Nature's guards after all, ensuring that the world continued to rotate on its axis and maintain peace.

Sophia smiled, grateful to be a part of something so important. Thankful for whatever came next. If the world required her to take on more, then that's exactly what she'd do—to ensure the planet was safe.

SARAH'S AUTHOR NOTES
DECEMBER 17, 2020

Thank you to everyone out there who has supported the books and LBMPN. We can't do this alone. I really value all you readers, your input, your ideas, your encouragement and more! Thank you.

It's hard to believe this is book 11 in the series. And each book is two in one, so it's really book 22, if I'm honest.

What a year it's been and I'm not entirely saying that for the reasons some might think. Yes, the world is a different place and everyone's lives have changed, but I signed on to write this series with crazy deadlines and all before I knew I'd spend most of the year in lockdown. In hindsight, Past Sarah was super smart, committing to writing books when really there wasn't much else I could be doing.

Ironically, when Mike and I had the meeting in Las Vegas where it was decided we would do 24 books in the series, the day before I was dressed as a ninja and wearing a mask. That was November 2019. I remember thinking, man, wearing a mask over my face is difficult... Oh, Past Sarah, if you only knew...

This year I have one more book to write, then the final part of book 12 will be done by mid-January. That makes for 18 books I've written in 2020. In 2019, I wrote 15. In 2021, I plan to write 10. I heard all you readers just mutter, "Slacker." And it's true. Total slacker.

What do I plan to do with all this free time? Well, I got Lydia a Nintendo Switch for Christmas. Yes, that's right, it's totally for Lydia.

When I started writing books years ago, I gave up video games. Before that, I used to spend weekends playing computer time management games and whatnot. I heard a bunch of you readers just mutter, "Nerd." It's true. After a long work week of meetings and deadlines and soul crushing tasks, nothing was better than sitting on my couch and virtually fulfilling tasks as I ran my restaurant or farm or whatever it was.

My point here is that when I decided to make a go of this whole author thing, I gave up games, knowing that it would cut into my schedule. I knew I'd be working from home and it would be hard to put boundaries on things. So besides from a few occasions when I've schooled Lydia in Mario Kart, I haven't played video games.

That's all about to change.

Santa is going to get me Zelda for Christmas. And I'm going to play the hell out of that and Animal Crossing and all sorts of other things. So, that's what I'm doing when I'm not writing 8 extra books this next year. It won't be activities that enrich my life and hopefully yours by creating fiction that will never die, but it will make me happy and I sort of need the break.

I'd also like to see the Scotsman a bit more, so hopefully that gets to happen in 2021 and not just because I won't have tons of crazy deadlines. Hopefully the world will open up. Just today, I had my third trip to Scotland postponed. The world is dumb, but he and I are resilient.

I have plans to take off upwards of a whole two weeks when I finish this series. It will be nuts, like that one time when I was a corporate professional and the university required me to take off Fridays due to a union agreement. I literally stared at my boss and said, "B-B-But what am I supposed to do…?"

All my friends all had regular jobs so I knew that they weren't going to be able to hang out with me on my Fridays off. So guess what I started doing to fill the time? I started a blog, which turned into a book, which I didn't publish because it was silly. But still, I can probably thank having those Fridays off for preparing me to write real books that are still silly but hopefully much better than my first one.

I'd actually written a book prior to that called One Day Hill. I, like many authors, had woken up from a dream where I'd gotten this idea for a novel. I started taking my lunch breaks to write it. I didn't outline at that time because I was insane. And guess why you'll never see that book? Because it doesn't have an ending. Well, it doesn't have a good ending. It actually has like three endings that I've written but none of them fit because I don't think I was ever supposed to do anything with the book. Like the blog, it was just priming me to one day write real books that have endings and hopefully are good enough that readers pick up the next one or hopefully the next 11.

Seriously, right before I sat down to write these author notes, I was like, I've got nothing to write about. And then 2k words later and I'm talking about video games and blogs. Is it ever a wonder that my daughter is never quiet? I wonder where she gets it from...

Speaking of never quiet, let's discuss Ramy Vance and how he got to be killed *twice* in a book. So Martha Carr has these really fun Zoom luncheons each month. She made the mistake of asking Ramy and I to host one. Anyway, during one of these lunches, he all but begs me to bring him back in the books and kill him off, but only in ridiculous ways.

The idea was that his deaths would always be totally avoidable and a total inconvenience to others (especially because he didn't really die and would come back). In the past, I've actually had trouble with the idea of killing off a friend in a book. Yes, I called Ramy-Cans a friend. Do not tell anyone!

However, after coming up with the new Ramy storyline, I realized that I could kill him since he didn't really die. So that's how we got the Ramy-Cans who is accident prone and can't be killed, but is constantly splattering his guts all over everything.

To make things even darker, I asked the Scotsman how Ramy should die and he supplied the idea of him making fun of a vegan and then poisoning himself with meat or cheese. Yes, that's how we romantically spend our time, crafting the fictional deaths of our friends. Just imagine if you're not my friend!

If you're not my friend, then you go into a book as a villain, where you are hated and die an even more horrible and permanent death. Versalee was a real bearded girl I knew from Arkansas. She wasn't bright or especially talented and she cheated on my brother (her husband at the time) and then tried to sabotage me. It's all water under the bridge. I forgive Versalee for being a first class Hooker Shoes (yeah, I'm bringing that one back for those of you who get the reference). I forgave her, but then I also put her in a book and who knows what will happen to our villain. Spoiler alert! She won't go on to rule the world or break hearts or succeed in bringing me down.

Okay, I'm off to start book 12 and a little sad as I realize that it will be the last one, but as you all know, I'm never really done with characters or settings. I've got the ability to bring back Ricky Bobby, the House of Fourteen, the Lucidite Institute and many characters. So be prepared to see our friends again, possibly in the next series: The Inscrutable Paris Beaufont. Looking forward to visiting Happily Ever After College after this.

Until then, take care of each other and yourselves.

Much love and peace,
Tiny Ninja

PS Manderle, I let you off the hook on this one, but just you wait... More teasing at the end of book 12. That's a promise!

MICHAEL'S AUTHOR NOTES
DECEMBER 28, 2020

Thank you for not only reading BOOK 11(!) but also my author notes in the back after Sarah 'What do have I to talk about?' Noffke's novellete before me.

Not that I'm saying she has a problem with lockdown and going stir crazy (and just how far apart is crazy from stir crazy anyway?)

But I totally am.

She and I spoke the other day for a few minutes to catch up on a subject or two and if you ever get a chance to jump on a phone call with her...

Do it.

I promise, the call will be EXACTLY like her author notes in this book.

So, I'm starting to cook more (something I did a lot of back in my teens and early twenties). For the last few years (especially since 2016) I have exchanged money for someone to cook and clean at restaurants. The reason was time.

As in, I haven't had enough time since 2016 to slow down.

Now, about five years later, I have set up stuff in the company in such a way that I'm looking forward to getting some time to dabble in other areas besides books and publishing. I've kinda decided that healthy eating (well, healthier eating because me...) is what I hope to do.

So, be prepared for more discussions about my little jaunts into cooking and things I have learned. For example, I'm a HUGE fan of chili oil at Chinese food restaurants.

Now, I thought that it was little more than oil and red chili flakes mixed together and let it sit.

Spoiler – It's not.

So, I was on Amazon a couple of weeks ago and decided I'd try to start buying some of the food that I can't find easily while re-heating fried rice from Ping Pang Pong. Of course, I was running low on chili oil from a bottle I purchased at the local large grocery store.

I had an iPad, and a reason to go shopping for something cool.

I found two different types of chili oil (one with the flakes as a component and one that was clear red) PLUS a 7-Pepper Japanese mix that you shake onto your food.

For those who are interested, here are the products:

S&B Layu, Chili Oil, 1.11 fl oz
  S&B - La-Yu Chili Oil With Chili Pepper 1.11 Fl. Oz
  And
  House - Shichimi Togarashi - Japanese Mixed Chili Pepper 0.63 Oz

Now, I haven't tried the first oil (only the second) nor the mixed chili pepper yet. The 'With Chili Pepper' oil was ...ok. It wasn't as good as what I get at the restaurants and had a slightly odd flavor that was kinda meh.

I've tried the Japanese spice on the tip of my finger – it promises to burn the @#%@# outta my mouth. Not really jumping on that wagon at the moment. Plus, I haven't cooked anything I'd want it on.

Oh, and I bought something besides ground meat for the first time in a while. I grabbed the Smith's Carne Asada and grilled it for tacos yesterday. Wasn't a huge fan of the spice they used. So, I'll have to find a recipe to use.

I also had leftover brisket (from the day before – Dickey's BBQ. I didn't go to Jessie Rae's because now I live pretty far away.) The restaurant did NOT provide much sauce so I bought Stubb's BBQ sauce and tried it.

Pretty good, nice hit of spice but a bit sweet for me. I need to plan a trip over to Jessie Rae's to buy a bottle or two of God Sauce.

I found a book on wood-pellet grill and smoking and bought it last night. I felt like Tim 'the Tool Man' Taylor as I'm reading all of the specifics of how wood pellet cooking makes BBQ and smoking a Texas brisket much easier.

I'm from Texas, I have a desire to at least cook one damned brisket that can be described as meat butter before I die.

I realized that for the cost of everything (that I wanted) I could order a @#%@# ton of brisket from the local BBQ joint for three years so is that really practical?

Who said loving to make BBQ was practical?

I'm eyeing a part of the back yard where the pit could be stashed. If my wife finds me out there with a tape measure, she should get worried.

Ok, I need to go eat, I'm starving!

See you next book.

Ad Aeternitatem,

Michael

ACKNOWLEDGMENTS
SARAH NOFFKE

I feel like I'm on the stage at the Oscars, accepting an award when I write my acknowledgments. I stand there, holding this award, my hands shaking and my words racing around in my mind. I'm not an actress for a reason. I'm a writer and talking to people in "real life" is hard. Not to mention a ton of people all at once.

I picture looking out at the audience and being blinded by spotlights and forgetting every word of the speech I memorized just in case I won. The speech would go like this and it's meant for all of you, not the guild. For the fans. The supporters. The people who are the reason I would ever stand on any stage, ever.

Okay, here we go. I clear my throat and smile, looking up at the camera, holding the little golden man. And then I begin:

This was never supposed to happen. I was never meant to publish a book and then another one. And then another. I was supposed to write in private and live a life that Henry David Thoreau called a life of "quiet desperation." I would always hope to share my books, but never bring myself to do it. And you would never read my words. But then, in a crazed moment of brashness, I did share my books and you all liked them. And because of that, I've never been the same. And here I am feeling grateful all just because…

That's why I'm here. Because of you. Thank you to my first readers. The ones who picked up those books that I didn't even outline and you still liked them. You messaged me and maybe you thought it was no big deal, but when your ego is new to the publishing world, it's a big deal.

I can't thank you readers enough. I've found that reading your reviews helps me to start a chapter when I'm stuck or lazy.

I really need to thank someone who has made this all possible and that's my father. I was going to quit. I can't tell you how many times I quit. But when I wasn't making it, he was the one who told me to not throw in the towel. "Give yourself a timeline," he suggested. If I didn't get to my goal by then, I'd quit. And apparently there was magic in that advice, because I'm still doing this. Dad, you're the pragmatic one, but when you believed in me enough to tell me to not quit, I knew I had to follow your advice.

And I thank all my friends who are constantly supporting me with thoughts of love and encouragement. Most don't read my books. I'm sort of self-deprecating, although I'm working on it and will be the first to tell my friends, "My books probably aren't for you." However, every now and then a friend surprises me and says, "I was up all night reading your books." It's always a total shock. But my point is, that even if they didn't read, I still have the best friends ever. Diane, you're my rock. And I love you, even though you will probably not read this.

Thank you to everyone at LMBPN. Those people are like family to me, although I'm not sure if they'll let me sleep on their couch. Well, who am I kidding? They totally will. Big thanks to Steve, Lynne, Mihaela, Kelly, Jen and the entire team. The JIT members are the best.

Huge thank you to the LMBPN Ladies group on Facebook. Micky, you're the best. And that group keeps me sane.

And a giant thank you to the betas for this series. Juergen you are my first reader and friend. Thanks for all the help. And thanks to Martin and Crystal for being some of the best people I know. What would I do without you? A huge thanks to the ARC team. Seriously, if it weren't for you all I might pass out before release day, wondering if anyone will like the book.

And with all my books, my final thank you goes to my lovely muse, Lydia. Oh sweet darling, I write these books for you, but ironically, I couldn't write them without you. You are my inspiration. My sounding board. And the reason that I want to succeed. I love you.

Thank you all! I'm sorry if I forgot anyone. Blame Michael. For no other reason than just because.

BOOKS BY SARAH NOFFKE

Sarah Noffke writes YA and NA science fiction, fantasy, paranormal and urban fantasy. In addition to being an author, she is a mother, podcaster and professor. Noffke holds a Masters of Management and teaches college business/writing courses. Most of her students have no idea that she toils away her hours crafting fictional characters. www.sarahnoffke.com

Check out other work by Sarah author here.

Ghost Squadron:

Formation #1:
Kill the bad guys. Save the Galaxy. All in a hard day's work.
After ten years of wandering the outer rim of the galaxy, Eddie Teach is a man without a purpose. He was one of the toughest pilots in the Federation, but now he's just a regular guy, getting into bar fights and making a difference wherever he can. It's not the same as flying a ship and saving colonies, but it'll have to do.

That is, until General Lance Reynolds tracks Eddie down and offers him a job. There are bad people out there, plotting terrible things, killing innocent people, and destroying entire colonies. **Someone has to stop them.**

Eddie, along with the genetically-enhanced combat pilot Julianna Fregin and her trusty E.I. named Pip, must recruit a diverse team of specialists, both human and alien. They'll need to master their new Q-Ship, one of the most powerful strike ships ever constructed. And finally, they'll have to stop a faceless enemy so powerful, it threatens to destroy the entire Federation.

All in a day's work, right?

Experience this exciting military sci-fi saga and the latest addition to the expanded Kurtherian Gambit Universe. If you're a fan of Mass Effect, Firefly, or Star Wars, you'll love this riveting new space opera.

NOTE: If cursing is a problem, then this might not be for you.

Check out the entire series here.

The Precious Galaxy Series:

Corruption #1

A new evil lurks in the darkness.

After an explosion, the crew of a battlecruiser mysteriously disappears.

Bailey and Lewis, complete strangers, find themselves suddenly onboard the damaged ship. Lewis hasn't worked a case in years, not since the final one broke his spirit and his bank account. The last thing Bailey remembers is preparing to take down a fugitive on Onyx Station.

Mysteries are harder to solve when there's no evidence left behind.

Bailey and Lewis don't know how they got onboard *Ricky Bobby* or why. However, they quickly learn that whatever was responsible for the explosion and disappearance of the crew is still on the ship.

Monsters are real and what this one can do changes everything.

The new team bands together to discover what happened and how to fight the monster lurking in the bottom of the battlecruiser.

Will they find the missing crew? Or will the monster end them all?

The Soul Stone Mage Series:

House of Enchanted #1:

The Kingdom of Virgo has lived in peace for thousands of years...until now.

The humans from Terran have always been real assholes to the witches of Virgo. Now a silent war is brewing, and the timing couldn't be worse. Princess Azure will soon be crowned queen of the Kingdom of Virgo.

In the Dark Forest a powerful potion-maker has been murdered.

Charmsgood was the only wizard who could stop a deadly virus plaguing Virgo. He also knew about the devastation the people from Terran had done to the forest.

Azure must protect her people. Mend the Dark Forest. Create alliances with savage beasts. No biggie, right?

But on coronation day everything changes. Princess Azure isn't who she thought she was and that's a big freaking problem.

Welcome to The Revelations of Oriceran. Check out the entire series here.

The Lucidites Series:

Awoken, #1:

Around the world humans are hallucinating after sleepless nights.

In a sterile, underground institute the forecasters keep reporting the same events.

And in the backwoods of Texas, a sixteen-year-old girl is about to be caught up in a fierce, ethereal battle.

Meet Roya Stark. She drowns every night in her dreams, spends her hours reading classic literature to avoid her family's ridicule, and is prone to premonitions—which are becoming more frequent. And now her dreams are filled with strangers offering to reveal what she has always wanted to know: Who is she? That's the question that haunts her, and she's about to find out. But will Roya live to regret learning the truth?

Stunned, #2

Revived, #3

The Reverians Series:

Defects, #1:

In the happy, clean community of Austin Valley, everything appears to be perfect. Seventeen-year-old Em Fuller, however, fears something is askew. Em is one of the new generation of Dream Travelers. For some reason, the gods have not seen fit to gift all of them with their expected special abilities. Em is a Defect—one of the unfortunate Dream Travelers not gifted with a psychic power. Desperate to do whatever it takes to earn her gift, she endures painful daily injections along with commands from her overbearing, loveless father. One of the few bright spots in her life is the return of a friend she had thought dead—but with his return comes the knowledge of a shocking, unforgivable truth. The society Em thought was protecting her has actually been betraying her, but she has no idea how to break away from its authority without hurting everyone she loves.

Rebels, #2

Warriors, #3

Vagabond Circus Series:

Suspended, #1:

When a stranger joins the cast of Vagabond Circus—a circus that is run by Dream Travelers and features real magic—mysterious events start happening. The once orderly grounds of the circus become riddled with hidden threats. And the ringmaster realizes not only are his circus and its magic at risk, but also his very life.

Vagabond Circus caters to the skeptics. Without skeptics, it would close its doors. This is because Vagabond Circus runs for two reasons and only two reasons: first and foremost to provide the lost and lonely Dream Travelers a place to be illustrious. And secondly, to show the nonbelievers that there's still magic in the world. If they believe, then they care, and if they care, then they don't destroy. They stop the small abuse that day-by-day breaks down humanity's spirit. If Vagabond Circus makes one skeptic believe in magic, then they halt the cycle, just a little bit. They allow a little more love into this world. That's Dr. Dave Raydon's mission. And that's why this ringmaster recruits. That's why he directs. That's why he puts on a show that makes people question their beliefs. He wants the world to believe in magic once again.

Paralyzed, #2

Released, #3

Ren Series:

Ren: The Man Behind the Monster, #1:

Born with the power to control minds, hypnotize others, and read thoughts, Ren Lewis, is certain of one thing: God made a mistake. No one should be born with so much power. A monster awoke in him the same year he received his gifts. At ten years old. A prepubescent boy with the ability to control others might merely abuse his powers, but Ren allowed it to corrupt him. And since he can have and do anything he wants, Ren should be happy. However, his journey teaches him that harboring so much power doesn't bring happiness, it steals it. Once this realization sets in, Ren makes up his mind to do the one thing that can bring his tortured soul some peace. He must kill the monster.

Note This book is NA and has strong language, violence and sexual references.

Ren: God's Little Monster, #2

Ren: The Monster Inside the Monster, #3

Ren: The Monster's Adventure, #3.5

Ren: The Monster's Death

Olento Research Series:

Alpha Wolf, #1:

Twelve men went missing.

Six months later they awake from drug-induced stupors to find themselves locked in a lab.

And on the night of a new moon, eleven of those men, possessed by new—and inhuman—powers, break out of their prison and race through the streets of Los Angeles until they disappear one by one into the night.

Olento Research wants its experiments back. Its CEO, Mika Lenna, will tear every city apart until he has his werewolves imprisoned once again. He didn't undertake a huge risk just to lose his would-be assassins.

However, the Lucidite Institute's main mission is to save the world from injustices. Now, it's Adelaide's job to find these mutated men and protect them and society, and fast. Already around the nation, wolflike men are being spotted. Attacks on innocent women are happening. And then, Adelaide realizes what her next step must be: She has to find the alpha wolf first. Only once she's located him can she stop whoever is behind this experiment to create wild beasts out of human beings.

Lone Wolf, #2

Rabid Wolf, #3

Bad Wolf, #4

CONNECT WITH THE AUTHORS

Connect with Sarah and sign up for her email list here:

http://www.sarahnoffke.com/connect/

You can catch her podcast, LA Chicks, here:

http://lachicks.libsyn.com/

Connect with Michael Anderle and sign up for his email list here:

Website:
http://www.lmbpn.com
Email List:
http://lmbpn.com/email/
Facebook
https://www.facebook.com/LMBPNPublishing

www.ingramcontent.com/pod-product-compliance
Lightning Source LLC
Chambersburg PA
CBHW020229110726
47898CB00004B/1208